FOUR-FOOTED ANGELS

THE HEAVENLY GRILLE CAFÉ - BOOK TWO

Four-Footed Angels
The Heavenly Grille Café Book Two

This is a work of fiction. All names, characters, businesses, places, events, and incidents, are products of the author's imagination or used in a fictitious manner. Any resemblance to actual persons, living or dead, or actual events is purely coincidental.

Published by Piscataqua Press

An imprint of RiverRun Bookstore Inc.

142 Fleet Street | Portsmouth, NH | 03801

www.riverrunbookstore.com

www.piscaaquapress.com

Printed in the United States of America

ISBN: 978-1-939739-96-4

FOUR-FOOTED ANGELS

THE HEAVENLY GRILLE CAFÉ - BOOK TWO

By

J. T. Livingston

AUTHOR'S NOTE

The first book in The Heavenly Grille Café series introduced the reader to three special angels: Maximus, a former Gladiator; Bertie, whose boisterous personality has earned her the proprietary title as Heaven's naughty angel; and, Doug, a young soldier who died in battle in 1953. These three angels run the Heavenly Grille Café, currently located in the middle of nowhere, in the small town of Monticello, Florida. The café is famous for the golden halo that seems to float miraculously above it. The first book also introduced us to Amanda Turner, a young girl from Tampa, Florida who found refuge, and a new family, at the Heavenly Grille Café. Amanda has moved back to Tampa to pursue a career in law enforcement, and the angels have decided to remain in their current location for the time being.

Book Two in the series begins in October 2013 and introduces the reader to a different kind of angel…a four-footed angel. His name is Sam, and he was Amanda's dog for 10 years before he died. Sam and his human angels at the cafe are on a mission to do what they can do to help those who cannot help themselves…bait and fighter dogs. If you have ever wondered whether or not we will be reunited in Heaven with our four-legged companions, then you will most certainly enjoy the angels' second book of fiction…or…is it really fiction?

Special thanks to my dear friend, Elizabeth Radabaugh, for giving me the idea for Book Two!

CHAPTER 1

A Late-Night Visitor

It was almost midnight on a Friday night in October 2013, when the Heavenly Grille Café closed its doors behind the last customer of the night. Bertie locked the door behind the young man and shook her head. "Something about that young man…" she mused.

Doug was clearing the table that had just been vacated by the young man with the surly attitude. "Talking to yourself again, Bertie?" he teased.

Bertie raised her eyebrows and punched Doug on the arm as she walked past him toward the kitchen. "Watch it, handsome," she grinned. "Besides, I'll have you know that some of my best conversations take place with myself." She walked into the kitchen where Max was wiping down the stove and countertops. "Isn't that right, Maximus?"

"You'll get no argument from me, Bertie. So…what was it about that young man that has you talking to yourself?"

Angels have an extraordinary sense of hearing, so Bertie was not surprised that Max had heard her mumbling at the front door. The three angels who currently ran the Heavenly Grille Café often read one another's thoughts, so they really did not need to rely on their keen sense of hearing.

Bertie shrugged and reached for the broom that leaned

against the refrigerator. "I'm not sure; I can't quite put my finger on it, Max. I mean…he was here for almost an hour, he barely touched his food, and he kept looking over his shoulder…kind of like he was expecting someone to show up, you know?"

Doug strolled into the kitchen with the last of the dishes. He rolled his broad shoulders and stretched his neck from side to side. It had been a long day, and even though angels did not require food or sleep, he was looking forward to some quiet time in his small apartment above the café. "I heard him talking to someone on his cell phone," he offered.

"About what?" Max asked.

"Something about a dog," Doug replied. "He told whoever he was talking to that he hadn't been able to find it, but that he would keep looking."

"Humph…" Bertie grunted. "Who looks for a dog in the middle of nowhere, at almost midnight? Yep…there's something fishy about that young man."

"I'm not sure how long he's been looking for the dog…sounded like maybe it's been most of the day, though," Doug said. "I did notice that his hands were trembling…a lot…while he was talking to whoever was on the phone. He seemed really nervous…or, either really angry…I'm not sure which."

The angels were each lost in their own thoughts, so all was quiet for a few moments, until Max looked puzzled and shook his head. "He barely touched my food?"

The three angelic friends looked back and forth at one another for a few more moments until they burst out in simultaneous laughter.

The young man sat inside his pick-up truck that was still parked outside the café. He ran his hands over his dark buzz cut, reached for an Atlanta Braves baseball cap that was lying on the front seat, and slapped it on his head. He stared off into the dark wood line that surrounded the café and lit another cigarette. He pinched the bridge of his nose and absently rubbed the small two-inch scar that ran down his right cheek. He watched the wood line for the slightest movement, but everything was calm and quiet on this balmy October night. Even though the weather had cooled considerably throughout other parts of the country, the Florida nights were still a bit on the warm, humid side. He wiped a line of sweat off his brow. Suddenly, with no warning at all, the young man deliberately banged his head against the steering wheel and hissed, "Damn you to Hell, Spartacus…where are you!" It wasn't a question.

He continued to watch while some of the lights went out inside the café, and he slid down in his seat when the muscular man who had been bussing tables exited the front door and glanced at the pick-up truck. The young man watched and stayed hidden until the busser made his way up the stairs that were located on the right side of the building. When a light came on inside the upstairs apartment, the young man finally released a deep breath. It was time to leave. He started the pick-up truck and rolled down his window while he drove slowly out of the parking lot.

His attention was once again drawn to the dark wood line that bordered the back of the café. Chills ran up and down his spine. He couldn't shake the feeling that it felt like he was the one being hunted, rather than the other way around. He rubbed the bridge of his nose again and blew out an exasperated breath. "I know you're out there somewhere, Spartacus, and…I will find you…"

Back inside the café, Bertie and Max were sharing a final cup of coffee for the night. Doug, who lived in one of the upstairs apartments, had left them a few minutes earlier to turn in for the night.

Bertie sighed. "Sure doesn't feel the same since our Amanda moved back to Tampa, does it, big fella?"

Max shook his head and grinned. "No, Bertie, it doesn't.

I have to admit, I miss that girl a lot. Have you talked to her lately?"

Amanda Turner was the young woman who the angels had literally taken under their wings during the summer of 2011. She had arrived at the café homeless, jobless, and with no family to call her own. They had offered her one of the upstairs apartments, as well as a waitressing job at the café.

"As a matter of fact, I talked to our bundle of joy just after supper time tonight. She sends her love to you and Doug. I meant to mention it to you both earlier but things got hectic in here and I forgot. Hmmm…I didn't think we angels ever forgot anything…and, when that young man came in, well…I really got side-tracked and distracted."

"Not a problem, Bertie…but you are right…angels aren't supposed to forget anything. Maybe it's time I sent you Home for a tune-up!"

Bertie threw a wet dishrag at Max and feigned offense. "Tune-up, my ass! I'll have you know I had the sharpest mind in my family, never forgot a thing."

Max threw up his hands and laughed. "Kidding, Bertie…just kidding! So…is everything going okay for Amanda in Tampa?"

Bertie nodded. "I'm afraid so, Maximus…I don't think there's any chance she'll be giving up her life in Tampa to move back to Monticello any time soon. She did have some news, though…really surprised me, too."

Max waited a few moments and when Bertie didn't immediately continue, he asked, "Care to elaborate on that last statement? Has she met someone special, maybe?"

Bertie pursed her lips to form a pout and raised her brows. "She's met someone, alright, but it's not what you're thinking. It seems our little girl may be having a change of heart about her choice of career fields. She's been volunteering at some animal rescue place, and said she's thinking seriously about quitting the police force to go back to school and become a veterinarian."

Max was dumbfounded. He had been so sure that

Amanda would make a career out of law enforcement. She had breezed through the Police Academy and loved working in the area of New Tampa. "Care to run that by me again, Bertie?"

Bertie grinned. It wasn't easy to surprise Max, but she could tell that this bit of news was definitely not what he expected to hear. "You heard me right, big fella. Seems that someone brought in a small, bullie-mix puppy to the rescue one night; whoever brought it in said it had been thrown out the window of the car in front of him and he had almost ran over the little fella. It was touch and go for a few days, but the pup made it. Needless to say…Amanda fell in love with the little fella and adopted him."

"Amanda got herself a dog…you don't say!" Max laughed out loud. "Well, it's about time. I don't think she's had one since her dog, Sam, died a few years ago. I remember her talking about him once…I think she was around seventeen when he died…it broke her heart and she said she didn't want to suffer that kind of loss again."

"Yeah," Bertie nodded. "She said it hurt too much to lose Sam, but…it looks like time has finally healed that wound. You seemed surprised about the dog, but you didn't say anything about her wanting to quit the police force."

Max shook his head and took a final sip of coffee. "Well, I am surprised she would consider leaving law enforcement, but, in a way…I guess I'm not really all that surprised after all. She's good at her job, but she's young. I don't think she really knows what she wants to do long term, career-wise...can't say that I'm surprised about her wanting to go to school to become a vet, though…somehow, it seems like a good fit." He rinsed out his mug and smiled. "You know…animals are with us for such a short amount of time on earth…God means for us to open our hearts to as many as possible while we're here, so I'm really glad that Amanda has seen fit to do that again."

"Did you get that tidbit of information straight from the boss, Himself?" Bertie punched his shoulder and placed her own mug in the empty sink.

"Well...as a matter of fact..." Max began, but stopped when he heard a strange scratching noise coming from the back entrance.

Bertie heard the noise, too. Her posture stiffened and she whispered, "What was that, Max?"

"Probably nothing...just a raccoon or 'possum...I'll have a quick look."

"I'm coming with you," Bertie continued to whisper.

"Why are you whispering?" Max grinned down at her from his seventy-six inch height.

"Hell, I don't know...go on...open the damn door..."

"You know He doesn't like it when you curse, Bertie."

"Yeah, yeah, right...but, He also knows that I'm a work in progress, so I gotta believe that He gives me a little slack in that department."

"Guess we'll find out on Sunday when we visit Home," Max grinned again.

"Oh, shush, and open that door!" Bertie spoke in her normal, loud tone. She took time to grab the broom as her choice of weapon and followed Max's lead.

"What are you going to do with that broom, Bertie? Sweep dust into the poor creature's face?"

Bertie punched him on the back of his right shoulder.

The soft scratching noise sounded again.

The door knob became quickly lost within Max's large, black hand; he grasped the knob and slowly pushed it outward. The light from the floating halo above the café provided a soft glow that spread across the back yard. There was a full moon out which helped to accentuate the multitude of shadows that played host to the back of the property.

Bertie gasped when she peeked from behind Max's massive shoulders and saw the large, dark lump on the back porch. "What is it, Max? It's too big to be a 'possum or raccoon..."

The large, dark lump raised its head, and two soulful eyes met Max's concerned stare. Max bent down and squatted before the matted lump that was…a dog. It was hard to tell what color the dog was since it was covered in mud and, what appeared to be, dried blood. What was left of the dog's ears flinched when Max reached out to it, and it trembled so badly that it urinated on the old, wooden porch. Max's touch was gentle when he lifted the dog's chin; its trembling ceased immediately upon Max's touch.

"I'll be damn…" Bertie whispered once again. "Poor baby…who could have done this to him?" The dog was a broad-shouldered, black pit-bull mix with the saddest and largest brown eyes Bertie had ever seen on a dog. There were cuts and bite marks all over his head, face, shoulders, and legs. A dog this size should have easily weighed seventy to eighty pounds, but this poor soul did not appear to weigh more than fifty pounds, at the most. Every rib showcased against his dull, loose skin.

Max continued to stroke the dog while huge tears rolled down his face. He immediately recognized the dog for what it was. "I think he might be a bait dog, Bertie…"

"A what?" Bertie cried. "What the hell is a bait dog?"

The dog whimpered when Max's thumbs rolled across its bruised ribcage, but it immediately relaxed. "They go a long, long way back," Max sighed. "We even had them back in my Gladiator days. They were a source of *entertainment* for our Roman society."

Bertie wiped the tears from her own eyes and said, "Well, you can tell me all about that later. Get that poor baby in here now and let's get him cleaned up and something to eat."

Max took the dog's large head between his two hands and looked deeply into its eyes. "It's going to be okay, boy…" He positioned himself so that he could easily lift the dog into his arms. "There should be an old blanket on the top shelf of the pantry, Bertie."

Bertie rushed back inside. "I'll get it," she replied quickly. She spread the blanket out in the corner beside the back door. "Ready, Max…lay him down. I'm going to get him something to eat."

"He needs water first, Bertie…then, please heat up some milk. I'm pretty sure milk is on a dog's DO NOT FEED list, but it's a quick way to get some warm nutrients in him. There are some hamburger patties in the fridge. I don't want to give it to him raw…"

"Hey, don't think that you're the only one around here who knows how to cook, big fella. I'll get it ready. Why don't you get some old rags and see if you can clean up some of those wounds?"

While the two angels bustled about the kitchen carrying out their respective duties, the dog never took his eyes off them. He lifted his nose when he smelled the beef cooking. His eyes closed and he appeared to take a deep, repressed sigh.

Spartacus rested. This was the first time in his two years of life that he finally felt…safe.

CHAPTER 2

According to Spartacus

Spartacus sighed deeply and without fear for the first time in the memory of his two short years. *"It feels so good to be free of that heavy chain around my neck. I know Little John used it to build my strength and make me a better fighter, but there were so many days that it felt like it was choking the life right out of me."*

He continued to watch the two humans moving around the big room with the wonderful smells and the soft blanket. *"I wonder who these people are…I don't see a chain anywhere, so maybe they will let me sleep on this soft blanket tonight. Something sure smells good. I wonder if that loud woman will give me something to eat. Maybe I'll just rest my eyes for a little while…maybe I won't dream those bad dreams again…"*

"Little John" Abbott owned a hundred acres of land just over the Georgia-Florida state line in Thomasville, Georgia. He had inherited the land from his father, "Big John," who was currently serving time in Thomas County Prison for repeated assault and battery offenses. The ruling judge had looked the other way for as long as possible, but county residents had finally had enough of the Abbott family and their connections. Big John and the hardened misfits that worked for him had been locally described as Thomas County's "Redneck Mafia." They controlled a good portion of southern Georgia's illegal gambling niche. If a bet could be placed on it, there was a high probability that "Big John" was behind the means of debt collection. However, there was a new generation taking over in Thomas County, and it was a generation that had no use for Big John and his crew. It had taken three years, but Big John's entire establishment had been disbanded and all participants now received their daily meals, courtesy of the Thomas County taxpayers.

There was nothing little about Little John Abbott. His height measured just under six feet, but his weight was tremendous. He weighed in at almost three hundred pounds, but his was not sloppy, unattractive fat; the man was built solid as a rock - the extra weight on his frame was similar to that of a professional body-builder. The flames from the pit reflected off his shiny, bald but perfectly shaped, head. His eyes appeared to be as black as the night that surrounded the back forty acres of his 100-acre ranch; there was no human emotion reflected in those eyes. He had high cheekbones, thanks to his distant, Cherokee-Indian heritage, and a thick black mustache that was always meticulously trimmed.

He stood erect, arms crossed and legs slightly apart, and watched three of his crew as they performed their assigned duties. One operated the dump truck, one tossed the carcasses into the 20-foot pit, and the third man monitored the fire to ensure that the contents of the pit burned properly.

The man operating the dump truck got out and came around to where Little John stood. "Any word from Tyler yet, Boss?"

Little John's eyes glazed over the driver and dismissed him without a word.

The man rubbed the back of his neck and shuffled his feet.

"Sorry, Boss…it's just that I wasn't here when Spartacus took off, and I haven't heard anyone say anything about him…I was just wondering if Tyler had tracked him down yet."

Little John decided to grace his employee with an indifferent response. "No…not yet. He thinks the loser probably died in the woods. He tracked him to Monticello before he lost his trail."

The driver offered up a nervous smile. "Wow…Monticello, huh? Spartacus covered some good ground in less than twenty-four hours. He got chewed up pretty bad in that last fight…"

Little John stared down the driver. "I'm well aware of how he performed in his last fight; that's why he should be in that damn pit tonight, instead of wandering around free." Little John had invested a lot of time and money in training Spartacus to be a grand champion of the southern-Georgia underground dog fighting rings; a grand champion was an undefeated fighter dog with five wins. He had remained undefeated until the fight that took place late Friday afternoon. Little John had placed a ten-thousand dollar bet on Spartacus to defeat the second-ranked pit-bull in the area, Czar. He stared back at the pit and said, "Make sure nothing is left…" He turned back to his own pick-up truck.

"Sure thing, Boss…you can count on me," the driver mumbled. He covered his nose and mouth with his bandana to reduce the nauseating smell of burning fur and skin.

Spartacus' eyes were closed but he was aware of everything going on around him. *"The tall dark man with the kind eyes and gentle hands sat down on the floor beside my blanket. I pulled back when he started to rub my head, but the second he touched me, my entire body relaxed in a way that I've never felt before. I've only felt the touch of kindness once before, and although it felt good, it was nowhere close to what this man's touch felt like. I felt a tingle that started at the tip of my head, spread to my shoulders and down to my belly, and ended at the very tip of my tail. I've never felt a tingling sensation like that before, but something told me that it was a good, safe feeling; something told me that I had nothing to fear from this man and woman."*

"The patties are ready, Max; I'm going to break them up in smaller pieces for him," the loud woman yelled from where she was standing in front of the big white box…the box from where all the good smells seemed to be coming.

The dark man's hand moved back to my mouth. He looked into my eyes and smiled. "I just want to check inside your mouth," the man whispered. "Is that all right with you, fella?"

I closed my eyes in passive submission, which seemed to go against everything that Little John had trained me to do. The man opened my upper and lower jaws. I heard a small gasp escape from him, so I opened my eyes to see what the problem might be. The woman walked over with a bowl of some wonderful-smelling food. "What are you doing, Max?" she asked. At least now I know the dark man's name…Max…I like that name, and I like this man.

"I was just checking his teeth, Bertie," the man replied softly. "His teeth would tell me if he was used as a bait dog, which I thought was the case at first…or if he was trained to be a fighter dog, instead."

I looked at the woman and willed her to put the bowl of food on the floor. She did and I looked toward the dark man for permission to eat it. "Go ahead, fella…eat it all…but try to eat slowly if you can…" Shucks…slowly? Really? He's a nice man but he doesn't have any idea how long it's been since I've had anything to eat, but…okay…slowly it is…

Max rubbed my head while I managed to eat as slowly as I could. He looked at the loud woman…Bertie, yes that was her name…and said, "Judging from his wounds, I first thought he was a bait dog, but their teeth are usually filed down to the gum line and their nails are pulled out. This fella has extremely sharp teeth that have been filed to make them even sharper than normal, and he still has all his nails. He's been used as a fighter dog; a bait dog wouldn't stand a chance against this one. No…some of his wounds are old…maybe from fights…maybe from being beaten by his owner…" Max stopped talking and rubbed my head again. I stopped eating long enough to look at him…water was falling from his eyes. I thought he looked very sad.

"A fighter dog?" Bertie questioned. She put her hands on her hips and looked down at me. At first, I thought she might be mad at me because I had not eaten the food slowly enough, but it didn't take me long to realize that her anger was not directed at me. "What the hell are you talking about, Max? Are you telling me someone out there actually trained this poor pup to fight? Why would they do that?"

"Dog fighting is a popular sporting event in many states, Bertie...especially the southern states. Some dogs are stolen from their owner's home or yard; some are gotten from the free classified section of the paper or on that web site that Doug told us about...Craigslist...or something like that. Some are even adopted from pounds and shelters. The leaders of the fighting rings will make the determination on whether or not the dog is a prospect and has gameness..."

"A prospect...and what the hell is gameness?" Bertie pouted.

Max smiled, sighed and continued rubbing the top of my head. "Well...a prospect might be a young, aggressive pup that the ring leader has identified as being a potentially good fighting dog. Gameness is a critical quality for any fighting dog; it shows the dog's willingness and his tenacity to fight. If the stolen or adopted dog does not show gameness, then the leader will, most likely, use it as a bait dog instead."

Bertie bent down to rub my head, too. "I can guess what you mean when you say bait dog, Max...and I am not liking what I'm thinking."

"The life of a bait dog is not a good one, Bertie," Max sighed. The ring leader will use any kind of animal as bait...puppies, kittens, rabbits, squirrels, or any dog that turns out not to be a good prospect to become a fighter dog. These bait animals are often beaten and starved, their mouths are taped shut, and their legs bound together so that they cannot escape when they are put into a crate or ring with a fighter dog. If the fighter dog does not instinctively kill the bait animal right away, the leaders will poke the bait animal with a knife causing it to bleed, which will attract the attention of the fighter dog. At this point, the bait animal is horribly savaged by the fighter dog. If the bait dog does not die immediately from its

wounds, the leaders sometimes complete the torture by breaking all its bones, stabbing it, hanging it, dragging it behind vehicles…well…you get the picture…until it is dead."

I looked from the dark man to the loud woman, who was no longer loud. She had lots of water coming from her eyes, just as the man did. They both looked very sad. I did not understand all the words they said to each other, but I hoped I was not the reason they were sad. Maybe that meant they would turn me away into the night, but if they were going to do that, I wonder why they fed me and cleaned the sore and hurting spots on my body. Humans were such strange creatures at times. I continued to look back and forth between the two of them until the woman finally stood up and wiped her nose.

"I've heard enough, Maximus…for the life of me, I can't understand what would motivate someone to treat one of God's creatures like this." Bertie was quiet for a few moments before she continued. "Max…that young man that was in here tonight…do you think he had anything to do with this?"

Max shook his head and said, "I've been wondering the same thing, Bertie, but…I honestly don't know. Maybe we can find out some more information about him when we go Home on Sunday. Martin might be able to help us with that. Who knows…maybe the young man will come back here…"

"Well…I still haven't decided what it was I was feeling about him…I don't know if he had good intentions or bad ones…I just know that something didn't feel right. I hope he does come back in…"

"Why don't you go home, Bertie? I'm going to stay the night with this fella…I want to clean those wounds up some more and make sure he gets the rest that he needs."

Bertie placed her hands on her hips and stared down at the dark man. "You're crazy as hell if you think I'm going anywhere. I'm staying here, too. We can take turns keeping an eye on him. Maybe tomorrow will bring us the answers to some of our questions."

It quickly became obvious to me that these two humans were not going to throw me back outside to fend for myself. I think it might be safe for me to close my eyes and really sleep. It's been so long since I've been able to do that…

□ □ □

Tyler Foster waited patiently until his boss left the main ranch. He knew that Little John was riding to the back forty acres to check on the disposal of the latest batch of bait dogs killed in the training of his best fighter dogs. Tyler looked around to make sure no one else was within hearing distance of the phone call he needed to make.

It was three o'clock in the morning, Saturday, but the phone at the other end was answered on the third ring. "Hello…" the man's deep, raspy voice echoed through the phone line to Tyler.

"Dad? Hey…it's Tyler…really sorry to be calling you so late, but I needed to let you know that I wasn't able to find Spartacus…at least not yet. I'm going back out tomorrow…there's a place I want to check a second time."

B.B. Foster rubbed his large nose between his thumb and index finger. "I'm really sorry to hear that, son. I was hoping you would find him. Keep looking and if you do find him, just remember to call me right away and I'll meet you at the half-way point that we discussed."

Tyler sighed. "He's hurt pretty bad…he could be dead in the woods by now, but…"

"But…something tells you that he's a survivor, right?"

Tyler smiled into the phone. "Yeah, something like that. Anyway…I won't quit looking until I know for sure."

"No chance of your cover being blown, is there?" the elder Foster asked.

Tyler shook his head before remembering his father couldn't see that motion. "No…at least not yet. Little John thinks that I've been taking his losers, torturing them for losing their fights, then killing them slowly. He always wants a detailed description of how they suffered at my hands."

"Well, as long as he continues to believe that you're as evil as he is, then we're okay. The authorities are still working things at this end. They're close to getting all they need, but it could be another week or two before they're able to close in on him, so it's important that you keep your cover, okay?"

"You know I will. We're going to get this son-of-a-bitch, and all the other ones connected to his ring of horrors. Hopefully, we can rescue more than he kills…"

"That's what we're here for, son. That's what Foster Farm is all about. You take care now and call me if you need anything."

"I will…love you, Dad…"

"I love you, too, son…God Bless…"

Tyler Foster closed his cell phone and stuck it in his back pocket. He looked around him into the black midnight that surrounded the Abbott ranch, and listened to the whining of the dogs in the far-off kennels. Their sounds were pitiful, pleading, and…heartbreaking. He knew that he could not save all of them, but he was determined to save as many as he could. "I will find you, Spartacus…I promise…" He closed his eyes and offered up a silent prayer to the Father above him.

"Give ear, O Lord, to my prayer; and attend to the voice of my supplications. In the day of my trouble I will call upon You, for You will answer me." Psalm 86:6-7 (NKJV)

CHAPTER 3

Amanda Visits the Foster Farm

Amanda Turner closed the sliding door to the van that belonged to Pet Haven Rescue, a Tampa organization that rescued cats and dogs at the last minute from high-kill animal shelters. She lifted her face upward and breathed in the cooler, October breeze. The summer of 2013 had been a scorcher, and the clear, pleasant days of Fall in Florida were a constant reminder to her of why she lived in that wonderful state. Life in Florida during the months of October through April made the scorching, humid days of summer worth it.

The owners of Pet Haven Rescue were an elderly couple by the name of Earl and Sharon Stocker, who had dedicated their lives, and their 40-acre ranch, to rescuing as many animals as they could from the high-kill shelters surrounding the Tampa Bay area. They had no children of their own, but had grown extremely attached to Amanda during the few months she had been a volunteer at the ranch. Pet Haven depended heavily on the work of volunteers and private donations. The ranch had the capability to comfortably care for about sixty to seventy-five animals at any given time, but they were currently at the top of their intake limit.

"Are you all set, Amanda? Are you sure you can handle this load by yourself? If you want to wait until tomorrow, I'm sure Earl will be feeling well enough to go with you." Sharon Stocker wiped her hands nervously against her apron and blew a strand of wispy, gray hair off her forehead.

Amanda began volunteering at Pet Haven several months ago, shortly after her twenty-third birthday. She had been an only child and both her parents were dead now, so it had not taken her long to warm up to the kindness and compassion that came so generously from the Stockers. She had never volunteered at any animal shelter in the past, but her parents had come to her in a dream and told her she was needed at Pet Haven. The *heavenly* dreams with her parents had begun during the summer of 2011 when she left Tampa and ended up at a small, out-of-the-way café in Monticello, Florida…the Heavenly Grille Café. It was there that her life had been changed forever by the three angels who operated the café…Max, Bertie, and Doug.

Amanda walked over to Sharon Stocker and gave her a quick hug. "I'm fine, really. I can handle this load by myself; there are only six dogs, and Brooksville is only an hour away. I've never been to Foster Farm, but I've got their address loaded into my GPS. They do know that I'm coming, right?"

Mrs. Stocker nodded and smiled at the young woman who already felt like a part of their family. "Oh, yes, indeed…they'll be waiting for these handsome fellas. You'll like B.B. Foster…just wait until you see the Foster Farm!"

The six pit-bull mixes inside the van were barking, but Amanda had all the van windows down, so she knew they were as comfortable as they could be for the time being. "From what you and Mr. Stocker have told me about it, I'm really looking forward to meeting Mr. Foster and checking out his ranch. I Googled it last night, though, and couldn't find *anything* at all about it."

Mrs. Stocker shook her head and grinned. "And you won't find anything about it on the internet, my dear...no...word of mouth...that's the only way someone would find out about Foster Farm. They intentionally keep a low profile, you see, because their primary goal is to rescue dogs used as part of dog fighting rings. They're actually doing us a favor because they know we're at full capacity right now, and they have a lot more room than we do for these animals. Not many groups want to help the pit-bull mixes these days, but that's what Foster Farm is all about. I don't know if it's true or not, but rumor has it that B.B. Foster won a large sum of money in a lottery several years ago, and saving the pits is what he spends that money on."

"I love the bullie mixes," Amanda sighed. "I had one when I was younger...his name was Sam and he was a HUGE shiny, black pit-bull/lab mix. He looked like he could take you down with one swipe of his paw, but he was really just a big, teddy-bear of a thing."

"How long was he with you?" Mrs. Stocker asked.

Amanda sighed again. "About ten years or so...my Dad got him for me when I was about seven...right after my Mom died. Sam helped us both get through a pretty difficult time in our lives."

"He sounds like he was a very special pet, Amanda...speaking of which...where is Buster?"

Buster was the small bullie-mix pup that had been delivered to Pet Haven in the middle of the night a few weeks ago. It had been love at first sight for Amanda when she held the brown and white puppy in her arms, and she had been quick to adopt Buster for her very own.

Amanda grinned and gave Mrs. Stocker another quick hug. "Yep, Sam was very special, for sure, and...Mr. Buster is waiting patiently for me in the front seat; he's riding shotgun on this trip."

Mrs. Stocker moved to the front passenger door and peered inside. The subject of their conversation lay on his back with all four paws splayed in different directions. He was snoring soundly, and was oblivious to the barking of his six, fellow riders. "Riding shotgun, huh?" She laughed and shook her head. "Good luck with that!"

Amanda slid into the driver's seat, and reached over to rub Buster's rounded belly. The four-month-old pup yawned and stretched, and opened one eye. He licked Amanda's hand and immediately fell fast asleep once again. "Thanks, Mrs. "S"...we won't be long...it's an hour there, maybe an hour to look around Foster Farm, and an hour back...so, we should be back before supper time."

"I'll make sure I save you both a plate," Mrs. Stocker grinned and waved.

"Tell Mr. "S" to get some rest!" Amanda yelled back.

The only thing that B.B. Foster and his wife, Jean, loved more than their 200-acre farm was their God and their family. They had been blessed with four handsome sons, good genes and equally good health. They had also been blessed with an abundance of faith that had carried them through some lean and difficult years before they won a substantial landfall in the state lottery ten years ago. B.B. Foster had been a hard-working mechanic before he won $200 million off a single quick-pick lottery ticket. It was the first, and last, time he had ever played the lottery; it was not something his church believed in or supported, but...it had happened, and B.B. had won. He donated half of his winnings to various religious organizations and used the remainder to buy the 200-acre ranch that was now a safe-haven for all animals, but most especially, for rescued pit-bulls.

His four sons...Scott, Rick, Matthew, and the youngest, Tyler...were all dedicated to ensuring that Foster Farm would be around for generations to come. Each of them had their individual roles in keeping B.B.'s dream, which was to provide a permanent safe-haven for neglected and abused animals, alive and functioning. Scott was an accountant and kept the books; Rick was the most outgoing of the four sons and used his people skills to continuously, and discreetly, raise donations to help support Foster Farm; Matthew was a writer and photographer, and it was his job to write the biographies for each animal and select just the right picture to post to prospective adopters; and, Tyler...the youngest at age twenty-five...was the most adventuresome of the four brothers. Tyler had taken it upon himself to incorporate himself into a dangerous liaison with investigators looking into the southeastern states' dog fighting rings. He was currently working as a crewmember for one of the worst ring leaders in Georgia...Little John Abbott.

B.B. Foster sat in one of the many rocking chairs positioned on the log home's wrap-around porch. Three pit-bulls lay comfortably at his feet while he watched the mile-long driveway for an approaching vehicle. He was expecting a van from Pet Haven Rescue and he wanted to be onsite when it arrived.

Jean Foster opened the screen door and walked out onto the porch. She wiped her hands on the apron tied around her waist and asked, "Any sign of them yet?" She bent down to scratch behind the ears of the oldest of the three dogs that stood to greet her.

B.B. smiled at the woman he loved more than life itself. "Not yet, but you never know what kind of traffic you're going to hit coming from Tampa."

"That is so true...and, all the more reason I love living out here away from all that commotion." Jean stood up and leaned over to kiss the top of her husband's head. She had married him when she was eighteen; he had been ten years older than her, but she knew the moment that she first laid eyes on him that she would be spending the rest of her life with B.B. Foster. That was thirty years ago. They had their first son when she was nineteen, and their second son when she was twenty. Jean had a miscarriage when she was twenty-one...a little girl, but popped out their third son when she was twenty-two, and their last son when she was twenty-three. She had wanted to keep trying until she had a girl, but after two more miscarriages...both of them little girls...they had finally given up on that dream.

B.B. covered Jean's hand with his own, calloused one. "You and me both, Babe...it just doesn't get any better than this, does it?"

Jean looked out at the 50 acres that blanketed the front part of their 200-acre ranch. She shook her head and smiled. "Nope...we are so very blessed to have our own little piece of heaven right here on earth." She sighed and looked at her watch. "Have you talked to Tyler today? I thought he would've checked in with us by now."

B.B. blew out his cheeks and closed his eyes. "Ah, Babe...I'm sorry...I forgot to tell you that I talked to him early this morning. He called around three, but I didn't want to wake you."

"Is everything all right?" Jean asked and tensed up. "Why was he calling at three in the morning?"

"He's fine...don't worry...that son of ours can take care of himself. No...he was just calling to tell me that he wasn't able to find Spartacus, but that he hasn't given up. He was going back out today to search some more. He's got the day off...guess there aren't any dog fights scheduled for the rest of this weekend."

"I wouldn't bet on that," Jean grunted. "From his description of that Abbott fellow, I'm surprised he would take a day off from making money off those poor dogs. Spartacus? That's the one that Tyler's been trying to help for a while now, isn't it?"

B.B. nodded and squinted his eyes at the puff of rising dust, less than a mile down the driveway. "Yep...the dog has been Abbott's biggest money-maker for more than a year now, but he lost his last fight and cost the man about ten grand. Abbott wanted to kill him on the spot, but Tyler convinced him to hold off a couple of days to see if he had any fight left in him." B.B. cocked an eyebrow and grinned. "Well...wouldn't you know it...lo and behold...that dog went and managed to escape shortly after the fight..."

"Uh-huh...no doubt that dog escaped without any help from our son, I bet..." Jean smiled and looked down the driveway. "Looks like the Pet Haven folks have finally arrived. I'll get the boys to help us get their dogs settled in." She went back inside the huge, log-cabin home.

B.B. stood and stretched out his bum leg…the one he almost lost the day he and Tyler crashed on their motorcycle three years ago. B.B. had ended up with a permanent limp, and the scar on Tyler's right cheek sported as a painful reminder of the accident. It could have been much worse. B.B. knew that Tyler blamed himself for the accident, and that was why his son had never wanted to have the scar removed, but it wasn't anyone's fault. Tyler had simply over-corrected the bike when he tried to avoid hitting a stray dog that had run out onto the highway. The stray turned out to be a bait dog that had escaped its intended destiny…only to be killed when it became entangled with the crushing bike. The connection was made; that was the day Tyler committed himself to helping every bait and fighter dog he could to escape their tormented lives.

The van slowed down in the circle driveway and finally came to a complete stop. B.B. didn't recognize the driver; it certainly wasn't old-man Stocker, whom he had expected. The driver took off a Tampa Bay Rays baseball cap and shook loose a mass of long, blonde hair; no, it most definitely was not Earl Stocker who grinned up at him now.

"Hi there!" the young woman beamed as she moved quickly to the porch to shake hands with B.B. "You must be Mr. Foster…I'm Amanda Turner from Pet Haven Rescue…you probably gathered that, though, huh? I mean…it's written all over the van and all. Anyway…Mr. "S" is a little under the weather today, so I volunteered to deliver some precious cargo to you. By the way…this place is totally AWESOME!"

B.B. grinned down at the vivacious young woman who had made her way quickly to the top step of the porch. "That would be me, yes…but you can call me B.B.; everyone around these parts does. Can I offer you something to drink, Miss Turner?"

"Well, you can call *me,* Amanda, and yes…thanks…I would love something cold to drink after I help get these guys situated."

"No need for that," B.B. smiled at her. "I have a crew that's gotten everything ready for them…and, here they come now, along with the missus…"

Amanda turned to look behind her at two, good-looking men who walked toward them with an attractive, older woman between them. "Hi!" she said. "Name's Amanda Turner." She held out her hand to shake hands with Jean and the two oldest Foster sons. "I'll be glad to help y'all get them settled."

Scott Foster was quiet and reserved, but his more outgoing brother, Rick, was quick to say, "Nice to meet you, Amanda. I'm Rick Foster, this is my brother, Scott, and…" he turned to hug the petite woman between them. "This is the beautiful matriarch of the Foster clan, our mom…Jean."

Jean ignored Amanda's hand; instead, she reached out and gave her a warm hug. "Don't be silly, sweetie. Everything is all ready for these precious souls. Would you like to see where they'll be staying until we find them their perfect fur-ever homes?"

Amanda's eyes lit up. "Are you kidding? I would love to see it all! I didn't want to be rude and ask, but this place is absolutely beautiful…these dogs are so lucky to have ended up here. I thought they had it made at Pet Haven, but…"

B.B. laughed. "Pet Haven is a wonderful place and Earl Stocker is as good as they come. We're just glad we were able to help out. If Earl's place is full, that means there are too many strays looking for a safe place to lay their heads. We always have room at Foster Farm; if we don't…then we'll make room somehow. We've never turned a pet away…never will…"

A small bark from the front passenger seat got everyone's attention.

"And who might this ferocious one be?" Jean laughed as she leaned into the open van window to receive a dozen puppy kisses from Buster. "Oh, please tell, me he's going to stay with us!" she laughed again and rubbed Buster's soft head.

"Not a chance!" Amanda laughed back. "That one is mine. I adopted him a few weeks ago. His name is Buster. He's gone from being tossed from a moving car to being the most important man in my life."

"Is that so?" B.B. grinned. "So, young lady…I take it you're not married…"

"Here we go…" Rick laughed and Scott grinned, too. "Watch out, Amanda…our Mom and Dad are sorely determined to marry off the last of the Foster brothers before the year is out."

Amanda spent the next two hours touring the expansive Foster Farm and petting every rescued animal there; she lost count after a hundred…and that was just the dogs! *"Hmmm…"* she pondered, *"Amanda Foster does has a nice ring to it…I wonder what the last of the Foster brothers is like…"*

CHAPTER 4

-Heaven-
Sunday Visit Home

Martin was the lead mentor for recently deceased humans; it was his primary job to ensure those humans successfully transitioned into their next phase within their heavenly realm. The first transition usually went off without a hitch, with the deceased accepting the fact that they had left their human body, and, accepting their new, heavenly bodies. Of course, there was always the rare occurrence when one of the humans defiantly refused to accept that their lives had changed forever.

"Martin! Hey there, you old geezer! How's it hanging?"

Martin closed his eyes and shook his head when he heard the loud, boisterous voice coming closer from behind him. "Awwww, yes…it is Sunday, and…she's back…" he sighed and whispered. His right hand reached up to rub the left shoulder that took the brunt of the anticipated, sharp punch.

"I heard that, Martin! Yep…Max and I are Home for our Sunday visit. Damn, it feels good to be here again!"

"B-E-R-T-I-E!!"

There was no mistaking God's reprimanding voice, although, Bertie would have sworn she detected a slight twinge of humor in it, also. She knew that voice well. Heaven only knew that she had been reprimanded more than any angel there! "Oops…my bad…sorry, Lord…won't happen again…" she grinned and winked back at Max.

Martin spun around and looked over Bertie's head toward Max. Max grinned and shrugged his shoulders. "If I was a betting man, I'd have to get in on that one..." he said as he reached over Bertie to hug his friend, Martin. "How have you been this past week, my friend?"

Martin continued to rub his left shoulder but welcomed Max's hug. "It's been a busy week, Max, but all is well…at least it was…please try to behave yourself while you're here, won't you, Bertie?"

Bertie crossed her heart and laughed out loud. "I'll do my best, Martin…I promise."

Martin waved his hand and the black words on the huge white screen behind him disappeared. "I was just getting ready to take a break and check on the newly-transitioned ones…would the two of you like to come along?"

"Sure thing!" Bertie grinned. "I take it you don't have any stragglers this week, huh?"

"No, Bertie…" Martin puckered his thick, black lips. "There have only been a few of those in the hundred plus years since you died…and trust me, none of them have resisted their transition phase as much as you did."

Bertie wrinkled her nose and laughed. "That's because I didn't know where the hell I was at; I'd never seen so much white in all my life…at least until you entered the picture, Martin! Still haven't met any black folks as dark as you! Yeah, I know…it took me a while to accept the fact that I was too young to die…and you know, something else has always rubbed me the wrong way, but I'm not going to make a big deal out of it…"

"Please, do tell…" Martin replied as he hooked an arm through Max's and began walking forward to where the blinding whiteness began a gradual fade to blinding goldness.

Bertie tagged along behind the two black men. "Well, as you know, I was only in my twenties when the driver of that fancy new automobile hit me while I was walking to my friend, Fernie's house.

But then...I get here, get my new wardrobe, look into the water at those beautiful falls, and what do I see? Nooooo....not the twenty-six year old I was when I kicked the bucket, but instead, I see this!" Bertie spun around and put her hands on hips that were more ample than the day she died. "This heavenly body I got has to be at least forty-something! Tell me again why I ended up older in Heaven than I was when I died on earth?"

Martin stopped in his tracks and turned to face Bertie. "If you're not going to make a big deal of it, Bertie, then why does it matter?"

Bertie held her hands up in mock defense. "Just curious, that's all...I mean, I see all ages here in Heaven, from six years to about sixty...just wondering who decided I needed to be forty-something for all of eternity. I didn't have all this extra padding on me when I died either, you know."

There was laughter evident in Max's voice when he looked at Martin and shrugged again. "It's your job, my friend. I have to listen to her six days out of the week. Surely you can handle her questions and curiosity the one day that we return Home to visit?"

Martin rubbed at his shoulder again; it wasn't really sore because there was no pain in Heaven, but he thought that if he performed the gesture often enough, it just might reduce the chance of Bertie punching him again. "Very well..." he moved aside to allow Bertie to walk between him and Max. "As you know, Bertie, your heavenly body will usually be the point in your life where you felt your best, your healthiest. In your case, your best was yet to come, therefore...you are in the body we see before us now."

"But what about those poor souls who are born into imperfect bodies? The ones who are born deformed, either mentally or physically...what about them?" Bertie queried.

"There is no pain, no sorrow, no mental or physical handicaps in Heaven, Bertie," Martin continued. "The pain they suffered on earth was not in vain because our God has a purpose for each and every one of us. Some of us enjoyed life on earth in healthy bodies and minds, while others struggled daily for every word, for every breath, for every movement. It is not for us to know or understand WHY, but it is important that we BELIEVE that their condition did serve a useful purpose to someone else on earth. Those imperfect individuals receive a very special place in Heaven...a position in

which their bodies and minds are whole and completely healthy, and they are all usually transitioned into an age group varying from the twenties to the thirties, since that is determined to be the peak years in our human lives."

Max nodded and looked at his friend. "Beautifully said, Martin…I couldn't have explained it better myself."

"Easy for you to say," Bertie grunted. "You ended up in one hunk of a body while I ended up looking like…who was that woman Amanda's father said I looked like…oh, yeah…that actress, Shirley Booth. Not that she was a bad-looking woman, mind you…just sort of matronly if you know what I mean."

Max laughed and hugged Bertie against his side. "I'm not sure if the world could handle you in any other form than you are currently in, Bertie."

"Agreed!" Martin chimed in. "Look, my friends…we have arrived at the first of the transitioning stations."

The blinding whiteness had gradually evolved into a splendid gold that illuminated all around them. Several hundred souls stood around in groups, talking to one another, and staring in awe at the calm serenity that surrounded them.

"I remember this part," Bertie grinned as the trio walked among the newly transitioned souls. "It's like you finally know that you've died and gone to Heaven, and that you're really glad to be here because you weren't entirely sure that this was where you were going to end up!"

"You're just speaking from personal experience, Bertie," Martin puffed. "Trust me, not everyone is as surprised to be here as you were!"

Max laughed and shook his head. He was about to say something when he heard someone call out his name.

"Mr. Max? Bertie? Is that really y'all?"

The trio turned toward the thin, young black man running effortlessly toward them.

Bertie recognized Andrew Brown before Max and Martin did, and she broke away from their group and rushed into the strong arms of a thirty-something Andrew. "Oh…my…God…it is so good to see you again, Andrew!"

"Mighty good to see you again, Miss Bertie…yessirree…mighty

nice, indeed!" Andrew grinned as he scooped Bertie up into a tight bear hug. "Seems like only yesterday that I was sittin' in the café eating Mr. Max's buttermilk cake…I do miss that cake, Mr. Max!"

Martin and Max joined in the group hug and Max laughed out loud. "I was wondering when we would be seeing you again, Andrew…and don't you worry too much…you can have as much of that cake as you want when you get to your next phase. I have to say, though…I'm surprised to find you still in this first phase of transition."

Andrew Brown was the twin brother to Amos Brown, and they had both been frequent visitors to the Heavenly Grille Café. They had previously met Max when their father had taken them to a café to celebrate their seventh birthday. The white patrons did not want them eating in the café, but the owner had stood up to them and let them know, without a doubt, that the Brown family was more than welcome to eat there. Max served the boys their first taste of his famous buttermilk cake that day and had taken a picture of himself with the entire Brown family. Amos Brown still had that picture, which served as proof that Max had not aged one bit in almost seventy years. Amos was also with Amanda the day that Max showed himself to them in his heavenly form.

Andrew grinned widely and shook his head. "It seems like only yesterday when I arrived here; sometimes it's really hard to believe that it's been almost two years. I mean…I knows I'm dead, but...I been havin' a hard time not having Amos here beside me…we ain't ever been separated for too long, you know…so it's takin' me a while to let go of that feelin'…but I am ready now…yessirree…I can't wait to see what's next!"

Max hugged Andrew against him again and said, "You don't have to worry about Amos at all; he's fine. He misses you and your father a lot, but he's been keeping busy since you passed on. We were a little worried about him for a couple of months, but he is at peace with your passing because he knows the two of you will be reunited again with the rest of your family one day."

"I'm glad to know he's okay, Mr. Max. I was worried that Amos wouldn't want to go on after I died…he spent so much time taking care of me those last couple of years. Nobody could ask for a better brother. I miss him, but up here, it's not a sad kind of missing, if

you know what I mean."

"We know exactly what you mean, Andrew," Martin smiled. "That's all part of the first transitioning phase…letting go of that sadness we first feel in leaving our loved ones behind."

"Well," Bertie laughed as she punched Andrew on the shoulder, "One thing is for sure…since Amos is one of the two humans who know the truth about us, we can tell him that we saw you today and that you truly are in a better place!"

Andrew sighed deeply and showed a mouthful of healthy, white teeth – something he lacked during most of his human life. "You know, Miss Bertie…nothin' I ever read in the Bible prepared me for what this place is really like…I don't think they've invented words yet to really describe this place!"

"It does sort of leave you speechless," Max sighed as he looked around him. "And you haven't even experienced the best of it yet, Andrew…just wait until you move out of this phase."

"Which he is now ready to do!" Martin exclaimed. "You are free to move on today if you wish, Andrew."

Andrew looked around him and saw nothing but the beautiful golden glow that surrounded the area. "You mean, this isn't it?"

"Heavens, no!" laughed Bertie. "Did you really think this was all there was to Heaven? Oh, it's going to be fun watching you see what's coming next!"

Bertie grabbed hold of one of Andrew's arms and Martin took the other one. Max floated beside them as they moved through the crowd of souls waiting their turn to move forward to the next phase. "Excuse me!" Bertie bellowed. "Angels coming through, make way!"

Max smiled over at Andrew and said. "Just to make this even more fun for Bertie, why don't you close your eyes for just a moment Andrew…don't open them until Bertie tells you to…"

Andrew trusted the angels completely and did as Max requested. "Yessirree, Mr. Max…I am ready to see what's next…"

"Therefore do not worry about tomorrow, for tomorrow will worry about its own things. Sufficient for today is its own trouble." Matthew 6:34 (NKVJ)

CHAPTER 5

Spartacus Heals

Spartacus sighed and rolled onto his side. Once again he had received a good meal and a belly rub by humans who, obviously, meant him no harm. The two people who watched over him now were not the same ones who had taken him in a couple of days ago and cared for his many wounds, fed him a hot meal, and offered him a soft blanket on which to lay his weary head. His eyes opened when the old, dark man began to speak.

"I think he's gonna be jes fine, Mr. Doug…if he hadn't done got here when he did, though, those wounds woulda got really infected and he might not have made it…" Amos Brown spoke softly while stroking the dog's exposed belly. "My Daddy taught me and Andrew when we was boys how to take care of animal wounds."

Doug, the third angel in the trio of angels who ran the Heavenly Grille Café, squatted down beside Amos and rubbed the dog's head. "Your Daddy was a smart man, Amos; who would have ever thought of using sugar on open wounds!"

Amos nodded and grinned his toothless grin. "Yessirree…plain and simple granulated sugar works good for most wounds, but we always liked making a paste of powdered sugar and cooking oil cause it covers and sticks to the wound better than just plain 'ole sugar…that's all it takes to get rid of any infection in open wounds…lots cheaper than those high falutin' medicines they want you to use, too."

Spartacus licked one of those wounds and decided he liked the taste of this thing the old man called *sugar*. He closed his eyes again when the younger, white man rubbed his head. A feeling of calm and peace came over him, just like when the other black man had touched him that first night. He felt instantly safe.

"Yes, I think Max and Bertie will be very pleased with the progress he's made while they've been away today," Doug smiled over at the old man who had been a steady customer of the café since it first opened at its current location in Monticello, Florida. "They should be getting back here any time now, Amos, if you want to head home…I can watch over this fella until they get back."

Amos rolled his head from side to side, to get the kinks out, and nodded. "Well, if you be sure you don't mind, Mr. Doug, I am a bit tired. Might be a good idea if I took myself on home and got a little rest. I'll be back tomorrow, though, to check on him. Don't forget to use some more of that sugar paste on those legs wounds before you go to bed tonight; looks like his po' legs took the brunt of the fighting; he's lucky he didn't lose that front, right one…got tore up pretty bad, but it's gonna heal jes fine, yessirree…jes fine…"

It was almost eleven o'clock when Bertie and Max suddenly appeared before Doug and the dog. Doug was leaning against the wall with his eyes closed, and the dog's head lay in his lap.

"Well!" Bertie laughed when she saw the lovable duo, "Angels don't sleep, so I have to assume you're praying there, handsome!"

Doug opened one eye and grinned back at Bertie before

nodding in agreement. "Glad you two are back. How was your visit Home?"

"It was just what we needed, as usual," Max spoke softly. He bent down and placed his large hand upon the dog's head. "We saw Andrew Brown while we were there."

"No kidding!" Doug straightened up and repositioned the dog's head upon his lap. "That's great news. Amos will be glad to hear about that visit, for sure. He was here with me, all day, taking care of this fella. Have you ever heard about the healing powers of plain, old sugar…how it works wonders for healing open wounds? Check it out…"

Max moved his hands over the dog and sighed. "Unbelievable at how quickly he is healing…sugar, you say? You know…it's been centuries, but I do remember using a mixture of honey and grease back in my Gladiator days to heal wounds…for ourselves and the animals. Did Amos come up with that sugar remedy?"

Doug smiled and nodded. "Yes, he did…said it was something his Daddy taught him and Andrew a long time ago…looks like this fella is going to be just fine. Have you given any thought about what you're going to do with him?"

Max shook his head. "Not really…our primary concern was getting him healed…"

"The restaurant has been closed today," Bertie chimed in, "But…did you have any visitors?"

Doug looked at the naughty angel and grinned. "How did you know, Bertie? As a matter of fact, remember that fella who was in here Friday night…the one you had a bad feeling about?'

Bertie punched Max on the back of his shoulder. "See! I knew it! I knew he would come back! What did he want, handsome? He's involved with this dog somehow, isn't he? I knew it!"

Spartacus opened his eyes when he heard Bertie's excited voice. *"Oh no…what man…is someone looking for me? Are these people going to give me back to the Abbotts? Or maybe they're talking about that other man…the one who was nice to me when*

Little John wasn't looking…what's going on?"

Max comforted the dog when it was obvious their loud talking had startled him. "It's okay, boy…nothing for you to worry about…nobody is ever going to hurt you again…"

Doug moved to a standing position and stretched his arms over his head. "Well…he was looking for a dog, but I don't believe the story he told us. He drove up around two o'clock and peered through the front door. Amos and I were back here in the kitchen, but I sensed him at the front door. He walked around to the back wood line, then to the back porch. I think he was probably following the blood trail."

"Oh, no…" Bertie shook her head. "I knew it…I just knew he had something to do with this poor animal."

"The dog began whimpering when he sensed the man at the back door," Doug continued. "He didn't growl, didn't shake…just whimpered a little bit, but it was loud enough that the man must have heard because the next thing he did was to knock on the back door. Amos wanted to handle him, but I insisted that he stay with the dog and let me talk to the man."

Max took the dog's head between his two hands and looked deeply into its soulful, trusting eyes. "Go on, Doug…what did the man have to say?"

"He introduced himself as Tyler Jones…said he worked for a rescue organization that took in abused animals…specifically…pit-bull mixes, and that he had been transporting a dog there when he stopped for gas and the dog escaped from the truck bed."

"Did you believe his story?" Bertie asked.

"Not entirely," Doug answered. "I don't know…he was a little difficult to read, but I got the feeling that at least part of his story might be true. Anyway…while we were talking, the dog whimpered loud enough for the man to hear him. When I explained to him that we had found a hurt dog, he asked to see him."

"And you let him?" Bertie asked incredulously. "What were you thinking, handsome?"

Max stood to his full height and put a hand on Bertie's shoulder. "Calm down, Bertie. Doug did the right thing. We needed to find out what connection this man has to the dog." He looked back at Doug and asked, "Did the dog seem to be afraid of the man?"

Doug shook his head. "Not in the least. In fact, his tail began thumping against the floor and his ears, or at least what's left of his ears, laid back flat when the man bent down to talk to him. No...it was obvious that the dog knew the man and trusted him, but...something about the man's story just didn't ring true to me, so I told him no when he asked he if could take the dog to the rescue's farm...at least until I could do some research to check out the facts about the place."

"Did you check the information out?" Max asked.

"I tried, yes..." Doug answered. "I couldn't find anything on the internet or phone books about the place, but Tyler gave me the rescue's phone number and I called after he left. A man by the name of B.B. Foster owns and operates a place in Brooksville, Florida called the Foster Farm. Mr. Foster confirmed that Tyler did work for him, and that they did, indeed, rescue abused and abandoned animals. I went a step further and asked him if Tyler Jones was involved, in any way, with dog fighting rings."

Max raised his eyebrows in surprise. "You did? Didn't waste any time, did you?"

"I was able to get a good reading off this man over the phone," Doug explained. "This is a good man...an honest man. He did say there was more to Tyler's story, but that neither of them was at liberty to explain it just yet. He said he had a spot waiting for this dog...whose name is Spartacus, by the way..."

I heard my name and tried to stand up but my front legs were still weak from not using them for the past twenty-four hours. I lifted my head and whimpered. The kind, black man smiled at me and said, "Well...hello there, Spartacus...what a gallant name you have..." I looked at the loud, white woman who was also smiling down at me. I assumed that she must like my name, too. I was glad that the nice man who worked for the Abbotts told them what my name was…it sounds so much better than just "dog." It was good to see that nice man again, but I was also pretty relieved when the man they called Doug refused to let him take me away, because I was afraid he would take me back to the Abbott place. I was so tired of fighting…I never wanted to hurt another dog again like Czar had hurt me…never…

"He looks like a Spartacus," Bertie grinned. "Okay…so where do we stand now with this Tyler fella? Is he coming back to get Spartacus?"

"He wanted to," Doug continued, "But I told him we would call him once we had decided on what needed to be done. Funny thing, though…right after he left, guess who called?"

"Who?" Max asked.

"Amanda!" Doug smiled when Bertie began to clap her hands in delight. "Yeah…and you won't believe where she was at when she called…"

"You're keeping us in suspense on purpose, aren't you?" Bertie chastised him.

Doug laughed and shook his head. "Not on purpose, Bertie…it's just that…well…things really do happen as they are meant to, I guess. Today was Amanda's day off and she was helping out that animal shelter place she volunteers at; she offered to take a load of dogs to another rescue organization, located in Brooksville, Florida…care to guess which one?"

Max and Bertie stood dumbfounded for just a moment before staring at each other and bursting out in laughter. "No!" Bertie shouted. "Not the Foster Farm?"

Doug nodded. "Yep…she was just leaving Foster Farm, met the whole family, and verified that it is a rescue organization that goes out of its way to help abused and abandoned dogs and cats, but most especially…and get this…the owner has a passion for rescuing pit-bull mixes that have been victims of…dog-fighting rings…"

Bertie punched Doug on the shoulder and shouted, "Well,

praise the Lord! He truly is everywhere, isn't he…he knows what's going on everywhere, every second of the day…our God sent Amanda to that place…He knew that we needed her there to make this connection to Spartacus…truly amazing…"

"Well," Doug nodded as he pulled a piece of paper from the back pocket of his jeans. "Here's Tyler's contact information." He handed the paper to Max. "I told him you would be in touch after we had a chance to check out his information. I told Amanda about the situation we had here. She said that she's got a few days off coming to her and that she would be glad to drive here tomorrow and take Spartacus back to Foster Farm."

Max sighed and looked around the room. "Well…it's been a long day…let me think all this over tonight and I'll call Amanda in the morning with our decision. I'll call Tyler Jones, too, and let him know what we've decided. I'd like to meet this young man first, though, before I tell him anything about our decision. I trust Amanda's opinion of Foster Farm…it seems like a safe place for Spartacus to go. It's probably a good idea to get him as far away from Monticello as we can…we have no idea who was responsible for fighting him, or whether they are looking for him. We could be inviting a lot of trouble into the situation."

"Humph…" Bertie grunted. "None of us has ever run away from trouble, so I say, bring it on. We've got to do what's best for Spartacus, though…as much as I'd like to keep him here with us, I think he needs to get away from Monticello, too, and…as soon as possible."

Spartacus took a deep breath and pushed himself to a standing position. His front legs wobbled but he managed to maintain a standing position and lifted his head high. He looked into the eyes of the three people who had taken such good care of him. He trusted them explicitly and nodded his assent to them.

"Did you see that!" Bertie exclaimed. "I think he understood everything we just said!"

Max smiled. "I can assure you that he did, Bertie, and...you may eventually be able to know exactly what Spartacus is thinking."

Spartacus sighed. *"Well of course I understood everything you said...why is it that humans seem to think we animals are inferior to their intelligence?"* He wobbled over to each of them and licked their hands. *"I may not be able to actually talk to them, but maybe I can make them understand what they need to know...maybe they're smart enough to get what I need to tell them..."* He barked happily, turned around, lay back down on his soft blanket, closed his eyes, and fell fast asleep

CHAPTER 6

Amanda's Parents Contact Her

It was eleven o'clock, Sunday night, when Amanda took Buster outside to do his business. The young pup made his rounds, sniffing the fence line and checking to ensure his mistress was safe and protected. He may have been only four months old, but he already knew that his primary mission in life was to protect Amanda Turner at all costs; she had saved his life by adopting him and loving him like he was sure no other human ever could.

"Okay, come on, Buster…it's been a long day…time for bed," Amanda whispered loudly, trying to get the pup's attention without disturbing her neighbors.

Buster hiked his back, right leg one final time and watered his favorite palmetto palm bush. He ran quickly to Amanda when she opened the front door wider to allow him entry. He sat down and looked up at her while she secured the locks.

Amanda shook her head. "No, it's too late for another snack…time for sleep, little fella." She pointed upstairs toward her bedroom. She laughed when Buster appeared to pout before he finally turned and sprinted up the carpeted stairs. She turned off all the lights downstairs, and made her way to the single bedroom upstairs. Her one-bedroom condo suited her needs perfectly; it was large enough for what little storage she needed, and small enough that it was quick and easy to maintain. It only took Amanda a few minutes to wash her face, brush her teeth, and pull on one of her father's oversized, comfy tee-shirts. She looked down at her pillow to find Buster already comfortably splayed upon it. "Move over, Buster…you have to learn to share…" she smiled.

It really had been a long day. She had thoroughly enjoyed her visit to the Foster Farm and meeting the wonderful family who ran it. Mrs. Stocker had fed her and Buster upon their return from Brooksville. She had not left Pet Haven until almost nine o'clock, but had taken her time because she knew that she had the next two weeks off work and could sleep late the next morning.

Amanda fell asleep, to the sound of Buster's soft snoring, the moment her head hit the pillow. Her sleep was peaceful until the early hours of Monday morning; that's when her parents usually came to her in her dreams…usually within an hour before her awakening. It had been several weeks since she had dreamed of her parents but she smiled in her sleep when she heard her father's voice.

"Hey, there, Princess…guess who?" her father whispered. He looked over at his wife, Regina, and said, "She gets more beautiful every day, doesn't she?"

"Yes, she does…" Regina agreed, "But we don't have much time, Stephen…tell her what she needs to know."

"I hear you both," Amanda grinned in her sleep.

"Okay, Princess…here's the scoop. It would appear that you have some time off coming to you from work."

"Some much earned time off, I must say," Amanda mumbled with her eyes still tightly closed. Buster continued snoring soundly beside her and she draped an arm over him. "I haven't taken a personal day off since I started working for the Department, so I have two weeks coming to me. The Captain practically ordered me last week to find something else to do for two weeks."

"Well," Regina smiled down at her sleeping daughter. She wished that she could touch her golden hair and hold her in her arms, but she knew that was not possible…at least not yet. "It just so happens that we have a project that might interest you…"

"One that you, and Buster, will thoroughly enjoy…" Stephen chimed in.

"Are you listening, Amanda?" Regina grinned.

Amanda held up an index finger and shook it slightly. "Listening…you betcha…project for me to do…"

Stephen hugged his wife tightly against him and shook his head. The next couple of weeks should be very interesting. The last thing he whispered into Amanda's ear after they told her about the project was, "Be expecting a very unexpected visitor, Princess…"

Amanda's alarm clock clanged blaringly and jarred her awake at five-fifteen Monday morning. Buster barked and licked her face. Amanda searched blindly in the dark for the clock's OFF switch and hit it a bit harder than was necessary. Buster barked and licked her face again.

"Okay, okay…" she moaned as soon as she realized that she had, unintentionally, set the alarm for her first day off in eighteen months. She opened one eye and tried to focus. It was hard to see anything since it was still dark outside, but she did see Buster running around in circles on the bed. She immediately jumped up and yelled, "Don't you dare pee on my bed, Buster! Come on, boy, let's go pee-pee on the grass…come on!"

She felt her way blindly down the staircase and let Buster outside to explore his early-morning experiences. She rubbed her eyes and made her way into the kitchen, without turning on any lights. She felt for the coffee maker's ON button and plopped down into the worn-out, but comfortable recliner she had found at the local thrift store. She closed her eyes and suddenly remembered the dream with her parents. Her eyes popped open widely and she said, "Oh, crap! I've got to pack and get my butt back to Monticello!" She made her way to the front door and convinced Buster to give up on his dream of catching the rabbit who habitually ate all of Amanda's flowering plants. "Come on, Buster! We have an adventure to get ready for…you're gonna love my angels, fella!"

Little John Abbott's truck pulled up slowly outside the bunk house where most of his crew spent their nights. He spotted the lone silhouette leaning against the wooden fence outside the bunkhouse and knew immediately who it was. He cut the truck's engine and got out.

"You're up early, Jones…" Little John grunted.

Tyler thought he picked up a suspicious, accusatory tone to his boss's voice. He also thought he knew why. He lifted his baseball cap and nodded. "Morning, Boss…yeah…I thought if you could spare me this morning, I would get an early start looking for Spartacus again."

Little John moved closer to the young man who had come to work for him a few months earlier. He couldn't say why, but part of him didn't trust Tyler Jones…if that was even his real name. He had done a background check on Tyler, but nothing negative had turned up. It was a common name, and the references Tyler had provided offered satisfactory, albeit vague, comments about his previous job experiences. The fact that Tyler had never served any time in jail or prison was the first red flag for Little John; still…he sensed that it was better to keep Tyler close so that he could keep an eye on him. He stared hard at Tyler and said, "You've been looking for him since Friday…there's a lot of work to be done this week."

Tyler nodded. "I just need one more day, Mr. Abbott. If I don't find him today, then we'll have to assume that he died in the woods."

"I would prefer to *KNOW* what happened to him and not to *ASSUME* anything," Little John grunted. "One more day is all you've got, kid…that's it. That damn dog cost me a small fortune when he lost that fight, not to mention taking a hit to my reputation for having champion winners. By the way…the dog he lost to…Czar?"

"Yeah?" Tyler replied.

"I want him…I told Clint to make it happen, so make sure you do whatever he might need you to do to make that happen." Little John did not wait for a response.

Tyler watched while Little John turned abruptly and got back into his truck. He watched the truck until it turned right at the end of the long drive-way; Little John was obviously headed into town. "Yeah…that'll happen…" he muttered before pulling out his cell phone. He let the phone at the other end ring until the voice mail came on. "Hey…it's me…I'll get back to you in a couple of hours, but plan on meeting me today at the point we agreed on…" Tyler looked around the quiet, darkened ranch and exhaled deeply. He got into his own truck, driving south toward a small café in Monticello. If he had looked in his rear view mirror, he probably would have seen the shadows of someone stepping out from behind the bunk house.

Clint Meacham was Little John's second-in-command. It was his job to run a check on the crew they hired to work at the ranch, but he had been out of town the day that Tyler Jones had been hired. Tyler had already been on the job for a week by the time Clint returned to the ranch, and Clint's radar soared when he first met the young man. His instincts told him that Tyler should not be trusted, and he conveyed those feelings to Little John. The ranch had been extremely short-handed at the time, so Little John had told him to let Tyler remain on the job, but that Clint should keep a close eye on the kid.

Clint flicked his cigarette butt to the ground and stepped on it with his heavy, work boot. He replaced the cigarette with a preferred pinch of dried tobacco between his tongue and cheek. He watched Tyler's truck disappear down the drive-way and make a left-turn southward. "Now, I wonder who you might be meeting today, Tyler Jones…and why…"

Clint debated on whether or not he should follow Tyler, but Little John had another job for him to do today, so he knew he would have to put his suspicions about the young man on hold…for now. "Another time, kid…another time…"

The breakfast crowd at the Heavenly Grille Café were all enjoying the fruits of Max's labor this fine, Monday morning. The visit Home, as usual, had energized Max and Bertie, so the two of them relished in their work and their conversations with their customers. The café was alive with the enticing aromas of creamy cheese grits, buttery-fried eggs, sausage, bacon, ham, biscuits, and the never-ending cups of richly-brewed coffee. Max's breakfasts were famous for being the stick-to-your-rib kind, and truckers from all walks of life made it a point to eat at the café whenever their routes allowed them. Max cooked the delicious food, and Bertie kept the refills coming. Nobody ever had to pay extra for seconds; Max's only request was that the patrons not request more than they could actually eat, because he felt it was sinful to waste food when there were so many people around the world going without it. There was always a money jar on the counter where truckers gladly put extra tips for whatever family Max and Bertie were trying to help out at the moment; the voluntary giving of those donations made them feel less guilty for asking for free seconds of Max's delicious food.

Bertie was making her rounds, punching an available shoulder here and there, and keeping the coffee cups filled. Doug was cleaning the tables as quickly as possible when customers left so that the truckers waiting in their rigs could take their turn inside the café. The truckers could have easily gone a little farther down the interstate and stopped at one of the many fast-food restaurants, but word-of-mouth kept them coming…and waiting their turn…at the Heavenly Grille.

Doug caught Bertie's eye as she approached the table he was wiping down. He glanced out the window toward the parking lot and tilted his head in that direction. Bertie felt a chill run down her spine and turned to see what had captured Doug's attention. She almost dropped the coffee pot when she saw the dark pick-up truck pull into the last empty spot in the parking lot. "Well, I'll be damned…" she whispered to Doug. "Look at what the dog dragged in…"

"No pun intended, I'm sure," Doug grinned back at her. "Keep an eye on him…I'll let Max know."

Tyler looked up at the golden halo that floated effortlessly above the café. It still puzzled him as to how the halo was attached; he couldn't make out any wires or cables holding it in place. He took a final look at it before making his way to the front door, and automatically wiped his feet on the welcome mat provided. The mat was in the shape of angel wings with the phrase, "GOD LOVES YOU AND SO DO WE!" emblazoned around the bottom edge. He removed his baseball cap upon entering the café and looked around for an empty seat. The middle-aged waitress, who Tyler thought resembled the actress who played on re-runs of an old television show called "Hazel", stood behind the counter and motioned him forward.

"Take a load off, young man," Bertie grinned and nodded toward the last empty stool at the counter. "Don't worry none about a menu…you like grits? Cause that's what we got for breakfast…cheese grits…all you can eat, along with all the fixings that come with it."

Tyler recognized the waitress as being the same one who had served him on Friday night. There was something about the way she looked directly at him when she spoke to him that made him squirm in his seat; he was sure that she was the type who could see through any bull of a story he might have thought to offer. He smiled back at her and said, "Yes ma'am, thank you…sounds good…I'll take one of everything, I guess."

"Figured you would…" Bertie grinned again as she leaned across the counter and gave him a playful punch against his shoulder. "No need to beat around the bush either, 'cause I know why you're really here...but, you go ahead and eat first. Max will talk to you later when this crowd thins out some. You got some time to kill, don't ya?"

Tyler nodded and rubbed his shoulder. She had a pretty strong punch for such a little woman. He was momentarily speechless because she had caught him off-guard. Did she really know why he was here? He looked around the café and quickly recognized Doug as the man he had talked to on Sunday about Spartacus. He nodded at Doug and turned back to Bertie. "Yes, ma'am, I do..."

"Good," Bertie said. "That's good...it'll give us a chance to get to know one another a little better..."

Tyler looked over Bertie's shoulder, toward the partly-open kitchen area, and saw the largest black man he had ever seen in his life smiling back at him. He suddenly felt all the stress and tenseness that had imprisoned his body over the past few months evaporate into the air around him. He had not felt this peaceful since he first set out on his latest adventure to put an end to the Abbott's dog-fighting establishment. He looked back at Bertie and sighed. "Yes, ma'am...it will..."

CHAPTER 7

Spartacus and Tyler Reunite

It had taken longer than usual for the breakfast crowd to thin out, but Tyler had been patient. He had spent the last three hours eating the best breakfast he had had since leaving home a few months ago; in fact, the food at the Heavenly Grille Café was probably *better* than his mom's cooking. However, he would be the last person to ever admit that to her.

"You had better tell Bertie that you've had enough...else, she'll keep loading that plate up over and over again until you literally burst...the woman doesn't know the meaning of the word STOP", Doug whispered as he stood behind Tyler. He sat the tray of dishes he had carried from a dirty table onto the counter and grinned at the young man who was sopping sausage gravy from his empty plate.

Tyler choked on his last bite of biscuit and looked over his shoulder at the tall, muscular man who stood quietly behind him.

Doug thumped him on the back. "Sorry...didn't mean to sneak up on you like that."

Tyler shook his head and grinned. "It's okay...I was so

busy cleaning my plate I didn't even realize that breakfast must be over. They must think I'm a glutton. I don't usually eat this much food, especially in the mornings, but, well...damn...this is the best food I've had in a long, long time."

Doug took the young man's offered hand and shook it firmly. "It's good to see you again...Tyler *Jones*, right?"

Tyler squirmed beneath the lie he had told Doug the day before, but he couldn't take any chances that the truth might somehow get back to Little John. He didn't want to think about the ensuing consequences if that were to ever happen. It would be bad for him, undoubtedly, but he knew that Little John would make sure that the dogs suffered, too...especially, if he ever found out about Tyler's familial connection to Foster Farm. "It's good to see you again, too...I'm sorry...I'm terrible with names..."

"It's Doug, and that's okay. I wasn't sure if you would really come back today or not." Doug sat down on the empty stool beside Tyler and stared unabashedly at the young man.

Tyler had the decency to flinch but felt compelled to return Doug's imploring stare. He couldn't explain why, but he suddenly had the feeling that his secret would be safe with this man. He also had the strangest feeling that he would end up telling these people the truth about his mission. Tyler finally nodded and said, "I...had to come back...I have to convince your boss to release Spartacus to me. How is he? Spartacus, I mean?"

Doug grinned. He had liked this young man when he first met him, and he liked him even more now; but, it wasn't up to him...it was Max's decision. "You may not recognize him."

"Who?" Tyler asked.

Doug grinned again. "Spartacus...oh, trust me, you'll have no problem recognizing the boss. He's the huge Gladiator in the kitchen."

Tyler glanced over to the open serving window that separated the kitchen from the rest of the restaurant. He gulped without realizing it. "Yeah…I kind of thought that might be him. You're right…I can almost picture him strutting around the Coliseum…"

"Oh, you have no idea!" Doug laughed out loud now, which brought Bertie marching toward them.

"There's probably a few grits left in the pot, Tyler Jones," she smiled and cocked her head sideways.

Tyler got the impression that she was sizing him up and the only way to find out his true mission in life was to feed him bowls and bowls of cheese grits. He held up both hands in mock defense. "No, ma'am, thank you…I really couldn't eat another bite."

Bertie pursed her lips together and continued to watch Tyler with an inquisitive look. "Hmmm…okay, then. Don't forget the jar on the counter there…you can do your good deed for the day and help the Wooten family raise enough money to pay for George Wooten's gall bladder surgery. They don't have any insurance and I doubt if this silly thing they call Obama Care is gonna do a damn thing to help them with it."

Tyler reached into his back pocket for his wallet and took out a ten dollar bill. "Yes, ma'am, glad to help out."

Bertie nodded and moved toward the kitchen. She looked back and said, "Max will be ready to see you soon. Don't you move, you hear?"

Tyler nodded. "Yes, ma'am…I wouldn't think of moving…"

Doug waited until Bertie was in the kitchen with Max, and then burst out laughing. He patted Tyler on the shoulder and said, "Don't worry…you're certainly not the first person not to be able to say NO to that woman. Her name is Bertie, and, I wish I could say her bark is worse that her bite, but…I couldn't really swear to that, so…"

Max stepped out of the kitchen, wiping his massive black hands on the dish towel that was tucked inside his belt. He was smiling as he moved toward Doug and Tyler; he had been watching and listening to Tyler all morning, and had not picked up any threatening vibes about the young man. "Tyler Jones?" his deep voice reverberated throughout the almost-emptied café.

Tyler gulped and quickly pushed off the stool that he had sat on for the past three hours. He held out his hand and almost stuttered, "Yes…yes, sir…that's me…" He felt guilty again at the white lie he had told about his name.

Max took Tyler's offered hand and cradled it between his own two hands. "Very nice to meet you, young man…I am Max, the owner of this café."

Tyler was momentarily speechless when he saw how small his hand appeared between the black man's grasp. He had never seen hands that huge before, and he hoped and prayed that he would never find himself on the receiving end of this man's ire. It had, also, not escaped his attention that neither Doug, Bertie, nor Max had offered any last names; but, he certainly was not going to question them on that small fact. "Very nice to meet you, Max…yes, sir…very nice…"

Max still held Tyler's hand between his own and was learning much more about the young man than Tyler would have realized. He smiled again and looked over at Doug. "Why don't you take Tyler into the back and let him see for himself how well Spartacus is doing?" He finally released Tyler's hands.

Tyler didn't realized how peaceful he had felt while Max held his hand…until the large, black man released it. Tyler shook his head and tried to focus on why he was there. "Thank you, Max…I would love to see Spartacus again."

Spartacus was lying on his blanket and licking the last of the sausage gravy from his bowl, but he stopped suddenly when he sensed movement in the doorway. *"Hey, I know you! You're that nice man who helped me get away from my master! You were supposed to take me to the pit…yeah, we all knew about the pit…but you didn't take me there. I sure hope you're not here to take me back now because I really don't want to fight any more…"* He pushed himself to a standing position while the young man who had saved him made his way slowly toward him.

"Spartacus? Hey there, fella..." Tyler spoke softly as he reached out to rub the dog behind his ears.

"Oh, I love it when you do the ears...yep, yep, yep...a little to the left, please..." Spartacus licked the hand of the young man. *"Hope you tried some of that yummy brown stuff they call gravy, cause it sure was good!"* He wagged his tail and leaned in for more of the young man's rubs and hugs. He couldn't remember a time when he had experienced so many rubs and hugs from humans. He liked it...he liked it a lot!

Bertie stood behind Tyler and watched how he interacted with the dog. "So...Tyler *Jones*, is it?"

Tyler continued rubbing Spartacus. He couldn't believe how quickly the dog's wounds were healing, and he was so thankful that his prayers for the dog's well-being had been answered. Tyler gave Spartacus a final rub behind the ears, took a deep breath, and turned around to face the no-nonsense waitress. He looked her squarely in the eye and knew that he could not lie any longer to these people, but more importantly, he knew that there was no need to lie to them. "No, ma'am...I wasn't completely honest about that, but...there's a reason for the lie..."

Everyone was quiet for a moment and you could literally hear the proverbial pin drop if you listened closely enough.

"Today would be nice!" Bertie bellowed. "You'll find that the truth works better for you here than any lie ever would. Spit it out! We're listening..."

Tyler took another deep breath and faced the trio. "I work for a man who uses dogs for fighting purposes; he makes a lot of money off these dogs. Spartacus is one of his champion fighters, but he lost a major fight on Friday night, and it cost my boss a lot...and I do mean...a lot of money. It was my job to make sure Spartacus suffered before I finally killed him off..." Tyler waited for the shocked expressions that never appeared on the trio's faces. "Well...I couldn't do it...no, wait...I *wouldn't* do it! The truth is...I am actually working, sort of undercover, at the Abbott ranch in Thomasville to help the state's animal protection inspectors expose the owner for his role in operating a large dog-fighting ring. Tyler Jones is just a name I used to get a job at the ranch…my real name is Tyler Foster and my family owns and operates a sanctuary in Brooksville for abused bait and fighting dogs. If you decide to return Spartacus to me today, it is my intent to transport him to Foster Farm for his protection and eventual re-homing to a family who will love and appreciate him for the loyal soul that he is…" Tyler took a deep breath, unaware that he had not breathed while giving his spiel.

Spartacus moved forward and licked Tyler's hands. He looked up at the trio of angels who had nursed him back to miraculous health in just two days. *"Hey…I trust him! No reason the three of you shouldn't trust him, too! Besides, this Foster Farm place seems like a much better place to be than the Abbott ranch. If my vote counts, I'm with this guy!"*

Max smiled down at the dog. "Your vote definitely counts, Spartacus." He looked at Tyler's wrinkled brows and knew that the young man had no idea what had just transpired between the angels and the dog. "Well…it's very nice to meet you, Tyler *Foster*…and, I see no reason why you shouldn't take Spartacus with you to Foster Farm. I think he will be safer there than he would be here. You've been patient in waiting, but, do you think you could wait another hour before you leave?"

Tyler looked at his watch. It was almost noon and it would take him almost two hours to meet up with his father at their designated half-way point, but that should still allow him enough time to get back to the Abbott ranch and concoct a story about Spartacus' demise. "Sure thing, sir…no problem…I'll just wait back at the counter…maybe have some more of that delicious coffee…call my Dad and let him know the plan." He knelt down again and took Spartacus' head between his palms. He kissed the top of the dog's head and whispered, "It's going to be okay, fella…everything is going to be okay…"

The angels watched as Tyler returned to the dining area. Doug knew better than to question Max as to why he wanted

Tyler to wait another hour before leaving; he knew that Max always had a reason behind his requests.

Bertie, on the other hand, needed an explanation. "Why the hell are you making that young man wait another hour, Maximus? He's got a long ride ahead of him. He needs to get going."

Max shook his head and said, "He only has to drive half way to Brooksville, Bertie; someone will meet him at the half-way mark and take Spartacus the rest of the way. He has plenty of time."

"Still..." Bertie commanded, "Why the delay?"

Max stood silent for a moment and Doug turned to leave the kitchen. The café phone rang just as Doug reached the doorway. He looked back at Max who nodded at him. Doug picked up the phone. "Heavenly Grille Café...Doug speaking..." A smile spread across his chiseled, handsome face and he looked back at Max, who was grinning at him. "Well, it's good to hear your voice, too! What? Really? Hey, that's the best news I've heard all day. Okay...okay...I'll tell them...good-bye."

Doug hung up the phone and rubbed the back of his neck. He was still smiling when he turned back to face Bertie and Max. He shook his head and stared at Max. "That was Amanda...she's on her way to spend her two-week vacation with us. She'll be here...within the hour..."

"Well, hot damn and hallelujah!" Bertie bellowed. She punched Max on the shoulder and looked at him sternly. "But you knew this all along, didn't you, big fella?"

A scratch at the back door stopped them all in their tracks. Spartacus' ears perked up and he barked softly. It was not a threatening bark, rather, more of a welcoming one.

"Ah..." Max whispered while he moved to open the back door. "There is one other surprise I haven't mentioned.

Bertie gasped when she saw the huge black dog standing outside the screen door. Her hands flew into the air and she laughed out loud. "Sam! Well, I'll be damned again...what a sight for sore eyes you are...and won't our Amanda be surprised to see you!"

Spartacus moved closer to where Sam, Amanda's first dog, stood guard in the doorway. *"Wow…if I'm going to look anything like you when I get to Heaven, maybe I should've died in those woods a couple of nights ago! Nice to meet you, Sam!"*

Sam walked slowly into the kitchen and rubbed heads with Spartacus. This was his first assignment as an angel dog and he couldn't wait to see his sweet Amanda again!

CHAPTER 8

-Heaven-
Andrew Brown Moves On

Martin was watching his huge monitor as the scene unfolded in the kitchen of the Heavenly Grille Café. He clapped his hands and then folded them in prayer when Sam and Spartacus rubbed their heads together. Dogs and cats were often sent back to earth to complete various assignments, but he was especially looking forward to Amanda's reaction to seeing her long-lost pet again. He almost wished he could be there with them for the reunion, but he knew that he could better serve his God doing what he loved to do…overseeing the transition of the newly departed.

Even though time was not of the essence in Heaven, it was Martin's primary job to ensure that the newly departed advanced, in a timely manner, to phase three of their heavenly transition process. Phase one occurred immediately upon the last breath of the deceased; if they were a believer in Christ, then their souls went immediately to Heaven's Waiting Room. It did not matter what condition their earthly bodies were in when they took their final breath, or what age they were when they died…once they entered the Waiting Room, their bodies were whole and healthy and at the age in which they would have been at their best on earth. An infant who died prematurely might be a 12-, 22-, or even 32-year old in

Heaven, while a 90-year old who had been crippled and deformed with arthritis on earth, would be a vibrant and energetic 25-, 35-, or 45-year old in Heaven. There was no rhyme or reason involved; it was all in God's hands; He, and He alone, made that determination for each and every soul who entered His Home.

The majority of phase one participants quickly and eagerly accepted their new transition; they more than welcomed their good fortune in being able to spend eternity with their Lord and Savior. However, every once in a while, Martin came across a stubborn participant, who was not ready to accept the fact that their earthly body was gone and that they were, indeed, DEAD. Bertie had certainly been one of his more frustrating cases; it had taken years for her to move on to phase two.

Souls who advanced to phase two replaced their simple white robes and white sashes with a more elaborate white robe…accented with a beautiful, colored sash. They left the peaceful, white serenity of phase one and found themselves engulfed in the brilliant gold that surrounded the holding area of phase two. Phase two allowed them the time they needed to learn the basics of Heaven. They learned about the different colored sashes and how they depicted a soul's educational advancement in Heaven; only one person was allowed to wear a gold sash and that was God Himself. They learned that any food, except meat, was available for their enjoyment – even though their new, heavenly bodies did not require food or water. The hardest thing they learned was that the factor of time was very different in Heaven than it had been when they lived on earth. One hour in Heaven might be the equivalent of one week, one month, or even one year on earth. It usually did not take them long to realize that it was not worth the effort to try to correlate the time in the two locations. Although it surprised many souls that they could not immediately reunite with their loved ones until much later in the transition process, they did not question that fact. It might be fifty minutes or fifty earth years before they were reunited, but it did not matter to them. They knew that they would eventually be able to hold their loved ones in their arms once again; but, they also knew that their time would be blissfully filled and occupied until that moment arrived.

Phase three was the final phase in the overall transition process.

This was the phase in which each soul was provided their own mansion in which to live, began their daily conversations with their Lord, were assigned their "job" in Heaven, learned about the hierarchy of angels, and countless other things which only served to enlighten them and bring them an extraordinary feeling of love and joy.

Martin sensed the footsteps and waved his hand across the huge screen. The images of the angels and the dogs quickly faded away as Andrew Brown approached his mentor. Martin turned and held out his arms in welcome. "Andrew! Just look at you…I see you have already earned a green sash. I am very impressed…very impressed…but, then, I knew it wouldn't take you long."

Andrew grinned, flashing his full set of pearly whites – he was still trying to get used to seeing them in his reflection when he looked into the clear ponds. He looked down at his green sash and nodded. "Yes, sir…I just got it a little bit ago. Red, blue, green…only one more to go until I learn all the basics…purple…they say that could take a long, long time."

"There is a lot to learn, Andrew. You will have daily studies with your peers and your mentors. It's all part of the process so that those of us who are already here can be ready to assist the millions that will arrive in a short span of time when the Rapture occurs. There will be no need for the three phases of transition at that point, but we will need everyone here to be ready to help out when that time arrives."

"I sure wish I knew when that might be, Mr. Martin, sir…" Andrew sighed wistfully. "I just wish that everyone was here with us now, because…well…I just can't imagine being anywhere else, to tell you the truth..."

"Aww, my boy, but you certainly know that no one knows the exact day or time that will occur. All we can do is to continue to pray for those who are not ready when the time comes…pray that they will be ready when that final trumpet blows. My heart bleeds for what those left behind will have to endure during the Tribulation…it will not be a pleasant existence for any of them…"

"Yes, sir…I know that…I just wish there was a way to convince folks down there now to accept Jesus before the Rapture takes place. I'm truly glad that what's left of my family will not be left behind…I

wish there was some way to warn all them others…"

Martin sighed. "But there is a way, Andrew…all they have to do is to have faith and to believe. It truly is as simple as that. If they read their Bibles, especially the book of Revelation, then they would know what awaits the non-believers. They all have free will, and have total control over whether or not they choose to believe."

The two men held hands for a moment longer and prayed silently together. They prayed for the millions of souls who would find out, too late, what fate had in store for them if they chose not to believe the written word of God.

Martin opened his eyes and smiled at the strong, 35-year old man standing before him. "So, Andrew…tell me…what do you think of your new living quarters?" In the blink of an eye, they had both transported from Martin's work area to the front porch of Andrew's own mansion.

Andrew shook his head and his grin spread from ear to ear. "Mr. Martin…never…never did I ever expect to live in a place like this. It's so big and spacious, but what I'm still trying to believe is the outside…the grounds are…well…I can't even find the words to describe it."

"Well," Martin smiled back. "There's a reason your grounds are even more spacious than your mansion, Andrew."

Andrew blinked. "Why might that be, Mr. Martin?"

"Well, we all know about your love for animals, Andrew, and…you have been chosen to be one of the many caretakers of the animals."

Andrew looked confused. "But I haven't seen any animals since I got here…I was thinking that it must be true what folks use to say…that animals don't go to Heaven…"

Martin made a shushing sound and waved his hands in protest. "I never understood why people would believe that humans would be the only recipients of Heaven's welcome. What? Do they put themselves above other living creatures? God created ALL living life, so it is only natural that ALL living life be given the opportunity to share eternity with their Creator. Yes, Andrew, there are animals in Heaven…many, many different kinds of animals, and you will see them all, but in your case…well, you will be in charge of a very select group of cats and dogs."

Andrew threw his folded fist into the air in glee. "YES! You're right, Mr. Martin...I do love the animals, especially the dogs, but...what do you mean by a SELECT group?"

Martin put an arm around Andrew's shoulder. "Close your eyes, Andrew."

Andrew did not question why. He closed his eyes and when he opened them again, he and Martin were standing in the middle of the back yard. The yard was no longer empty; instead, hundreds of formerly abused animals were lounging in Heaven's glow, rolling on the soft grass, playing with the fluttering butterflies, and chasing their tails. They were all healthy and happy...they were finally at peace in their final, fur-ever Home.

Andrew pumped another victory fist into the open air. "Lawdy, lawdy, will you just look at all of them!" He ran forward to join the playful dogs that gathered around him and welcomed his loving strokes and hugs. He looked back at Martin and asked, "But what exactly do I need to do? What is my job? They don't have to be fed and watered, they don't have to be exercised, and they don't even have to sleep if they don't want to. What exactly is my responsibility to them, Mr. Martin?"

Martin sighed again as he approached the group of animals that surrounded Andrew. He petted their heads as he made his way to the center of the group. "You're right, Andrew...they don't have to do any of those things if they don't want to, but...these particular dogs are the ones who never experienced a loving touch during their lives on earth. They were born into neglectful and abusing situations. Most of them were starved and beaten all their lives, and their deaths were not easy ones. There was no one to meet them when they crossed over what humans refer to as the Rainbow Bridge. Your job, Andrew...is to simply...love them. Show them what they missed on earth and assure them every day that they will never again experience a harsh word or a painful blow. You see, this select group of dogs never belonged to a family on earth, so they have no one in Heaven to be reunited with...that's where you come in...you are now their family...at least until they find another family here that they choose to live with..."

Tears of happiness flowed down Andrew's cheeks and he simply nodded. "Yes, sir...thank you, sir. I won't let you down, and...I won't let them down." He wiped the tears away and a glint of confusion was evident in the scrunching of his brows. "But what about all of my own pets that I loved and cared for, Mr. Martin? I haven't seen any of them yet. I remember them all...Brownie was my first one...she was just a mutt; and there was Sophie, Ellie, and Rags, and...well, there were a bunch of them...what about them?" He looked around the back yard that was filled mostly with various sizes of pit-bull mixes.

Martin motioned him back toward the beautiful mansion behind them. "Come inside, Andrew."

Andrew followed Martin onto the expansive brick veranda and stepped inside the large downstairs area. There were windows throughout the mansion, but there was no glass inside those windows, nor were there any screens on the windows. Those items were not needed in Heaven, where the temperature and weather was always perfect. There was no need for drapes and blinds. The climate was ethereal and there were no machines or engines required to maintain the temperatures.

Andrew looked around the empty room before looking at his mentor again. "I don't understand, Mr. Martin, sir...what is it I am supposed to see inside?" He turned when he heard a clacking noise behind him. It sounded as though it came from the massive staircase that led to the large living quarters upstairs. The sound grew louder and louder until the first large, shaggy mutt came barreling down the stairs, rounded the corner, and flew hard enough into Andrew to knock him down.

Andrew sat on the marbled floor and the tears began to flow again. "Brownie! Girl...is that really you?" Brownie had been his very first pet, and Andrew was only 10 years old when Brownie died from being poisoned by the white man his father worked for at the time. Brownie planted her two large paws on Andrew's shoulders and licked his face profusely until a dozen other former pets came barreling down the same staircase to take their turns in his lap. "Oh, sweet, Jesus!" Andrew laughed. "It just can't get any better than this..."

Martin closed his eyes and clasped his hands in front of him. "Oh, yes it can my dear friend...yes, it can..."

"And after my skin is destroyed, this I know, that in my flesh I shall see God, whom I shall see for myself, and my eyes shall behold, and not another." Job 19:26-27 (NKJV)

CHAPTER 9

Amanda's Vacation Begins

Amanda turned off the interstate and sighed deeply. She looked over at the passenger seat where Buster stood on his short hind legs and licked the window. His tail wagged in time to the windshield wipers that swooshed away the light mist that Amanda had driven in for the past four hours. "It won't be long now, Buster…we're almost there."

Buster turned his head at the sound of his master's sweet voice. *"Okie dokie…that would be great, 'cause I gotta go pee pee on the grass!"* A grin spread across his face and he bounded onto Amanda's lap.

Amanda laughed out loud and rubbed his head. "I know that look, and don't you worry, little fella…just a few more minutes, and then you can go pee pee on the grass. Is that what you want? Is it?"

Buster ran back to the passenger seat and leaned forward on his front paws, his back end lifted high in the air. His tail continued to wag and he began barking profusely.

Amanda reached into her sweater pocket and tossed him a treat. He loved the pepperoni sticks made especially for dogs, but she was careful to limit him to just one per day.

Buster caught the treat in mid-air and jumped down onto his blanket that Amanda had placed on the front passenger floorboard. She knew that she should have put him in his crate for the long ride, but he had already learned not to jump around inside the car when it was moving, so she had opted to allow him the freedom of the front seat.

Once she had pulled off the interstate, traffic had slowed considerably, even at lunch time on a Monday. She saw the familiar curve up ahead, surrounded by tall oaks on both sides of the road. Amanda sighed softly and whispered, "I'm home..."

She slowed at the curve and immediately saw the huge, golden halo up ahead. She was surprised to see the parking lot almost empty. She glanced at her watch and nodded. "Well, that explains it...looks like we're just ahead of the lunch crowd. That's great, Buster. That will give you a chance to meet my angels. You're gonna love them, fella...and they're gonna love you. I'm not exactly sure why my parents told me to get here as soon as possible, but you can bet there will be an adventure waiting for us. How about it fella? Are you ready for an adventure?"

Buster looked up at her from his spot on the floorboard and moved his head from side to side. *"Hey, I'm not sure what an adventure is, but as long as I get to stay with you, I'm game. Sure hope I get to pee pee on the grass soon, though..."*

Doug positioned himself behind the counter and smiled at Tyler. "I'm not sure if you can hold anything else, but let me know if I can get you something else to eat or drink."

Tyler looked down at his flat stomach and marveled that it didn't show how full he really was. He shook his head. "No more food, please...but, I will take another cup of coffee. I need to call my father and let him know when to meet me."

"Go ahead and make your call," Doug said. He glanced out the window and saw the familiar black Trooper pull in and park beside Tyler's pick-up. "I'll get you that coffee in just a second."

Bertie strolled out of the kitchen and slapped Doug on the shoulder as he came from around the counter. "I'll get the coffee, handsome." She followed Doug's gaze to the parking lot. "Oh! To hell with the coffee!" Bertie pushed Doug out of the way and practically ran to the front door. She threw it open and bounded outside to the parking lot.

Amanda had not even had time to turn off the car's ignition when she felt her door being pulled open. "Bertie!" she managed to gasp before being pulled into a bear-hug.

Buster growled when the stranger pulled his master out of the car and wrapped her arms around her. *"Hey! You better not hurt her!"* He barked and growled some more until he saw his master wrapping her arms around the stranger.

Once outside the vehicle, the two women began bouncing and twirling, all the while never releasing their hold on one another. Bertie was the first to release her embrace but still held Amanda at arm's length. "Let me look at you, princess…oh, you look wonderful! It's so good to see you again!"

"It's only been a few months, but it's really good to see you again, too, Bertie." Amanda hugged the angel…her angel…again and immediately felt that sense of calm and serenity that always came over her whenever she touched one of them. "I didn't really know that I was coming, you know, until this morning."

Bertie laughed out loud. "Let me guess…another dream from your parents?"

Amanda nodded. "Yep, they didn't really give me much to go on though, but I was able to add a few extra days to the ten days off I had coming to me, so I'm all yours for the next couple of weeks." She glanced past Bertie and nodded toward the apartment on the left side of the building. It was where the angels had given her refuge when she first met them a little over two years ago. "I…uh…I don't suppose my old apartment is vacant, is it?"

"What do you think?" Bertie laughed as she thumped Amanda against the shoulder. "Of course, it's vacant. This visit may have caught me...and Doug...off guard, but you can be sure that our favorite Gladiator knew about it. Besides...hasn't been anyone in that apartment since you left it. It's clean, though...I always make sure of that."

Buster growled and barked again. *"Hey! Did you forget that I need to go pee pee on the grass?"*

Bertie laughed again and squatted down to look the puppy in the eye. "Well, why didn't you just say so, little man? Come on...let's take you around back." Bertie hugged the dog to her when he practically jumped into her open arms.

Amanda raised her eyebrows and shook her head as she closed the car door and followed them. "Why am I not surprised that the two of you understand each other? His name is Buster, by the way..."

Bertie looked back at Amanda and grinned. "Like I didn't already know that, huh? By the way, princess...you are in for one hell of a surprise...so, don't say I didn't warn you!"

Max was alone in the kitchen with Sam and Spartacus. He wasn't entirely sure why Sam had been sent to them, but he had a pretty good idea; just as he, also, knew that Amanda's arrival would somehow contribute to whatever lay in store for all of them. He bent down to stroke Spartacus and ran his large hands over wounds that had miraculously closed up during the past two days. "Sugar...who would've thought..." he mused.

Sam came over to him and looked him in the eyes. *"Spartacus will leave with Tyler today, but don't worry...you will see him again very soon."*

"So..." Max smiled. "He will play a part in all of this, will he?"

Spartacus licked Max's hand. *"I just need a few more days to completely heal and then, yes...I will be back. I have to...I have to be there at the end of it all..."*

A single tear fell from Max's eye. "I know...I know..." He continued to rub Spartacus' neck. "You remind me so much of one of the dogs who used to fight beside me...not in looks so much, but in spirit. He was a brown, Neapolitan Mastiff...we called him Brutus. He was a survivor, too...like you, my friend. He was one of the lucky ones...the Emperor allowed him to retire from fighting rather than to feed him to the lions. He saved my life on more than one occasion, for sure..."

Sam laid his head against Max's shoulder. *"I've met Brutus and he does have some good stories to tell. They considered sending him down for this assignment but thought he might draw a little too much attention, if you know what I mean."*

Max grinned and nodded. "I do, indeed, know what you mean, Sam. Brutus was a true warrior and I am sure that Mr. Little John Abbott would love to get his hands on a fighting machine like that. No...you were the right selection for this assignment, my friend. Are you ready to see Amanda again?"

Sam stood proud and erect. *"It's been six years since I had to leave her and I know she has grieved and suffered a lot in that time. I was glad to hear that she finally opened her heart up to another pet."* Sam turned to look at the back door. *"They're here!"*

Max pushed against Sam's strong chest. "Quiet, boy...she's not expecting to see you." Max stood up and looked out of the small window beside the back door. "Yes, there she is with Bertie, and...well...I guess that would be your replacement, Sam...he's just a little thing..."

Sam moved beside Max and stood up on his hind legs. He watched the pup running around in circles before it finally hiked his short leg to pee against the group of small palmetto palms. He allowed his gaze to drift to Bertie and, finally, to the young woman who stood beside her, laughing at the pup's hyper antics. Sam looked deep into Max's eyes; no words were needed.

Max nodded and opened the back door. "Okay, fella...now is as good a time as any, I guess..."

It took all of the angelic willpower Doug had to contain himself. He had watched while Bertie and Amanda embraced before walking around to the back of the café. He really wanted to be there for the reunion between Amanda and Sam, but he knew that one of the angels had to remain with the humans that were still dining. He might not be able to watch their reunion, but he could at least tune in to *hear* it!

Tyler hung up his cell phone and looked over his shoulder at Doug, who was looking out the window to the parking lot. He got off the stool and made his way over to where Doug stood. "I spoke with my Dad and told him I would be bringing Spartacus to him in a couple of hours. Spartacus will be in good hands..."

Doug turned at the sound of the young man's voice and nodded. "Yes...I know he will be. If your father is anything like you, then I have no doubt that Spartacus will be fine." He was talking to Tyler but he was eagerly listening to the reunion that was now taking place in the café's back yard.

Bertie and Amanda had their backs to the door and were watching the playful puppy as he ran excitedly around the yard. "It was a long ride for him," Amanda laughed. "I think he really needed to stretch his legs."

"What legs?" Bertie bellowed. "That mutt has the shortest legs I've ever seen on a dog!"

"He's just a puppy, Bertie," Amanda grinned. "His legs are supposed to be short. Don't worry, they'll grow...won't they, Buster?"

Buster ran and jumped up into Amanda's open arms. He gave her some of his best puppy-dog kisses and looked sideways at Bertie. *"You're kinda short, too, you know..."*

Bertie laughed and muffled his face between her open

palms. "Yes, I am…yes, I am…but we all know that good things come in small packages, now, don't we?"

Amanda felt Buster tense up in her arms, and felt a small growl growing deep in his belly. "Hey there, little fella…whatsamatter…hmmm?" It wasn't cold outside on this second Monday in October but Amanda felt a shiver travel up and down her spine, nonetheless. She sensed a slight movement behind her and began to turn slowly, all the while, holding Buster tightly against her chest.

"You're kinda squishing my nose…I can't breathe too good like this…" Buster tried to move his nose from beneath Amanda's arm pit. He glanced over his shoulder and saw the largest, scariest black dog he had ever seen, moving slowly toward them. He growled again. *"I'll protect you, 'Manda…don't you worry none…"*

Amanda completed her turn-around, and stared into the eyes of the only other pet she had ever owned and loved. Her father had brought Sam home to her a few days after Amanda's mother had been killed in a car accident. Amanda had only been seven years old at the time, and Sam had been the best medicine for the emptiness and heartache she had felt when she learned that her mother would never come home again. The two of them had been inseparable for the ten years they had been together. "Oh…my…God…" she cried, and released Buster at the same time.

"Whoaaaaa!" Buster yelped as he felt himself freefalling briefly.

Bertie was quick to catch him. "Don't worry, little fella…I've gotcha!" She held him close to her and kissed the top of his head while she watched Amanda move in slow motion toward the massive black pit-bull/lab that was moving just as slowly toward them.

They were within two feet of each other when Amanda dropped to her knees. The tears flowed freely down her cheeks but she was momentarily speechless. She pressed her fingertips against her tightly closed mouth as the dog…*her* dog…continued to close the short gap between them.

Sam watched Amanda fall to her knees, so he did the same. He covered the last two feet on his belly as he pulled himself into her waiting lap. He sighed deeply when she dropped her hands from her mouth and held his face lightly between her hands. He closed his eyes in total bliss when she planted a soft kiss upon the top of his head. *"Aww..."* he sighed. *"Heaven is truly wonderful, but nothing compares to being touched again by you, Amanda..."*

CHAPTER 10

Little John Grows Suspicious

Little John had been busy in town since early morning, making arrangements for the next big fight. It was scheduled for Friday night, two weeks from now, and he needed to find a replacement dog for Spartacus. He was at the end of the long drive-way that led to the Abbott family home when he spotted his foreman, Clint Meacham, waiting for him at the wooden gate beside the crew bunk house.

Little John got out of his truck and took a quick look around. He flicked the blunt that he had been smoking and rubbed it into the ground. A blunt is a cigar in which the normal tobacco has been replaced with marijuana, and it was a staple for Little John Abbott. "Has Jones made it back here yet with Spartacus?"

Clint spat out juice from the wad of tobacco he had been babying inside his mouth for the past hour. "No…I haven't seen neither hide nor hair of him since he left here early this morning."

"Is that right?" Little John mused. "You know…you may have been right about him, Clint…there is something about him that doesn't feel altogether right, isn't there?"

"That was my feeling, Boss, but..."

"I know, I know..." Little John interrupted. "But...you weren't here that day and we were short-staffed. I tried to do some more checking on him today while I was in town...still can't find anything on the kid."

"I'm keeping an eye on him, Boss. He's pretty good with the dogs, I gotta say, but..."

"But, what?" Little John raised bushy eyebrows and smoothed down his meticulously-trimmed mustache.

"Well," Clint shook his head. "It feels like the kid is too...*sympathetic*...with the mutts. I've watched him when he's supposed to be training them against the bait dogs...when he thinks nobody is looking, and he's a little too easy and soft with them, if you know what I mean." He shook his head again.

Little John rubbed the back of his neck and looked toward one of the secluded training areas that was located inside a grove of large oak trees about a half-mile behind the bunk house. He could hear loud barking coming from the area now. "Doesn't matter...we'll only need him for a couple of more weeks, at the most."

"Why is that, Boss?"

Little John stared hard at Clint. He trusted this man who had been with the Abbott family for more than twenty years, but he had never really liked him much. "I heard something in town this morning that's got me a little worried. I'm thinking we might need to finish up the next couple of fights and then lay low with the dogs for a while."

"What did you hear?"

"There were a couple of strangers...two men...in the diner this morning. They looked...out of place...you know?"

Clint spat another mouthful of tobacco juice behind him. "Cops? In Thomasville...really?"

Little John nodded. "Maybe...yep...just two of them, but McAlister told me that they've been hanging around for a few days now. They don't look like street cops, though."

Clint grinned and showed a mouthful of tobacco-stained teeth. "McAlister would definitely be able to spot 'em, that's for sure…he's been locked up enough…"

Jerry McAlister owned a small farm a few miles past the Abbott ranch. He raised some of the bait and fighting dogs that Little John used in his illegal dog-fighting business. He had spent half of his life locked away for one petty crime or another, and nobody expected that he had not seen his last of the inside of a cell.

Little John stretched his arms above his head. "McAlister seems to think they might be private investigators instead of cops…seems they've shown a lot of interest in dog fighting…been asking a few too many questions…"

"You must be worried about 'em if you're thinking of closing up shop for a while…" Clint nodded.

Little John was quiet for a few moments before replying. "There's just the two of them, best I can tell…I can take care of them if I have to…just keep your eyes and ears open…let me know if you hear or see anything that doesn't feel right to you. If they're stupid enough to show up here, I want to know."

"I can do that…" Clint shrugged.

Little John lit another blunt and took a long drag from it. "And keep an eye on Tyler Jones, too…I'm not entirely sure that we need to keep him on, but for now…well…just keep an eye on him. He hasn't been back at all today?"

Clint shook his head. "Nope…he left right after you did early this morning. Took a left out of the driveway…"

"Hmmm…" Little John muttered. "Let me know the minute he gets back."

Amanda and Sam's reunion was a joyful one. Max came outside to join in and to answer what questions he could that Amanda had about Sam's presence. He explained to her that Sam was there to assist in the secret and unlawful dog-fighting ring that was prevalent in the neighboring town of

Thomasville, GA.

Amanda pulled Sam toward her in a protective hug and shook her head. "No, Max…what do mean…to *assist*? It sounds dangerous…he could be hurt…"

Bertie laughed out loud, "Hell, Princess...it's not like he's gonna get himself killed. In case you've forgotten, he's already dead…you know…angel-dog and all!"

Buster stopped chasing a batch of yellow butterflies and bounced toward them. He jumped onto Sam's back and grabbed hold of a shiny, black ear. *"Come play with me, Sam…p-l-e-a-s-e!"*

Spartacus had remained in the kitchen, but the sound of the puppy's pleading reached his ears and his curiosity finally got the best of him. His legs felt stiff and sore, but he knew that he needed to move around on them. He ambled onto the back porch and sniffed the fresh air. It felt good to be outside again, free of the heavy chains that always hung around his neck. He watched the young pup they called Buster and a wave of sadness coursed through him. He had never been allowed to run and play freely like that; he had never known a kind touch or a soft-spoken word; and, he had never had a human love him the way the young woman seemed to love Sam and Buster.

Amanda saw the thin, scarred dog standing on the porch and her heart filled with even more love. "Oh, my God…" she cried as she moved toward Spartacus. "What on earth happened to him?"

Spartacus' tail thumped softly against the wooden columns. *"Oh…look…she's coming over to me…I…I think she's going to touch me…"* He tucked his tail between his legs, lowered his head, and looked at her feet. *"She must think I'm pretty ugly and scary-looking with all these wounds…nobody like her would ever want to touch an ugly dog like me…"*

Sam barked loudly until Spartacus looked over at him. *"She's unlike any human you have ever known, my friend. You can trust her…"*

Amanda looked at Max. "Max?"

Max nodded and motioned for Amanda to join him on the porch with Spartacus. "Come here, Amanda. I want you to meet Spartacus..."

Amanda sat on one side of Spartacus while Max sat on the other. The dog looked at her with the saddest eyes she had ever seen. She reached out and rubbed the top of his head. "Well, hello there, Spartacus. That's a strong and beautiful name…just like you…"

Spartacus closed his eyes when she touched him. He felt the warmth in her hands flow through his body. He had never felt so alive before. *"She thinks I'm beautiful…"* He looked at Sam and Buster. The pup was still gnawing on the big dog's ear. Spartacus rolled the pup onto its back and placed a large paw over him. He returned Spartacus' look and barked loudly.

"He came to our back door a couple of nights ago, Amanda. If you think he looks rough now, you should have seen him then. I wasn't sure if he would make it through the night or not, but he did. He's a fighter…in more ways than one. Amos Brown helped out, too. He showed us the miraculous power that simple sugar has on open wounds."

Amanda continued to stroke Spartacus, all the while inspecting the newer wounds that appeared to be healing nicely. She ran her hands across other scars that, apparently, had been there for quite a while. "This dog wasn't hit by a car, was he?"

Bertie placed both hands upon her ample hips and said, "No, Princess…these wounds definitely were not caused by any car! Trust me…I know how it feels to be hit by one, too! No…Max seems to think that Spartacus' wounds are the result of dog fighting…and not just your run-of-the-mill, neighborhood dog fighting, either…"

Amanda closed her eyes as she quickly made the connection. She opened her eyes and looked at Max. "That's what you meant then…when you told me why Sam was sent here…to help Spartacus…so, what? Is Sam supposed to magically end the fighting in Thomasville…all by himself?"

She turned back to Spartacus and looked deeply into his dark, soulful eyes. "I can't begin to imagine what you have been through, fella, and I am so sorry that you have been treated so badly..." Tears flowed down her cheeks and she choked on her sentence.

Nobody seemed to notice when Tyler stepped onto the porch. "I'm sorry to interrupt," he began, "But...Doug said it would be okay if I came out back to see..."

Spartacus turned his head at the sound of Tyler's voice and his tail thumped louder than ever. *"Hey! It's the nice man...the one who fed me extra food and only pretended to beat me when my master told him to train me."* He looked at Sam. *"Hey, Sam...look!"*

"He's here to help you, Spartacus," Sam confirmed. *"Don't worry...he's going to be taking you some place safe, but we'll meet up again in a few days. It's important that you heal quickly because we don't have much time."*

Max stood up, while Tyler bent down and lowered his head toward Spartacus. "Hey there, fella...how are you doing? You look stronger..." He gave Spartacus another quick rub and then stood up. He held out his hand to Amanda, who was still sitting on the stoop beside Spartacus. "Hi...I'm Tyler Foster..."

Amanda placed her hand in Tyler's and shivered involuntarily when he helped her to stand. She looked at Max, who was smiling broadly and nodding his head slowly. She looked back at Bertie who raised her eyebrows and wiggled her shoulders. She looked at Sam, who released his hold on Buster, and walked toward her while Buster ran off to chase butterflies again. Her dream with her parents echoed within her brain...all these individual actions occurred within a few seconds in time...which was all it took for Amanda to, once again, make a quick connection. "Tyler Foster...no...this is too much of a coincidence...*you're* Tyler Foster?"

Tyler looked confused but continued to hold on to Amanda's offered hand. "I am...and you are..."

Amanda grinned and shook her head. "Well…if fate has anything to do with it, I'm probably going to be your wife someday soon!"

Tyler quickly released Amanda's hand!

CHAPTER 11

A Plan Takes Form

It was almost one o'clock before Tyler loaded Spartacus into the front seat of his truck and began the almost two-hour trip to rendezvous with his father. The angels were busy with the lunch crowd for a few hours, and Amanda took the opportunity to unpack and relax in her old apartment. Sam had gone off on his own into the woods, but Max had assured Amanda that he would be fine and that she would see him later.

She lay horizontally across the twin size-bed with her feet dangling toward the floor. She was still in the comfortable jeans and thin sweat shirt she had donned earlier that morning. Buster ran circles around her feet, attempting intermittent swipes to grab hold and pull off her socks. Amanda was oblivious to the pup's humorous antics. Her eyes were closed but there was a smile upon her face...a smile that ended abruptly when Buster bit her little toe as he successfully managed to finally pull off one sock.

"Ouch!" she laughed and sat upright. She picked the pup up and put him on the bed beside her. She rolled him onto his back and began tickling his belly. "That hurt, Buster! How would you like it if I bit your toe?"

Buster wriggled free and backed up to the pillows at the

head of the bed. He crouched down with his butt in the air and squinted his eyes at her. He offered her one of his most fearsome puppy growls and wiggled his butt to show that he was serious.

Amanda laughed at him and threw the sock at him. "Okay, okay…here…take it! I'm going to jump in the shower and then head downstairs to see what Max has cooked for dinner. If you're a good dog, I might even sneak something back to you. What do you say?"

"I say you need to get a move on it! There were some mighty good smells coming from that big room behind the porch. Okay…I promise to be good…but I wish I could go with you…" Buster lowered his raised butt and shook the sock from side to side. He rushed to the end of the bed and jumped into Amanda's lap.

Amanda kissed him on the head and stood up. She reached back for him and placed him on the floor. "Okay, you be a good boy now…I really need that shower, and then I'll take you out to pee pee on the grass before I go back to the café. I'll leave the TV on to that doggie channel that you like so much, okay?"

Buster barked loudly and took his prized sock off to his own bed.

It was almost three-thirty by the time Tyler and his parents were ready to say their good-byes. The van door was open and Tyler was bent over whispering into Spartacus' ear. "You're going to a good place, Spartacus…a really good place. These people will take good care of you, I promise. You be a good boy, now, you hear?" He planted a kiss on the dog's lumpy head.

"I'm not worried one bit," Spartacus sighed. *"I wish I could tell you what's going on, though. I wish I could tell you what Sam told me. You don't know it yet, but I have to go back to that place one more time. I don't want to, but…I have to."* He closed his eyes when Tyler kissed the top of his head. The lumps and

old wounds didn't seem to faze the young man who had been so kind to him the past few months.

Jean Foster walked around to the back of the van and wrapped her arms around her son. She sighed against his back and whispered, "God, I wish you didn't have to go back to that place. I wish you had never gotten involved in all of this, son..."

Tyler placed his hands on top of his mother's and raised up. "I know...me, too. It's been hell watching how they treat all those poor animals, especially the baiters. I wish I could save them all, but, Mom...so many of them have ended up in that pit. I die a little bit inside every time I have to take one there. I want to give them all a proper burial, to let them know that someone cared about them, that their lives weren't in vain, but...well...I think the foreman is already a little suspicious about my true feelings for the animals."

B.B. Foster had joined his wife and son at the back of the van. He looked inside at Spartacus and smiled. "We can't save them all, Tyler...but you've done one helluva job in saving this one. He is a true survivor, and I promise you that the rest of his days on this earth will be good ones. I'm thinking that this one might need to stay with us instead of being adopted out. I'm not sure if I could let him go now; there's something about him that tears at my heart strings. If each of those wounds could tell a story..."

Tyler slipped from his mother's embrace and placed a hand upon his father's shoulder. "It might not be a story we would want to hear, Dad. Little John raised Spartacus from a pup, and he's two years old now, so you can just imagine what his life has been like. I've told you before about the abuse that goes on at that ranch."

"Well..." B.B. sighed, "Hopefully, that is about to come to an end very soon. I, uh...I heard that the two men I told you about are in Thomasville now. They're feeling folks out, letting it be known that they're interested in betting on the next big fight."

"That's great," Tyler nodded. "I've been expecting them

for a few days now, but haven't met them yet. I've talked to them both on the phone, working out the final details on what's about to go down. They told me again that I don't need to be involved if I don't want to, but..."

Jean sighed. "I wish you would listen to them on that score, Tyler. There really is no need for you to be any more involved than you already are...especially if that Meacham fella and Abbott are the least bit suspicious of your intentions."

Tyler shook his head. "I doubt Meacham has a clue, Mom. He just thinks I'm a little *soft* when it comes to disciplining and *disposing* of the animals. No...I'm pretty sure nobody suspects anything yet. But...as for Little John...well, he isn't as country and backward as some folks may think he is; he's actually pretty sharp and intuitive, but, I don't trust anything he says or does. Hell...I may not even have a job when I get back there. I was supposed to check back in with Clint Meacham a couple of hours ago."

"Then you had better get going, son," B.B. said. "Don't worry about Spartacus. We'll take good care of him. You won't recognize him the next time you see him...and, thanks for that info about the powdered sugar mixture for open wounds...we'll keep doing that until he's healed completely."

Tyler bent down and gave Spartacus a final kiss on the head. "I know he'll be safe with you, Dad." He exhaled deeply and turned toward his truck. "By the way...I meant to tell you both about this really strange girl...woman...I met earlier today."

Jean's eyebrows raised in eager anticipation. "Oh? You've met someone?" she asked hopefully. "Who is she?"

Tyler shook his head and smiled. "She scared the crap out of me, to tell you the truth; her name is Amanda Turner and when I met her, she informed me that she was probably going to be my wife one day real soon. Really, really strange..."

Jean managed to keep the smile off her face until after she and B.B. had hugged their youngest son good-bye and watched him drive away. "Well, well…" she smirked.

B.B. laughed and pulled her toward the van's passenger door. "Come on, beautiful. I know exactly what you're thinking. This is the same young woman we all met yesterday, isn't it?"

"Why, you know…I believe it must be," Jean smiled back. "I knew it! I knew when I met her that there was something special about her. Come on…you have to admit it…fate works in mysterious ways, doesn't it?"

"I'm not sure if fate has anything to do with their chance meeting," B.B. laughed again. "Poor Tyler doesn't stand a chance!"

The lunch crowd had thinned out considerably by four-thirty; there were only a half-dozen customers who remained at the blue- and white-checkered tables. Amos Brown was the only person sitting at the counter seats. He was at the café every day for a late lunch, but when he found out that Amanda was back for a visit, he stayed later than usual so that he could see her again. He and Amanda shared a very special bond since they were the only two living humans who knew the truth about the angels of the Heavenly Grille Café. They had been witness to Max's transformation when he had revealed his true identity to them.

The angel chimes sounded when Amanda breezed through the café's front door. "Oh, my God! What smells so good…" She stopped in mid-sentence when the old black man at the counter turned around and grinned at her. "Amos!!" She let the screen door bang shut behind her and literally flew into the arms of the sweetest man she had ever known, besides her own father.

Amos stood up in time to welcome her fierce hug and grinned a toothless grin. "Lawdy, Miss Amanda…it's really good to see you again…yes, it is…" He eventually held her at a distance and said, "Let me gets a good look at you…why you look fine, girl…just fine."

A tear ran down Amanda's cheek and she grinned back at him. "So do you, Amos...so do you. It feels like it's been years instead of just months since I've seen you. How are you? Are you feeling okay? Taking care of yourself?" She hugged him again.

Amos laughed and sat back down on his stool. He patted the empty seat beside him. "Oh, I's be just fine for an old man, I guess. Can't complain none and ain't no one to complain to if I wanted to. So, as long as the good Lord sees fit to keep me here, then I guess this is where I'll be for a spell. Mr. Max and Miss Bertie sees to it that I eats right, though."

"Well..." Amanda sighed. "If anything can keep anyone going strong, it would be Max's cooking for sure! Speaking of which, I am *starving*!"

Bertie came out of the kitchen, her arms loaded down with a tray of steaming food. "I heard that!" she bellowed. "And...I've got just the thing you need to get your vacation started off on the right foot. Take a look at this meal!"

Amanda closed her eyes and inhaled the delicious aromas of some of her favorite foods. Her plate was filled with three large pieces of crispy, buttermilk-fried chicken, mashed potatoes with bacon and cheese, fried collards seasoned with fat back, and large chunks of Max's famous jalapeno-cheese cornbread. "Oh, my God...do they cook like this in Heaven? Please tell me they do!"

Bertie laughed as she placed the food, along with a large glass of cold milk, in front of Amanda. "Well, Princess, you don't require food there, but you can eat anything you want, whenever you want, and never have to worry about gaining weight. However...you might want to consume all the fried chicken you can while you're here because there won't be any meat!"

Amanda's eyes widened in shock. "Oh, no...please tell me you're kidding!" No meat? But...I love meat. Meat is...like...protein...don't we need lots of protein?"

Bertie punched Amanda's shoulder and grinned. "Trust me, Princess...you'll get everything you need, and then some…you won't miss the fried chicken at all…"

Amanda nodded and exhaled. "Well then…I guess I'd better do all the damage to my arteries while I can." She picked up a thigh and bit into it. She licked the juice from her lips and closed her eyes. "You just don't know how much I've missed this…nobody in the Tampa area knows how to fry chicken this crisp…and don't even get me started on the collards and cornbread!"

"Well, you go ahead and eat to your heart's content," Bertie laughed. "I'll fix something special for you to take back to Buster for later." She grinned at Amanda's raised eyebrows. "Don't worry, it's not fried chicken. I boiled some especially for him and Sam."

"Who's Sam…and Buster?" Amos asked politely.

"Oh, you'll be meeting them soon enough, Amos," Bertie informed him. "As a matter of fact, we need to have a long talk with you before you leave today. We might need you to…uh…provide shelter for a couple of our guests."

Amos rubbed the back of his neck. "Well, Andrew's room is empty, Miss Bertie, so your friends are more than welcome to stay there for as long as they needs to. Yes, ma'am…your friends are always welcome in my home."

"Hmmm…" Bertie sighed. "You may not want these friends sleeping in Andrew's bed, dear friend…they have eight legs between the two of them."

Amos wrinkled his brows and looked totally confused.

Amanda swallowed a mouthful of mashed potatoes and patted him on the back. "Don't worry, Amos…Buster will be staying with me, if that's okay with Bertie and Max, so you'll only have one guest. You see…Sam and Buster are *dogs*."

The wrinkle in his forehead relaxed and Amos grinned broadly. "Oh, I sees what you mean. Well, it don't matter none how many legs they have between 'em…they are more than welcome to stay as long as you need them to. I promise I'll take good care of 'em for you."

Bertie touched the old man's bony shoulder. "You're a good man, Amos. Max will fill you in on what's going on.

It's okay if Buster stays with Amanda upstairs, but we might need for Sam to stay somewhere else…off the premises. Only one dog needs to go home with you tonight, but there may, or may not, be another one in a couple of days…before Friday, for sure."

Amanda watched Bertie closely. Who, besides Sam, was going to be involved with this adventure her parents had sent her on? "What other dog are you talking about, Bertie? Not my Buster, I know, because…"

Bertie shook her head. "Don't be silly, Princess. We would never subject that sweet pup to what needs to be done in the next couple of weeks. No…you see…Spartacus will be returning to the area. I'm not sure of where he will stay, so there's a chance that he may need to stay with Amos for a few days, too…we're still not entirely sure of what accommodations might be needed yet."

"Do you mean that poor dog that was on the back porch earlier today!" Amanda exclaimed. "God, no! You can't mean that. Hasn't that poor animal been through enough?"

"Amanda…calm down," Bertie began. "Yes, Spartacus will be a part of the plan. I don't know how things will play out in the end…I'm not privy to that information…but I do know that he has to be part of it all. Now, go ahead and finish your food…there's buttermilk cake for dessert…Max will explain everything to you later."

Amanda took another bite of collards and chewed slowly. She was deep in thought, and worry, about what roles Spartacus and Sam would play in busting the dog-fighting ring in Thomasville.

Amos did not appear to be worried about anything. He trusted the angels completely and knew that, whatever lay in store for the dogs, the angels would do their best to ensure their safety. He raised a long finger at Bertie before she turned to leave. "Don't suppose I could get another slice of that buttermilk cake, could I, Miss Bertie?"

CHAPTER 12

Finding Czar

Tyler heard the door to the bunk house squeak open. His back was to the door but he could hear boots shuffling toward his bed. He flinched when the toe of one of those boots pushed against his kidneys.

"Wake up, Jones…" the raspy voice was just above a deep whisper. "You're coming with me today to persuade Czar's owner that he needs to sell the dog to Little John. You awake, kid?"

"Damn…" Tyler thought. *"I was hoping to avoid this one…"* He rolled over on his back and looked up at Clint Meacham, who was leering down at him with what Tyler swore must have been pure unadulterated contempt. "I'm up, Boss…I can be ready in 15 minutes…"

Clint resisted the urge to kick the young man again, harder this time. "You've got 10 minutes…I'll be waiting for you outside."

Tyler waited until he heard the bunk house door squeak shut before fumbling, in the dark, for his cell phone. He punched in his father's quick-dial number and hoped he would answer; the voicemail picked up on the third ring, so Tyler left a hurried message. "Hey…it's me…looks like the man will have a new champion for the next fight. I'll be gone most of the day…I was hoping to avoid it, but it looks like I have to help bring the dog back here…I wanted to touch base with the people we talked about yesterday, but, I guess that will have to wait. Okay then, I'll try to call back tonight if it's not too late…talk to you soon…" Tyler ended the call to his father and slid quickly into the well-worn jeans laying on the wooden chair beside his bunk. He looked around the darkened room and wondered why he had been singled out to go with the foreman to collect Czar. The other workers continued to snore soundly in their own bunks.

Clint Meacham had never left the bunk house. He had simply closed the bunk house door and waited inside. The room was so dark that he knew Tyler could not see him. He had listened quietly to the phone call Tyler had made. *"You little prick…I knew you were bad news…question is…how bad…and what do we need to do about you?"* He knew that Little John would want to hear about the phone call, but he decided that could wait until they returned from their mission to obtain Czar. Clint waited until Tyler went into the washroom before he opened the squeaky door to wait outside. He spat a wad of nasty tobacco juice onto the ground and thought, *"Your ass is gonna burn, Tyler Jones…and I hope I'm the one to light the match…"*

Sam lay curled up at the foot of Amos' bed. He listened to the old man's snoring with one ear, while the other ear listened to the conversation taking place in the Abbott bunk house. *"So…it looks like Czar will be Spartacus' replacement…that's going to be tough…Spartacus has already lost one fight to that dog…but, if Abbott buys Czar, then he won't be able to pit his own dogs against each other…"* He lay on the comfortable bed for a few more minutes before sliding off gracefully and walking silently into the kitchen. His body tensed at the moment when he realized that the foreman had only pretended to leave the bunk house. *"Great...he was already suspicious of Tyler...looks like I may need to speed up the timing of my arrival."* Sam knew what he had to do, but he had to let Max know about the change in plans. *"I'll talk to Max whenever Amos heads that way for lunch today...I'm sure he won't mind an extra passenger tagging along."*

Amanda had put on an apron when she arrived for breakfast Tuesday morning at the Heavenly Grille. She knew that Bertie would say she didn't have to help, but she didn't want to feel like she was free-loading off the kindness of the angels. It was true that this was her vacation, her much-needed time off from work, but she also knew that she was there to help with the dog-fighting ring situation. She just wasn't sure what her role would be.

The breakfast crowd finally began to diminish when Bertie punched Amanda's shoulder and said, "Take a load off, Princess. Amos should be in soon, but you can sit at his stool until he gets here. Let me get you a cup of coffee."

"I can get my own coffee, Bertie...you don't have to wait on me, you know..." Amanda smiled at the small bundle of energy that never seemed to slow down. "But, thanks...that sounds good. Hey, Bertie...tell me something?"

Bertie poured the coffee and placed it on the counter. "I'll tell you anything you want to know, Princess. That's one good thing about having you and Amos know the truth about us...we don't have to worry about what we say! What's on your mind?"

"Well," Amanda began. She blew out a deep breath that she hadn't been aware she had been holding in. "You were married, right? I mean, before you...died?"

Bertie cocked her head sideways. "You bet I was, Princess...married myself the kindest and sweetest man on the face of the earth. I just wish we would've had more time together before that damned automobile decided to plow me down!"

"But you get to see him...your husband...in Heaven, right? When you and Max go Home to visit?"

Bertie nodded. "Oh, Hell, yeah...I see him all the time...and I still love him more than anything, but...well...and don't tell Max I said this...although, I bet he's listening in on our conversation anyway...but...well...hell, I can't help but remember the great sex that me and my old man used to have. Man, we use to rock the walls in that old shack we lived in!" Bertie's laughter filled the café when Amanda's jaw dropped open and she sputtered hot coffee all over the counter.

A few customers turned in Amanda's direction when she started coughing. Bertie waved at them and said, "She's all right, folks, go on back to your meals." Bertie waited until Amanda regained control of herself and then leaned both elbows on the countertop. She grinned widely and stared directly into Amanda's still-shocked eyes. "Best I ever had, Princess...of course, my old man was the only person I ever had sex with, and I died young, so I never had anyone else to compare him to, but..."

Amanda held up one hand and used her free one to wipe up the spilled coffee. "I get the picture, Bertie...trust me...I get it. Wow...I guess I just never thought of angels having...you know...*sex*..."

"Angels *don't* have sex, Princess...that desire is gone once you hit the Pearly Gates, but in case you forgot, we were all just as human as you, once upon a time. You young people don't have a license on the stuff, you know. From what I hear on all those talk shows, folks today are having sex into their eighties and nineties. What about you? Have you had sex yet...or are you a *virgin*? You can tell me, Princess."

Amanda grinned at the Shirley Booth look-a-like bent over with her chin perched in her open palms, and elbows on the counter. "Well...if you must know...and, I am not ashamed to say it...I am twenty-three years old and still a virgin. I made a promise to my Dad...and to myself...that I would wait until I found the person I wanted to spend the rest of my life with before I got my...*license*."

Bertie raised her brows and grinned. "Hmm...nope...can't say that I'm really surprised by that revelation. I bet you've taken a lot of heat for that over the years though, huh? I mean, looking like you do and all...people are quick to judge the book by its cover, if you know what I mean."

Amanda motioned toward the coffee pot. "Could I get a refill, please? I seem to have spilled most of mine." She shook her head while Bertie turned to grab the coffee pot. "It really hasn't been all that difficult. I mean...there have been a few guys who thought they could have a quick roll in the hay and then be on their way...some who have called me a tease because I wouldn't put out when it got down to the nit and gritty, but...I don't know...I keep thinking about what my Dad would say if I slipped up and gave in to the temptation. He would be so disappointed, and...well...even in death...I don't want to disappoint him if I can help it."

"So you've never met anyone who made your toes curl up?" Bertie poured them both a hot cup of strong coffee. "What about that little hunk that was here yesterday to pick up Spartacus? You forget that we angels can hear anything we set our minds on hearing..."

Amanda laughed. "So, you heard me tell him that I was probably going to be his wife one day soon, huh?" She covered her eyes with both hands and shook her head from side to side. "Oh, God...I can't believe I said that to him." She uncovered her eyes and grinned at Bertie. "I don't think I got a chance to tell y'all...it is the weirdest coincidence, but...I was at the Foster Farm on Sunday delivering an overflow of rescue dogs to Tyler's father!"

"Max knew that...he told us. So...get out of here!" Bertie whispered loudly. "You mean, you've already met your future in-laws?"

Amanda shrugged. "Well, I didn't know it then, but...you know...I think there might be forces at work here that will be beyond both mine and Tyler's control. I just hope he's ready and can handle all *this*!" Amanda stood up and ran her hands along her sides until they rested on her hips.

Bertie laughed out loud again and came around the counter to give Amanda a strong bear hug. "Is that what started this conversation, Princess? When you asked if I had been married?"

"I don't know, Bertie. I've never really had anyone to talk to about these things, you know. I mean…my Dad…well, he tried. He gave me the *talk*…stumbled through it somehow, but I didn't dare ask him any questions. I've listened to other women over the years and tried to pick up some pointers; Kris has been a big help in that department. She's like the sister I always wanted and I can talk to her about anything."

Kris DeVone-Hall was the young woman that Amanda and the angels had rescued in 2011. She had been seven months pregnant when they first met and had been left stranded and abandoned by her live-in boyfriend.

"How are Kris and the baby? Is Officer Hall treating them right?"

Amanda nodded. "Oh, yeah…they are deliriously happy and Charlotte Grace is getting so big. She just turned two, you know…oh, I wish all of you could have been there for her party. It was a blast! We had a bounce house on the front lawn and all the neighborhood kids took turns using it. Yeah…Kris and Dean are very happy. Nobody would ever guess that Charlotte Grace wasn't his own, biological child. He adores her and is very, very protective of them both."

"I'm glad you have Kris to talk to, Princess. Have you called her yet to tell her that you've met Mr. Right?"

"You think you're kidding, but I wanted to! I really did, but I think I had better hold off on that for a while. So…you don't think I'm crazy then? I mean…is it possible to know right off the bat, when you meet someone…that you're going to marry that person?"

"It's an old cliché," Bertie replied. "But, I think they might still refer to that as love at first sight. This should be interesting to watch unfold, yessiree…"

"Tyler's part of my adventure, isn't he, Bertie? Max hasn't told me all that's going on yet, but I know that's why I'm here…why my parents told me it was urgent that I get here as soon as possible. I don't know how that's going to work out, though…I doubt if I'll ever see Tyler Foster again."

"I don't know everything that's going on either, Princess. All I know is that there is a dog-fighting ring that needs to be disbanded. That's why Sam was sent back down. Now…what part he'll play in all this, I don't know yet, but…" Bertie's thoughts were interrupted when she saw a familiar dark truck pull into the parking lot. "Well, well…I'll be damned…looks like you're gonna see your future husband a lot sooner than you may have thought. He's got someone with him, though…"

Amanda turned to look out the large window beside the café's front door. Once again, her jaw dropped open and she sputtered coffee…this time on the floor in front of her.

"Damn!" Bertie laughed. "I hope this fella realizes what a slob he's gonna be marrying!"

Clint Meacham closed the passenger door and stared at the floating halo above him. "What the hell is this place, Jones? Looks like a damn church…I thought you said you knew a place we could grab a quick sandwich…" He spat a juicy wad of chewed tobacco onto the paved lot.

"It's not a church, Boss…I promise…and once you smell the food that's cooked in here, a sandwich will be the last thing on your mind. I found this place by accident when I was out looking for Spartacus. The folks who run it said they saw a dog that matched his description heading south down the side road over there." Tyler pointed to the curved road that brought people, headed north, to the Heavenly Grille.

"So you don't think he died in the woods, then?" Clint asked. That was the story Tyler had told them when he arrived back at the ranch after dark on Monday night.

Tyler shook his head. "Hard to tell for sure…no…at first, I was positive that he had to be dead, but I checked those woods thoroughly and there was no sign of him."

"Maybe the buzzards finished off the loser," Clint muttered.

"I don't think so, Boss. I'm thinking he kept wandering away. Maybe someone felt sorry for him and picked him up…he could be anywhere, but…I don't think we'll ever see him again, or, know for sure exactly what happened to him."

Clint stared at Tyler without saying anything in response. He hoped his silence would make the kid nervous and scared of what the consequences might be for him, since he had not been able to locate Spartacus.

Tyler was anything but nervous and scared; instead, he was infuriated with the man who stood beside him. He wanted to bash Clint's head in, to file his teeth down to nubs, to wrap masking tape around his nose, mouth, hands, and feet, to cut off his ears with scissors, to break every bone in his legs…he wanted to do all the things he had seen Clint do to the bait dogs used to train Little John's champion fighters. Instead, he just nodded toward the café and said, "Come on…my treat…you'll be glad we stopped here." He also wondered if he would see the cute blond again…the one who insisted she would become his wife one day soon.

CHAPTER 13

Amanda and Tyler Meet Again

Bertie greeted them at the door. The worried look in Tyler's eyes when he saw her confirmed her ethereal thought that he did not want the man with him to know that Tyler was on friendly terms with anyone in the café. "Come on in fellas…take a load off." Bertie led the two men to a corner booth. "I'm guessing you two will be wanting the cook's special?"

Clint glared at the overly-friendly waitress and snarled. "Then you'd be wrong, lady. How about a menu?"

Bertie pursed her lips and somehow found the required restraint to remain pleasant when all she really wanted to do was to punch the hell out of this jerk. "We don't have any *menus*," she almost snarled in return. "You can have a burger and fries, peanut butter and jelly sandwich with chips…or, you can have the cook's special. Just so you know…we don't sell a lot of burgers or sandwiches."

Tyler cleared his throat and smiled over at Bertie. "We'll take two of the cook's special, ma'am."

Bertie glanced quickly at Tyler but returned her glare to

the man across the booth from him. "Smart choice...I'll be right back with your sweet tea..." Bertie turned to leave but stopped and looked back at the man. "And don't you go spitting that crap in your mouth anywhere in here. Restroom's over there," she indicated to the far right corner of the café.

Clint started to offer a retort, but changed his mind. He looked around the café and saw that several customers were looking in his direction. "What the hell y'all looking at?" he bellowed in his raspy, loud voice.

Bertie was almost to the kitchen when she turned and marched back to Tyler's table. She placed her hands on her ample hips and looked calmly into the cold, dead eyes of Clint Meacham. "There ain't no cussing' allowed in this establishment...unless it's done by me, so I suggest that if you can't keep a civil tongue in your mouth, then maybe you and your friend should just be on your way."

Clint started to stand up. He wanted, more than anything, to spit his wad of tobacco juice into the insolent face of the smart-ass waitress; however, the sudden arrival of a tall, muscular man at their table made him think twice about that desire.

Doug had been working with Max in the kitchen. They had both been eavesdropping on Bertie's conversation with Tyler and Clint Meacham. Max had nodded to Doug and said, "I doubt if she needs your help, but why don't you go on out there anyway?"

Doug touched Bertie on the shoulder and said, "Max needs you in the kitchen, Bertie." He looked directly into Clint's eyes and spoke calmly. "Why don't you go place these gentlemen's order and I'll get their drinks?"

Bertie grinned at Clint Meacham because she knew what he had been thinking. "Don't forget what I said about that crap in your mouth..." She sashayed away with her head held high.

Amanda was doing her best to suppress a grin when she caught Tyler staring at her. She clamped her lips together and nodded at him before turning back around to finish her coffee. "Way to go, Bertie!" she whispered when Bertie breezed past her.

Clint Meacham started to stand but Doug placed a firm hand on his shoulder. "I'll be glad to get your drink order, fellas…do you both like sweet tea?"

Clint flinched but then immediately calmed at Doug's touch. The anger and tenseness he had felt toward the waitress suddenly evaporated into thin air. He should have felt intimidated at the man's firm grip on his shoulder, but, instead he felt calmer than he had in years. He looked up at Doug and said, "Tea's fine…thanks…" He stood up when Doug left the table. "I'll be right back," he said to Tyler before heading toward the restroom.

Amanda watched while Doug's touch calmed the rough waters once again. It wasn't the first time she had been witness to the power of controlled calm that emanated from his firm but gentle touch. She locked eyes with Tyler and smiled.

Tyler waited until Clint was behind closed doors before he stood and made his way to the counter. His returned smile was hesitant. *"I have no idea why I'm heading in her direction,"* he thought. *"No idea, whatsoever…"*

Amanda scooted off the stool and placed her hands on her hips. "Hello again, Tyler Foster…you're about the last person I expected to see here today."

Tyler raised his brows and shook his head. "Likewise…by the way…the people I work for know me as Tyler Jones, so…"

Amanda nodded. "I know…Max told me a little about what's going on with you and your Dad…that the two of you are working with the authorities to disband a big dog-fighting ring over in Thomasville."

"He told you about that?" Tyler's look of chagrin expressed his concern. He had told Max a little about what was going on, but he had also stressed that it was extremely important to keep his cover for another couple of weeks.

"Yep...Max knows more than you might think he knows about what's going on. You might even say, he's got *inside* information."

"Really?" Tyler asked, surprised. "He's a cook...what possible involvement would he have in busting a ring like this?"

"Well..." Amanda replied, mad at herself for possibly revealing too much information about her angels. "Don't mind me...I tend to ramble at times when I'm nervous. I doubt Max knows anything important, other than what you've already told him, but, *me,* on the other hand...well...in case you didn't know, I'm on the Tampa police force and they've been keeping files on some of the people associated with this Thomasville ring." Amanda hoped her lie would appease Tyler's sudden suspicious mind about Max's involvement. She knew that she had already said too much.

"*You're* a cop?" Tyler was genuinely surprised. "But you're so..."

Amanda cocked her head to one side. "I'm tougher than I look." She hesitated briefly before expanding her lie a little. "Actually, Max and Bertie are old friends of my father's and they think I'm here on a two-week vacation. I'd rather they not know the truth about why I'm really here, so if you'll keep it to yourself, I would appreciate it."

Tyler looked back toward the restrooms. "Keep what to myself?"

"Well," Amanda began the lie. "I happen to know that you've positioned yourself at the Abbott ranch in order to help bust this ring. I've been assigned to do what I can to assist you."

Tyler's look of total perplex said it all. "What the hell are you talking about? Who told you I was involved in anything like that?"

"Well...that's confidential information, Tyler Foster, on a need-to-know basis only..."

"Let me guess," Tyler countered. "You don't think I have

a need to know, right?"

Amanda stared at Tyler's broad shoulders, suppressed a gulp, and nodded. "You might want to get back to your table…I think your friend is looking for you."

Tyler looked behind him and saw Clint glowering at him. "I can't get back here tonight, but I'll be back after work tomorrow. Maybe we can continue this conversation then…"

Amanda shrugged and sat back down on her stool. "Maybe we can. I'll be here around seven…so, I guess we'll see…"

Clint returned to his table at the same time that Amos Brown pulled into the parking lot; a very special passenger shared the front seat with him. Amos rolled down the windows and patted Sam on the head. "I'll be right back, big fella. You stay right here, now…"

Sam waited until the front door closed behind Amos before he hopped gracefully out of the passenger window and made his way around to the café's back door. He barked in welcome when he saw Max waiting on the porch for him. He quickly told Max about the sudden change in plans.

Max sighed and shook his head. "I can't say that I am thrilled about this, Sam, but…I understand what you mean and what has to be done. Just remember, my friend…it's important that none of the humans guess the truth about you…"

Sam licked Max's extended hand. *"I know…and I will be careful. I know what needs to be done until Spartacus returns. The important thing is that I be there for those fights…even for Czar's."*

"That's right, my friend. Czar has been treated badly his entire life. All he knows is violence and killing. He will not be an easy one to convince."

"Just leave Czar to me...I've got to go now. Your friend, Amos, will be upset when he finds me missing, but I want to make sure I'm a few miles up the road by the time Tyler leaves to return to the ranch."

Max nodded and took Sam's face between his two hands. He stared into the angel-dog's soulful eyes. "Man's best friend does not begin to describe you and your kind, my friend. God be with you…"

Sam looked back at Max once before he dashed into the dense woods behind the café. *"He is always with me, Max…always…"*

Clint looked at his watch. He and Tyler had been at the café for almost an hour. He had to admit that the food was the best he had ever tasted. His stomach was full and his demeanor was a lot calmer than when he first arrived. "We need to get going, Jones. There's a new delivery of bait dogs coming in this evening. Czar will be delivered tomorrow morning and I want to see for myself what he's made of…finish up with your meal, but get a move on it. I'll wait for you outside. You're paying for this, right?"

Tyler nodded. "I got it, Boss…gonna hit the John before I leave...I'll be out in five minutes."

Amanda and Amos sat side-by-side at the counter. Their friendly chatter stopped when they saw Clint leaving the café. Amos saw the slight movement of Amanda's eyes as she glanced quickly at Tyler and blushed. He, nor his twin brother Andrew, had ever married, but he recognized the look he saw reflected in Amanda's eyes. He glanced back at Tyler and could have sworn that he saw the same look in the young man's eyes. "Lawdy…lawdy…this could get pretty interesting, yessirree…"

Amanda quickly averted her look toward Tyler. "What?"

Amos grinned and said. "If I was a bettin' man, and I ain't…then I'd be bettin' that you're sweet on that young man…yessirree…I think you both might be smitten'…"

Amanda feigned an air of nonchalance. "I'm sure I have no idea what you're talking about, Amos Brown."

Max came out of the kitchen and moved to the empty stool beside Amanda. "I don't want either of you to get upset about this, but…there has been a change of plans. Sam is gone…"

Amanda turned sharply to face Max. "What do you mean? He's gone back Home? I didn't get to say good-bye!"

Max shook his head. "No, Amanda...that's not what I meant. Sam left right after Amos got here; he's headed toward the Abbott ranch. As a matter of fact...Tyler and Clint Meacham will spot him on their way back to the ranch. I don't have to tell you what thoughts will be going through Mr. Meacham's head when he sees a dog like Sam..."

Amos shook his head sadly. "Lawdy, lawdy...I hates to hear that, Mr. Max...I surely do..."

"No..." Amanda groaned hoarsely. "No, Max...you've got to stop him...you can't let him go to that place. He'll be..."

"Killed?" Max smiled. "No, Amanda...trust me...Sam knows what he is doing, and...there's only one person we know of who has total control of this situation."

"But what can Sam do?" Amanda cried. "He's only a dog!"

Max shook his head. "You underestimate Sam...he may have been only a dog at one time...when he belonged to you, but...He belongs to God now, and Sam is following God's will and command. We have to trust them both..."

"Oh, Lawdy!" Amos grinned widely. "You mean, our Sam is an...*angel* dog? Well, I'll be..."

Tyler placed several bills on his table and moved toward the front door. He spotted Amanda talking to the owner of the café and another elderly, black man. He wanted to say good-bye to her, but he could tell the three of them were in deep conversation about something and he didn't want to interrupt. *"I'll see you tomorrow night, Princess..."* he thought. He shook his head and rubbed the bridge of his nose. "Princess? Now, where the hell did that come from?" he muttered.

CHAPTER 14

-Heaven-
Regina and Stephen

"I wonder how Sam is doing down there?" Stephen sighed wistfully. "He's only been gone a couple of days, and I know he can take care of himself, but..."

Regina Turner walked up behind her husband and wrapped her arms around his waist. "You know you don't have to worry about his safety, right?"

Stephen smiled and turned around to face his heavenly wife. He loved her as much today as he had during their short time on earth together. He had missed her terribly after she had died and had never become involved with another woman; however, he never thought about those years of celibacy, and they seemed like they were a lifetime ago. There was no physical intimacy between husbands and wives in heaven, but the special bond and closeness remained. His heavenly body became warmer and more sensitive to touch whenever he was close to Regina. The sensation was unlike anything he had ever experienced on earth, and it could not be described in mere words.

He held her tiny face between his hands and kissed the top of her head. "Yes…I do know that, but…it would be nice if Martin would tell us exactly what is going on down there."

"Hmmm…" Regina smiled and placed her hands upon her husband's shoulders. "Somehow, I don't believe Martin is obligated to keep us informed of anything. This is where our faith comes in handy, you know? We just have to have faith that whatever plan has been laid will work out…and, Martin did tell us that Sam wouldn't be gone all that long…no more than a couple of weeks, right?"

Stephen nodded and kissed the tip of Regina's nose. "Yep…that's what he said." He sighed again and looked around at their beautiful mansion and grounds. "You know…I still can't believe that this is ours. I never get tired of looking at all this…it's beyond anything I ever thought I would ever have…"

"Well…" Regina laughed. "It's not exactly ours, now is it?"

Stephen looked perplexed. "What do you mean, it's not ours? We built it ourselves, we work the garden every day…"

Regina shook her head. "Remember, Stephen…there are no possessions in Heaven. Yes…it is true that God has gifted us…and everyone else…with a mansion full of blessings…but, we are not to think along the lines that it belongs to us."

Stephen shrugged. "Well, I agree there's no mortgage attached to it, but…okay, okay…I've got to study up on this a bit more. It's obvious I missed a lesson along the way. Anyway…what do you say we take a long walk to take my mind off Sam and Amanda?"

Regina nodded and smiled. "Today is my day to assist with the children's Bible studies, but that's not until much later, so…yes…I would love to take a long walk with you. Where would you like to go today?"

Stephen thought for a moment before replying. "The Golden Falls…I've heard so much about them since I got here, but I haven't been yet."

"Oh, you're going to love them, Stephen! I won't even bother to describe them to you because my words would not do justice to them. Oh…I'm so excited that I'll be with you when you see them for the first time. Come on, let's go!"

"Lead the way, beautiful lady!"

Regina grabbed his hand and they skipped down the seven steps from their veranda to their immaculately-manicured grounds. Regina's favorite flower was the yellow rose, and they bloomed everywhere on the grounds. Ten acres of their assigned property was dedicated to growing luscious fruits and vegetables, but the remaining acreage was home to a beautiful array of flowering plants, bushes, and trees. Rabbits and squirrels played together, chasing each other across the lawn; birds and butterflies shared leaves and branches; cats and dogs who had crossed over the Rainbow Bridge and had no earthly owners of their own, rolled and relaxed on the soft and luscious turf; and, the occasional elephant, giraffe, lion, and bear also made daily appearances to the property.

Golden cobblestones served as a sidewalk that took them to the edge of their property. A dirt trail took its place once Regina and Stephen got to the end. Other mansions were so spread out that they could not see their neighbors' homes, but, once they were on the dirt trail, they saw several other couples walking hand in hand. They spoke to everyone they met along the trail.

They came upon one of their closest neighbors, a couple by the name of Minnie and Donnie, both of whom appeared to be in their fifties. "Where are you young people off to today?" Minnie asked after giving Regina a quick hug.

Regina returned the older woman's hug and said, "I'm taking Stephen to see the Golden Falls!"

"Oh, my!" Minnie laughed. She looked at Stephen and said, "You are in for a treat, young man. Donnie took me to see them shortly after I got here. He spends most of his free time there, don't you, 'ole man?"

Donnie feigned shock and answered, "Who are you calling 'ole man, woman?" He grinned and pulled his wife in for a tight hug. "But, yes…the Golden Falls are unlike anything you've ever seen before, Stephen. I wish we could go with you since this is your first time, but…you two should be alone for this trip. Maybe we can all go together some other time."

Stephen hugged Donnie and smiled back at him. "I would like that, Donnie. I've been excited to see them, but after hearing all of you talk about them, well, now I really want to get there."

"Well…" Regina spoke softly. "We could just think ourselves there, you know, and get there a lot quicker."

Stephen shook his head. "No, I don't want to do that. I want to enjoy every step there. These woods are amazing, so full of beauty and so much to see…I don't want to miss any of that."

"Well, you two run along, now," Minnie said. "But be sure to let us know what you think about the Golden Falls. I love hearing from people who see them for the first time. I can't wait to go again."

"Okay," Regina waved back at them. "Maybe we can all visit them again in a few days…together."

"It's a date!" Donnie laughed. "Have a great time!"

Stephen and Regina lost all track of time as they walked, hand-in-hand, along the dirt track. They stopped several times along the way to sit and lower their feet into cool spring waters. Deer and possums moved around them, eating flowers and playing in the streams.

"I don't think I'll ever get use to all this," Stephen said during one of their stops. "I've never experienced this kind of beauty or peace before. I mean…I thought earth was pretty awesome, but nothing…absolutely nothing…compares to all this. Just look at the animals! That still blows my mind…how all the different species just walk along, side-by-side, sharing everything."

Regina turned when she heard a loud purr behind them. A majestic lion looked at her for a moment before moving to stand beside her. Regina reached down to stoke its soft fur. "Yep, pretty amazing, isn't it?"

Stephen froze for a moment and was utterly speechless. "Okay…now that was scary…I've seen the lions moving around before, but I've never seen one come right up to a human like that. Why didn't he attack us?"

"Everyone…and everything…shares Heaven, Stephen. God didn't create all this just for us humans to enjoy. He loves every living thing that he created, right down to the ants over there building their own mansions." Regina pointed to a large ant hill to her left.

"Don't tell me," Stephen said while shaking his head. "Even the ants don't bite, right?"

"That's right!" Regina laughed as she locked arms with him. "Come on, we're almost there. Look up ahead...can you see how much brighter it is around that last bend?"

Stephen took a deep breath while the lion walked slowly around and in front of them. The sky seemed brighter here than it had on the trail through the woods. Even though there was no darkness, no sun or moon, and no severe weather of any kind in Heaven, there were still shadows and shade provided by the voluminous trees. He looked behind him and then looked ahead. "Yeah...I can see that it is getting brighter...hey...that looks like golden sunshine coming from behind that bend."

"That's a good way to describe it...I like that...golden sunshine..." Regina pulled him along the trail. She reached down and patted the lion's head as it purred at her one more time before wandering off into the woods. She watched while the lion stopped long enough to allow a group of field mice to cross in front of him. The closer she got to the falls, the more immediate the need she felt to be there. "Come on! Enough walking, let's run!" She let go of his arm and took off at a slow sprint.

Stephen caught up with her in time at all. Neither of them became out of breath and they laughed as they ran faster and faster until they finally reached the final bend in the road.

Stephen stopped suddenly in his tracks, but Regina kept on running when the trail ended at the final bend. She wanted him to be alone when he saw the falls for the first time; she remembered her own experience well, and she didn't want to be a distraction for him.

Stephen forgot to breathe for a moment; the brilliant beauty of what lay before him literally took his breath away. He blinked his eyes repeatedly to help them adjust to the sudden golden brilliance that surrounded him on three sides. The trail behind him dimmed in comparison to the entrance to the Golden Falls. The dirt trail was replaced with the bright, golden bricks. "Wow," he whispered into the air. "This gives new meaning to the Yellow-Brick Road..." He followed the brick trail for about a quarter of a mile before it expanded into a larger, circular road. The circle was about five miles in diameter, and, in the center of it was the Golden Falls.

Stephen stopped and looked upward. A gold-mirrored wall surrounded him on all sides and reflected the falling, golden water as it flowed from some infinite origination high above him. He looked at the walls and saw hundreds of reflections of himself as he spun himself around and around with his arms extended upward. The glow from the walls and the bricks warmed his body and every nerve in him tingled with energy. He suddenly felt more alive than he ever had in his life time. He closed his eyes and felt the strangest sensation course through him. It felt as though something…or someone…was inside him, providing him with a strength, and a peace, he had never before experienced. He dropped his arms and hugged himself hard. Tears of bliss and pure, unadulterated joy poured down his cheeks. The mist from the gentle splashes of the golden waters splashed him and cooled the intense heat that seemed to emanate from within his body. There was nobody there beside him, nevertheless…he felt strong arms wrapped around him…and he felt another heart beat against his chest. He didn't know how he knew it, but he did…he knew that God had just wrapped his arms around him.

"Oh…my…God…" Stephen continued to cry. He dropped to his knees and bowed his head. "Oh, my God…"

"WELCOME HOME, MY SON… WELCOME HOME…"

Stephen didn't have to ask; he knew from whom that voice had come. His Father had chosen the Golden Falls to provide his official, welcoming homecoming.

Regina watched from a distance. Stephen couldn't see what she saw because he had closed his eyes before he dropped to his knees. She, too, dropped to her knees and cried tears of happiness and joy. "Thank you, Father…thank you so much for loving us…"

"The wolf also shall dwell with the lamb, the leopard shall lie down with the young goat, the calf and the young lion and the fatling together; and a little child shall lead them. The cow and the bear shall graze; their young ones shall lie down together; and the lion shall eat straw like the ox…" Isaiah 11:6-7 (NKJ

CHAPTER 15

Sam Infiltrates the Ring

Tyler was smiling to himself when he closed the café door behind him. His smile faded when he saw Clint Meacham standing on the passenger side of Tyler's truck; he was talking to someone on his cell phone. He quickly averted his gaze when Clint turned to stare at him.

Clint closed the cover to his flip-phone. "Let's get going. The Boss is waiting for us; there's a new supply of baiters coming in. We'll need to sort them out tonight and decide which ones to try out on Czar tomorrow." He snorted an evil laugh. "From the way he tore at Spartacus the other night, I have a feeling he'll go through this batch of baiters in no time. We'll probably need to find some more before the next fight."

Tyler bit on his bottom lip to keep from saying what he so desperately wanted to say to the scumbag foreman. He simply nodded and moved into the driver's seat.

They pulled out of the parking lot and turned north onto the road leading back to Thomasville. They had been driving for fifteen minutes before either of them spoke.

"I saw you making eyes at the sweet piece back at the

café," Clint mocked. He puckered his lips into a smooch before licking them with his tobacco-stained tongue.

Tyler was repulsed but refused to let the foreman bait him into a confrontation, so he offered no response.

"Whatsamatter, kid? Cat got your tongue? Can't say that I blame you for checking her out, though. I wouldn't mind getting me a piece of that..." Clint stopped in mid-sentence when he spotted the large, black dog sitting on the side of the road. "Stop! Pull over, quick!"

Tyler had been staring straight ahead, trying his best to tune out the offensive innuendos from Clint, so he had not seen Sam sitting on the side of the road. "What..."

Clint looked over at him and barked an order. "I told you to stop the damn truck!" He had his door opened before Tyler had even come to a complete stop. "Bring that leash and chain with you," he demanded without looking back at Tyler. The black dog seemed to be taunting him as he moved toward it. The dog stood up and moved backward each time Clint took a step forward. "Bring me that damn chain, Jones!"

Tyler opened his door and grabbed the choker chain and leash from the back floorboard. He finally spotted the large, black dog and immediately recognized it as being the one he had seen in the back yard of the café the day before. He had been so focused on rescuing Spartacus that he had not asked about the large, black dog that had stared soulfully at him from the back yard. He was sure that it, most likely, belonged to the people who owned the café...probably, to the no-nonsense waitress who punched him repeatedly on the shoulder. "We can't take that dog, Clint...I'm pretty sure it belongs to someone back at that café."

Clint looked back at Tyler with a sneer. "And how the hell would you know that?"

Tyler knew he had said too much, and needed to cover his tracks. He could not let Clint suspect that he had any connection to the owners of the café. He did not want to do or say anything to put their safety in jeopardy. He shrugged his shoulders and said, "I think I saw him hanging around there when I was looking for Spartacus. He's well-fed, so he must belong to someone; it's obvious he's not a stray."

"You've got a lot to learn, kid…" Clint spat out a wad of tobacco juice and turned toward the dog again. "This dog looks like a golden opportunity to me...stray or no stray…he's coming with us. Now help me get him."

Sam lowered his head and emitted a low, threatening growl. Tyler took a step backward and Clint grabbed the choker chain from his hand. He spotted a thick, wooden stump on the ground and picked it up as he took another step toward the dog. Sam lunged at him and Clint swung the wooden club in a reflexive manner. He made quick contact with the side of Sam's head.

"Stop it!" Tyler shouted. "You don't have to do that! He withdrew a syringe from his back pocket and quickly inserted it into the back of the dog's neck, as it lay on the ground whimpering from the stunning blow. "He won't be good to anyone if you bash his brains in…" Tyler fought the urge to pick up the club and give Clint a taste of his own medicine.

"Well, why the hell didn't you tell me you had a syringe!" Clint shot back. "Hurry up, get him into the back before someone drives by…"

The drive back to the Abbott ranch was a tense one; neither man spoke nor made eye contact with the other. Tyler listened closely as the black dog whimpered where it lay on the back floorboard. All he could do was to grit his teeth and hope he could find a way to help the dog escape before any more harm came to it.

Little John Abbott was waiting for them as they pulled near the bunk house. His muscular arms bulged beneath his signature black tee-shirt. He nodded to Clint when he got out of the truck. "You made the deal on Czar…no problems?"

Clint nodded and spat tobacco juice on the ground. "No problems...everything went smooth. The owner said he'd been wanting to get out of the business anyway and was going to be looking to sell Czar soon."

Little John nodded and watched Tyler exit the truck. He thought the young man looked flustered and uptight about something. He waited until Tyler was looking at him and asked, "What's wrong with you, Jones? You look like you could bite someone's head off right about now."

Tyler shot a quick glance at Clint and pursed his lips together. It was imperative that he keep his emotions under control.

Clint pursed his lips in another mock kiss and said, "Pretty boy here got his panties in a wad because I spotted something on the side of the road that I thought you might be interested in; he thought it might belong to someone else and didn't want to take it."

"What's that?" Little John asked. He never took his eyes off Tyler. He thought that if looks really could kill, then he was convinced that Clint Meacham was a dead man walking.

Clint opened the truck's back passenger door and bent over. When he stood back up, he had the choker collar wrapped around his hand and pulled Sam roughly to the ground. Sam landed on his side with a hard, solid thump. Clint kicked his backside. "Found this mutt just sitting on the side of the road...like he was just waiting for us to pick him up. He's big and strong...I figured if we couldn't train him to fight, then he would still make one helluva baiter...what do you think, Boss?"

Little John walked closer to where the massive black dog lay on the ground. The dog's hair was too long for it to be a pure pit. "Looks like he might have some lab in him, but...he definitely has some pit, too." He bent down and pulled its lips up. "Nice, sharp teeth...no scars...so, either it's never been in a fight, or...it's never lost one." He didn't show how excited he really was at Clint's latest find, but he was already thinking that between this dog and Czar, he might be able to make enough money in the next two weeks to shut down the business for several months if he had to. "Good eye, Clint."

He stood up and looked at Tyler, who was standing rigid and tense. "Okay, Jones, put him in a cage and let him sleep it off. Let me know when he starts coming around…I want to see him in a standing position. Make sure you don't give him any food…you know the drill. Water's okay, but no food until I see what he's made of…"

Tyler clinched his teeth together and tried to relax some of the tension in his arms and shoulders. "Yes, sir…I'll take care of it." He walked around to where the two men stood. He bent down and picked up the seventy-pound dog with ease, and returned him to the back floorboard once again. He nodded to Little John but managed to avoid any further eye contact with the foreman. He got back inside his truck and drove a half-mile past the bunk house toward the grove of trees that surrounded and housed some of the baiters and fighters.

Little John watched him drive away. "What's really going on with him?"

Clint shook his head. "I told you, Boss…I think the kid is too soft. He doesn't have what it takes to get these dogs in fighting condition."

"He might be," Little John conceded and shook his head. "We should probably cut him loose right now. I really don't have a good feeling about him, but…we're still short-handed. Just remember what I said…keep a close eye on him. We only need him for a couple more weeks; you can fire him then."

"I'd like to do more than that…" Clint mumbled.

Little John heard him and said, "Once we don't need him anymore, do whatever the hell you want to with him…just make sure he gets off and stays off this ranch. If it seems like he's going be shooting his mouth off to anyone about what he's seen here, then…you know what to do about that…"

Clint spat a watery wad onto the ground and grinned. "I know exactly what to do…"

Tyler pulled into the grove of trees and was glad to see

that none of the other workers were there. Training had stopped early today and most of the workers were at the receiving station, waiting on the new load of bait animals that were due to arrive. The receiving station was located at the other end of the ranch, closer to the burning pit. Tyler carried the huge, black dog from the truck to an empty cage at the end of the circled grove. He laid the dog gently on the ground and quickly gathered extra pine straw to place inside the cage. He filled up the water bowl with fresh, cool water before picking the dog up and placing him inside the 3x3x3 metal cage. He took a handkerchief from his back pocket, dipped it into the cool water, and wiped the dried blood from the dog's ear, the one that had made contact with the wooden club.

"I'm so sorry this has happened to you, big fella, but…I'm going to do my best to see that they don't hurt you. I hope you believe that…" A single tear escaped from the corner of Tyler's eye and he quickly wiped it away with the back of his hand. He dipped the rag again and ran it over the dog's neck and chest. He was so concerned about what might happen to this beautiful creature that he didn't notice the moment when the dog's eyes opened.

"Oh, Tyler...please don't worry about me…I wish I could tell you that this is the way it has to be for now…" Sam watched while Tyler wiped away the tear. He waited until Tyler dipped the handkerchief into the water again. He sighed when he felt the cool water against his neck and chest. Just as Tyler started to pull his hand away, Sam's tongue darted out and licked it.

Tyler jumped, jerked his hand away, and fell flat on his best feature – at least, that's what his own mother had always told him. "Jesus Christ, you scared the crap out of me!" he practically yelled. He scooted backwards and slammed the cage door shut. He remembered how the dog had lunged at Clint and he wasn't convinced that it wouldn't do the same to him. He grasped the back of his neck and squeezed it between his open palms. "Damn…you shouldn't be coming out of it, already. There was enough in that dose to keep you knocked out for another two or three hours."

Sam lifted his head and stared deeply into Tyler's worried eyes. *"You've got to have faith, Tyler. I know what I'm doing, and everything is going to work out..."*

The dog's gaze was hypnotic and Tyler found it hard to look away. He watched in awe and wonder as the dog pushed itself easily to a standing position. His massive size did not leave him much room to move about inside the largest cage they had. Tyler waited for the dog to growl at him, to show some sign of aggression, but it was soon obvious to him that he would not be witness to that. He got to his knees and crawled closer to the cage. "Hey, boy..." he spoke softly while reaching his hand between the bars of the cage. "Please don't eat me, okay?" Tyler's eyes widened in disbelief when the dog's eyes appeared to twinkle with a hint of mischief.

"I like you, Tyler Foster..." Sam thought as his long tongue reached out to lick Tyler's nervous, shaking hand. *"And so does my sweet Amanda..."*

CHAPTER 16

The Bait Dogs Arrive

Tim Breydan and Ross Taylor lay on their bellies, hidden by the thick covering of underbrush that overlooked the circular grove on the Abbott ranch. They each had their own set of binoculars and watched intently while Abbott's crew herded thirty small-to-mid-size dogs into an enclosed arena.

Tim and Ross had worked together for three years on cases like the one they were on now; they were both dedicated Animal Protection Inspectors who were part of an undisclosed division within the USDA's Center for Animal Welfare Department, and had been extremely successful in helping to shut down dozens of dog-fighting rings during that time. Although this department's primary mission was to collaborate with other animal welfare entities to ensure that federally established standards of care and treatment of animals were enforced, Tim and Ross had been eager to sign up for the special assignment to help shut down dog-fighting rings across the United States. They had both been trained extensively by members of ASPCA's anti-cruelty team.

Tim stared through his binoculars and pointed. "There's

our contact...the young man squatting next to that last cage on the left...the one with the large, black dog in it...see him?"

Ross nodded. "Yeah, I see him...that's B.B. Foster's son...we're supposed to meet up with him tonight. From what I hear in town, there's another fight scheduled for next Friday night."

Tim was quiet for a moment while he continued to watch some of the crewmembers moving about the closed arena where the latest batch of bait dogs had been secured. He winced when one overweight, belligerent ranch hand kicked a small terrier-mix that had come over to him to be petted. "Son-of-a-bitch..." he muttered beneath his breath.

"Easy, Tim...we can't get to them now...nor will we be able to save them all...but, if everything goes according to plan, we can lock these assholes up soon and throw away the key...at least for a few years..."

The terrier-mix was slow to get up, but it eventually managed to crawl itself into the far corner of the arena. Tim and Ross were both so intent on watching the other bait dogs that neither of them saw Tyler running to the small dog's rescue. They also did not see the latch on the cage that housed the large, black pit slide open, apparently, all on its own.

"Hey!" Tyler yelled. "You didn't have to kick him!" He marched up to the overweight crew member who was a younger, flabbier version of Little John Abbott, and quickly felt the crunch of the massive blow to his belly.

The crewmember who had kicked the pup glowered at Tyler. "Don't tell me how to do my job, Jones..." He didn't have a chance to say anything else.

Sam approached quickly and attacked the brute before he could turn back around. He growled and jumped on the man's back and knocked him to the ground. When the crewmember, whose name was Bubba, turned over on his back, Sam was quick to go for his throat. He could easily have ripped open the man's exposed throat, but Sam knew that the angels...and God...would be disappointed in him if he reacted in that way; instead, he growled and slobbered onto Bubba's trembling face, got off him, and ambled slowly over to where the terrier-mix lay trembling in the corner. *"Don't worry little one...you are safe with me...I'm going to have to do something to you, but I need you to just go along with me, okay?"*

The small dog continued to tremble, and did not respond to Sam's soothing words.

What happened next was a horrible sight to witness...if you were human. Sam moved quickly and grabbed the small dog by the throat. He shook him violently for several seconds until those humans who were watching in awe, heard the snap of the pup's neck.

"Damn...did you see that?" Bubba blubbered as he pushed himself up and stumbled to a standing position. He was oblivious to the dog drool that covered his face and shirt.

Nobody answered him; instead, they all backed away nervously when Sam turned and moved toward them. Tyler tried to shake the horrible death scene from his mind and quickly hooked a heavy-duty leader leash around Sam's neck. "Easy, fella...come on, now...let's get you back inside your cage."

Bubba had recovered his wits about him by that time and charged at Tyler. "I'm going to kill that mother right now...I'm going to bash his head in with my bare fists..."

Tyler dropped the leash and turned quickly to administer his own belly-crunching blow to Bubba's massive gut. "I wouldn't do that if I were you...this dog is important to Little John, and I doubt he would react favorably to anyone who bashed his head in with their bare fists." He looked back at the small, lifeless form of the terrier-mix. "And, don't touch that one...I'll take care of him myself."

Bubba clenched his fists but quickly turned away when Sam growled and lunged at him again. "Get that mutt outta here now! How the hell did he get out of his cage, anyway?"

Tyler picked up the leash and led a seemingly subdued Sam back to his cage. He turned to look at the other crewmembers who were laughing at Bubba's reaction to the attack. He watched while they continue to separate the bait dogs into groups of four; none of them bothered the limp terrier that lay dead in the far corner of the arena. Tyler closed the cage and secured the lock. He knew he had locked it behind him and could not fathom how the dog had managed to escape. He reached through the bars and rubbed the top of Sam's massive head. "I wish you hadn't done that, fella…it was just a pup…it didn't deserve to die that way…"

The crew members all dispersed after the bait dogs had been separated; there were other chores that had to be done before the training commenced later that afternoon. When they had all left, Tyler returned to the arena and went to where the terrier-mix lay on the soft red clay. He stroked its side, noting that the pup could not have weighed more than fifteen pounds. "I'm so sorry, little guy…so very sorry this had to happen to you…" He bowed his head and said a silent prayer for the pup who had probably been someone's pet at one time. He fell flat on his butt again when he felt a cold nose press against his arm. "Damn!" he yelled when he saw the black pittie-mix standing directly behind him. "How the hell *are* you getting out of your cage?"

Sam moved to stand beside Tyler and stared directly into his eyes. *"I shouldn't let you see this, but Max said you could be trusted, so…"* Sam walked slowly around to where Tyler still sat on the ground, until he came to the lifeless pup. He lay down beside the terrier-mix and placed one large paw on it; it appeared that he was hugging the dog to him.

Tyler watched in total awe as the huge dog gently took the lifeless body and folded it into what appeared to be an embrace. He watched the larger dog lick the terrier's face until…

"Oh…my…God…" Tyler whispered beneath his own shattered breathing. He could not believe what he was seeing. He knew the terrier had been dead; he had heard the snap of the pup's small neck when the pit shook it to its death…yet…now…the eyes of terrier slowly opened and a tiny whimper escaped him. Tyler held his breath and brought both palms together, pressed against his mouth. "Oh...my...God..." he repeated.

Sam lifted his massive paw off the resurrected pup and allowed it to crawl toward Tyler, onto his waiting lap.

Tim gasped and dropped his binoculars. "Jesus Christ!" he rasped. "Jesus...did you see that, Ross?"

Ross continued looking through his binoculars. He had been watching the other bait dogs being maneuvered by the crew. He had seen the large black dog shake and kill the small terrier, but he had not witnessed the subsequent resurrection of the pup.

Both men had been so engrossed in what they were witnessing, that they did not hear the first crackle of leaves behind them. They both heard the second crackle, however, but it was too late for either of them to reach for their guns. They each felt the cold end of a rifle against the back of their necks.

"Well, well..." Clint Meacham grinned and spat a wad of brown juice from his mouth. "What do you suppose we have here, Pete? Looks like a couple of trespassers, wouldn't you say?"

Clint's second in command, Pete Ratchett, hacked up phlegm and spit it out. "Yep...that's what they look like to me. What do you think we should do with 'em, Boss?"

Clint thought the two men might be the ones that Little John had mentioned earlier...the ones who had been asking too many questions about dog-fighting. "Get up slow...both of you...and don't try anything, 'cause I'd just as soon blown your brains out right here and now...come on, up slow...very slow..."

Tim and Ross pushed themselves up on their knees and into a standing position.

"Put your hands behind your head," Clint barked. He noticed the side holsters on each man. "Get their guns, Pete."

The inspectors complied but did not say anything. They

had both removed all forms of identification before they left their hotel room that morning. They knew this would buy them some time if they were caught spying at the Abbott ranch, but wondered if that would be enough. The only person in town who knew where they were staying was Tyler Foster, and they were supposed to meet him in person later that night. They could only hope that when/if they didn't show for the meeting, that Tyler might put two and two together, contact the authorities, and ensure their identifications did not fall into the wrong hands.

Clint nodded to the path behind him. "Get moving, *gentlemen…*"

Tim caught Ross's eye and shook his head slightly, silently warning him not to say or do anything.

Pete hacked and snorted again. "Why can't we just kill 'em here? It's not like we ain't done it before…"

"Shut your damn mouth, Pete." Clint motioned for the two men to follow after Pete. "Hog-tie them and throw them in the bed of your truck. I'll get their vehicle and follow behind you. Take them to the cabin at the pit. It's your job to make sure those ropes are good and tight because if these fellas get away, your ass is mine, and I'll throw you in the pit with the rest of the garbage."

Pete knew that Clint Meacham would do just that, so he was quick to follow orders. "I got it covered, Boss…"

Clint looked back and retrieved both sets of binoculars. His gaze darted briefly down the hill to the hidden grove where the dogs were caged. He had not witnessed the miracle that Sam had administered, but he watched while Tyler petted one of the mutt-bait dogs and lifted it to his chest; it looked like he was comforting the dog. "Maybe I'll toss you inside the pit along with these two sissies…" He spat and turned around; he held his rifle to the backs of the two men who were following Pete to the truck he and Clint had parked a quarter-mile away.

Sam stopped in his tracks on his way back to his cage. He turned and looked up toward the brushy meadow at the top of the hill, about a mile away. *"That's not good..."* he thought. His gaze then drifted to the enclosed arena, where Tyler stood, holding the small terrier-mix to his chest. *"But...that is good..."* he sighed, walked back inside his cage, and lay down on the extra bedding of pine straw Tyler had provided the night before. He closed his eyes and the sliding lock engaged on his cage.

CHAPTER 17

Tyler Confides to Amanda

Bertie placed the Italian sausage, peppers, and cheese omelet in front of Tyler, and poured him a cup of coffee. "Surprised to see you back here so soon…" she said. She had watched him intently since he entered the restaurant twenty minutes ago. "You're white as a sheet, boy…do you want to talk about it?"

Tyler snapped out of the fog he had been in ever since witnessing the resurrection of the small dog that had been killed by the huge, black dog he and Clint had picked up the day before. He had immediately placed the resurrected dog inside his pick-up truck and instinctively headed toward the little restaurant with the floating halo. He had not told anyone that he was leaving, so he knew he might not have a job to go back to; but, sheer instinct had told him to gather the pup up and bring him to the Heavenly Grille Café. He did not remember ordering anything to eat, but he must have, because the bossy waitress had just placed the mouth-watering meal on the counter in front of him. He turned his head and glanced backward toward his truck in the parking lot. The small black and white terrier was barking and hanging his two front paws over the open driver's window.

Tyler looked back at Bertie and shook his head. "You wouldn't believe me if I told you, but…do you think I could get a plain burger to go…for him?" He nodded back toward the parking lot.

"I'll take care of that for you. Is he yours?" Bertie replied softly, which was totally uncharacteristic of her.

Tyler removed his cap and ran his hands over his dark, buzz-cut hair. "I guess he is now, but…"

The front door opened and the angel chimes welcomed Amanda inside. She immediately saw Bertie standing at the counter with a customer. She waved quickly and made her way through the crowded restaurant. The only empty seat at the counter was beside the man Bertie was talking to. "Morning, Bertie! Hey, did you see that cutie in the truck out there…" She sat down on the empty stool and finally recognized Tyler when he turned to face her. "Oh, hey there! It's you! I didn't expect you back here until later tonight."

Tyler grinned and shrugged; the mental fog he had been in during the drive to the café was lifting, and he knew he had to come up with a good excuse for leaving the ranch like he had. He inhaled and pursed his lips together. Amanda looked beautiful and refreshed. He looked back and forth between her and Bertie.

"I can take a hint," Bertie mocked. "I'll leave you two alone to *talk*…and I'll get you some breakfast, Princess. Go ahead…have a seat and take a load off."

Amanda blushed and looked at Tyler. "Okay…she's gone, and you're white as a ghost…what's going on? Is everything okay at the Abbott ranch? I was going to drive to Thomasville and get a room tomorrow so that I could be closer to the action…you know…to help you with whatever needs to be done. I was going to talk to you about all this when you came back here tonight, though…"

Tyler rubbed the bridge of his nose and shook his head. "I was going to have to cancel tonight anyway, Amanda. I got a call late last night from the two investigators in charge of busting this dog-fighting ring…I'm supposed to meet with them at seven o'clock tonight. They said they had reason to believe that next week's fight may be moved up to this Friday. Oh…and, do you remember that big, black pit-mix dog that was in the back yard the day I met you? Well…you're not going to believe this, but, he's locked up in a cage right now, at the Abbott ranch. Little John wants him ready to fight in the next fight…and, you're going to think I'm crazy, but…I…watched that black dog bring a dead dog back to life about an hour or so ago…"

Bertie and Max listened from the kitchen and exchanged surprised glances with each other.

"Sam showed himself to Tyler…" Max spoke softly and smiled. "Now, that surprises me…"

"Surprises you?" Bertie whispered back loudly. "Well, it shocks the hell out of me! What are we going to do, Maximus?"

Max put an arm around his favorite naughty angel and laughed. "*WE* are not going to do anything, Bertie. I knew Sam's plan to infiltrate the Abbott ranch had to be speeded up, but I'm still not sure what's going to happen there. So…*WE* don't do anything. If Sam needs our help, he'll let us know. In the meantime, I have a feeling this whole situation is going to bring Amanda and Tyler a lot closer together."

Bertie grinned. "Well, I'm all for that…I think…"

The two angels continued to eavesdrop on the conversation between the young couple.

Amanda's jaw fell open and she started to say something, but then closed her mouth again. She spun the stool around and looked out toward the parking lot at the happy dog barking from what she now recognized as Tyler's truck. "So…you've got Sam at the Abbott ranch, and…I assume that the eager fella in your truck is the one that Sam brought back to life?"

Tyler picked up his coffee cup again and took a long swig.

He shook his head and stared hard at Amanda. "Sam? You know his name? Of course, you do. Do I even want to know why you don't seem surprised that the dog I kidnapped yesterday somehow, miraculously, brought a dog with a snapped neck back to life?"

Amanda stood up and placed her hands on both hips. "That's a conversation for another time...okay? Suffice it to say that...no...I am not surprised to hear this about Sam...you will find out...no, forget that, you've already found out...that Sam is...*special.*"

"Special?" Tyler nodded his head. "Okay...special...how?"

Amanda waved her hands in dismissal. "Never mind about that...I'll tell you later, I promise, but, right now...I'm going to eat some breakfast and then you're going to call your Dad to tell him to meet us half-way. We're going to take that cute fella out in your truck...does he have a name...to your Dad, who will keep him safe. Then, you and I will head back to Thomasville and find me a place to stay. If you don't mind, I would like to go with you to meet those investigators tonight."

Tyler didn't know what to say, but he instinctively knew that he could trust Amanda Turner completely. "I'll call my Dad and let him know to meet us...why don't you go ahead and eat that omelet? I'm not really hungry..." Tyler was at the front door when he turned and said, "That little guy doesn't have a name yet..."

Amanda pulled the breakfast plate toward her and took a huge bite of the delicious omelet. She turned and watched while Tyler walked outside to his truck, petted the eager pup, and punched a number into his cell phone. Amanda grinned when the little pup jumped up and down, and washed Tyler's face with puppy kisses. She smiled, took another bite of the omelet, and chased it with what was left of Tyler's coffee. "I think we'll call him Licker..." she smiled. She looked up and saw Max and Bertie grinning back at her.

Max offered a thumbs-up signal, and Bertie mouthed, "*Be*

careful!"

Amanda returned the thumbs-up gesture and blew them a kiss.

"Hold up!" Bertie yelled from the kitchen. Max had already prepared two beef patties for the pup and placed them in a paper bag. "You're going to need this!" She ran to the front door and gave them to Amanda. She pulled the young woman to her in a bear hug and whispered in her ear, "We love you, Princess...you call us at the first sign of trouble!"

Amanda returned the hug and said, "You know I will, Bertie...I love you, too! By the way...Buster is upstairs...please take care of him until I get back...maybe Doug can take him out back to play later!" She waved to Max and was out the door by the time Tyler had finished his phone call.

"Dad will be waiting for us," he reported while he walked around the truck and opened the passenger door for Amanda.

"Ohhh..." Amanda teased. "My future husband is such the gentleman, isn't he?" She laughed when the terrier-mix pup rushed onto her lap and pushed his nose toward the greasy bag she held in her hand. Amanda returned his puppy kisses and broke the patties into small pieces for him. "Here you go, Licker...enjoy..."

Tyler returned to the driver's side, opened the door, and slid inside quietly. He looked over at Amanda and the pup. He didn't know which comment to address first...the dog's new name...or the comment about him being Amanda's future husband. He played it safe and did not say anything for the first half of the trip.

They were half-way to their destination point when Tyler finally said, "Okay, Amanda...we have another forty-five minutes to go, so that should be plenty of time for you to tell me why Sam is so...what did you say...*special*?"

Amanda looked over at Tyler's handsome profile and grinned. "We're going to have some really nice-looking kids, aren't we?" Licker had snuggled comfortably in her lap and was sound asleep.

Tyler looked sideways to see what he hoped was a teasing expression on her face; instead, he thought that she looked completely serious. For reasons that he could not, and would not even begin to explain, he felt resigned to accept what fate might have in store for them both. The connection he was feeling toward her warmed him from the inside out, and he could only nod his affirmation. "Yeah...yeah, I believe we will..."

Amanda's comment had served its purpose and she smiled inwardly. She would be able to put off her explanation about Sam for the time being.

The small, one-room concrete house was upwind from the burning pit that the Abbott ranch crew members used to discard dead, or semi-dead, bait dogs. However, the lingering smell of their burned fur and skin still managed to seep through the walls of the house where Tim Breydan and Ross Taylor had been savagely beaten and bound.

Tim was the first to regain consciousness. One eye was swollen completely shut, but when he heard groaning coming from the opposite corner of the room, he was able to open the other one wide enough to make out a crumpled form; and, he had to hope and assume it was Ross. His hands were tied behind him, and the rope extended and connected to his bound ankles. *"I guess this is what being hog tied means..."* he thought. He tried to call out Ross's name, but no sound came out at first. He remembered being choked from behind by one man while another one beat his face to a bloody pulp. He squinted through the darkness again, trying to focus on the crumpled form in the far corner; it was impossible to determine whether or not his friend was still alive.

Tim was not able to get into a sitting position because of the way he and Ross had been tied, so he turned on his side and tried to get a better feel for their surroundings. It was no use; there were no windows, and the room was too dark to make out anything other than what looked like a crumpled form in the far corner. Where were they? He vaguely remembered the older man telling Pete to take them to the cabin at the pit. What pit? Were they still on the Abbott ranch?

The darkness within the room prevented Tim from knowing what time of day or night it might be. He had no idea how long he and Ross had been there. He listened for any sign of movement inside or outside the cabin; he heard absolutely nothing…the eerie quietness of the place worried him more than the men who had beaten and discarded them. He turned his head sharply back toward the crumpled form when he heard a low moaning coming from that direction. He used his knees and shoulders to scoot sideways toward the sound.

"Tim…." The voice was cracked and weak, but Ross Taylor managed to get it out. His voice wasn't the only thing that was cracked; when he tried to turn toward the dragging sound he heard, he knew immediately that he, most likely, had some broken ribs. The pain was excruciating and it hurt like hell trying to breathe. "Tim…?"

"I'm here, buddy…I'm here…" Tim rasped hoarsely, as he made his way slowly across the room. "You okay?" His throat burned like a furnace, but the words came easier now.

"Yeah…yeah…I'm okay…" Ross groaned back. "We've got to get out of here…before they come back..." It was a struggle for Ross to get the words out. "I heard them say something about throwing us in the pit…"

Tim had managed to scoot closer to the corner where Ross's battered body lay. The closer he got, the more he was able to see the damage that had been inflicted upon his friend. Ross had put up more of a fight, and had been beaten more severely than him. Tim did not think his friend and co-worker looked good at all. He listened to Ross's raspy and labored breathing, and wondered if his lungs had been bruised or, worse, punctured. "They don't know who we are," Tim croaked. "I don't think they'll do anything until they find out for sure." He was quiet for a minute or two. "We're going to get out of here, Ross...you've got to hang on...do you hear me?"

It was another full minute before a sigh of relief escaped Tim's parched throat...a blessed sigh of relief when he heard Ross's tortured inhalation of air.

"I hear ya...I hear ya..." Ross answered back with forced determination. He closed his eyes and suppressed a scream that threatened to escape when he attempted to reposition himself. The burning in his rib cage and lungs was beyond any pain he had ever before experienced. He wanted to believe Tim's words, but he didn't have Tim's faith. He wished he knew how to pray because he had a feeling they were going to need all the help they could get in order to get out of the predicament in which they now found themselves.

CHAPTER 18

Spartacus Returns

Tyler and Amanda made small talk for the remainder of their trip to meet up with B.B. Foster. They both had so much to confide to the other one, but neither of them felt confident or secure enough to trust the other with all the information they had to share.

Licker, on the other hand, was thoroughly enjoying his first freedom ride. His short life had been lived on the streets as a stray, scrounging food from any place he could find, trying to keep dry from pounding rains, and constantly outguessing the local animal control officers. He had thought he was a pretty smart canine when he hooked up with a pack of stray dogs on the outskirts of Thomasville. Their luck ran out the evening before when a truck from the Abbott ranch pulled up beside the alley in which they were playing and hiding out. There had been seven of them, and only one had escaped the loops that the Abbott crew expertly tossed around their necks. Licker shook his head from side to side. He had not had time to get over the shock of being captured and thrown into a ring with a mass of other dogs when that big, black dog had attacked him and...*killed him.* Licker looked over at the man driving the truck...the man who had picked him up and held him after that same big, black dog had licked him back to life. He looked over to the pretty woman whose hand was trying to catch the wind outside the truck window...the woman who had fed him those delicious and juicy brown things. He wished he had two more of those now. He slipped onto the woman's lap and lifted his nose to the wind. It felt good to feel the breeze blowing against his face.

"I think he likes you," Tyler spoke softly.

Amanda held Licker up so that he could enjoy more of the breeze blowing into his face. She laughed out loud when his little tongue tried to lap and capture the wind. "He's a sweetie, for sure. I should have brought Buster along for the ride."

"Buster?"

Amanda looked over at her future husband and grinned. "He's the main man in my life these days."

"Oh..." Tyler paused. "I...see..."

Amanda threw back her head and laughed again. "Don't go getting all jealous on me, Tyler Foster. Buster is my...puppy. I brought him with me. He's back at the café."

"Oh...well, yeah...you should have brought him along. What kind of dog is he?"

"He's a pittie-mix, my favorite kind," Amanda said. "Someone threw him out of a moving car. He's lucky to have survived, but he did, and...I adopted him. I knew his chances for adoption would be slim-to-none, I mean...being the breed he is and all."

"Well, whatever you do, *don't* bring him anywhere near the Abbott ranch." Tyler's face tensed at the thought of what Buster's short life would be like if he were unlucky enough to end up as one of the Abbott's bait or fighter dogs. "Little John especially likes that breed."

Amanda was quiet for a few moments. "How did you ever get involved with all of this, Tyler? I mean, you live in

Brooksville, right? How did you end up working for Little John Abbott?"

"You met my parents, didn't you?" Tyler asked.

Amanda smiled broadly. "I did, yes…and fell instantly in love with them. You can tell they are huge animal lovers."

Tyler nodded. "Well, my father has a lot of connections with animal enforcement agencies, as well as most of the rescue organizations throughout the southeast. This bust is part of a larger one that has been in the works for over a year now. Little John's ring is only one of several that the agencies are working together to bring down. Dad is good friends with one of the investigators I'm supposed to meet tonight…Tim Breydan. Tim and my Dad go way back, but I've never met him face-to-face. He works mostly out of Atlanta, Georgia. Anyway, Mr. Breydan told Dad about the Abbott ranch and how they wanted to send in someone to infiltrate the group…someone to feed them information about upcoming fights, the condition of the dogs, you know…"

"And you volunteered to do that, huh?" Amanda's eyebrows rose in surprise.

Tyler looked over at her and appreciated her simplistic beauty. There was nothing made-up or pretentious about Amanda Turner…from her flawless skin, to her long, thick blond hair, to her upturned nose and infectious grin…yes, he definitely appreciated her outward shell, but he was also beginning to appreciate the gentle genuineness of her soul. "I did volunteer, yes. My parents were against it at first, but…I can't explain it…something just led me to believe that I needed to be that inside person."

"So…how is it…working at the ranch, I mean?"

Tyler shook his head. He didn't want to remember some of the things he had witnessed, but he owed it to all the dogs who had not survived, to tell their story. "It's horrible, Amanda…it's horrible. The dogs they bring in every week are either strays, pets that are stolen from someone's yard, gotten from the free classified ads…you get the picture.

They're caged or put into the ring when they first arrive. That gives the crew a chance to separate the potential fighters from the bait dogs. Those that survive the first few days are taken to the next phase for training, where they are all bound with heavy…and I mean, heavy…chains around their necks. The chains are ten feet long and there's only about one or two feet separating the dogs from each other. Some of them get food and water…some don't. The ones that don't get anything try to survive by attacking the ones that are given food and water. Trouble is, they aren't close enough to actually get at each other…just close enough to make them mean…and hungrier. It's not just older dogs that are trained, either…there are pups as young as three months old being chained to these posts."

Tears were falling down Amanda's cheeks. "Puppies…"

"The thing is…" Tyler continued, "Late at night…when I go alone to check on these dogs...I can go right up to them, even the fighting dogs, and the first thing they do is wag their tails and lick my hand. They want nothing but to give and receive a little love and kindness, and I'm their only link to that emotion. It takes everything in me not to release them all into the wild and high-tail it out of there."

"Then why don't you?" Amanda gulped back a tear. She stroked Licker and kissed the top of his head, thankful that Tyler had saved him from what surely would not have been a peaceful ending, if the Abbott crew had realized he had not died after all.

Tyler shook his head. "I talked to my Dad about that very thing. I wanted to suggest it to the investigators that I'm meeting tonight, but…Dad said they are so close to this coming to an end. He begged me not to do anything like that…told me to remember that those we do save will have a place to come to when it's all over."

"Your Dad plans on taking them all in, doesn't he?"

"Maybe not *all* of them; this is going to be a multi-state sting," Tyler smiled. "But, yes…he will be taking in all the ones we rescue from the Abbott ring." Tyler pointed to a rest area up ahead. "We're here."

Amanda wiped her tears away and smiled at Licker. "I want to be a part of this, Tyler. I want to help you stop these people."

Tyler shook his head. "It's not safe...it could get dangerous and not end well...I don't think you should get in the middle of..."

"Let me clarify myself, Tyler Foster. I *will* be a part of this...I have to be...it's why I'm here..."

Tyler saw the Foster Farm van parked beneath a huge, shady oak tree and pulled up beside it. "We'll talk more about this later," Tyler promised. "Hey...look who's with Dad!"

Amanda waved back at Tyler's parents, who stood outside the van. A stunning, shiny-black, broad-shouldered pit sat between the couple and stared straight ahead. Amanda felt a slight tremble in her lap when Licker spotted the huge pit. "That's...*no*...it can't be...is that...Spartacus?"

Tyler was grinning from ear to ear. "Yes, indeed...it is. Will you just look at him! He doesn't look like the same dog I dropped off here just a few days ago, does he?"

Spartacus recognized Tyler immediately and rose to meet him when Tyler opened his truck door and jumped down. Tyler bent down and allowed Spartacus to sniff his hand. "Hey there, fella? Remember me?"

Spartacus lifted his huge head and stared directly into the eyes of the man who had helped him escape from the brutal life he had endured for two years. *"I could never forget you, Tyler...never."* He licked Tyler's hand and allowed Tyler to embrace him. It seemed like the embrace would never end. *"Okay, okay, need a little breathing room here..."*

Tyler released Spartacus and jumped up to hug his mother and father. "Man, it's good to see you two again. I can't get over how much he's healed since...what...two...three days? What kind of miracle meds did you give him?"

Jean hugged her son against her, reluctant to release him. "Sorry...wish we could take credit for it, but we can't really explain it. All we did was to continue the sugar paste for the open wounds. The old scars will always be there, but the latest ones have healed almost completely."

B.B. Foster waited for his turn for a private hug with his son. "Doc got him started on some antibiotics and inflammatory meds, but other than that, well…the healing process went well beyond anything we could do for him. B.B. lifted his eyes toward the heavens and grinned. "If you know what I mean…"

Spartacus moved slowly toward Amanda, who had stood at a distance, holding Licker in her arms. *"Calm down, little fella, I'm not going to eat you. You're coming to a safe place. I wish I could stay and show you around, but you'll be safe with these people. They're going to make sure you end up in a good home."*

Licker barked happily and squirmed in Amanda's arms. She was reluctant to release him with Spartacus so near, but one look into the soulful eyes of the huge, black pit told her that her fear was unwarranted. She knew, without a doubt, that Licker would be safe. She bent down and allowed Licker to run toward the pit.

Licker continued to bark and jump excitedly as he circled the larger dog. He nipped playfully at Spartacus' heels and ears.

"Amanda! I thought that was you!" Jean Foster rushed excitedly to where Amanda stood beside the passenger door of her son's truck. "It's so good to see you again!"

"It's good to see you again, too, Mrs. Foster…" Amanda grinned as she was engulfed in a warm hug from her future mother-in-law, and blushed at this private thought.

"B.B., look who's with our son…you remember Amanda Turner, don't you?"

B.B. grinned and walked over to his wife and Amanda. He looked back at Tyler and raised his eyebrows in query.

Tyler shrugged with feigned aloofness.

B.B. embraced Amanda and said, "Well, now…this *is* a pleasant surprise…it's really good to see you again, young lady."

"It's wonderful to see you again, too, Mr. Foster," Amanda accepted a bear hug from the gentle giant. "You're probably both wondering why I happen to be here…with…your son…"

"The thought had crossed my mind," B.B. grinned when he saw Tyler rubbing the back of neck and looking uncomfortable. "But…that's not important right now. I just have to assume that you are helping Tyler with what's going on in Thomasville…is that it?"

"Yes…" Amanda said.

"No!" Tyler chimed in.

Jean and B.B. looked at each other and smiled in silent acknowledgement.

"Well, now that we have that question cleared up…" B.B. cleared his throat. "Let's take a look at this little fella." He bent down and clicked his tongue at the small terrier, who was bouncing from one human to another, accepting strokes and hugs.

"You can change it if you like, but I named him Licker," Amanda offered. She smiled broadly when Licker bypassed B.B. and jumped immediately into Jean Foster's arms.

Everyone's attention was focused on the latest rescue, so they did not notice when Spartacus moved slowly toward the open door of Tyler's truck and jumped into the front seat.

"Interesting name," Jean laughed, as she snuggled against the pup's neck. She looked at Tyler and her expression turned serious. "Your Dad told me…about…what happened with this little fella."

Tyler grabbed the back of his neck with both hands. "If I told anyone else about what I saw, they would probably lock me up for observation, but…the three of you…all seem to take it in stride…like it happens every day. I'm still in shock…still trying to sort out…"

B.B. touched his son's shoulder and said, "Some things are beyond our explanation, son. Some things are just meant to be…believed."

"Amen to that!" Amanda chirped in. "Who are we to

question God's will…?"

Jean looked back and forth between Amanda and her son. She smiled a mother's smile and cocked her head sideways to catch her husband's eye. "Yes, indeed…who are we to question God's will?" She smiled again.

B.B. Foster shook his head and whispered into his son's ear. "You don't stand a chance, my boy…"

Spartacus sat inside the truck and watched while the happy scene unfolded before him. He was glad that Licker would have a happy-tails ending. He wasn't so sure about his own, but he knew what he had to do. He had to return to the Abbott ranch; he had to fight one last fight…

CHAPTER 19

Little John Interrogates

The lunch crowd had thinned, and Bertie poured herself a cup of coffee and sat down on a corner stool beside Amos Brown.

Amos had never seen the naughty angel so quiet…for so long. She had not spoken a single word in more than five minutes. "Seems like you may be worried 'bout something, Miss Bertie."

Bertie didn't hear him; she really was wrapped up in her own thoughts. She sipped at the rich, black coffee and closed her eyes in silent prayer. She had been having concerning thoughts about Amanda for several hours now, ever since the young woman had left with Tyler Foster to drop off the rescued pup.

"Miss Bertie?" Amos cleared his throat and placed his huge, black hand across her shoulders. "Is you okay, Miss Bertie? You looks like someone just walked across your grave…"

"What…" Bertie turned to look at the old man sitting next to her. Amos was almost a permanent fixture at the café and she sometimes forgot that he wasn't one of *them.* She shook the cobwebs from her thoughts and punched him against the shoulder. "Don't you worry none about me, Amos Brown. Anyone dares walk across *my* grave, I'll just give them a good punch!" She punched him again for good measure.

Amos grinned, showing the three remaining upper teeth in his mouth. He rubbed his shoulder and said, "Yes, ma'am, I bet you would." He smiled again before continuing, "It's just that I ain't use to seeing you so quiet and all. I figured if there was something you needed to talk about, then, I'd be mighty glad to listen to your troubles."

Bertie watched him for a moment and thought about what a genuinely good person Amos Brown was, just as his father and brother had been before him. He came from good stock. "Don't you know by now, Amos, that angels don't have any troubles?"

Amos looked confused. "Is that right, Miss Bertie? You mean, none…none at all?"

"Well," Bertie laughed. "None of our own, I should say. We worry about all of the living souls here on earth…worry about *their* troubles and how we can best help them, but, no…once you die and go to Heaven, you truly never have *anything* to worry about ever again."

"That's a pretty wonderful thought," Amos sighed. "I have to say…I look forward to that day."

"Why, Amos!" Bertie punched him again. "What kind of troubles do you have? Just lay them on me and we'll take care of every one of them before you leave here today."

Amos grinned and rubbed his shoulder. "You punch pretty good for a little thing, Miss Bertie."

"I've had years of practice," Bertie laughed. "So…what worries you, my friend?"

Amos picked up his coffee cup and took a long sip before he answered. It did not escape him that Bertie had managed to turn the topic of conversation back on him. "Well…Miss Bertie…the older I get…and the closer I get to meeting my Maker…I finds myself worrying that I may not be good enough to spend eternity with Him. I mean…all my life, I tried to help folks and to be a good friend and neighbor, but…well…I done some things in my past that I ain't too proud of…when I was younger…"

Bertie covered the old man's trembling hand with her own. "How old were you, Amos, when you accepted Christ?"

"How old?" Amos scratched his head. "Well, Andrew and me…we were brought up by God-fearin' parents, but you probably already knows that. I mean, we went to church every Sunday and we was both baptized when we was about seven or eight, but…well, that didn't mean much to us at the time. I left home when I was seventeen…didn't contact anyone in my family for almost ten years. I think the young folks today would call it rebellion." He looked over at Bertie and shook his head. "I did a lot of things in those ten years that I'm not proud of, and I ain't going to tell you what those things were, but…well, I finally came back home when Mama was dying. I'm so glad I got to see her before she passed. She whispered something to me the night she died."

Bertie already knew what his mother had whispered to him that night, but she wanted to hear Amos say it. "What did she say, Amos?"

A single tear rolled down his cheek and he wiped it away with the back of his weathered hand. He looked over at Bertie and shook his head. "She told me that she loved me, and that God loved me, no matter what I had done those past ten years…and, she told me that He was waiting for me to let Him in again."

"Is that right?" Bertie smiled.

"Yes, ma'am…Mama died in her sleep that night. Two weeks later I walked into her church and turned my life over to God…again. I know He forgave me, but, it was harder for me to forgive myself. I guess I still have a little doubt as to whether or not I'm really good enough to spend eternity in His presence."

Max had been listening to their conversation and came out

to stand behind the counter.

Amos looked up at him and nodded. "I'm guessing you heard that conversation, Mr. Max?"

Max nodded. "I heard, Amos." He reached across the counter and took Amos' hands into his own.

Amos shivered at the immediate warming sensation that coursed through his hands, up his arms, and across his chest. He inhaled sharply until the warming sensation turned into a tingling, peaceful vibration that soared through his entire body.

"Trust me, Amos...you have absolutely nothing to worry about. Your mama was right. God loves you no matter what you did yesterday, what you did today, or what you may do tomorrow. He loves you, unconditionally, and wants you to feel that love every day of your life. You must learn to turn all your worries and fears over to Him, and not to keep them buried inside your soul."

Amos closed his eyes. "But all those things I did...all those people I used...all the pain and worry I caused my mama and papa, and Andrew..."

"All of that is truly forgiven, Amos..." Max released his grip.

Amos sighed again and opened his eyes. His spirit felt lighter and more secure. He nodded and smiled. "It really is, isn't it...thank you, Jesus!"

Ross Taylor's spirit was definitely not as light and secure as Amos Brown's. His bruised and battered body still lay crumbled in a corner of the darkened cabin. His lungs burned with every shattered breath he attempted to take. He didn't know what time it was, what day it was, or how long they had been in the cabin. "Tim..." he croaked. "Tim...?"

A chair pushed backward from across the room.

Tim lifted his own head when a cigarette lighter flickered on and illuminated the face of the massive man that stood before them. He immediately recognized Little John Abbott.

He tried to swallow but couldn't produce enough spit to do so. Instead, he coughed loudly and croaked, "Are you okay, Ross?"

Little John lit a blunt and inhaled deeply. He walked a couple of feet forward and lit the kerosene lantern that hung on a huge nail on one of the room's exposed beams. "You're both awake...that's good. What do you say we have ourselves a little talk?"

The sudden light hurt their eyes and both Tim and Ross squeezed their eyes tightly shut to block it out. Tim was the first to ease open his good eye. He didn't want Little John to know that he knew who he was. "Who are you?" he choked out the question. "Why are we here?"

Little John took another long drag on the blunt before walking over to where Tim lay on his side. He removed a short machete from a side holster and squatted down. "Oh, I think you already know who I am..."

Ross opened his eyes, saw the machete, and managed to scream out. "Don't you hurt him!"

Little John shot a cold, irritated look in Ross' direction. He looked down at the man called Tim and expected to see fear etched upon his face; that did not happen. Little John was impressed with the calm expression the man before him maintained. The man did not even flinch when Little John whipped the machete around and expertly cut the ropes that bound his hands to his ankles. "Sit up..." Little John walked back across the room and dragged the chair over to where Tim was trying to get the circulation to return to his hands and feet.

His hands and feet were still tied, but the rope no longer connected them, so Tim was able to sit up and roll his shoulders and neck. He stretched his legs out before him and was relieved to see them both still attached to his body. It had been several hours since he had been able to see or feel them, so he hadn't been sure. He looked Little John squarely in the eye and said, "There's been some mistake...I don't know who you think we are, but..."

Little John took a long toke off the blunt and continued to stare into Tim's good eye. "Doesn't really matter who you are, does it? You were trespassing on my property. Folks around here don't take kindly to that. As you can see…we take the law into our own hands when that happens. I heard him call you Tim…got a last name?"

Tim did not hesitate in his reply. "Smith…Tim and Ross Smith. We're cousins…we heard there was going to be a good dog fight and we just wanted to get an up-close, personal look at the dogs before we placed our bets. That's all…I'm sorry we trespassed…"

Ross lifted his head and added, "Just let us go…we're really sorry…we didn't mean any harm…"

Little John looked at the man called Ross, who still lay on his side. "Smith, huh? Cousins, you say?"

Tim nodded. "Yeah…second cousins, actually…" He never expected the kick to his face, so it caught him completely off guard.

Little John walked over to Ross, bent down, and cut the rope that connected his hands and feet. "You two may as well make yourself as comfortable as possible…for whatever time you have left, because, you see…I don't believe anything you just said. One thing I can't stand is a liar and a cheater. You two are both those things. You'll see soon enough how we deal with liars and cheaters in this county. In the meantime, you can try to get those ropes off if you want, but it won't do you any good…the door is bolted from the outside, no windows, and no way off this property. There are two bottles of water beside the door. I suggest you make it last. I'll be back later…while I'm gone, maybe the two of you can come up with a better story, or, maybe…I don't know…even the *truth*?"

Tim had managed to upright himself again. "You can't just leave us here…" he started.

Little John spun around and kicked him hard against the head again.

Ross could have sworn he heard Tim's teeth rattle. "Leave

him alone, you son-of-a-bitch!"

Little John looked over at Ross and spat. "You don't know anything about my mother, so I suggest you be very careful about what you say next..." He turned to leave. "I'll leave the light on for you, but be careful...one stray flame could burn this room up in a matter of minutes..."

Tim and Ross listened to the door being bolted and locked from the outside. They heard a truck, with a loud muffler, start up and drive away slowly. The stench of burned flesh and fur had rushed in when Little John opened the door, and Ross leaned over, gagged, and retched the almost-empty contents of his stomach onto the wood floor beside him.

Ross watched while Tim had managed to crawl closer to him. Now that there was light from the lantern, he saw how badly his friend had been beaten. Blood trickled from his nose and mouth, and sure enough, when Tim opened his mouth, Ross noticed at least two teeth missing. "You look like shit, buddy," he tried to smile.

Tim wasn't smiling. He just nodded when he managed to collapse beside Ross. "I think we may be in trouble, Ross..."

"Yeah..." Ross groaned when he tried to take a deep breath with his bruised lungs. "I don't think he believes that we're cousins..."

CHAPTER 20

The Truth About Sam

Spartacus sat stoically on the front seat between Tyler and Amanda. He stared straight ahead and thought about what he had to do next. *"I wish there was some other way..."* he thought. *"I sure don't want to go back to the ranch, but...Sam said that's the way it has to be."*

Amanda draped her left arm around the pit's broad shoulders. She kissed the top of his head when he turned to look at her. "Why do you think he jumped into your truck, Tyler? I mean, he was stubborn when your Dad tried to coax him out...I was afraid Spartacus might bite him."

Tyler's mind had been churning since early that morning when he witnessed the resurrection of Licker. He kept thinking about what Amanda had said about Sam being *special*, but she had never gotten around to elaborating on that statement. He couldn't shake the feeling that, somehow, Sam and Spartacus were connected by fate or destiny. He glanced down at Spartacus, who seemed to be listening intently to their conversation.

"Go ahead...tell her, Tyler...tell her that I would never, ever bite

anyone…that would be so wrong of me. Tell her…" Spartacus' look was imploring.

Tyler blinked hard and shook his head. Spartacus appeared to be using his soulful eyes to tell him something…something important. "I don't know why he insisted on coming back with us, Amanda, but I'd be willing to bet our family farm that this dog would never bite anyone. If he was ever going to do that, trust me, he would have done it to those assholes who work at the Abbott ranch…excuse the language, but it's hard to think of them as anything other than that."

Amanda smiled. "I've heard worse…so, will you be taking him back to the ranch with you?"

Tyler nodded. "Yeah…I think that's probably his plan. I want to drop you off at the café first and maybe talk to Max about some things."

"But I wanted to go with you to meet those investigators tonight…" Amanda almost pouted, but caught herself in the nick of time. The last thing she wanted was for Tyler to think of her as a clingy, pouty female.

"No…I don't think that's a good idea, Amanda. Let me meet them first and hear what the plan is. There's a big fight scheduled for next Friday night, and I still don't know when the bust is going to take place. I was hoping it would be before that fight…especially now…" He glanced down again at Spartacus. "If he goes back with me, I know Little John will use him in that fight, even if he doesn't expect him to win…it would be just like Little John to want to get even with Spartacus for costing him so much money during his last fight. Trust me…nothing would make Little John happier than to see Spartacus suffer a fatal loss."

"What other dog do you think he will place in that fight?" Amanda asked, but she was pretty sure she already knew the answer to her question. "Never mind…he's going to fight Sam, isn't he?"

"I'm pretty sure he will, yeah…" Tyler sighed. "He's already purchased the dog that beat Spartacus in the last fight; his name is Czar and he really is one helluva fighter. At first I thought Little John would pit Spartacus against Czar…just to see Spartacus torn to bits. There's not another dog in this area that could beat Czar, but after seeing what Sam did this morning, well…I'm having second thoughts on that score. It's against the rules for owners to pit their own dogs against each other, though…redneck rules…so Sam, Spartacus, and Czar will probably all face champions from other counties or states."

Amanda knew that Tyler was providing an opening for her; he had been patiently waiting to hear her explanation as to why Sam was *special*, and he deserved one. She wasn't sure how mentally capable she would be if she had witnessed what he had, and not knowing what she knew. She took a deep breath and prepared for whatever might happen next. "There's a small rest area up ahead, Tyler. Why don't you pull in and we'll let Spartacus stretch his legs; and, besides…I don't think you should be driving when I tell you about Sam…"

"Well…this should be interesting…" Spartacus almost smiled.

Two minutes later, Tyler turned into a small, shaded rest area. There were no other cars in the parking lot, so they had the area all to themselves.

Amanda opened the passenger door and hopped down. "Come on, Spartacus…time for a break."

Spartacus looked over at Tyler.

"Go ahead, fella…I'm right behind you," Tyler rubbed the back of the dog's neck and opened the driver's door.

Spartacus exited on Tyler's side. *"No offense, pretty lady, but I think I'll stick close to Tyler while you tell him your story…after I go pee, that is…"* He trotted over to the first bush he saw and paid his respects. He walked and sniffed around for a couple of minutes, and finally spread out beneath a wooden picnic table.

"I think that's our cue," Tyler grinned. "After you…" he motioned Amanda ahead of him.

Amanda locked her hands behind her neck and turned side-to-side a few times. "It feels good to get the kinks out." She sat on top of the wooden table and patted the empty space to her right. "Take a load off, Tyler...you're going to want to be seated when I tell you about Sam."

Tyler sat beside her, but left a good foot of distance between them. "After what I saw Sam do this morning, I'm not sure if what you have to say can surprise me any more than that did."

Amanda nodded. "You said that Sam snapped Licker's neck, right?"

"Yeah...he did...no doubt about that...everyone there heard it."

"Well..." Amanda began. "What if I told you that...maybe...that didn't really happen...that...what you *think* you saw wasn't actually the real thing."

"No offense, Amanda, but you're not making any sense. I thought you had something insightful to tell me about Sam."

"I do," Amanda nodded. "And what you *think* you saw is all part of it; it's what Sam *wanted* you to think. Actually, it's possible that Licker wasn't really dead at all..."

"I heard his neck *SNAP*!" Tyler insisted. "You're trying to make me think I imagined all of what I saw, is that it?"

Amanda touched his shoulder and felt a tingling sensation travel from the tips of her fingers, down her arm, and into the pit of her belly. "No, Tyler...you didn't imagine it. Let me just spit it out, okay? Let me just say what I need to say, and then...we can discuss it a little more."

"Oh, this is getting good," Spartacus grinned and closed his eyes.

"I'm listening..." Tyler encouraged her to go on.

Amanda turned sideways and propped her right knee on the table top. She looked Tyler squarely in the eye and did not hesitate. "Sam is my dog. My father got him for me when I was seven years old, shortly after my mother was killed in a car accident..."

Tyler shook his head. "No, no...wait a minute, how old

are you?"

Amanda never took her eyes from his. "I am twenty-three…"

Tyler rubbed his face and squeezed his mouth between his palm. He did the mental math and said, "That would mean that Sam would have to be…"

Amanda raised her brows and puckered her mouth. She nodded and said, "Yep…sixteen…yep."

"But…he…" Tyler stopped to refocus. "That dog cannot be more than five years old, Amanda; I would have guessed closer to two or three…"

Amanda wrinkled her nose. "Yeah…he looks pretty good for his age, huh? Except that…well, he's not really sixteen either." She inhaled a deep breath and released it slowly before she continued. "Tyler…and, please promise you won't freak out on me when I tell you this…but, Sam died when I was seventeen years old. My Dad and I were with him when he took his last breath; we had him cremated and buried his ashes in our back yard, in my Mom's favorite flower bed." When Tyler didn't respond, she pushed on. "I never saw my Sam again until two days ago…on Monday…when I arrived at the café…"

"I told you this was going to be good!" Spartacus opened his eyes and crawled from beneath the table. He thought the look on Tyler's face was priceless. *"Heh, heh…I wish Sam could've been here for this!"*

"Tyler?" Amanda lowered her head so that she could see his face better.

Tyler lifted his head and stared at her. "Do…you…honestly…expect…me…to…believe…that? Do you have any idea how *crazy* that sounds?"

Amanda nodded in agreement. It would be easier, not to mention more believable, if she could tell him the truth about the angels at the Heavenly Grille Café, but she knew that she could never reveal that particular fact; Max was the only one who could make that decision. She knew how risky it could be if too many people learned the truth about her angels.

"Yeah…yeah, I do, actually…"

Tyler was shaking his head. "No, you're mistaken, that's all. He's a black pit-mix…do you know how common that breed is? How many of them are roaming the world as we speak? No…he just *looks* like your long, dead pet, Amanda."

Amanda waited for him to collect his thoughts and said, "Actually, Sam has more black lab in him that he does pit…I'm not entirely sure if he has any pit in him at all, but, I can see where you would think that, Tyler, but then…you would still have to explain to yourself how Sam resurrected Licker this morning. You said you saw it with your own eyes."

"I did…" Tyler mumbled.

"Well…all I'm saying is that there is no doubt in *MY* mind that Sam is my dog. I believe he is an *angel* dog who has come back to help out with what's coming down at the Abbott ranch. Maybe Sam did not really kill that pup this morning, Tyler; maybe it's just what he wanted you and everyone else to believe. It was important that those other men thought the dog was dead; otherwise, they may have thrown him into that burning pit you talk about, or worse, tortured him even more until he really did die. I can't say with one hundred percent certainty…yet…whether that's exactly what happened or not, but I do believe that Sam sort of *suspended* things for a bit and when the timing was right, he woke Licker back up…or…maybe he really did snap the little booger's neck and licked him back to life." She shrugged and offered a weak grin.

Spartacus came out from beneath the table, stood up, and stretched his hind legs, one at a time. He took one look at Tyler's open-mouth expression and thought, *"Oh, Sam…you would've loved this!"* He finished his stretches and reached out to nudge Tyler's boot. *"Okay, you two, it's getting late, and I'd really like to get something to eat before going back to that place…what do you say, can we go now, can we…"*

Tyler stared at Amanda, opened his mouth as if to respond, closed it, and shook his head. "I need some time to think about what you've said, Amanda; and, I need to get you back to the café." He looked at his watch. "We can get something to eat before Spartacus and I head back to the ranch. As much as I hate to do it, I'm going to have to get him settled and let Abbott know that I found him…before I head into town to meet the inspectors." He shook his head. "You do know how crazy your explanation sounds, right?"

Amanda shrugged her shoulders again. "If it's any consolation, crazy doesn't run in my family, so…our kids should turn out okay!"

Clint wiped his feet and knocked on the massive oak door of the Abbott home. He spat a wad of tobacco juice into the flower bed just as the door swung open.

Little John looked down at the brown liquid mess for a long moment before looking back into his foreman's wary eyes. "Pick it up…"

Clint wiped away a drop of juice from the corner of his mouth. "What…"

Little John continued to stare at him. There was no doubt to the intentions behind the stare. "I said…pick it up…"

Clint pushed some mulch around the spat juice, bent down, and wadded it up into his ungloved hands. He knew how stupid he must look just standing there, and he resented Little John Abbott for making him feel that way. Big John never would have treated him like this. "Sorry, Boss…"

Little John did not invite him inside his home, nor did he offer up a trash can in which to dispose of the nastiness that Clint held in his left hand. "Did you go through the car like I said?"

Clint nodded. "We just finished. It's a rental car, but there's nothing inside it, except the rental contract in the glove compartment. Those guys didn't bring any identification with them."

"A rental contract?" Little John asked. "Did you think to look at it to see what names might be on it?"

Resentment was a mild feeling to describe what Clint really felt toward Little John Abbott. Did the man really think he was stupid, or did he just get a kick out of treating people that way? Maybe twenty years was long enough on this job…maybe it was time for Clint to move on to bigger and better things. He bit his tongue to prevent anything that might be interpreted as a retort from erupting. "Tim Smith is the name on the rental contract."

"Is that right…" Little John mused. Could it be possible that the two men locked in the cabin had been telling him the truth earlier that day? "I checked on them earlier and had a little chat. They said they were cousins…that they were just trying to check out the merchandise before placing their bets for the upcoming fight."

Clint shifted his weight to the other foot and avoided the temptation to spit out another wad of juice. "You believe 'em?"

Little John didn't answer. He just looked over Clint's shoulder and said. "Just keep doing what needs to be done…for now. What do you have that Jones kid working on today?"

"He's supposed to be working with the new batch of bait dogs that came in last night, Boss. I've been tied up all morning taking care of those trespassers and their vehicle, so I haven't really had time to check up on him."

"I've got my own ideas about him. I want to see if he can be trusted, so when you see him, you tell him to drive that rental car back to town. Tell him I want him to find out where those two fellas are staying and to go through their room…find out who they really are. One of our dump trucks is parked at the Shell station…oil change supposed to be done on it tomorrow. Give him a spare key to the truck and tell him to drive it back here when he finds out what I want to know."

"You can't be serious…" Clint began, but stopped when he saw the deadly, steel glare from Little John Abbott. "Sorry, Boss…but…I thought that we've already agreed that the kid can't be trusted..."

"*WE* haven't agreed on anything...last time I checked, I was still in charge of this ranch. I've given you a direct order, Clint. I expect you'll carry it out...tell Jones to report directly to me when he gets back...no matter how late it is..." Little John slammed the door in his foreman's face.

Clint's bottom teeth bit hard against his upper lip. He waited until he heard Little John's receding footsteps; then, he turned to the right and spit an especially large dose of juice back into the prized flower bed, along with the wad he held in his left hand.

CHAPTER 21

-Heaven-
Martin Does Some Research

"The more and more I learn about this despicable sport, the more I worry about the heartless souls who find it so easy to carry it out..." Martin mumbled to himself. He was alone in his quiet work space. He placed his hands behind his back and began pacing back and forth, thinking about everything he had learned about the sadistic sport of illegal dogfighting. He had learned that most fights average one to two hours, and did not end until one of the dogs could not, or would not, continue the fight. He learned that the majority of the dogs used in these fights died from exhaustion, infection, blood loss, and/or shock. One of the dogs – named Boomer – had been in a fight where he spent the majority of the time on his back, while the champion fighter broke one of his front legs high up in the shoulder, as well as one of his back legs, at the knee joint. Boomer only had one leg that the champion dog had not broken, and it had been chewed and punctured beyond repair. If that had not been torture enough, the owners had allowed the fight

to continue until the champion dog had literally scalped Boomer by tearing a large chunk of skin alongside one of his ears. Boomer had been tossed from the ring, into a pit, and left to take his last breath alone, and in extreme pain. Like Boomer, some of the dogs used for fighting did not die right away; it often took some of them several hours, or even days, to die from their wounds. They all died thinking that this was how ALL mankind treated animals; most of them never knew the loving and kind touch from someone who truly cared about their welfare.

Martin waved his hand and the research vanished from the white screen before him. "I cannot bear to read any more of this today..."

"Excuse me, Mr. Martin, sir..." Andrew Brown cleared his throat. He thought that the angel looked extremely agitated and he felt uncomfortable now, having interrupted him. "I'm sorry to bother you...I can come back later..."

Martin spun around when he heard Andrew speak and quickly spotted the shepherd/lab-mix dog that sat obediently at his side. The dog looked directly into Martin's eyes, and Martin could have sworn that the dog smiled at him. He stared back at the dog for a few moments before he realized that this dog was the same dog he had been researching a short while ago. "Well...hello there, Boomer! It's so nice to finally get to meet you. I see you have found one of our caretakers..."

The dog's coat was magnificent and his eyes and teeth were healthy and bright. His legs were strong and he held his head high with confidence. "It's nice to meet you, too..." he transferred his thoughts directly to Martin. "I see you've read my story?"

Andrew stood quietly and watched while Martin interacted with the dog he had found waiting on his front porch just that morning. They appeared to be having an actual conversation. "Can you understand him, Mr. Martin?"

Martin walked over to Boomer and kneeled before him. He took the dog's head between his hands and lowered his head to Boomer's head. "I can, indeed, Andrew. It broke my heart to read about the way he lived...and the way he died...but, that is all in his past now. He's been here for a while now, but he did not want to leave the Rainbow Bridge. Since he's with you, I am assuming he found his way to you?"

Andrew grinned and nodded. "Yessir, I found him sitting on the porch this morning. I sat down beside him and he laid his big, 'ole head in my lap. He's a beauty, isn't he?"

"Yes, he is!" Martin shouted and raised his hands upward. "Praise, God…praise, God…" He stood up and placed a hand on Andrew's shoulder. "So, how are things going for you, Andrew?"

"Well, Mr. Martin…to tell you the truth…if I'd known Heaven was going to be like this, I would have wanted to leave my earthly body a long, long time ago. My Mama and Daddy have decided to move from their own mansion soon and to share mine. It's just so good seeing them both again. Daddy comes over every day to study God's word with me and to play with all the pups…last time I counted, there's 312 dogs and 97 cats on my grounds now…and they all want love and attention. Daddy was always a huge animal lover, so he suggested that we all stay in one place so we could take care of the animals. I just wanted to check in with you and make sure that was alright…I mean, I don't know all the rules and all…"

Martin laughed out loud. "Oh, my sweet boy…there are absolutely no rules in Heaven! No…there is nothing in writing that says anyone even has to live in a mansion; they can all live out in the open if they so choose…it is their choice. You and your parents are free to go and live anywhere you want, but we knew about your love for animals, so we thought you might want to be actively involved with those who never had a real home on earth."

Andrew nodded. "I guess I'm having a hard time not thinking about all this as a…job. I feel like I need to be contributing something for being allowed to spend eternity here."

Martin disregarded that idea with a forward flick of his wrist. "Nonsense…no, no, no. It's true, though, that everyone is very productive in Heaven, but that is of their own choosing. There are no jobs, no time clocks, no reports to fill out, nothing of the sort. Your…job…if you want to call it that is to simply continue your studies about your Maker and Heaven, so that you will be prepared to help all the souls who arrive during the Rapture and afterwards. It's going to be a very hectic and busy time up here when that happens, and everyone is going to have to pitch in and help. In the meantime…you should continue to care for and love these lost, abandoned, neglected, and abused animals. When they are ready to leave your sanctuary, they will choose their own heavenly fur-ever family with whom they will spend eternity."

Andrew nodded again. "That's pretty much what my Daddy said, too, but I just wanted to double-check with you. I am so thankful for everything that's been given to me here…I don't want anyone to think I take things for granted…know what I mean?"

"I do, yes...and nobody thinks that, Andrew. Your heart is pure…you were a good man on earth and you are an even better man in Heaven. Things are so perfect here, I can see where it might be easy for people to eventually take things for granted, but so far…no one has."

Boomer walked over and licked Martin's hand. "I sure don't take anything for granted. This place rocks!"

Martin smiled at the dog and said, "Well…yes…I guess it does, Boomer!" He looked back at Andrew. "Anything else on your mind, Andrew?"

Andrew grinned. "No sir, just wanted to check with you about sharing the mansion with my parents. Oh…did I tell you that I met the parents of my friend, Amanda? You probably already know that, though, huh?"

"No, I didn't know you had met Regina and Stephen…contrary to popular belief, I do not keep tabs on everyone!" Martin laughed out loud. "I have enough to do just keeping an eye on our own little naughty angel"

Andrew met Martin's laugh with one of his own. "You must be talking about Miss Bertie." He nodded his head again. "She's one in a million, alright."

"So, Andrew…where did you meet Amanda's parents?"

"At the community Bible study meeting last night. They said they thought they recognized me 'cause they had seen me and Amos on one of your screens here a couple of years ago. They wanted to thank me for being nice to their daughter."

"They are fine folks," Martin said.

Andrew cleared his throat. "Mr. Martin…they said that they get to see and talk to Amanda through her dreams?"

"Yes, that is true," Martin acknowledged.

"Well…I was wondering if all of us can do that…I mean…can we appear to those we left behind in their dreams?"

"You're hoping you could do the same to Amos, I'm guessing…right?"

Andrew sighed deeply. "Oh, I would give anything to see my brother again…twins share a very special bond, you know. I would just love for him to know that I ain't in any pain no more and that I love and miss him."

"I'm sure he knows that already, Andrew…but, the answer to your question is…yes; provided, of course, that the earthly being is a true believer. They must believe, beyond a shadow of a doubt, that Heaven is real. If they believe that, then, yes…if they want…and if their heavenly family wants to…then they are able to communicate via dreams. It cannot happen too frequently, however, and they cannot just pop in to say hello or have a good day. There must be an emotional need for the souls to appear to their loved ones in a dream. However, with that being said, you must always remember that the Bible teaches that spiritual guidance should be sought from God alone, through Jesus Christ and the Holy Spirit. He has provided everything we need for this life in his Word."

"Oh…okay, then," Andrew mumbled. He looked more confused than ever, but he didn't want to take up any more of Martin's time. "I know that Amos is okay, for now…so I probably won't be seeing him in no dream anytime soon. Okay…I'm gonna go now, Mr. Martin…I want to show Boomer around a little…or maybe let him show me around. I'm not really sure which one of us got here first."

"Time is irrelevant in Heaven, Andrew…so never fear that you are taking up too much of my time. I hope you and Boomer have a glorious day!"

Boomer barked happily and strutted off. He turned to look at Andrew, who was still standing beside Martin. "Hey, you…Andrew! You coming or not? We passed a cool spring that I want to go play in!"

Andrew's mouth dropped open and he stared, dumbfounded at Martin. "Did…did…you hear that, Mr. Martin? Did you hear? Boomer talked to me…I actually heard him…did you hear him? Of course, you heard him…oh, my goodness, this is wonderful…just wonderful…" He ran to catch up with the energetic pup. "I'll see you later, Mr. Martin!"

Martin watched the happy duo running off into the distance. He sighed and closed his eyes. "Silly, silly humans...where is it written that only angels can speak to the animals..."

"But as it is written: Eye has not seen, nor ear heard, nor have entered into the heart of man the things which God has prepared for those who love Him." 1 Corinthians 2:9 (NKJV)

CHAPTER 22

Tyler Meets the Inspectors

It was shortly after five o'clock when Tyler left the Heavenly Grille with Spartacus. He had shared a quick meal with Amanda, while Spartacus played in the back yard with Buster and Doug. He had managed to persuade Amanda that her presence might be more of a hindrance than a help if she went with him to his scheduled rendezvous with the inspectors; that had not been an easy feat because she was one stubborn female.

Tyler pulled into the entrance to the Abbott ranch at five-thirty and was glad to see that the foreman and crew were still out and about. His intention had been to throw on a quick change of clothes and stash Spartacus in one of the pens until he could discuss his "finding" with Little John or Clint Meacham.

Tyler parked his truck in front of the crew's bunk house. Spartacus jumped out just before the truck door closed shut. Tyler looked around nervously and tried to get him back inside the truck, but Spartacus obviously had different plans.

He announced his return to the Abbott farm by barking loudly and profusely.

Little John opened the front door to the main house and stepped outside. A partially-clothed woman stood behind him with her arms wrapped around his bare waist. Little John squinted his eyes, unable to believe what he was seeing. "Well…I'll be damned…"

"Come back inside, lover…" the woman cooed. "We still have some time left…"

Little John looked back at her with a cold and menacing glare.

The woman released her hold on him and backed away. "Fine…but you still gotta pay for the full two hours…" She retreated back inside the house.

Little John closed the door and began walking toward the bunk house.

Spartacus finally stopped his incessant barking when he saw Little John. *"I wonder if it's too late to change my mind."* He offered a soft whimper and moved to stand behind Tyler.

Little John walked toward them and Tyler exhaled deeply. He couldn't help but notice the granite six-pack that Little John sported; the man looked like he was sculpted from stone. He removed his Atlanta Braves cap and ran his fingers over his head. *"So much for hiding Spartacus away…"* he thought. He felt Spartacus trembling against his leg, and heard his slight whimpering. He took a deep breath and plunged into his concocted spiel. "I…uh…I just had a feeling that maybe I missed something in those woods back in Monticello, so I went back today for a final look. I…uh…found him in someone's fenced back yard. It looks like they nursed him back to health. Nobody was home, so…"

Little John was within two feet of them when he stopped and looked at the cowering dog. "It's him, alright… Spartacus…hard to believe that's the same animal that took off from here Friday night, though." He saw the dog trembling and grunted, "From the looks of him, he's still a loser, too...he's healed, but he sure doesn't look like he has any fight left in him." He walked around Tyler for a closer look at Spartacus. The scars were still there, but all the open wounds were completely healed. "Unbelievable..." he mused. He walked back to face Tyler and said, "Get him settled. He's probably useless as a fighter, but there are a couple of new champions from North and South Carolina that I might be able to pit him against. If I could pit him against Czar, I would, but now that I own Czar, that's not an option. I'll just make sure I don't bet on the wrong dog this time. If he manages to live through the fight, I want him used as bait for training the big black one you just brought in. I need to come up with a name for that one. I'm thinking of using him in the finale fight; he's an unknown, and people will probably place their bets on his opponent, but I have a feeling Big Black will surprise us all."

It took all the restraint Tyler could muster not to punch the smirk off Little John's chiseled face. "I'll get Spartacus settled in..."

One of the large dump trucks rolled into the drive-way just then. Little John nodded toward it and said. "Never mind...someone else can take care of that. Turn Spartacus over to one of them and then come inside. I have a job I want you to take care of tonight..."

"Tonight?" Tyler stumbled, thinking feverishly of an excuse to get out of whatever Little John had in mind. He *had* to meet the inspectors tonight. "But...I've already made plans..."

"Change them," Little John ordered. "You've got 15 minutes...I'll leave the front door unlocked for you."

Doug and Amanda remained in the back yard after Tyler had left to return to Thomasville. It was almost six o'clock and Amanda grew more restless with every minute that ticked by.

"I don't see why I couldn't go with Tyler to meet those

inspectors tonight. I mean...what harm would that do? He just doesn't realize how much help I could be to him; he doesn't need to be in this by himself. From everything I've learned about that monster that he works for, it's not safe for him to be on that ranch."

Buster enjoyed the last few sun rays of the day and spent his time profitably, by chasing a lone butterfly. *"Oh, boy, I almost had him that time, but...geez...what do I do with him if I actually catch him?"* Buster stopped chasing the butterfly and shook his head. The butterfly had landed on a large rock, and Buster crawled on his belly to get a closer look. He finally nudged the butterfly with his wet nose. *"Naw...you need to fly away, little friend...I don't want to hurt you by playing too rough. Shoo...go on now...fly away..."* He watched the butterfly lift up from the rock and fly off into the wood line. Buster sighed, turned, and walked toward his beautiful owner.

Doug was sympathetic, but firm. "He has your best interest at heart, Amanda. It's important for him to know that you are safe. Quite frankly...I have to agree with him on this. Even though you're a cop and trained to handle yourself...well, I don't think it's safe for you to get too involved with busting up that dog-fighting ring. Besides...you might even be a dangerous distraction for Tyler."

The look on Amanda's face grew indignant. "Really, Doug? My parents came to me in a dream, remember? They pretty much gave me the green light to come here and get involved with this *adventure*!"

Doug scratched his head and tried to suppress a grin. "That is true, yes. I think they felt it was important that you be here for all of this, but...maybe...your involvement was meant to be more of a *supportive* role for Tyler..."

"Whoa! Stop right there, big fella!" Amanda stood up and placed her hands on her hips. "Do you honestly think they intended for me to stay on the sidelines and play the helpless female by offering *encouragement* for whatever Tyler has gotten himself mixed up in? Really! Me…the helpless female?"

Doug laughed out loud. "Okay, okay! I admit it…that's not a natural role for you, but, I don't think you fully realize how barbaric Little John Abbott and his crew are."

"Hellooooo…I am a cop!" Amanda's stance was indignant.

"But…let's face it, Amanda…you're still a rookie. There's a television series on now about rookie cops…it's really good in case you haven't seen it yet…and, there are all types of very bad people out there, most of whom you haven't yet had to handle…Little John Abbott is a tyrannical mad man. Did you know that forty-eight percent of all Americans between the ages of 15 to 54 experience a psychological disorder during their life time? Trust me on this…Abbott is high on that list. These kinds of people project themselves into believing they are king of the mountain, they have serious control issues, and a total lack of respect for other human beings. People like Abbott have become more willing to kill because of desensitization, conditioning, and denial. No…I have to agree with Tyler on this one. I think you should take a step back and monitor things from the café, rather than being front and center with Tyler."

A sharp reply slithered to the tip of her tongue, but Amanda managed to keep it to herself; instead, she pursed her lips together, nodded, picked up Buster, and marched up the stairs to her room.

Doug watched her climb the stairs and rubbed the bridge of his nose. He waited until Amanda slammed her door shut and assumed she was in for the night. "Well…I can see how well that went over…"

Little John had ordered Tyler to follow him to the cabin by the burning pit. Tyler kept looking at his watch. It was almost six-thirty. If he hurried, he might still be able to make his meeting with the inspectors, and still take care of Little

John's *errand.*

Little John met Tyler outside the cabin and handed him the key to the cabin's padlock. "Go ahead. Open it."

Tyler preferred not to have Little John at his back, but he took the offered key and turned it in the padlock. Dusk was approaching and shadows lined the porch to the small cabin. Tyler opened the door and took a few minutes to adjust his eyesight to the darkness within the cabin.

The door slammed closed behind him and he glanced back at Little John, whose huge silhouette blocked the cabin's door. He was fairly certain that Abbott did not know why Tyler was really working for him, but, that didn't do anything to curb the sinking feeling that Abbott had brought him here to confront and, possibly, kill him. "Why did you bring me here, Boss?" Something didn't feel right, and Tyler felt a layer of sweat beading up across his back and under his arms.

Little John didn't say anything for a long minute. He was about to test Tyler to see if he could be trusted; he still had serious doubts about the young man, but he needed to know for sure whether or not the doubts were warranted. He took out a match and lit the kerosene lantern he had left hanging on a nail. "Over there…on the floor…"

Tyler turned to look in the direction Abbott had indicated. It took a few moments before he was able to make out the two dark lumps that appeared to be sitting on the floor, and leaning against the back wall. Tyler moved forward for a closer inspection. It only took a few seconds to determine that the two lumps were human beings. He only hoped they were *living* human beings, but the closer he got to them, the less hope he had for that being true. He was within a foot of them when he squatted down to look at their battered faces. An eyelid opened on one of the forms and startled Tyler so much that he fell backwards. He jumped up immediately and walked backwards toward Little John. "Who are they?" he asked, never taking his eyes off the two men huddled together on the floor. "Why are they here? What have you done to them?"

Little John had watched closely to see if any recognition registered between Tyler and the two men. He saw nothing to indicate that these three men knew one another. "They're trespassers…said they were on the property to get a closer look at the dogs…to give them an advantage when they placed their bets…" Little John walked forward and kicked Ross in his already-bruised ribs. He smiled when Ross groaned and inhaled sharply. "What do you think we should do with these *trespassers*, Tyler?"

Tim managed to keep his face expressionless, but his entire body tensed when he heard Tyler's name mentioned. It only took him a few seconds to see the resemblance between Tyler and B.B. Foster. He was thankful that he and Ross had never met Tyler in person; otherwise, he knew, without a doubt, that Little John Abbott would have been able to sense a connection between them. He shifted his position to keep Ross from tumbling over on his side. "We said we were sorry about trespassing on your land…please, mister…you need to let us go…my cousin needs medical help…"

Tyler was speechless. He turned around and walked quickly back outside. It was important that he keep his anger under control. He didn't know who those two men were, but he did know that no human being deserved to be treated the way they were being treated…and for what…trespassing?

Little John followed Tyler outside and secured the padlock once again. He lit a blunt and blew the smoke in Tyler's face. "Clint was supposed to go over all this with you, but you've been missing most of the day. He hid their vehicle in the woods behind the cabin. I want you to drive it back to town, find out where they're staying, and stash the car somewhere…it doesn't really matter where you leave it. Make sure you wipe it down good; I don't want any prints leading back to anyone on this ranch. Find out all you can about these two *cousins*…I want to know who they really are. Your job, Jones, is to give me a reason *not* to kill them for trespassing on my land. Personally, I don't believe anything about their story, but I am willing to reserve judgment on them until you get back. When you're finished, you can use our dump truck to get back here; it's parked out front of Smitty's Garage, at the Shell station." Little John reached in his pocket and retrieved a key. He grabbed Tyler's hand, slapped the key onto his open palm, and said, "You've got twenty-four hours, boy, to find out the truth about these two. You might say that their lives depend on what you find out. Report to me…and only me…when you get back. You've got until seven o'clock tomorrow night, Jones. Get going…"

CHAPTER 23

Amanda Doesn't Listen

Amanda kept watch from the small window in her apartment that faced the back of the café property. She waited until Doug went back inside the café, before stuffing a change of clothes and a few puppy snacks into a small duffel bag. "I can't leave you here by yourself, Buster, so you're gonna have to come with me." She changed into a pair of black jeans and a black tee-shirt, tied her long hair into a loose ponytail, and slapped her Tampa Rays ball cap on her head. She turned on the lamp beside her bed, grabbed her shoulder bag, and whistled softly. "Okay, come on, fella…we're taking a ride to Thomasville…"

Tyler drove the cousins' rented vehicle past the police station. He fought with his conscience, repeatedly, about pulling in and telling the police about the two men locked away in the small cabin on the Abbott ranch. He circled the block and parked in front of the police station. It would be so easy to tell them what was going on at the ranch, what his part in all of it was, what was coming down in the next few days…it would be so easy to tell them everything, but…telling them might also jeopardize any chance the higher authorities might have in making the dog-fighting charges stick. He, also, could not be sure of how many of the local police were in Little John's back pocket; if he confided to the wrong officer, it could blow the entire operation for the authorities.

He shook his head and rubbed the bridge of his nose. He wondered what advice his father might give him; he had tried calling B.B. Foster on his way into town, but his call had gone straight to his father's voice mail. He had twenty-four hours to come up with something that would convince Little John that the cousins were harmless; otherwise, he knew that Little John would not hesitate to kill the two men. Tyler didn't want to leave this type of information in a voice mail message; he would try his father again later on, after he had more information about the situation. He looked at his watch; it was a little after seven and he was late for his rendezvous with the two investigators. He was supposed to meet them at their hotel; they told him they were staying at the Econo Lodge off Highway 19 South, in room 109.

Tyler took a last look at the police station before pulling out into the slow, oncoming traffic. "I'm going to keep that meeting," he spoke to his reflection in the rear-view mirror. He figured he would have plenty of time after the meeting to hit a few bars and find out what he could about the cousins. Thomasville was a relatively small town, with a population around 20,000, so Tyler felt confident he would be able to find out something about the two battered strangers. He would make something up, if he had to…anything to keep Little John from killing them.

He was so engrossed in his thoughts that he didn't notice the older-model Trooper that drove slowly by him just before he pulled out into traffic.

The driver of the Trooper, however, recognized Tyler immediately, pulled off to the side of the road until he passed, and then quickly pulled back in behind him. "Tyler Jones…"

Amanda whispered while she reached over and patted Buster, who sat quietly in the passenger seat, and chewed on a large dog biscuit. "Well, that was easier than I thought it was going to be, Buster…figured I'd have to drive around for a couple of hours before I spotted his truck. Good thing I went past him when I did, though…cause, he's not driving his truck…"

Buster looked over at her and growled softly.

Amanda smiled down at him and said, "We're gonna follow him, okay. I think he's going to meet up with those inspectors, and, well…I tried to tell him I wanted to be there for that meeting. He's not going to like it, but…we'll cross that bridge when we come to it, won't we, fella?"

Buster offered up one more supporting growl before returning his attention back to the dog biscuit. *"Hey, I'm just along for the ride, remember!"*

Tim nudged Ross. "Hey, Buddy…you awake?"

Ross groaned as he tried to sit upright against the wall. His chest was burning with pain, and every time he inhaled, it felt as though he was being hit with a wrecking ball. "Hell…I'm afraid to go to sleep…might not wake up again…" he tried to joke. "I think I might have one rib left that they haven't broken yet."

Tim looked at his friend and co-worker through the one good eye he was still able to use. Tyler and Abbott had left them at least thirty minutes ago, and Ross had not said anything about the visit. "You do realize that the kid was Tyler Foster, don't you?"

Ross looked sideways in Tim's direction. His friend's battered face made him almost unrecognizable. "The thought had crossed my mind, yeah…do you think he knows who we are?"

Tim shook his head. "I don't think so…and, I hate to say it, but he might be our only chance of getting out of this alive. If he goes to the hotel room tonight, as planned, there's a chance he'll find our I.D. cards, put two and two together, and realize what's going on...provided he can find a way inside the room."

"Well..." Ross groaned again as he tried to find a more comfortable position. "I'm not sure what my own face looks like, but...I know for a fact that you don't look anything like the picture on your card." He tried to laugh, but the pain in his chest was excruciating, and it came out more of a croaked groan. He began to cough and tried to get his labored breathing under control. "He really is our only hope, isn't he? That crazy son-of-a-bitch, Abbott, is going to kill us..."

Tim remained quiet. He knew he should say something comforting and reassuring, but he had been thinking along those same lines for most of the day. Nobody knew they were here...their bodies would never be found...he was sure of that. "Ready to pray yet, my friend?" was all he could think to say.

Ross closed his eyes and shook his head. "Prayer isn't going to get us out of this cabin, Tim...so, no...I don't want to pray, but...if it works for you...by all means, be my guest."

Tim was quiet for a few moments. He decided to change the conversation to help get their minds off their impending predicament. "Ross...earlier this morning...on the hill...when we were watching Tyler and the dogs..."

"Yeah?" Ross mumbled. "You talking about when that monster dog snapped that little pup's neck? Damn...I heard that snap all the way up the hill...sent chills down my spine."

"No..." Tim spoke softly. "I'm talking about what happened afterwards..."

"What do you mean?" Ross asked, puzzled. "That's about the time I heard the leaves crunching behind us. Wish I'd heard them sooner...we might not be in this predicament if I had..."

Tim smiled. "So...you *didn't* see what happened afterwards?"

"What are you talking about, Tim" Ross mumbled. "We got caught by these assholes afterwards."

"No..." sighed Tim. "I'm not talking about that...you missed it...you missed seeing that little terrier dog come...back...to...life..."

Ross shook his head closed his eyes again. "I think you got hit harder in the head than we thought, my friend..." He waited for Tim's reply but when none came, he exhaled a short, painful breath. "Tim...we've got to find a way out of this cabin...before Tyler reports back to Abbott. Even if the kid learns the truth about who we are, I can't imagine what he could say to Abbott that would make him change his mind about killing us."

Tim sighed deeply. "The best thing Tyler could do, for himself, would be to tell Abbott the truth about us. He needs to protect his own cover until this operation is finished."

"So...you do have a death wish, huh?" Ross kept his eyes closed and concentrated on taking short, shallow breaths that seemed to hurt a lot less than deeper ones. "Because...if you think, for one minute, that Abbott is going to let us go after he finds out who we really are, then..."

"No...I'm sure that he plans to kill us, regardless, Ross..." Tim smiled. "That's what he does...that's all he knows how to do. Once he finds out what we're really in town for...and he will...he'll have no choice. He can't let us go, and...he can't allow anyone to ever find our bodies."

"Well...you're just a ray of sunshine, aren't you?" Ross grumbled. He couldn't argue with his friend, though, because he was beginning to feel the same way. He sighed deeply, in spite of the effort and pain it took him to do so, closed his eyes, and thought about his wife and two boys. He was almost twenty years younger than Tim Breydan; he had people who depended on him to come back to them.

"Sorry," Tim smiled absently. He glanced sideways and saw the worried expression on Ross's face. "I lost my faith for a little bit there, but I know for a fact that if He brings us to it...He will bring us through it...one way or another."

"Oh, yeah...one way or another, huh?" Ross smirked. "Well, *if* your God is real, then I wish he'd hurry up and bring us through it before Abbott comes back here. I don't like the looks, or the smell, of that pit out there. I sure as hell don't want to spend my last hours on earth roasting over it..."

Tim didn't respond. He was deep in silent prayer to the one person who had never let him down. His previous conviction that Abbott would kill them regardless of what Tyler told him, dissipated into the darkness of the claustrophobic room. He was ashamed that he had allowed his faith to falter, even momentarily.

Tim's eyes remained closed in prayer, but a smile crossed his lips when he heard a lone, deep howl that echoed from a distance outside the cabin. He couldn't explain how he knew, but he suspected that the howl belonged to the large, black dog that had miraculously brought the small terrier back to life. He knew that he had not imagined it; he knew he had witnessed one of God's miracles. He, also, knew that he and Ross were not alone in this room...God was with them, had been with them all along, and, Tim Breydan's faith would not allow him to believe that they would be forsaken.

It was completely dark outside by seven-thirty when Tyler pulled into the parking lot of the Econo Lodge. He rode around to the side of the building and found Room 109; there were no other cars in the side parking lot. He rode to the end of the building and parked the rental sedan on the other side of the dumpster; he figured this would be as good a place as any to park the cousins' vehicle. He removed the rental paperwork from the glove compartment and wiped down the seats, steering wheel, and door handle, so that his prints would not show up once the police found the car. He threw the keys into the dumpster, pushed his hands deep into his pockets, and walked slowly across the parking lot to Room 109.

An exterior light burned beside the room's door; the drapes were closed. Tyler put his ear to the door, but didn't hear any noises or voices coming from inside. He knocked lightly upon the door and waited for a response that, for some strange reason, he didn't really expect to receive. He felt the hairs on his arm stand up and knew, instinctively, that he was no longer alone. He spun around quickly, fists raised to protect his face.

Amanda was the last person he expected to see standing behind him, and she wasn't alone. Buster positioned himself bravely between her arm and chest, and growled defensively when Tyler raised his fists.

"What the hell are *you* doing here?" he whispered loudly. "I thought I told you to stay put at the café and I would let you know how things went."

"Hmmm..." Amanda pondered, while rolling her eyes. "Nope...I guess I don't follow *orders* all that great, do I? I told you I want to meet these investigators. I can help, Tyler. You don't have to do this all by yourself."

"And why on earth would you bring *him* with you?" Tyler demanded.

"Because I couldn't very well leave him by himself, now could I? And I couldn't ask Max and Bertie to watch him while I galloped off after you because they agreed with you that I should stay there, so..."

"I don't have time for this, Amanda...you have to go *now*...please." He turned to knock on the door again.

"I don't believe anyone is home," Amanda sighed. "Why don't we go inside and wait for them? You're late, so maybe they went to get something to eat."

"We can't go inside because the door is locked," Tyler stated the obvious and wondered again about her qualifications for being a cop.

Amanda pulled what appeared to be a dry eraser marker from her back pocket. "Oh...ye of little faith. Check out this neat gadget that I pulled off some jerk a few days ago. Silly me forgot to log it into evidence; I'll have to do that first thing when I get back to work..."

"You're going to open the door with a magic marker?" Tyler pushed his face between his hands and sighed.

"Scoot over, handsome...and hold Buster while I show you how this little contraption works." She handed the pup to Tyler. "You see...it acts as a master key for hotel room door locks. Most of these key card locks have a power jack on the bottom that doubles as a 1-wire communications port. Crooks are using this little gadget to unlock hotel doors in less than one second; it's that easy. Let's face it...nobody is going to be suspicious if they see someone holding a dry eraser marker, now are they?" She removed the tip and inserted the marker into the hole beneath the lock.

Tyler was about to voice another objection when the green light appeared on the lock.

Amanda turned the handle, opened the door to Room 109, and stepped back. She bent at the waist and smiled. "After you..."

CHAPTER 24

Amos Collapses

The dinner crowd was in full swing by seven-thirty; every table was filled and the counter seats were all taken by the usual trucker crowd, with the exception of the end seat - the one closest to the kitchen - where Amos sat talking to Doug.

Amos looked around the crowded room and grinned. "Lawdy, this place sure does a good business at dinner time, don't it?"

Doug was working behind the counter while Bertie made easy work keeping the table customers satisfied. Doug had a special connection with the truckers and he especially enjoyed those who stopped by for their dinner meal on their way to designated stops across the nation. "Yes, it does, Amos." He looked at the empty dinner plate that sat before the old, black man. "Looks like you didn't have any trouble finishing your meal," he laughed. "Your favorite is on the dessert list tonight, you know."

Amos dabbed his thick lips with a napkin and grinned back at Doug. All his upper teeth were missing now, but he still had three on the bottom that allowed him to continue to enjoy Max's celebrated meals. "Buttermilk cake… yessiree… that is my favorite, for sure…" He stopped in midsentence and caught his breath.

Doug's natural instincts kicked in; he could feel that something wasn't quite right with Amos. He moved to stand beside him and put an arm around his shoulder. "Amos? What's wrong, my friend?"

Several truckers at the counter stopped talking and watched Doug tilt the old man's head back so that he could look into Amos' eyes. One of the truckers slid off his stool and moved quickly to stand on the other side of Amos. "What's wrong with him, Doug? He's sweating like a pig."

Amos was taking short, shallow breaths but managed to smile at the trucker. "Actually…pigs don't sweat, so…"

"What?" the red-neck trucker, named George Hickson from Opps, Alabama, asked.

Doug didn't like the sensation he was absorbing from Amos, but he knew that Amos would not want to be the cause of any disruption, so he clarified Amos' response. "It's true, George…pigs don't sweat…they don't like hot climates for the simple fact that they have very few functional sweat glands. So you see…they're hardly able to sweat at all. They are also not very good at dumping heat from their wet mucus membranes in the mouth by panting…you know…like dogs are able to do. Long story short…pigs are not very good at handling heat stress.

George looked back and forth between Amos and Doug. It appeared that the old man's breathing was becoming more regular and since Doug didn't seem to be overly concerned, he figured everything must be okay. He shook his head at Doug's explanation about pig sweat and heat stress. "Yeah…right…okay, then…" He returned to his seat.

After George sat back down, Amos stared directly into the eyes of an angel and whispered. "I don't want to cause no ruckus, Mr. Doug, but…I's not feeling all that good…do you think…"

Doug helped Amos off the stool and walked him toward the kitchen where Max was already wiping his hands on his apron. "Grab a chair, Doug..." he said as he guided Amos into the kitchen, toward the back door. He opened the door to allow in the fresh, cool October air.

Doug returned with a chair and placed it on the back porch. "Sit down, Amos," he offered. "Tell me...are you feeling any tightness in your chest, any pain at all?"

Max provided Amos with a glass of water and wiped his forehead with a cool rag. "Here, take this, Amos." He also pulled a bottle of aspirin out of his pocket. "I want you to chew this aspirin, too...don't just swallow it...make sure you chew it." He put his hands on Amos' shoulders and closed his eyes. When he opened them, he looked at Doug and said, "Call 911, Doug..."

Amos moved to stand up, and shook his head when Max gently pushed him back into a sitting position on the chair. "No sir...no ambulance...I don't like them...folks die in them things...please, Mr. Max..."

Max squatted down so that he was eye-level with Amos. "Amos...be honest with me...how long have you been hurting?"

"It ain't nothin', Mr. Max...really...probably just indigestion cause I ate too much of your good food...I's be fine in a few minutes," he rubbed his jaw absently.

"Jaw pain?" Doug asked.

"Just a little," Amos replied, while rubbing his left arm. "And, it feels like my arm has gone to sleep...been feeling like this for a few hours...before I got here this evening, off and on."

Doug looked toward Max, who gave him the signal. "Stay seated, Amos. I'm calling 911," he held his hand up at Amos' forthcoming objection. "No argument from you, my friend...and, don't you worry...one of us will ride with you all the way to the hospital. We won't leave your side...you will not be alone, okay?"

Amos took a deep breath and closed his eyes. He simply

nodded and said, "Will you pray with me, Mr. Max?"

Max took the old man's withered hands into his own and bowed his head. "Heavenly Father...we ask that you be with Amos and heal him...you are the One we turn to for help in moments of weakness and times of need. We ask that you be with your servant in this time of illness. Psalm 107:20 says that you send out your Word and heal. So then, please send your healing Word to your servant. In the name of Jesus, drive out all infirmity and sickness from his body."

Amos heard the sirens coming from a distance. He opened his eyes and smiled into Max's all-knowing eyes. "Thank you, Mr. Max...thank you..."

It was very dark inside Room 109, so Amanda felt for a light switch on the wall and flipped it on. The entire room lit up with bright, fluorescent lighting.

Tyler kicked the door shut behind them and put Buster down on the floor. He quickly turned off the light. "Are you crazy!" he whispered loudly. He moved in the dark until he found the switch for the table lamp on the nightstand between two queen beds.

"What!" Amanda exclaimed. "We can't very well search the place in the dark, can we?" She began looking through the two suitcases in the corner. "Go ahead, look in all the drawers."

Tyler stared at her with a dumbfounded expression. "What are you doing, Amanda? I'm just here to meet these fellas, not to discover their innermost secrets. What do you think we're supposed to *search* for anyway?"

Amanda placed her hands on her hips and returned his dumbfounded stare. "Tyler...you have to admit it, something feels off about this whole thing, doesn't it? I mean, these guys are here to bust up a dog-fighting ring, and you're supposed to meet with them, promptly at seven o'clock. It's past that time now, they haven't called you to cancel the meeting, and they're nowhere to be found..."

Tyler looked at his watch and rolled his eyes. "Amanda, it's only forty minutes past the time we were supposed to meet. Anything could have happened to delay them. That's certainly no reason for us to go rummaging through their personal belongings. I say we go back outside and wait for them there. Come on..." He moved to open the door but stopped when he saw Buster dragging something from one of the suitcases on the floor. "Amanda, get him quick before he destroys something..."

Amanda squatted on the floor and urged Buster to release the piece of plastic he had in his mouth. "Come on, Buster...what do you have there, huh? Come on...give it to me..."

Buster backed away from Amanda, preparing to play their "catch-me-if-you-can" game. *"Oh, no...that's not the way the game goes...I found it first...you have to try to get it from me..."* He scooted backward on his butt, dragging the plastic card with him.

Amanda reached out quickly and pulled it from his grip. She wiped his mini-drool off the plastic, which appeared to be some sort of identification card. She looked at the picture and handed it to Tyler. "Hmmm...nice looking...for an older fella...says his name is Tim Breydan...is this one of the men you're supposed to meet?"

Tyler took the card from her and said, "Yeah, it is...I've never met him, but Mr. Breydan is a friend of my father's." He looked more closely at the picture of the investigator. He moved closer to the lamp, sat down on one of the beds, and held the picture under the lamp's light for a closer look.

Amanda pulled the second suitcase away from the wall and found another identification card. She brought it over to the bed and sat down beside her future husband. She wiggled against him and grinned, "Well, this is cozy, isn't it?"

Tyler looked over at her briefly before scooting over enough to force a few inches between them. "We're not here to get cozy..." he said before returning his full attention to the picture of Tim Breydan. "You know...I've never met Mr.

Breydan before, but…I swear…he looks really familiar to me…"

Amanda closed the short distance between them until their hips and shoulders touched again. She grinned at Tyler's obvious discomfort at being so close to her. "Well, they say everyone has a double, right? Here's another one." She handed him the second identification card. "Says his name is Ross Taylor…now, he *really* is a nice-looking man!"

Tyler looked at Ross's card and shook his head. "No…no way…"

Amanda leaned her head against Tyler's left arm for a closer look at the pictures. "What?"

Tyler tried to ignore how good it felt to have Amanda pressed so close to him, but she was making it hard for him to concentrate. He gently prodded her away from him. "Amanda…can I have some space…please?"

"Oh, I get it…I get you all hot and flustered, don't I? Make it hard for you to focus on whatever it is you're trying to focus on, right? Yep…I'm thinking we probably need to have a really short engagement. I mean, the quicker we get married, the quicker your brain returns from mush, huh?"

"You really *are* crazy, you know that, don't you?" Tyler replied. He rubbed the bridge of his nose and shook his head. "Seriously, Amanda…I think you're right…something doesn't feel right about all this…" He held the two identification cards out to her. "Remember that I told you I've never met these men before?"

Amanda took the cards and looked at them again. "Yeah?"

Tyler stood up and looked nervously around the room. "We've got to clear this room of everything that belongs to these two men."

Amanda sighed. "Well…we're already guilty of breaking and entering…why not throw in a little theft to seal the deal. I'm game, but do you mind telling me *why* we need to do this?"

Tyler was already going through drawers and removing

any evidence that Tim Breydan and Ross Taylor had ever occupied the room. He stopped for a moment and looked back at her. "I *have* met these men before...earlier tonight as a matter of fact..."

Buster sat on top of one of the suitcases that Tyler had zipped up and placed by the room's door. He didn't really understand what was going on, but he did sense an adventure. *"Oh, this is fun! I think I'm gonna like being a cop dog!"*

Amanda was clearing out the men's few toiletries from the bathroom and poked her head around the corner. "Okay...slow down for just a minute...explain yourself, please!"

Tyler exhaled deeply and a worried frown creased the space between his brows. "Little John captured two trespassers earlier today. That's why I'm here...to hide their rental car and find out what I can about them. I'm supposed to report back to him before seven o'clock tomorrow night." He looked at Amanda and shrugged. "Those trespassers are Tim Breydan and Ross Taylor. They've been severely beaten, Amanda. Little John has them locked in a cabin on his ranch. He took me to see them tonight before I came here. One of them...Tim...said that he and Ross were cousins. I'm guessing that he knows who I am."

Buster emitted a low growl. *"Let me at them, Amanda...I'll bite them real hard and make them let those men go. I can do it, Amanda! I can save them!"*

Amanda looked over at Buster and held her finger to her lip. "Shhh...Buster...no dogs are allowed in here. We don't want to draw any attention to ourselves, so be a good dog and keep quiet..." She stared at Tyler while a determined look spread across her face. "Oh, my God...Tyler...we've got to do something. What can I do to help?"

Tyler closed all the drawers and smoothed the beds. "*You're* not going anywhere close to the Abbott ranch, Amanda. Little John is one crazy son-of-a-bitch, and if you think for one minute that he wouldn't hurt you because you're a woman, then you are dead wrong. It would not faze him one bit, and if he found out you were a *cop*...well, then he would take extreme pleasure in bringing you pain. The man is a psychopath. I can tell you...if he finds out who these two men really are, he will not hesitate to kill them."

Amanda's shocked expression covered her face. "I...I knew he was a bad person...fighting the dogs and all, but, wow...I guess I never thought he was a killer..."

"From what I've heard around the ranch, this wouldn't be the first time that trespassers have *disappeared*. I've got to find a way to buy some time for them...I've got to...

"CALL YOUR DAD!" Amanda beamed. "He'll know what to do, who to notify...from what you've said about Little John Abbot, there really is a good chance that those men won't survive long enough for the authorities to be notified and brought in."

"You're right about that," Tyler agreed. "I actually thought about going to the local police and telling them everything, but...that might have sealed the investigators' fate. Little John has a good portion of the local police in his back pocket; they look the other way because he keeps their pockets greased. He keeps the ones who can't be bribed in line by threatening to hurt their families. The man is insane. No...I have to think about this. I need Dad's help...I could never live with myself if my actions resulted in those men's deaths..."

"That's not going to happen, Tyler. Come on, let's get out of here...call your Dad...then we'll figure out our next move."

Buster was running around in circles. *"Oh, boy...oh, boy...my first real adventure! I can't wait!"*

CHAPTER 25

Sam's Healing Powers

Two truckers were exiting the café when Tyler, Amanda, and Buster reached the front door. They stopped in their tracks when they heard one of the truckers say, "Sure hope the old fella makes it; he didn't look too good when the ambulance drove off."

Amanda held onto Buster with one arm and grabbed the trucker with her free hand. "Hey! What did you say? What old man? What ambulance?" She looked behind her at the parking lot that held only a half-dozen vehicles. "What are you talking about? Tell me!"

"Whoa there, little lady! Take it easy, now..." George Hickson answered back as he grabbed the tiny hand that clutched at his bicep.

Buster growled and wiggled in Amanda's arms.

George removed Amanda's firm grip and reached out for the pittie-pup. "Well...what do we have here..." He stopped in mid-sentence when the pup lunged and snapped at him. A scowl quickly appeared on George's acne-scarred face.

Doug's towering form quickly appeared in the doorway,

and George felt the man's hand wrap firmly around the same bicep that the young woman had just released. His first instinct was to turn and swing at Doug, but that thought dissipated as quickly as it had first formed. Instead, he took a deep breath and felt a tremendous feeling of calmness surge through his body. He felt the physical tension and frustration of the past week evaporate through the skin that the waiter still held firmly onto.

"I see you've met Buster," Doug smiled down into George's bewildered face. "Here…let me have him, Amanda. Why don't you go inside? Bertie is in the kitchen…"

"But who was hurt?" Amanda began. Her mind was spinning cartwheels. The look on Doug's face confirmed to her that it was someone close to her. It didn't take her long to figure out who that someone was. "Oh, no…oh, my God…Amos…" She pushed past Doug and rushed inside.

Doug released his grip on George's arm and said, "You fellas have a safe trip…make sure you stop and see us again on your way back home."

George rubbed his arm and stared into emerald-green eyes that seemed to burn into his very soul. "I…I wasn't gonna hurt the pup," he said. He looked down and moved to leave, but turned back around to look at Doug. "What…what did you do to me?"

Tyler stood in the same spot he had been in for the last few minutes. He had felt compelled to watch the scene unfold before him, but had not felt the need to come to Amanda's rescue. He, somehow, knew that no harm would come to any of them as long as Doug was there. He had sensed the sudden change in the trucker's demeanor the moment Doug had clasped the man's arm.

Doug smiled but never took his eyes off George. "I didn't do anything, George…you did it all yourself. Go on now…you fellas have a safe trip…" Doug watched until the truckers drove out of the parking lot.

Tyler never took his eyes off Doug.

Once the fading tail lights left the parking lot, Doug

exhaled softly. He knew that Tyler was watching him. He turned to look at the young man and reached out to touch him.

Tyler drew back quickly. "Oh, no, you don't…"

Doug threw back his head full of jet-black hair and laughed softly. "You don't have to be afraid of me, Tyler."

"I'm not afraid of you," Tyler said, keeping his back to the door and never taking his eyes off Doug. "What *did* you do to that man? Because…something just happened…that man looked like he wanted to hurt Buster, and maybe Amanda, too, but…you touched him, and, he…*changed…*"

Doug continued to smile at Tyler. He liked this young man and he had a good feeling about what might happen between him and Amanda. "I didn't do anything to him, Tyler…really, I didn't. Sometimes, the calm approach works with people who normally react rashly to things. I just tried to calm him down a bit, that's all."

Tyler shook his head. "No…no, you did something else…you calmed him down alright, but, it wasn't by anything you said to him. It was in your *touch*…you could see the change come over him the second you touched him…"

Doug took a step toward Tyler and placed a firm hand upon the young man's shoulder. "You mean…like *this…*"

Tyler was about to jerk away when that same feeling of calmness that overcame the trucker immediately settled within him, too. His anxiety about what he had seen vanished. He shook his head. So much had happened in the past twenty-four hours. The day had started out with him witnessing the resurrection of a dead dog, discovering the truth about the trespassers, and now…well…he wasn't sure exactly what he had just witnessed between Doug and the trucker, but, he knew it was something beyond mere mortal explanation. Tyler exhaled deeply, closed his eyes, and surrendered briefly to the most intense peace and calm he had ever felt. When he opened his eyes, Doug was smiling at him.

"Come on, let's go inside. You could probably use a cup of coffee right about now." Doug removed his hand from Tyler's shoulder, turned, and walked back inside the café.

Tyler watched the gentle giant re-enter the café. He shook his head and thought, *"Truth be told, I could use something a lot stronger than coffee right about now..."*

Three hours later...Amos Brown's heart stopped beating, and he died on the operating table.

Complete darkness surrounded the small cabin that stood a hundred feet from the burning pit on the Abbott ranch. A lone screech owl hooted from one of the massive oak trees surrounding the cabin, and an orchestra of tree frogs croaked in solidarity while searching for their evening meal of gut-loaded crickets, tadpoles, guppies, spiders and worms. The small, mosquito-infested pond in back of the cabin provided a smorgasbord for these tiny, green members of the Bufonidae family.

Two golden eyes glowed from the tall hedges that grew along one side of the burning pit. Sam was just about to step into the clearing when he heard the rumbling of an engine coming slowly toward the cabin. He back-stepped into the bushes, and hunkered quietly down on all fours. Spartacus had wanted to come with him to check on the two strangers, but he had convinced him to stay behind and keep the other dogs quiet. If they barked too much, the crew never hesitated to beat them into submissiveness.

The pick-up truck rolled to a slow stop and the engine shut off. The driver's door opened and Clint Meacham stepped out. Sam watched intently as the foreman grabbed two guns from inside the truck. One was a tranquilizer gun that was frequently used on uncooperative animals; the other was a Smith &Wesson-357 Magnum that Clint always carried with him. He holstered both guns and moved to the back of the truck.

Sam's ears became erect when he heard a slight whimpering coming from the bed of the pick-up, but he never took his eyes off Clint.

Clint dropped the tailgate and retrieved a shovel he had thrown into the bed. "Damn idiots," he mumbled. "I'm stuck doing manual labor while those damn idiots are in town getting laid and wasted..." He spoke out loud as a way to vent his anger. Little John was treating him more and more, lately, like the minimum-wage losers they hired to handle and dispose of the dogs. He didn't know what he had done to earn the man's ire, but he was quickly getting tired of being treated like a general flunky, especially, when he had been a loyal employee to Big John Abbott for so many years.

He grabbed a pair of thick work gloves and put them on; dark stains covered every inch of the gloves. He pulled on the first pair of legs he came too and dragged the dead shepherd off the truck; it landed with a hard plop on the ground. Clint bent down and began rolling the dog toward the open pit. Top soil and quicklime pellets had been dumped on top of the last truckload of deposited animals in order to speed decomposition of any remaining, unburned body parts, and to deter any wildlife scavenging efforts. More and more lately, the crew were adding extra dirt and quicklime to the pit, rather than burning off the evidence, because the smell of burning flesh and fur tended to linger longer than they liked.

It was only a few feet to the pit's edge, but Clint was no longer the young twenty-year old who had come to work for Big John Abbot in the mid 90's. He took a deep breath and used his boot to push the shepherd the last few inches, into the pit. He thought he heard a rustling in the bushes on the other side of the pit and looked up quickly. He backed up to the truck and grabbed a flash light from the small toolbox he kept in the bed. He waved the light back and forth across the bushes, but did not see anything, so he placed the flash light on the ground and continued hauling the bodies of bait dogs into the pit. Three of them were not completely dead and he knew he should complete that task before disposing of their bodies, but he decided they would be dead by morning, anyway…so, why waste a perfectly good bullet on them.

It took him thirty minutes to dispose of all the dogs. There might have been a time in his life, a very long time ago, when it would have bothered his conscience to hear the final, whimpering pleas that the still-alive dogs were making; he knew it was inhumane to leave them to die in a pit with the remains of their dead, mangled counterparts. Instead, when he kicked the last body into the pit, he followed it with a large spit of the chewed tobacco that was a permanent part of the inside of his left cheek.

He went back to the truck and pulled a large paper sack and a lantern from the front seat. He kept the bloodied gloves on and unlocked the door to the cabin. The oil from the lantern was almost gone, so the light was dim. His eyes adjusted quickly to the semi-darkness of the room; the dark never seemed to bother him like it did some people. One of the trespassers was attempting to stand up; the other one was still on the floor and attempting to assist his friend.

"Well, what are you two fellas up to?" Clint mocked as he took the almost-empty kerosene lantern off the hook and replaced it with the refilled one. "What? You need to take a piss…is that it? Kinda hard to do with your hands and feet all tied up, ain't it?" He stepped closer to them and spat another wad of juice at their feet. "In case you ain't already discovered it, there's a hole in the far corner over there," he nodded to his right. "I expect you can figure out a way to help each other get your zippers undone…smart fellas that y'all are. Oh…what the hell…I'm feeling generous tonight…" He moved behind them and flipped open the pocket knife he always kept in his back pocket. It was extremely sharp for such a small knife, and it made quick work of cutting loose the rope that secured the men's hands behind them. He walked back in front of them, and spat a wad of tobacco juice at their feet. "I'll send someone by later to re-tie your hands and feet, so enjoy the freedom while you can." He opened the bag and threw two bologna sandwiches, in plastic sandwich bags, on the floor in front of them. The bloody glove left streaks of evidence across the plastic. "Oh, hey…will you look here…the cook even threw in a bag of chips for y'all to share." He tossed the small bag of chips alongside the sandwiches, followed by two plastic bottles of water. "Don't get to use to this service, fellas…you might even want to savor this meal, cause…it just might be your last…"

He placed his hand on top of the revolver he had stuck in his waistband. "Yep…only a few more hours to go before the boss decides what to do with you two…sweet dreams, fellas…" Clint turned, grabbed the empty lantern, exited the cabin, and secured the padlock on the outer door.

Tim managed to push himself up and stood erect, while Ross crawled over to the food and water. He picked up one of the sandwich bags and saw the red streaks across them. "What the hell…" he said, as he held the bag up to his nose. "Oh, God…that's blood…" he moaned just before turning and dry-heaving the watery contents of his stomach alongside the wad of spit tobacco.

Tim had untied the rope around his feet and lurched over to the door and listened while the truck drove away. He could hear the crickets and frogs, but after the truck was gone, he thought he heard something else. He was torn between helping his friend and trying to figure out what sounds he was hearing just outside the door. He turned to help Ross, but stopped when he recognized the sound of toenails clicking on the small, wooden porch of the cabin. He pressed his ear to the door and could have sworn he heard the heavy breathing of an animal. He waited until the clicks moved off the porch before turning again to help Ross up off the floor. "Something is out there…" he whispered to Ross, while he tried to side-step the vomit and tobacco at his feet.

Ross took a deep breath while Tim helped him to a standing position. "He probably left someone out there to guard us…"

Tim shook his head. "No…I don't think so…if so, then it sounded like that guard had more than two feet…"

Sam waited outside the cabin door until he felt sure that the men inside were okay. He knew they were good men and he wished he could help them, but he had more important things to do right now. He trotted over to the pit and looked down. His canine heart broke when he saw all the lifeless forms of his comrades. The corner of his eyes became wet with tears, but he had a busy night ahead of him and not much time left to get his work done. He quickly jumped into the pit but did not land on any of the dogs; instead, his massive body hovered an inch or two above them. He floated around the burning pit until he found the source of the whimpering. One by one, he grabbed three dogs by the nape of their necks and floated them to safety, above and then beside, the open pit. The three dying dogs had all been someone's beloved pet at one time in their lives. Two of them were less than a year old, but the third one was a special-needs senior, a Golden Labrador, whose untreated cataracts had left him blind years ago. The three dogs lay side-by-side, gasping their last few breaths. Their bodies had been badly mangled by Czar during an earlier training session that evening.

The old dog, whose former owner had named him Bingo, tried to lift his head when he sensed Sam near him. He had no fight left in him, and he hoped this new fighting dog would kill him quickly. However, instead of the throat-ripping he expected, Bingo's cloudy vision began to lift when Sam laid down beside him and covered him with one of his huge paws. The old dog sighed deeply when Sam laid his head on Bingo's stomach. The cataracts evaporated from Bingo's eyes, and he watched in awe as the huge, black dog performed the same healing effects on the other two surviving bait dogs.

Sam gave the dogs a few minutes to adjust to their miraculous healing before he stood proudly before them.

Bingo was the first to see the small, golden halo appear above Sam's head. He had heard stories about angel dogs before, but he never believed they were real. He believed now!

"Come on, everyone…" Sam spoke to them. *"We don't have much time…I'll show you where you need to go, but you have to keep to the woods so that no one will see you. It's going to be a long walk for you, but the people at the Heavenly Grille Café will see to it that you get to safety. Come on now…follow me…"*

CHAPTER 26

-Heaven-
Amos Arrives

Amos was transported to Heaven at the exact moment that his heart stopped beating on the operating table. While the doctors attempted every measure to bring him back, Amos drifted slowly toward the brilliant beam of light that pulled him forward with a strong, magnetic force.

Martin's head snapped quickly around when he felt the presence of Amos. "Oh, my…you're not supposed to arrive here for several more years, my friend…"

Another voice suddenly boomed from behind Martin, causing him to snap back around in the opposite direction.

"Helloooo…Mr. Martin…" Andrew Brown called out. His genial greeting was cut short when he saw his twin brother, Amos, standing on the other side of Martin. Andrew fell to his knees and clasped his hands together in prayer. "Oh, Lawdy…Mr. Martin…that there is my brother!"

This situation had not happened in a long, long time, and it had Martin temporarily speechless. Once in a blue moon, someone appeared in Heaven before their time. When this happened, a select few might remain, but the majority of them would be returned to earth until their due termination date arrived.

Amos took two steps forward and stared intently at his twin brother…his very much younger twin brother. Tears began to flow freely down his cheeks as he got closer to Andrew, who was moving toward him at a quicker pace…but, then again…Andrew was now at least fifty years younger than Amos. "Lawdy…I guess I be dead, huh?" Amos whispered to his brother when they came close enough to touch.

Andrew looked back at Martin for assistance and clarification. "Is it okay, Mr. Martin? I mean…can I touch him? Can I hug my brother?"

Martin had regained his composure and reached behind him to flick on the huge screen that occupied most of his time. He directed his thoughts specifically to Amos Brown and the old man's bio quickly appeared on the invisible screen. "By all means, Andrew…yes…you may welcome your brother while I check something in his book…" He looked Amos squarely in the eye to reassure him. "Please don't worry, Amos…we will get this straightened out as quickly as possible. In the meantime, why don't you visit with your brother…let him show you around…"

Once they attained Martin's permission, the two brothers came together with a tremendous force of longing and love. Amos wiped the tears of happiness away and held his twin at arms' length. "Well…will you just look at yourself…I had almost forgotten how handsome we were when we were younger." He looked down at his own, seventy-decade body. "I guess I'm gonna have to keep the old vessel I finished with, huh?"

Andrew hugged his brother to him. "Lawdy…Amos…I don't cares what you look like…it's so good to see you again. I think about you every single minute of every single day. I don't understand why your body is still that of an old man, though…I arrived here looking like this…"

"Oh…it don't matter none to me, brother…" Amos laughed. "I've missed you so much…you have no idea…"

Andrew took his brother's hand. "Come on, Amos…I don't have any idea about what's going on right now, but I have a feeling that you ain't gonna be staying too long, and, I want to show you what you have to look forward to. This might seem a little scary, but you gots to trust me, okay? Hang on to my hand and close your eyes…"

Amos knew he should have been more bewildered and dumbfounded than he was, but…HE WAS IN HEAVEN, and he felt absolutely amazing. His arthritis was gone, his back felt strong, and his knees didn't creak one little bit. He felt a tingling sensation course through his body while the transportation was happening, and he kept his eyes tightly shut.

"Open your eyes, Amos!" Andrew released his brother's hand and lifted both his own hands upward. "Have you ever seen anything so beautiful?" Dogs of all shapes and sizes, with their tails wagging in happy greeting, bounded quickly toward them. Andrew dropped to his knees and allowed the multitude of the dogs to take turns in his lap to administer welcoming doggie kisses.

"Oh…sweet, Jesus…" whispered Amos. He wasn't looking at the dogs anymore; instead, his focus centered on the man and woman waving to him from the mansion's huge veranda. "Oh…sweet, Jesus…" he repeated as he began a slow sprint toward his mother and father.

Andrew rolled on the ground laughing and playing with all the dogs. He yelled after his brother, "Oh, yeah…I forgot to tell you that Mama and Daddy are living with me!" He continued playing with the dogs and allowed his brother to fully absorb and enjoy the reunion of a life time.

Meanwhile, back at Heaven's entry point, Martin scrolled down the large screen and clicked his tongue. "Oh, for Heaven's sake…" he mused. "Keep working, you fools…don't give up…his heart will re-start!" He watched what looked like a video clipping of the operating room where Amos Brown still lay on the table. One of the attending doctors was working fervently to bring Amos back, while another appeared ready to call "time of death."

"He's not coming back, Sorenson...if you don't make the call, I will."

Martin smiled at Dr. Denver Sorenson's firm reply.

"This is my patient, Dr. Bowman…I decide when it's time to give up on him." He adjusted the shock defibrillation paddles and

yelled back, "CLEAR!"

Martin flicked his hand across the screen to change scenes, and watched the happy reunion between the members of the Brown family. He sighed softly and shook his head. "If the choice was his to make, I'm sure he would remain right where he is at, but, alas…the choice is not his to make, and…it is NOT his time…not yet. No, Amos Brown, you have a surprise waiting for you back on earth, so I'm afraid you cannot remain with us today…"

The scene inside Andrew's mansion was one of pure, unadulterated love and happiness. Andrew stood in the kitchen, shoulder-to-shoulder with his twin while they watched their mother prepare a meal for them to share.

Amos leaned across the marble countertop to wipe his finger along the inside of the bowl that held the cake batter to his favorite chocolate cake his Mama use to make for him. He laughed out loud when the beautiful woman, apparently in her mid-forties now, slapped his wrist and grinned at him with a loving smile.

"Don't you remember, I always told you that eating raw batter wasn't good for you?" Mama Brown grinned mischievously.

Daddy Brown came up behind his wife, reached around, and quickly ran his own finger inside the bowl. He brought it quickly to his generous lips before she could swat him away. "I don't think we have to worry about that anymore, sweetie," he laughed and kissed her on the cheek.

Mama Brown sighed and looked around the room. "It's mighty nice to have all my menfolk together again. I has been waitin' a long, long time for this." She closed her eyes for a quick moment. She opened them and poured the cake batter in a baking dish. "I love you all…so very, very much."

Amos looked around the large, but comfortable, kitchen and noticed for the first time, the absence of any appliances. "Ummm…Mama…" he scratched his head. "How do you plan on cookin' that there cake? There ain't no oven in here…matter of fact…now that I be looking around…there ain't no refrigerator or freezer either…"

Mama Brown chuckled and pinched Amos' withered cheek.

"Oh, sweet boy…that's just one of the glories of this magnificent place. You see, son…food is not required, but you can make it if you want, or you can simply "think" about it and it will appear before you; but, for those of us who enjoyed cooking for ourselves and our families, well…we can still do it…we just don't have to wait hours for it to be finished! Watch this!"

Amos watched while his mother picked up the baking dish from the counter. She closed her eyes, turned around one complete cycle, and showed off the finished cake to her bewildered son. "Oh my, Lawd…will you just look at that…" he flashed his toothless grin and shook his head. "I guess that means I can ask you to cook all my favorites, doesn't it? Oh, how I miss your cooking, Mama…Mr. Max, at the café, is a good cook, but even his doesn't compare to yours."

"I've already prepared everything you loved most, Amos," his Mama smiled back at him. While you and Andrew were playing with all those pups, I came in here and whipped up EVERYTHING…all your favorites. Come on, now…I don't know how much time we have together before you have to leave, and I want to have all my men at one table again…"

Amos' head jerked up. "What do you mean…before I have to leave? I died…I'm in Heaven…with all of you. I don't want to leave. I've been looking forward to this day for longer than I can tell you. There's nothing left for me back there anymore…all of you are gone now…and it's mighty lonesome down there by myself. I don't want to go back, Mama." He looked pleadingly at his Daddy. "Please, Daddy…can't you do something…I want to stay."

The elder Brown motioned for all of them to come together and he wrapped his long arms around them all. He kissed the top of his wife's head before looking up to stare into Amos' pleading eyes. "That's not up to any of us, Amos…I think you know that. For some reason, we have all been granted this glorious reunion, and no matter how brief it is…that's what we're going to do...we're going to enjoy every blissful second we have together."

Amos nodded and wiped away a lone tear. "Yessir…" He looked over at the long, wooden table that had been positioned for a splendid view of the mansion's lush acreage. He could see that it now held bowls upon bowls of all his favorite foods. "It all looks mighty good, Mama…I can't wait to taste it all. No more sad talk…I don't know why the good Lord has allowed me to come see y'all like this, but I'm mighty grateful for whatever time He gives us…so, you're right, Daddy…let's not waste any of it."

Martin switched screens again and watched the determination and intensity on Dr. Sorenson's face. He could not suppress a smile when Dr. Bowman pursed his lips and rolled his eyes in frustration. "Oh, we have some serious work to do on you, Dr. Bowman…oh, yes we do!" Martin grinned. He turned at the sound of fluttering robes, and greeted the four members of the Brown family. "Ah…there you are, Amos. I was afraid I was going to have to come fetch you away from your beautiful family."

"What do you mean?" Amos took two steps away from his family. He immediately felt an electric shock surge through him and instinctively attempted to move back toward his family. His feet would not move backward. He took another two steps forward and felt another shock surge through his chest. He grabbed his chest, looked back at his brother, and reached out for him.

Martin sighed. "I'm sorry, but…your time is up, Amos. You must return now…one more shock should do it, I think."

"But…can't I hug them one last time…please?" Amos begged. Tears formed in his eyes as he tried in vain to move backwards; instead, his feet propelled him another two steps forward.

"We love you, Amos!" Andrew waved and shouted.

"We will see you again one day, son!" Mama Brown beamed as she held onto her husband for support. "We love you so very much!"

"Good-bye, Amos…please don't be sad…you know that we'll be waiting for you…" Daddy Brown choked on his own farewell and buried his face against Andrew's broad shoulder.

Amos' outstretched arms were the last thing that the three angelic members of the Brown family saw before they vanished.

"It was very nice to meet you, Amos Brown," Martin nodded. He took hold of Amos' hand and moved forward with him another two steps. "Please don't be sad…you were granted something that not many people ever get to experience…go and live the rest of your

life in peace and love. Something good is about to happen to you, my friend..."

Amos felt the final shock to his heart and heard a distant voice say, "Well...I'll be damned, Sorenson...you did it...you really did it!"

***"Wait on the Lord; be of good courage, and He shall strengthen your heart; wait, I say, on the Lord."* Psalm 27:14 (NKJV)**

CHAPTER 27

A New Plan Takes Form

The ambulance had taken Amos to the Archbold Memorial Hospital in Thomasville since it was closer than one of the larger hospitals in Tallahassee. Dr. Denver Sorenson pushed open the doors to Operating Room Number 7. He pulled the blue cap off his head, closed his eyes, and uttered a silent prayer to the person really responsible for saving Amos Brown's life. He never failed to give thanks to the true power behind it all. He opened his eyes and walked slowly toward the waiting room area. It was just after one o'clock in the morning, but there were several people waiting. He looked over the strange gathering…from the huge, black man who reminded him of a Gladiator, to the middle-aged woman who looked like Shirley Booth, to the virile-looking man who could easily have been a mercenary…there was something odd, yet special, about those three people, but he couldn't quite put his finger on what it was. There was, also, a young couple standing in the middle of the odd trio; their posture and stance suggested that they might be married.

Max noticed the doctor walking toward them, and

stepped out in front of the group. "Excuse me, sir…but we've been waiting several hours now…could you please tell us anything about Amos Brown? They said he was in Operating Room Number 7, and I saw you come out of there just now…"

Dr. Sorenson thought that the man's smooth baritone voice perfectly matched his massive physique. "Are you family?" he asked Max.

Bertie stepped around Max and punched the good doctor squarely against his shoulder. "Just because he's the only black person here doesn't mean he's the only family. Truth is…old Amos doesn't have any family left…all he has is us. We're the closest thing to family he has, so, spill it…is he okay?"

Doug grabbed Bertie's hand before she could administer another punch to anyone. "Sorry, Doctor…you'll have to excuse Bertie…she tends to be overly demonstrative at times, especially when she's worried about someone she loves…"

Amanda took her turn in front of the group. "Well? Is he okay?"

Dr. Sorenson smiled at the group and shook his head. "I would not normally discuss a patient's condition with anyone other than an immediate family member, but, it's obvious that all of you care very much about Mr. Brown. So…I will say that he is fine now. We had to insert three stents, and it was touch and go for a long while…in fact, we lost him once…his heart stopped, and I had a hell of a time bringing him back, but…"

The crowd of Amos' supporters jumped and yelled joyously, shouting praise to their Heavenly Father above for returning Amos to them.

"When can we see him?" Amanda asked.

"It will be quite a while before he wakes up," the doctor replied. "It's been a long night, folks. Why don't you all go home and get some rest? I'll be here the rest of the night and will keep a close eye on your friend. Come back tomorrow morning. I'm sure it will do him good to see all of you then."

He turned to leave but looked back at them. "He's lucky to have all of you…good-night, now."

It was almost two o'clock when the group arrived back at the Heavenly Grille. Amanda looked longingly at the steps leading to her apartment. "I'm sure Buster is about to burst, so I had better let him out to pee." She looked over at Tyler and asked, "What have you decided to do?"

Tyler had told the others about everything that was going on at the Abbott Ranch. He had also spoken with his father about the situation, while they waited for news about Amos. His father was working with the authorities on a new plan. "Well…" Tyler began but stopped when he saw shadows moving toward them from behind the café's building.

Max squinted into the darkness and was the first to realize what the shadows were. "More dogs…" he sighed as he walked toward the large Golden Lab and the two smaller dogs that hid behind it. "Come here…" he whispered. "Come…you don't have to be afraid…"

The Lab moved slowly forward, but the two smaller dogs scampered off and cowered behind a large bush. He dropped his head and stood still when the black man with the kind voice began to stroke his head. He lifted his head and stared into the black man's eyes. He conveyed to Max, telepathically, their story and how the large dog, named Sam, had told them to come to the café for help.

Max rubbed the dog's head again and whispered into its ear. "Everything is going to be all right; tell your friends to come out now." He stood and walked back to Bertie and the others.

Tyler met him half-way. "I recognize that dog…" he pointed to the Golden Lab, "But…he looks much *better* than the last time I saw him. I was going to treat his wounds earlier tonight, that is, until Little John took me to the cabin and gave me new instructions. Little John has been using him, and those two little ones, as bait dogs to train Czar; their mild temperaments make them easy prey for the fighter dogs."

Bertie exhaled deeply and grabbed Doug's arm. "Come on, handsome...I have a feeling this night isn't over for us yet. Help me get some coffee and food ready for Tyler and Amanda." She looked over at Amanda and winked. "Go let that mutt of yours out to pee, and then you and Tyler come inside to get some food to take with you to Brooksville. I'll watch Buster while you're gone."

"We're going to Brooksville?" Amanda raised her brows and looked back and forth from Bertie to Tyler.

Tyler nodded. "Looks that way...gotta get these three dogs to my Dad and go over whatever he and the authorities have come up with for a new plan. Just so I'm back at the Abbott Ranch before seven o'clock tonight. You don't have to go, Amanda. I mean...I know you're going to want to be at the hospital early to check on Mr. Brown."

"Is that your polite way of saying you'd rather I not tag along?" Amanda threw back at him. "Because, if it is...then, that's too bad...I'm coming with you." She looked at Max. "Amos *is* going to be all right, isn't he?"

Max nodded. "Yes, Amanda. You don't have to worry about Amos. I'm sure he will have a good story to tell you when you get back." He looked at Tyler. "I think it's a good idea if she goes with you, Tyler. It's already been a long night and it's not over yet. You haven't had any sleep and if there's one thing our Amanda can do, it is talking. She can help you stay awake."

Tyler offered an apologetic look to them both. "Sorry...I didn't mean that I didn't want her to ride with me; no...it will be good to have the company. I just know how close all of you are to Mr. Brown."

Amanda hooked her arm through Tyler's and shivered at the jolt that coursed through her body. She smiled up at him and said, "Great! Now that all that is settled, you can help me get Buster situated and then we'll meet Max inside to get some coffee and food for our little road trip."

Tyler had felt the same course of excitement travel up and down his own arm when Amanda touched him. He glanced, nervously, at Max and winced when the old man winked at him. He closed his eyes and allowed Amanda to steer him toward the stairs that led to her small apartment over the café. *"Why do I feel I have absolutely no control over my life anymore!"* he groaned inwardly.

Max heard his thoughts and turned his head so that Tyler would not see him smile in acknowledgement!

Cardiac patients were kept in the new North Tower addition on Archbold Memorial Hospital's campus. It had been a critical addition for advancing patient care, as well as being the hospital's largest capital investment in patient care and safety in 85 years. The eight-story, 247,000 square-foot tower boasted a larger Emergency Department with five more exam rooms, four fast track rooms, and two trauma rooms.

The new North Tower addition was, also, where Izabelle Ghent, known as Izzie to all her friends, spent the majority of her volunteer hours. Izzie had been a registered nurse for forty years. She had retired, reluctantly, four years ago at the age of sixty-five. Since that time, she had remained a constant source of delight throughout Archbold Memorial, serving in a volunteer capacity. She rolled the flower and magazine cart from floor to floor early Thursday morning, but stopped abruptly when she approached the closed door to Room 317. She felt a flow of warmness spread throughout her entire body when her hand wrapped around the door handle. She glanced at the patient's name outside the door…AMOS BROWN. She checked her list of newly admitted patients and saw his name at the bottom of the page. She ran her finger over his name and felt the strange warmness flow through her again.

She pushed the door open slowly and peered into the semi-darkened room. She moved closer to the patient's bed and sighed at all the machines he was hooked up to. "I think we could use a little light in here, Amos Brown..." she spoke softly within the confine of the small room as she moved to the window to adjust the blinds. She was careful not to allow too much sunshine into the room. "There now...that's so much better..." she whispered as she closed her own eyes and enjoyed the warmth of the sunshine as it flooded over her face.

"Better...than...you...could...ever...imagine..." Amos whispered back to her.

Tyler held the café door open for Amanda. It was a little after ten o'clock and neither of them had slept any over the past twenty-four hours. "After you..." Tyler smiled down at the young woman who had somehow managed to crawl under his skin.

Amanda smiled back and touched his arm. "Thanks...God, I can't remember the last time I felt this tired...what I wouldn't give for a hot shower and eight hours of sleep."

Tyler shook his head. "That's not going to happen, I'm afraid. Well..." he lowered his head to her shoulder and sniffed openly, "Maybe we *can* make time for you to get that shower..."

Amanda threw back her head and laughed. "You know...we could save time, and water, if we showered together!"

"AMANDA TURNER! I heard that, young lady!" Bertie's boisterous voice boomed from across the room.

Amanda raised her hands in mock defeat. "Kidding, Bertie! Just kidding! Hey, what's the news on Amos?"

Bertie glared at Tyler who had the decency to blush. "Have a seat, *Romeo*. I'll get you both something to eat." She grabbed Amanda in a bear hug and said, "Max just got off the phone with the head nurse on the cardiac ward. She said that Amos had a peaceful night and that he was awake now."

"Then we need to get over there ASAP!" Amanda rushed. "How about Buster? Where's my little fella?"

"Calm down, Princess," Doug smiled at them from behind the counter. "Amos is in good hands, and he knows that some of us will be there soon. Buster is in the kitchen with Max. What about the two of you? Did you get everything worked out with your father, Tyler?"

Tyler nodded. "Yeah, I think so…at least, I hope so. Could we get some coffee, please?" he asked Doug as he sat down on one of the counter stools. "Some with lots of caffeine would be great…" He spent the next few minutes telling Bertie and Doug about his father's plan to rescue Tim Breydan and Ross Taylor. "All I have to do now," he sighed, "Is to keep them both alive long enough for the authorities to carry out the new plan. The authorities got wind that Abbott is moving the fights up a week, so they're working on moving everything up at their end, too. The fights and the bust will take place this weekend rather than next weekend."

Bertie walked over to Tyler and placed his handsome, tired face between her palms. "You look so very tired, Romeo…here…this should help…" she said as she closed her eyes and continued to hold his face firmly between her palms. "Close your eyes…and no peeking!"

He had no clue as to why he complied with Bertie's order, but he did. Tyler felt a soft humming sensation that began in his toes and inched its way slowly upward to the top of his head. The sensation enveloped every square inch of his body, leaving it refreshed and energized as if he had rested for eight hours or more. He kept his eyes closed until the humming ceased, and when he opened them, Bertie released his face, looked him square in the eye, and punched him hard against the shoulder.

"There you go! Now you can go get that hot shower you wanted," she ordered. She glanced idly over at Amanda, pursed her lips, and said. "He can use Doug's shower, and you can use your own, young lady!"

CHAPTER 28

Izzie and Amos Bond

Tyler and Amanda used his truck to drive to Thomasville to check on Amos, while the three angels remained at the café to work the lunch crowd. It was just past noon when Amanda softly pushed open the door to Room 317. She was surprised to see that Amos was not alone; a beautiful, older black woman, sat by his bedside and held his hand. Their eyes were closed and they appeared to be in silent prayer.

"Oh..." Amanda gulped.

The woman's head lifted and turned toward her. She was even more beautiful than Amanda had first thought. "Hello, there...you must be Amanda. Amos told me a little about you. Come on in, dear. I can leave and let you visit with him..."

Amanda held up her hand in protest. "Oh, no...please...stay." She looked at Amos, who had lifted his left hand weakly in welcome.

"Mighty good to see you, Miss Amanda," he smiled. "Mighty good, indeed...hello, Mr. Tyler..."

Tyler closed the door behind them and walked over to

shake hands with the woman sitting at Amos' bedside. "Hello, I'm Tyler Foster…" He smiled down at Amos and said, "Hello, Mr. Brown…well…it looks like you're in good hands."

Amanda nodded to the woman but focused her attention on Amos. She moved to the side of the bed not occupied by the woman and laid her hand on top of Amos' arm, careful not to disturb the needles inserted in his left hand. "Oh, Amos…you gave us all quite a scare. We've been so worried about you, but the doctor said that you're going to be just fine…" She lifted his left hand and brought it gently to her lips. "I don't know what I would have done if anything had happened to you, too…"

Amos smiled back at Amanda and nodded. "Oh, I think you be right about that, Miss Amanda…I done went and seen the lights of Heaven, and they were the most beautiful lights I has ever seen…I gots to see Andrew…and my Mama…and my Daddy, too…"

Amanda glanced at the woman who had yet to introduce herself. "What kind of drugs do they have him on?"

Izzie stood up and stretched to her full height of five feet, two inches. She walked over to Amanda and put an arm around her. "My name is Isabelle Ghent, Amanda. I'm a volunteer here…worked here as a registered nurse for 40 years before I retired 4 years ago…you can call me Izzie…my friends call me Izzie." She glanced down at Amos and her face lit up with what could only be described as sheer affection and adoration. "Trust me, dear…that is not the drugs speaking…I believe Amos is telling the truth…I believe he visited Heaven when he died on that operating table."

Amanda looked back and forth among the other three people in the room. Strangely enough, they all had the same look of acceptance, and belief, on their faces. She shook her head and sighed. "Well…if that's what Amos says he saw…then…that's what Amos saw." She looked down at Amos again, at the restful and peaceful expression on his face, and smiled. "So, Amos…how is Andrew doing these days?"

Training was in full swing at the Abbott Ranch, and Clint Meacham was overseeing the current crew of dogs being tossed into the makeshift ring with Czar, the 110-pound, brown Mastiff that had defeated Little John's previous winning dog, Spartacus. A small pile of deceased dogs lay outside the ring, and four more had been tossed inside the ring with the massively-built Czar. Saliva drooled from his open mouth, and he pawed the ground with eagerness to get at the four mid-size dogs cowering in the far corner.

Clint shook his head and yelled out to the dog crew. "These dogs are worthless; there's no fight in any of them. We could sit here all day and watch him dispose of every single bait animal we have. We need to see how he's going to perform with one that will give him a real fight..."

"We could put the big, black dog in there with him," the crewman named Bubba mumbled. He was the one who Sam had attacked the day before. "Wouldn't mind adding him to that pile over there..." he nodded toward the pile of deceased dogs.

Clint looked over to where the large, black dog was crated next to Spartacus. A shiver ran up and down his spine when the dog immediately stopped his rapid pacing and seemed to glare at him. "Yeah, I'm sure that one would be able to hold his own against Czar, but...the boss doesn't want to pit them against each other until after the fight tomorrow night. Czar is already a champion fighter, and, the black one...well, something tells me he might be one, too, before long." He glanced at Bubba and nodded toward Sam. "Have you trained him against the bait dogs yet? We don't have much time left since the boss decided to move the fights up a week."

Bubba nodded and rubbed the back of his sweaty neck. "Yes, sir...well, at least we tried to fight him, but all he does when you put him in the ring with the bait dogs is sit and stare at them. We even picked the bait dogs up and threw them at his feet, but…all he did was growl…at *us*…not at the dogs."

"Really?" Clint spat a wad of tobacco juice into the red dirt and smiled. "Well…maybe he won't become a champion fighter after all; if that's the way he's going to be, then it will be an easy decision on where to place my bet tomorrow night." He turned to walk away and yelled over his shoulder. "Keep a close eye on that black dog, and give Czar a few more samples to whet his appetite. No food for any of them tonight or tomorrow. Those that survive tomorrow's fight can eat afterwards…"

Bubba adjusted the cap on his head and answered back, "Yes, sir, Boss…" He looked toward Sam and mimicked a snarl. "Your time is almost up, mutt…I can't wait to see you torn to pieces!" He looked at the rest of the crew and yelled. "Okay, let's give Czar another hour or so before we load up the quicklime and cart these dead ones to the pit. I don't know about the rest of you, but I'm looking forward to some drinking time in town tonight. The sooner we get this work done, the sooner we can get cleaned up and go make some women happy tonight!"

Amanda and Tyler arrived back at the café around two o'clock that afternoon. Tyler was still feeling refreshed from whatever Bertie had done to him, but Amanda's energy was almost depleted.

"You look exhausted," Tyler said before they got out of his truck. "Why don't you go lie down for a few hours?"

Amanda closed her eyes and sighed. "Maybe I can get Bertie to administer one of her *refreshment* sessions to me, too…"

Tyler rubbed the back of his neck and continued to stare at the pretty young woman who leaned her head back against the headrest. "Yeah…about that…I've been meaning to talk to you about what she did to me…and don't tell me she didn't do something, because, trust me…I could *feel* the change come over me…and it's still there. I feel like I could go another 24 hours without sleep."

Amanda opened her eyes and shifted sideways to look at Tyler. "God, but you are handsome…" she grinned sleepily. She held her hands up when it looked like he was going to interrupt her. "Okay, okay…yes…Bertie learned that refreshment technique years ago from one of her customers who practiced holistic medicine or something." The lie flowed freely from Amanda's lips, so much so, that she could almost believe her own explanation. "It has something to do with generating warmth from the hands to special nerves along the face…I can't explain how it works, but she used it on me once when I needed to stay up all night…"

Tyler watched her face closely. She was lying and he knew it, but since he couldn't fathom another explanation himself…at least one that did not involve the supernatural…he decided to let it go. "Okay, then…so…why don't you go grab a few hours of sleep…or see if Bertie can *refresh* your cheeks, too!"

"Hmmm…" Amanda pursed her lips together and looked at him through half-closed lids. "I'm thinking there is a possibility that you don't believe the explanation I just gave you, but…I don't have the energy to argue back right now, so…will you be here when I wake up?"

Tyler shook his head. "Probably not, Amanda. I'm going to get a bite to eat, but remember…I have to meet with Abbott before seven o'clock tonight. I want to check on Sam and Spartacus, too. They were supposed to be training Czar today, and I don't really trust Bubba and his crew not to use Sam before the fight. I'll try to come back later tonight if I can."

"Okay, then…but don't worry about Sam…trust me, he can take care of himself." Amanda smiled and yawned. "Be careful, Tyler…don't do anything stupid. I won't be there to have your back, you know." She yawned again and shook her head slowly. "Tell the angels that I'm going to lie down for a little while, and I'll see them in a few hours." She opened her door and ambled slowly across the parking lot and up the stairs to her room. She could hear Buster scratching at the door before she unlocked it. He bounced into her arms when she entered the room and gave her hundreds of puppy kisses. "Hey, sweet fella…oh…I missed you too, yes I did, but…you're going to have to use your pee pads for the next few hours. Come on…take a little nap with mama…"

Tyler took a few moments to enjoy the view of Amanda making her way up the long staircase to her room. He waited until she closed her apartment door before he exited his truck and walked to the café. He couldn't help but wonder if what Amanda said had any truth to it, or if she had simply been rambling; but, he found himself giving second thoughts to her reticent reference to the workers of the Heavenly Grille being *angels*! Tyler exhaled deeply before he opened the café's door. "Well, that would certainly explain a lot of things…" he sighed.

The first person he saw was Bertie standing at the counter, in animate conversation with one of the truckers. The halo headband she always wore bounced happily atop her head.

CHAPTER 29

Tyler Reports to Little John

It was a little after four o'clock when Tyler left the Heavenly Grille Café to return to the Abbott ranch. He had assured Max that the three dogs he and Amanda had delivered to the Foster Farm were already enjoying their newfound freedom and surroundings. They spoke briefly about the newly devised plan to rescue the investigators, and the necessity to move up the time frame for busting the dog-fighting ring. The success of both plans depended greatly on how well an actor Tyler proved to be once he was face-to-face with Little John Abbott again.

Tyler smiled to himself as he pulled out of the café's parking lot. He looked in his rearview mirror and saw that Bertie still stood at the door, waving good-bye to him. He watched as the sun glinted off the corny halo headband, and blinked rapidly to reassure himself that he had not seen the rest of her body become engulfed in a soft, golden glow. He squeezed his mouth, hard, between his thumb and forefinger. "Great…now I'm hallucinating…goes to show you the tricks your brain can play on you when you go this long without sleep." He took a final glance at Bertie before he turned left onto the highway. The glow that he thought he had seen was gone, so it was easy to convince himself that it had simply been the late afternoon sun and shadows that had made Bertie's body appear to emanate a golden light. "Maybe I should have asked for another one of her *refreshment* sessions..."

Tyler drove under the speed limit the entire way back to the Abbott ranch, to give himself some time to think about everything that had happened within the past week...Spartacus running away last Friday night, meeting Amanda Turner on Monday, finding Sam sitting on the highway on Tuesday, Spartacus returning to the ranch on Wednesday, witnessing the resurrection of a dead dog and learning that Sam could be an *angel* dog, learning the true identity of the two cousins beaten and locked in a tiny cabin on the Abbott ranch, and...rescuing another three bait dogs who looked amazingly more healthy on Thursday than they had the day before.

"Damn..." he sighed. "Ever since Amanda came into my life, everything seems to be on fast forward." He was talking to himself, but he needed to do this in order to mentally sort through these past events. "I feel like I've known her all my life, but, hell...it's only been, what...*FOUR* days...not only does she have me believing that we're going to be married one day...but she now has me wondering if an ordinary café, located in the middle of nowhere, is run by angels..."

The sound of a blaring horn jolted his attention back to the road. The driver of that car looked irritable when he honked at him a second time and shared an obscene finger gesture when he sped around Tyler's truck. Tyler looked down at the speedometer; he was surprised to see that he had only been going 30 MPH in a 55 MPH zone. He rubbed the bridge of his nose and lifted his shoulders in a shrug. "Sorry..."

It was almost five-thirty before Tyler finished up at the

Econo Lodge. He had to go dumpster diving to retrieve the keys to the rental car, but he was lucky that the bin had been fairly empty and he had been able to locate the keys before anyone saw him digging around in the dumpster. He used the eraser/door opener that Amanda had used earlier to open the door to Room 109, wiped down any areas that he and Amanda may have touched, and loaded all the men's personal belongings into the trunk of the rental car. He drove his own truck two blocks down the street and parked it in the parking lot of a busy diner, and walked back to the motel to retrieve the rental vehicle.

Although the cool air felt comfortable against his sweating skin, Tyler could not suppress the shiver that traveled up and down his spine when he thought about what he had to do next. He used the 20-minute ride back to the Abbott ranch to gather his thoughts. Max had advised him to have Sam with him whenever he talked to Little John; even though Tyler could not fathom *why,* he decided that it might not be a bad idea after all. Sam might be able to provide enough of a distraction from the conversation to enable Tyler to actually pull off the performance.

He pulled in to the Abbott ranch and drove directly to the training area. Several crew members were there, loading the bodies of dead-to-almost-dead bait dogs into one of the dump trucks. Tyler cringed when he heard a weak yelp come from a large shepherd that was the last dog to be tossed into the truck. "Dear, God..." he whispered, "Please let this all be over with soon...please be with these dogs, Lord...welcome them Home and make them healthy and whole again..."

Bubba watched Tyler pull alongside the dump truck. He removed his cap and spit a wad of chewing tobacco onto the hood of the rental car. "What are you doing with that car, Jones? Clint said you were supposed to dispose of it...he ain't gonna be happy to see that you couldn't handle a simple task like that."

Tyler fought the urge to drive his fist into the fat man's gut. "I didn't get that order from Clint, so that's no real concern of his…or yours, Bubba. What's going on here?" He looked over at the cages that held Spartacus and Sam, and was immediately relieved to see them both still there.

"What the hell does it look like?" Bubba sneered and spat another wad; this one almost hit the toe of Tyler's boot. "While you've been out taking it easy today, some of us have been training Czar and getting him ready for his fight tomorrow night."

Tyler looked over at the dump trunk before one of the crew raised the tail gate. He estimated there to be at least a dozen bodies piled on top of one another. He saw several bags of quicklime in the bed of the truck, too. "The pit is getting full again…" he said, trying to fight the lump that had formed in his throat.

"We'll use the quicklime for now," Bubba retorted. "We'll have plenty of time this weekend to burn down what's in there...don't suppose you want to come help us with that, do you, pretty boy?"

Tyler stared back, in silence, long enough for Bubba to have the good grace to snort and leave with the other workers. "Stupid, red-neck…" he grimaced as he watched the dump truck barrel down the dirt road toward the burning pit. He took a deep breath and walked the hundred yards to the cages that held the two black pittie mixes. He couldn't help but wonder about the similarity between the two animals. Sam was the larger of the two, no doubt; he outweighed Spartacus by a good twenty pounds. Other than their weight and the battle scars that Spartacus wore, the only difference between the two dogs was their eyes. He knelt down in front of their cages and reached his hands in to pet both dogs. He looked into the eyes of Spartacus and saw a life time of pain, abuse, and sadness. He looked into the eyes of Sam and saw hope, love, determination, and…Tyler shook his head and looked more intently at Sam.

The *angel* dog's eye color changed quickly from a brown-black, to an amber-gold, and back to a brown-black; and, Sam appeared to be *smiling* at him!

□ □ □

"I may do a lot of things," the dyed blond with heavy makeup snarled, "But, you can't pay me enough money to do *that*!" She slung her pocket book over her shoulder, while simultaneously buttoning-up the shear white blouse that she wore. The cooler October air provided sufficient evidence that she wore nothing beneath the top. "I've been hearing stories from some of the other girls, about you, John Abbott...you can bet your sweet ass that nobody else will be stupid enough to ride out here to service your sick needs!"

The door handle was jerked from Tyler's grasp; the dyed blond bolted in front of him and ran to her car. She looked back at Tyler and said, "You're crazier than he is if you have anything to do with that sicko!"

Sam sat at Tyler's side but turned to watch the woman leave. *"Evil deeds spurn evil results...whatever did you expect, lady?"* He looked up at Tyler and nudged him forward.

Tyler could have sworn that the dog was smiling *again*!

Little John's arrival at the front door caught Tyler off guard. He never heard the big man approaching.

"Jones," he said, looking at his watch. "You made it...with fifteen minutes to spare, no less. Come on in...wait a minute...why is that dog with you?"

Tyler looked down at Sam and fought the urge to rub the dog's head. He motioned toward the rental vehicle, where Spartacus sat in the driver's seat, waiting patiently. "I thought I'd get someone to drive me back to town to get my truck, and then take these two to the woods...to do some hunting...killing wild game really seems to stir up a dog's juices before a big fight."

"Really...to *hunt*?" Little John shook his head as an indication to ignore Tyler's explanation. He motioned toward the rental car. "Your instructions were to get rid of that car..." He turned to walk away. "Get in here and tell me what you found out about those two *cousins*...and chain that mutt up outside."

Sam arose and stood proudly. He uttered a single, low growl and strutted into the house. His nails clicked softly against the slate flooring in the foyer.

Little John turned around abruptly and said, "I told you to chain him up outside..."

Sam took two steps forward and growled again. He bared his teeth and took two more steps toward Little John.

Tyler hooked the dog's collar with the thick leash he had brought with him. "Sorry, Boss...I didn't want to leave him alone in the car with Spartacus, and I didn't want to take the chance of him breaking free of the leash if I chained him outside. I've got control of him. He won't bother you."

Abbott grunted and moved his hand to the side holster that was always at his hip. "Trust me, boy. I know how to control him myself if I need to." He sat down in one of the two large sitting chairs provided in the foyer area. "Sit down, Jones...I've been waiting for your report." He looked at his watch again. "You believe in cutting it close, don't you?"

Tyler swallowed hard and prepared to present the information that his father and the authorities had deemed necessary. They knew that Little John was too smart for anything other than the truth. In fact, they were hoping that the truth would shock him enough to allow them the time they needed to make the final preparations for busting one of the largest dog-fighting rings ever to have formed in the southeastern United States.

Tyler removed the two identification cards from his back pocket and handed them to Little John. "Their real names are Tim Breydan and Ross Taylor, and...they are *not* cousins."

CHAPTER 30

The Attraction Becomes Real

Bubba received the order to dispose of the rental car and to drive Tyler into town to retrieve his truck; chauffeuring Tyler and the two pit-bulls was a task that Bubba had not appreciated, and Tyler felt his silent ire and loathing during the short ride.

Tyler cringed when Bubba dropped him off; he thought, for sure, that Bubba would burn the rubber off all four tires when he pulled out of the parking lot where Tyler had parked his truck. He quickly opened the passenger doors and watch while Sam claimed the front seat, and Spartacus willingly hopped into the smaller back seat. He spent the next five minutes trying to regain his ability to exhale and breathe. He thought he had pulled it off...convincing Little John not to immediately kill the investigators; but, a tiny voice inside him wondered if Little John had not seen through his lies, and had secretly told Bubba to get rid of Tyler and the dogs. He knew that Little John would visit the men in the cabin before the night was over and dangle the truth before their eyes. Tyler wished he could be there for that meeting; he wished that he could somehow reassure Tim and Ross that he had not betrayed them. Most of all, he wanted to tell them not to lose faith, and that help was on the way. However, he knew that he couldn't take the chance of visiting the cabin alone and risking his cover being blown.

He looked at the two dogs and grinned. "Looks like we did it, fellas...we really did it. Now all we have to do is hold steady for another twenty-four hours or so. I don't know about the two of you, but I will be glad for all of this to be over."

Sam looked back and winked at Spartacus who had stretched out across the back seat. Sam leaned his head out of the open window and closed his eyes. *"The breeze feels great, Spartacus. Nothing makes a dog feel so free as to feel the wind blowing in his face and sitting beside someone who loves them. Let me know if you want to change positions..."*

Spartacus lifted his head and cast a sideway glance at Tyler. *"That's okay, Sam...I'm good back here. You know...I really like Tyler...do you think he'll miss me when I'm gone?"*

Sam looked back at his canine friend and tilted his head. *"What makes you think you're going anywhere, my friend?"*

Spartacus wrinkled his brows together and crossed his front paws. *"But I thought that's why I was brought back to the Abbott ranch...I thought I was going to have to be a last sacrifice before the good guys catch the bad guys..."*

Sam poked his head back out the window and closed his eyes again. *"You have nothing to fear, Spartacus. I will be with you the entire time, and...I will not allow any harm to come to you. You have suffered enough in your short life. God will see to it that you live out the remainder of your time here on earth with someone who loves and appreciates you."*

Spartacus lay his head on top of his paws and closed his eyes. *"I sure hope you're right about that, Sam...I sure hope you're right..."*

Bertie and Doug had left the café around seven o'clock to

visit Amos. Amanda had told them about Isabelle Ghent and was looking forward to their feedback about the woman. She had convinced Bertie that she should go along with Doug and not to worry about the customers; Amanda assured her that she and Max could handle the dinner crowd long enough for them to visit Amos.

The dinner crowd had thinned out considerably by eight-thirty, and there were only three of their regular truckers sitting at the counter talking to Max. Amanda was wiping down the tables and topping off the containers of condiments. She smiled when she heard the truckers trying to persuade Max to sing them one of his old-time gospel songs.

Max knew the words to almost every old gospel song of the past fifty years and one of his favorites had always been, "Grandma's Rocking Chair." He held up his hand to silence the burly truckers and said, "I'll be glad to sing for you, fellas, but only if you sing along with me. Wait right here." He disappeared into the kitchen and when he came back out he passed out sheets of paper to the three men sitting at the counter. "I figured y'all might not know all the words, so I keep a supply of my favorites in the back office. Get ready now…"

The truckers all cleared their throats and Amanda sat down in the booth closest to the front door to listen to them. She had heard Max sing this particular song many times before, so she already knew the words.

Max's deep, out-of-tune, baritone slowly began to reverberate throughout the café as he closed his eyes and began the first verse.

The truckers were all a little uncomfortable at first but were quick to join in, with gusto, when it was time for the chorus.

Max, the truckers, and Amanda all joined in for two more rounds of the chorus. None of them had seen or heard Tyler enter the café. He stood at the door with a broad grin on his face. He waited for them to finish and began clapping in earnest. "Man, that sounded great! I love that old song. It's been years since I heard it…as a matter of fact, I think my Grandma was the last one to sing it in our house…brings back some good memories…"

Amanda stood up and walked over to him. She put her arm through his and said, "Well, hey there, you. I was hoping you would find your way back here tonight." She whispered her next words. "How did it go? Did Abbott believe you?"

Tyler looked down at the perky blonde who had hooked arms with him. Something felt so *right* about it…about her. "I'll tell you everything when we can all sit down and talk, okay?"

Amanda nodded. "Sure thing…hey, are you hungry? Max cooked smothered pork chops and fried cabbage tonight. There's a pan of biscuits left over, too. Want me to fix you a plate?"

Tyler nodded. "Sure, thanks…uh…where's Bertie?"

Amanda led him to the counter and introduced him to the three truckers who were finishing their last cup of coffee with their desserts of homemade banana pudding. "She and Doug went to visit Amos, so I volunteered to hold down the fort for her while they're gone."

"*You*?" Tyler grinned.

Amanda planted her hands on her small but shapely hips. "I'll have you know that I know my way around a restaurant. Don't forget that I worked here for a while before I moved back home to become one of Tampa's finest!"

Max had already gone into the kitchen to fix Tyler a plate. He came out carrying a platter filled with three, thick pork chops covered in a rich brown, onion gravy, four biscuits, and a large serving bowl full of steaming, fried cabbage that had been flavored with pepper-bacon. "Have a seat, Tyler. You look like you need this." Max grinned at him and motioned for him to sit in Amos' vacant seat at the counter. "I don't think Amos will mind if you use his seat."

Tyler's mouth had begun to water at the sight of all that food. "Thanks, Max. I didn't realize how hungry I was until

I smelled all of that." He glanced at the large servings of banana pudding that the truckers had just finished. "Do you have any pudding left, or did they eat it all?"

The truckers all laughed and took their final sips of coffee. One of them slapped Tyler on the back and said, "Son, if you haven't learned by now…this place *never* runs out of food. I don't know how Max does it, but there's always plenty for everyone. I've never seen anyone leave this place hungry." He laughed again and shook Max's hand. "Thanks for the food, the company, and the song, Max. We'll see you again on our turnaround."

Max walked the three truckers outside and bid them all a safe trip. The parking lot was empty except for Tyler's truck. He peered through the darkness and saw a familiar dark shape moving stealthily toward him. He crouched down and reached out his hand. "Well…hello there, my friend. How have you been, Sam? Oh look…I see you've brought your friend, Spartacus, back to see us. Well…you two look hungry. Why don't y'all mosey around to the back porch, and I'll fix you a pork chop or two?"

"Thank you, Max," Sam answered back. *"I think we have some time to kill tonight. Tyler is supposed to be taking us in the woods to hunt wild game and whet our appetites for the fight tomorrow. Pork chops sound wild enough for me…what about you, Spartacus?"*

Spartacus licked Max's hand. *"I'm not sure what they are, but I'll try my best to force one…or two…down…"*

Max rubbed both their heads and said, "Okay, then…I'll meet you on the back porch. I'm going to put the CLOSED sign up early tonight. Things have been pretty slow tonight, so it shouldn't hurt closing a little earlier than usual." He watched the two dogs disappear around the corner of the building and sighed. He looked upward into a star-filled sky. "Please keep them all safe, sweet Lord…"

He went back inside and saw Amanda and Tyler sitting next to each other at the counter. Something was definitely happening between the two of them, and Max wanted to give them some time alone. He smiled when he passed them and said, "I'm going to leave you two alone for a while. It seems I have two hungry dogs waiting for me on the back porch, and I need to clean up the kitchen area before Bertie gets back."

Amanda started to get up and said, "I can help you Max…"

He turned back to her and said, "I can handle this, Amanda. Why don't you keep Tyler company until Bertie and Doug return. We can wait until they get back, Tyler, for you to tell us how things went with Mr. Abbott today."

"Okay," Tyler smiled at all the food on his plate. "I'll just keep on eating until everyone is here and then catch y'all up on what's going on."

Max disappeared into the kitchen and Amanda sat back down on the stool beside Tyler. She looked over at him and was surprised to find him staring at her. "What? What are you looking at? Did I spill something on myself?" She looked down at her frilly white apron and adjusted the halo headband.

Tyler put down his fork, smiled, and shook his head. He didn't know when it had happened exactly, but it had happened. This feisty specimen of the female population had gotten under his skin. He knew that he wanted to get to know Amanda Turner…he wanted to know everything about her. "No, you look fine…you look…beautiful…"

Amanda raised her brows and pursed her lips together in a happy-duck fashion. "Well, well…it's about time Mr. Foster. I was beginning to wonder if I was imagining all those feelings I've been having about you."

Tyler leaned closer to her and whispered, "What kind of feelings have you been having about me, Miss Turner?"

"Oh…the kind that I've read about in all those romance novels. Mind you now…I've only *read* about those feelings. I've never really experienced them with anyone…until I met you on Monday. Is it possible to have those feelings about someone you've only known for four days?"

Tyler leaned in closer to her and nuzzled a slight kiss against her neck. "If you had asked me that yesterday, I would have said, absolutely not," Tyler responded.

"But you feel differently today, huh?" Amanda grinned and closed her eyes, enjoying the feeling of his warm lips against her neck. She suddenly shivered and opened her eyes. "Oh..."

Tyler pulled back and stared. "What's wrong? Are you okay?"

"I'm not sure..." Amanda paused. "Maybe you should kiss me again so that...you know...so that I can be sure...that I'm...okay..."

Tyler stood up and pulled her up along with him. He took her face between his hands and smiled. "I don't know what kind of spell you've cast on me, Amanda Turner, but..." he stopped talking as he bent toward her and kissed her softly against her comically-puckered lips. He pulled back and looked down at her. He grinned again at the expression on her face, her eyes still closed and her lips still puckered up for another kiss. He waited for her to open her eyes and said, "Come on, let's go sit at a table and have some dessert. I want you to tell me everything about yourself."

"Everything? Really?" Amanda grinned back at him. She closed her eyes and immediately thought about her parents. *"Oh, I can't wait to tell you both all about Tyler Foster..."*

CHAPTER 31

Little John Confronts the Investigators

Tim Breydan sat on the floor with his back pressed against the wall. Their ropes had been retied shortly after Clint had cut them loose, and Tim's fingers tingled with the loss of circulation. He tried to wiggle his fingers but couldn't tell if they were moving or not. The ropes from the men's feet had been removed earlier in the day so that they could move around the small, dark cabin. He listened to the soft snoring of his fellow investigator. He knew that Ross' injuries were much worse than his own, and he worried that Ross might not last until they could be rescued.

Tim watched Ross' dark form curled up on the floor at his feet. They had both been in and out of consciousness so much over the past thirty-six hours; so, it had only recently dawned on him that they might be able to help each other untie the ropes that cut roughly into their wrists. "Ross? Are you awake?"

There was no answer, but relief spread quickly across Tim's face when he heard the soft intake of breath from his friend. He tried again to stir Ross awake, this time, with a gentle nudge of his foot to the top of Ross' head. "Ross...wake up..."

Ross had been lying on his left side, attempting to keep the pressure off his bruised ribs and lungs. "I wasn't sleeping...can't sleep...it hurts too much to even close my eyes for very long."

Tim thought that his friend's voice sounded weaker than it had since their last conversation. "Well, try to open them long enough to help me with something."

Ross sighed. "Hey...I've got nothing on my calendar...just name it..."

Tim smiled into the darkness and wondered what time it might be; the only thing he was certain of was that this was their second night of darkness. A meal of peanut butter and jelly sandwiches, chips, and bottled water had been delivered to them around dusk, but he didn't think that they had been asleep for more than an hour since then. "Well...it just occurred to me that we might be able to untie the ropes around our wrists...if you could loosen mine, I could get the circulation going in my hands again and get yours off."

Ross groaned into the darkness. "You're assuming, of course, that my circulation is working better than yours, huh, 'ole man? Can't believe we haven't thought to do this sooner...can you come to me? I don't think I can get to a sitting position by myself..."

Tim scooted down the wall, rolled onto his right side, and began to inch his way downward towards Ross. "I'm going to try to position us back-to-back. Try to find my hands and see if you can loosen the knot."

Maybe it was because he was younger, or maybe he just had better circulation than his friend, but Ross still had some sensation in his hands and fingers. It was the rest of his body that was pretty much useless to him. He waited until Tim had positioned himself against his back, and then began to search for the end of the rope that secured Tim's hands. He found the knot and wiggled it; the knot was looser than he expected it to be. It took a full ten minutes, but Ross smiled beneath a groan when he pulled the end of the rope through the knot. "I think I got it…"

Tim's hands were so numb that he was not even aware that the ropes had been loosened. "Okay…let me try to get them off…" He couldn't feel the rope, but he did his best to wiggle his hands around. He didn't feel the rope slide off, so he was startled when he saw his left hand come from behind and drop to the floor in front of him. "My, God…you did it…you did it, Ross…"

Tim maneuvered himself into a sitting position and shook his hands vigorously in front of him. He pumped his fingers in and out to help improve circulation to them. He grinned broadly when healthy coloring returned to the tips of his fingers. "I never knew something could feel so good…" He pushed himself to his knees and turned toward his friend. "Hold on, Tim…I can loosen your ropes now…"

Another ten minutes passed before Tim had assisted Ross to a standing position and they both began to move slowly around the room. It felt so good to feel the blood returning to their other limbs.

"I don't know if moving around is good for you or not," Tim said. "On a scale of one-to-ten, what's your pain level?"

It did feel good to be able to move, without constriction, around the room, in spite of the pain caused by his bruised and broken ribs. "It still hurts to breathe, but I'm thinking that it might just be fractured ribs…if the lungs had been punctured, I don't think I'd still be here…so…that being said…current pain level is around…thirteenish…"

The pair moved instinctively closer together when they heard the key in the padlock. They were standing side-by-side when Little John Abbott pushed open the door. He held a large, battery-operated lantern that filled the small room with bright light. They both shielded their eyes in a reflexive, protective manner. Little John removed the old, kerosene lantern off the hook and replaced it with the battery-operated one. "I'm feeling generous tonight, boys…thought I'd replace that old kerosene lantern with one y'all could use on your own...wouldn't want to risk you burning down my cabin with that old lantern, so couldn't leave you matches for it..."

Clint Meacham had accompanied Little John to the cabin, and started to enter the room with his boss.

"No...you wait outside...I can handle these two." Little John commanded as he kicked the door closed. He hung the lantern on a large nail that had been pounded into one of the load-bearing columns. "Well, well...it took the two of you long enough to figure out how to get out of those ropes...guess you college boys aren't as smart as you want folks to think you are..." The smile on his face never reached his eyes...eyes that bore into the two men with evil intentions. "But...I guess they don't teach you guys too many escape techniques in your animal advocate classes...now, do they?"

To their credit, both men remained expressionless. Ross could feel the tension in Tim's body as they stood side by side. "Don't say anything..." he tried to whisper.

Little John clicked his tongue and shook his head. "It's a small room...I heard that." He took three slow steps toward them. The younger man was slightly taller than he was, but Little John's solid 300-pound body weight gave him all the confidence he needed to know that neither of them was a physical threat to him. "Let's see...you...bent over in pain...you must be...Ross Taylor...and, you..." he pointed at Tim, "You must be Tim Breydan."

Ross tried to sound strong, but the pain in his broken ribs tripped him up. "Well, well...it took you longer than we thought to figure out we aren't really cousins..." He choked on the last of the sentence.

Little John shook his head. "Never believed that story for a minute, but, I didn't want to kill you without at least considering that it might be true. I mean, if it had turned out that you were cousins, then we could've just given you a good ass-kicking and threatened to kill your families if you ever stepped foot on my land again. No...it's too bad for you both that your story wasn't true. Instead…I find out that you are *investigators,* hell-bent on destroying something that brings an awful lot of financial security to this community."

Tim held his temper in check while he watched the big man strut back and forth in front of them. "You mean, financial security to yourself…so, now you know the truth…or at least you think you know the truth. What happens now?"

Little John's stare never wavered. "Who else is in on this with you? Tell me the truth and I just might let you live."

Ross grunted and spat at Little John's feet. "You know damn well that you're not going to let us live…" he gasped for a breath before continuing. "And Hell will freeze over before we tell you anything…"

Little John appeared to ignore the interruption. He directed his question to the older man. "Tell me…is the kid involved in your little operation?"

Tim stared back him with his one good eye. "What kid?"

"The one who was here with me last night…calls himself, Tyler Jones. I've had my suspicions about him, but I have no real proof that he's working with you on this. Hell…he's the one who confirmed your true identities…broke into your hotel room, he did…found your badges. I have some pretty good connections, so it didn't take long to find out who you work for and what you're really doing in our town. There have been a lot of rumors flying around the past few weeks about a possible sting to bust the dog-fighting rings around this area." He moved to within a foot of them and said, "That's *not* going to happen, gentlemen. From what I've been able to find out…your bust is scheduled to happen next weekend…that's why I've moved our fights up a week." He pulled Tim's cell phone from his back pocket and handed it to Tim. "But…to play it safe…you're going to call whoever is in charge and tell them that you haven't been able to find any concrete evidence of illegal dog-fighting in Thomasville. I don't give a damn what they do, or who they bust outside of this area, but you will ensure that they stay away from my city."

Tim stared at the cell phone in his hand and shook his head. He started to say something but Little John's rapid movement startled him into silence.

It happened in a split-second.

Little John lifted his pants leg and pulled an 8-inch hunting knife from a sheath strapped to his ankle. He moved swiftly behind Ross, jerked him backwards toward him, and held the glistening knife to his throat. "Do it, Breydan…do it now…and for your friend's sake…I suggest you be extremely convincing…"

Ross Taylor's agonizing scream echoed throughout the empty cabin.

Bertie walked ahead of Doug as they exited Room 317. She stopped at the elevator and waited for him to catch up to her. "Woo-hoo!" she exclaimed. "Who would ever have thought that our sweet Amos would have found true love in his late seventies!"

Doug ran his hands through his thick, black hair and was oblivious to the approving stares he received from the nurses' station. "I didn't see that one coming, did you?" he grinned at Bertie.

Bertie punched him against his solid bicep. "Ouch! Are you working out? Your arm feels like solid brick."

"Maybe you should take that as a hint to quit punching people, Bertie," Doug laughed as he tousled her short, pixie-styled hair. "I like your new haircut by the way." He received another punch for his conciliatory efforts.

Bertie touched her short hair. "I got tired of trying to keep the curls out of my face; now all I have to do is wet it and go!" She walked a few more steps before stopping and grinning up at Doug. "Seriously, handsome…don't you think those two were made for each other?"

Doug nodded. "It would seem that way…kind of like Amanda and Tyler, huh?"

The elevator doors opened and they stepped inside. Bertie shook her head and said, "Well, if you ask me, I think that relationship is moving *way* too fast."

"But not Amos and Izzie's relationship?" Doug queried.

"That's different and you know it," Bertie retorted and punched him again.

"Why is it different?" Doug knew what her reply would be, but he wanted to hear her say it.

"It's the whole age thing, if you haven't figured it out for yourself, handsome. At Amos' age, he's gotta just grab it while he can because, let's face it, he isn't getting any younger...but, our Amanda, well, she has her whole life ahead of her. She's only twenty-three and we don't really know all that much about Tyler Foster, now do we? I just wish things weren't moving so fast with the two of them."

The elevator doors opened onto the hospital lobby and the two angels stepped out. A little girl and her mother were sitting on one of the couches. The little girl tugged at her mother's shirt and pointed at Bertie. "Look, Mommy...it's that angel who works at the place where we eat sometimes!"

The mother never looked up from the book she was reading, "Uh, huh...that's nice, sweetie..."

Bertie recognized the little girl and winked at her. She and Doug were about to walk through the automatic doors when she looked back at the little girl and made the risky decision to share the "glow" with her. There were only a half dozen people in the lobby and they were all so engrossed in their cell phone conversations, playing games on their tablets, or reading senseless, romantic novels that none of them saw it; but...the little girl saw it.

The little girl waved to Bertie, and Bertie waved back. "See you soon, sweetie!"

Standing outside in the crisp October night, Doug glanced back at the little girl. He noticed how pale she was, something he had missed while they were inside. "Oh, no..."

Bertie sighed. "Yep...afraid so...and her mother can't get her nose out of that damn book long enough to see that something isn't quite right with her little girl. They were there to visit the little girl's grandmother…now, they're waiting for their ride to pick them up."

Doug felt helpless at times like these. He wanted to rush back inside and tell the mother to take a close look at her daughter, to schedule an immediate check-up, but he knew how insane that action would be. Parents today were so busy with their schedules and their own lives, that they often failed to notice the simple, warning signs that surrounded them every day. "I wish we had the power to change things like that…" he whispered.

Bertie shook her head. "You and me both, handsome…you and me both."

Doug opened the van's passenger door and waited for Bertie to get buckled in. "I don't know why I worry about seatbelts…it's not like we really need them…" He went around to the driver's side and took another look at the little girl, through the automatic doors.

A car pulled up in front of the hospital and the mother and daughter walked, hand in hand, to it. A man, who Doug assumed to be the father, came around and opened the back door for the little girl. He watched while father and daughter embraced and continued to watch until the little girl was secured into a booster seat. He saw the man's brows press together and heard him say to the woman, "Bella looks tired...is she feeling all right?" Doug watched the mother turn around and cast a cursory glance at the little girl, at the same time her cell phone rang. She waved her hand at her husband as she turned back around to answer her phone. "Oh, she's fine, don't be such a worry-wart…hello? Oh, hi, Patricia!"

The little girl turned slightly in her seat as the car pulled in front of the café's van. She smiled and waved at Doug as their car went past. Doug lifted his hand to return her wave, and, like Bertie, made the spontaneous decision to present her with another "glow."

The smile on the little girl's face lit up the night.

CHAPTER 32

-Heaven-
Stephen and Regina Discuss their Pasts

Amanda's parents walked hand-in-hand along one of the many golden paths. Heaven contained every species of flowering plants known to man, well over four-hundred thousand of them, and a wide assortment of them lined both sides of the walkway. Regina sighed deeply as she appreciated the horticultural beauty surrounding her…everything from pansies, alyssum, calendula, nemesia, tulips, marigolds, celosia, lobelia, begonias…they were all there, thriving together, and their aromas were tantalizing.

She was lost in her own thoughts when she felt Stephen lean down and kiss the top of head.

"You looked like you were a million miles away," he smiled.

She offered him a cock-eyed wink and answered back, "Well…we are in Heaven…it very well could be a million miles away, right?"

Stephen put on his best scholarly face and said, "Actually, the spiritual instructor I listened to earlier today explained the three heavens to us. I honestly can't say that I remember ever learning that in church; if I did, it didn't stick."

"Well, at least you attended church…" Regina frowned

wistfully. "I'm still amazed that I actually made it to Heaven at all. I mean, my parents never took me to church, and I never felt the inclination to go with you when you went. I hadn't made up my mind, back then, whether or not I even believed in all of this…do you remember?"

Stephen nodded. "Oh, yes…I do remember. I remember praying every night that you would have a change of heart and come to know and believe in God as I did…that never happened, did it?"

Regina shook her head. "No…well…at least not until the moment of impact, when that car crashed into me. I don't remember any pain, but I do remember seeing the most brilliant light I had ever seen in my life…it was so bright I couldn't have opened my eyes if I had wanted to…I don't think I had died at that point."

"What else do you remember," Stephen prodded.

Regina stopped and kneeled down to pick a handful of colorful pansies. "These will look so pretty on the kitchen table…" she spoke softly before standing back up. She turned and looked up into the eyes of the only man she had ever loved. "My eyes seemed to adjust quickly to that bright light and from a distance, I saw…a shadow…the form of a man…at least, I assumed it was a man…coming toward me. I never saw his face…just the outline of his body...but I knew beyond the shadow of a doubt that it was Jesus, Himself, coming toward me. He…held open his arms…and…" Regina took a deep breath before continuing. "It's hard to explain, but the moment He opened His arms, I knew the choice was mine, and mine alone. I could go to Him, or…I could turn away from Him the way I had my entire life on earth. Why He allowed me the choice, I have no idea…I was not a follower or a believer…but, well…I felt this calmness come over me…I knew I was dying, that I would never see you or Amanda again in that life time…I felt something, or someone trying to tug me away from Him, but the pull toward Him was stronger. I reached toward Him and said 'forgive me'…and…He did."

Stephen was quiet for a moment. "The coroner said you most likely died immediately upon impact…"

Regina shrugged and they continued walking toward their mansion. "I guess it's true that you never know what really happens between someone and God in the moments before they die.

I will never fully understand why He believed me in that last, split second, but…I am so thankful that He did. Otherwise…I would never have been able to see you and Amanda again.

"Well…let's hope that it will be a long, long time before Amanda joins us in Heaven!" Stephen laughed.

"Hmmm…" Regina said softly, "Could be sooner than you think if the Rapture comes. If the non-believers on earth had any real clue what was waiting for them here, they would be filling the pews of every church down there."

The couple walked in amicable silence for the next half-mile. Suddenly, Stephen stopped and spread his arms out wide. "Seriously, will you just look at all this! The walls surrounding us are what…two-hundred feet thick…and look at all the stones…jasper, sapphire, agate, emerald, onyx, ruby, chrysolite, beryl, topaz, turquoise, jacinth, and…amethyst…"

Regina laughed out loud. "Well…someone certainly paid attention in class today."

"Indeed I did, love, indeed I did. I want to learn everything there is to learn. But…I'm not sure what the last two stones are made of…they're absolutely brilliant and even more beautiful than the others…" Stephen smiled.

"That's because the last two stones that decorate these walls only exist in Heaven…the people on earth will never see them unless they end up here. So…what else did you learn in class today?"

"Oh," Stephen shrugged, "You know…standard textbook stuff…the twelve gates are actually twelve pearls, with each gate made of a single pearl…the great streets, as well as some of these beautiful walkways, are made of gold, pure as transparent glass…we don't need light because there is no night time in Heaven…the glory of God provides us all the light we need…the gates to Heaven will never be shut…and, nothing impure will ever enter into it…"

Regina nodded and added, "Nor will anyone who does anything shameful or deceitful…only those names written in the Lamb's Book of Life will enter Heaven's gates…"

"Okay," Stephen smiled. "That's enough of lessons for one day. Hey, I'm just thankful that we don't have to worry any more about overdue bills, going to the hospital for treatments, overdrawn bank

accounts…and best of all…there's no complaining, no hate, no crime, no fear, no back-talk…"

"Whoa!" Regina laughed. "You must be forgetting about Bertie!"

"You've got a point," Stephen exhaled. "Lots of sassiness and back-talk there!"

"She is definitely one spirited angel, for sure," Regina nodded. "I'm just thankful that Amanda has her three guardian angels watching out for her. When do you think we'll be able to visit her dreams again?"

"I was actually talking to Martin about that before class this morning. He told me that things in Thomasville will be coming to a head very, very soon."

"And, Sam…" Regina looked worried. "Is Sam alright?"

Stephen raised his brows in mock shock. "You're kidding, right? Have you forgotten that Sam is Amanda's angel dog? No…Sam is fine…he's doing what he was sent there to do. If everything works out according to plan, I expect Sam will be running in these fields with us again in no time at all."

"I miss him…you know…I wasn't there when you got him for Amanda, but I was here when he crossed over. There's a meadow over that hill there," Regina said pointing to the far left. "When animals die, especially the domesticated ones, that's the point where they enter Heaven. I know people on earth say that they cross over the Rainbow Bridge, but there is no such bridge. It's just this wide-open, beautiful meadow with a dense wood line surrounding it. There is a fairly large bridge the covers a gigantic koi pond, and that's usually where the pets' former owners wait for them to step forward out of the wood line. If there's no one waiting for the pet…think of all the abandoned and homeless pets…then they wander off to one side of the field and wait for someone here to come take them to their home. They don't usually have to wait very long."

Stephen listened with rapt attention. "Nobody has mentioned this to me…do you know where this meadow is…can we go there now?"

"Sure we can…come on, follow me…keep up if you can!" Regina challenged her husband as she took off toward a hill that

looked to be about five miles in distance.

"Can't we just teleport ourselves there?" Stephen laughed as he raced to catch up with his wife.

"No we cannot!" Regina chastised him. "Where would the fun in that be? Come on…it's closer than you think!"

The couple laughed all the way to the top of the hill, until Stephen stopped suddenly and looked down at the meadow below them. "Oh…my…God…" he whispered. "Look at them, Regina…"

Regina grabbed his hand and guided him down the hill. Dogs and cats of all sizes and shapes lifted their heads when they heard them approach. Some of them barked, some of them whined, and a large group to the left watched them quietly before lying back down upon the soft grass. Regina pointed to the quiet group. "Those are the ones who never knew love on earth, who never had a home, or a family, or a regular meal, or a safe place to lay their head…there are so many of them, but they will all eventually find a place here…I'm sure of that. The choice is theirs…we cannot pick them…they have to pick us…"

Stephen ran to the center of the field and got down on his knees. Hundreds of family pets ran toward him and offered kisses and their own version of lap dances before running off to continue their play. The quiet pack of pets did not move until Stephen stood up and walked over toward them. "Hello…" he said softly as tears flooded his eyes. He had to remind himself that they were not tears of sadness, but tears of happiness that these abused and abandoned animals would never be alone again. He wished he could take them all home with him, but he remembered what Regina had said…that he would have to wait for them to choose him…

One by one, several dogs and even more cats stood up and stretched. They lifted their noses into the air and decided that this was the person with whom they wanted to share their fur-ever lives…the person they would trust and love…for all eternity…

Regina stood off to the side petting an array of wild and domesticated animals. "Well…all I can say is that it's a good thing the Lord has provided us all with large mansions and plenty of acreage!"

"... that in the dispensation of the fullness of the times He might gather together in one all things in Christ, both which are in heaven and which are on earth—in Him. (Ephesians 1:10, NKJV)

CHAPTER 33

The Night Before

It was almost ten o'clock when the angelic chimes sounded at the front door to the Heavenly Grille Café.

Max sat at the counter with Amanda and Tyler. Tyler was on his third helping of banana pudding, and, although he felt a bit gluttonous, he did not feel guilty about all the food he had consumed. He convinced himself that he was providing his body the energy it needed for what was coming down in less than twenty-four hours from now.

Sam and Spartacus lay on each side of the front door and raised their heads when Bertie and Doug pushed open the door. Buster was curled up close, next to Sam.

"Well, it looks like the gang is all here!" Bertie spoke loudly. She bent down to rub the heads of the dogs. "I hope Max has given all of you plenty to eat..."

Sam's eyes turned to their golden shade as he nudged against Bertie's hand. *"I had forgotten how good Max's cooking was...yes...he fed us plenty..."*

Bertie nodded and whispered, "Well, that's a good thing, but there's plenty more where that came from, so you just let me know if you want some more."

Spartacus whined softly and licked her hand. *"Well…maybe one more of those pork chops before we leave…"*

Buster bounced around Sam's head. *"My favorite part is the bone…I'll take another one of those, please!"*

Bertie ruffled the tops of their heads again and laughed, "You got it, sweet things!" She stood up and made her way toward the counter where Amanda was already sliding off the stool and coming toward her.

"Well…" Amanda grinned. "Tell me…did you meet Izzie? What did you think of her? Is she going to be good for Amos?"

Bertie grabbed Amanda in a fierce hug and kissed her cheek. "You bet your sweet ass, she is!" she laughed.

"BERTIE!" Max scolded at her choice of words.

Bertie walked over to him and punched him against his massive forearm. "Ouch!" she said as she shook her hand. "I swear that both you and Doug are consuming steel and concrete…either that, or I'm losing my touch…that almost hurt!" She looked back at Doug and found him winking conspiratorially at Max. "I saw that, handsome…and if the two of you think you can change me after all these years, then you've both got another thought coming!" She pursed her brows together and stared back at Doug. "Why don't you make yourself useful and pour everyone some coffee?"

Doug shook his head and laughed softly. "Your wish is my command, Bertie." He touched Tyler's shoulder as he walked by. "Max makes great banana pudding, doesn't he?"

Tyler nodded. "Oh, yeah…it only took me three helpings to decide just how great it was."

Everyone returned to their stools at the counter. Bertie motioned for Max to scoot over so that she could sit next to Amanda. "And to answer your question, Amanda…yes…we met Mrs. Isabelle Ghent, and…I have to say…this looks like the real thing. I would venture to say that Amos Brown's single status will soon be coming to an end. Yep…she's a fine woman…Amos is lucky to have found her…"

Amanda took a sip of her coffee and mumbled beneath her breath, "I doubt if luck had anything to do with it..."

Bertie looked her square in the eye and shook her head in silent warning, while casting a sideway-glance toward Tyler. "It would seem that luck and love are in the air..."

Amanda blushed at Bertie's innuendo and smiled back. "Yep, so it would seem..."

Doug poured fresh coffee for everyone and Max stood to his full seven-foot height. "That's good news about Amos. No one is more deserving of love than he is, but...I think Tyler has been waiting for everyone to get here so that he can catch us up on the latest plans to bust the dogfighting ring. Tyler?" He motioned for Tyler to continue.

Tyler pushed the empty dessert bowl away from him and stood up to face everyone. "It took the help of a lot of people, but the bust that was scheduled for next week has been moved up to tomorrow night; the organization has another informant who told them that Little John has moved his fights up to tomorrow night, now that he thinks the bust is scheduled for next week. There will, also, be simultaneous busts taking place in North Carolina, Virginia, Alabama, and Florida. These busts have been in the works for almost a year now. The different agencies have been observing and gathering all the facts and information on everyone involved. They actually all liked the idea of moving the bust up one week...you know, in case word has gotten out that it was supposed to happen next week. I just hate that so many animals have already had to die while waiting for this to happen."

"Have you ever attended one of these fights, Tyler?" Amanda asked.

Tyler exhaled and nodded. "I hate to admit it, but...yes, I have...I've had to since I've been at the Abbott ranch...in order to keep my cover."

Max placed a hand on Tyler's shoulder and nodded. "We won't be there to witness what happens tomorrow night, Tyler, so...would you educate us a little on what Sam and

Spartacus will go through?"

The two dogs moved to stand on each side of Tyler, and Buster begged for Amanda's lap. Tyler flinched slightly when Sam's eyes glowed golden again for a quick second. Once, again, the dog seemed to be smiling at him. He knelt down and wrapped an arm around each dog. "Yeah…sure…" He kissed each dog on the top of their head and stood back up.

"You have to try to put your heads where these dogfighting professionals are…to them, a dog is not a domesticated pet. They are the main source of a $500 million industry. There are currently about 40,000 known dogfighting professionals across the United States. The sport used to be confined to the South, but it has become increasingly popular throughout the entire United States, Russia, Central Asia, and Eastern Europe."

Doug leaned his arms on the counter and folded his fists beneath his chin. "Forty thousand? I had no idea. I'm guessing this is not a new sport, is it?"

Tyler shook his head. "No, it isn't. In fact, the history of the sport in the United States can be traced all the way back to the early 1800s. People began to lose interest in it in the 1930s when their sense of humanity began to kick in, I guess. Anyway, it still continues, even though it is now illegal in all fifty states and in many other countries around the world. It's actually a felony in most states now, and…it is illegal to possess dogs for fighting in all states except for Georgia, Idaho, and Nevada."

Amanda's eyes began to tear up at the thought of how many animals were being abused across the nation. "We need to hear it, Tyler…what's going to happen tomorrow night?"

Tyler pinched the bridge of his nose and closed his eyes for a moment before answering. "Most of the fights in the South abide by what is known as Cajun Rules."

"What? They actually have damn rules for killing these dogs?" Bertie cried out.

Tyler nodded. "Yeah...the rules were created in 1952 by the late G.A. "Gaboon" Trahan...he was actually a police chief in Louisiana. He created a list of 19 rules that cover all aspects of professional dog fights...the last rule even specifies that a referee must organize a rematch if a bout is broken up by the police."

"Can you highlight some of those rules for us, Tyler?" Doug asked quietly. He kept his fists clenched together in order to contain the anger that was building up inside him. It had been many years since he had unleashed his anger upon anyone, so it was probably a good thing that Max had denied him permission to attend the fights scheduled for tomorrow night.

Spartacus' ears perked up and he looked over at Sam. *"I'm not sure if I want to hear this..."*

Sam moved closer to him and leaned his head down. *"It's probably a good thing that Tyler is describing what's going to happen...that way, you won't be caught off guard. I had planned on telling you about it later, anyway...chin up, Champ...I told you...I'm not going to let anything bad happen to you."*

"What about all the other dogs, though..." Spartacus sighed and flopped down on the tiled floor.

Tyler began pacing back and forth. "Okay...the fight will take place on the Abbott ranch. There's a large, secluded clearing in the backwoods. People will have to park their cars in another secluded area and walk about a half-mile to the fighting area. Some of these fights can go on for hours and can be pretty gruesome events, so most people will bring their own lawn chairs. Little John doesn't allow any alcohol at the events and everyone is checked for weapons before they're allowed to enter. Some professionals even allow children to attend these fights, but I guess that's one good thing about Abbott...nobody under the age of sixteen is allowed to view the fights...and they have to be eighteen to place any bets...we're not talking about fifty-to-hundred dollars bets either...the minimum bet for tomorrow night's lowest-ranking fight is set at five thousand..."

"Jesus Christ!" Bertie yelled. "Five thousand dollars to watch two dogs try to kill each other? Now I know these damn rednecks are as dumb as they act!"

For once, Max didn't stop to chastise Bertie's use of foul language. "That is a lot of money..."

Tyler nodded. "Yeah...and, like I said, that's just for the preliminary fights. The minimum betting usually increases with each advancing fight. Fighters across the U.S. will be bringing their best dogs to this fight. The highest bets will probably be on the last two fights of the night."

Amanda crossed her arms tightly beneath her rib cage. "You're talking about Sam and Spartacus, aren't you?"

Tyler nodded. "Spartacus is scheduled for the tenth fight. Since he lost his last fight against Czar, I heard that Abbot will probably pit him against a relatively new champion...that's a dog that has won three fights...from North Carolina. Czar is the standing champion in this area; Abbott wanted to pit Czar against Sam, but the rules state that the two fighting dogs cannot have the same owner, so he'll pick champions from other states for the two of them to go up against. I'm guessing he will save Sam for the last fight."

The night grew late as Tyler went on to describe, in detail, about the size of the ring, the roles of the referee, owners, handlers, and timekeepers; the required weigh-in and washings of the fighting dogs; how the winner is determined; and...what usually happens to the losing dog. It was eleven-thirty when he squeezed his eyes closed and shook his head. "It's late, folks, and I really need to get these two back to their cages so that we can all get some rest before tomorrow night. I just want you all to know that I will be with Sam and Spartacus the entire time and will do everything within my power to keep them both safe."

"When will the authorities step in?" Max asked.

"I don't really know...all I know is that they will be there...some may be part of the crowd, others may be hidden," Tyler said. "It's important that they get as much of the fight on videotape as they can…not only the dogs involved are video-taped, but the spectators, too. The owners of these dogs will be punished, but…so will everyone else who is there watching the fights. That's why they'll probably wait until the very end to make the bust."

"What time does it begin?" Doug lifted his head. The anger was still evident in his facial expression.

"There's no set time yet…that information may not be known until one or two hours before the fights are scheduled to begin. Most of them on Abbott's ranch take place just after dark…" Tyler answered back. "I'm guessing that folks will probably start arriving around seven, inspect the dogs that are scheduled to fight, place their bets…first fight should be ready to go by eight. It could be a long night…"

"I want to be there…" Amanda gushed. "I need to be there…for Sam…"

"**NOOOOO!!!**" came back the simultaneous and unanimous denial from the angels and Tyler.

Amanda flinched and bit hard against her bottom lip. *"Just try and stop me…"* she thought as she glared back with blatant defiance.

Buster felt the tension in his master's arms and jumped down from her lap. He nuzzled in close against Sam's side. *"Geez…I'm mighty glad that I'm too young for this particular adventure!"*

Sam licked the pup's head and said, *"Pups younger than you have given up their lives to this terrible sport, Buster…so, I'm mighty glad you won't be involved either…"*

CHAPTER 34

The Day of the Fight

Amanda had tossed and turned the night before, hoping her parents would come to her in her dreams, but they had not. Instead, her dreams had been filled with gory visions of Sam and Spartacus being torn apart inside a 16-foot by 16-foot ring, with canvas flooring. The yelping and whining from the discarded animals in her dream finally shook her awake at six o'clock. She knew she would not be able to go back to sleep, so she showered quickly, dressed in her oldest, most comfortable jeans and tee-shirt, and took Buster outside, behind the café, to do his business.

She was so deep in thought and worry that she never noticed Doug sitting on the back porch step.

Doug watched Amanda and Buster quietly for a few minutes before he stood up and walked over to the wood line where Buster was already chasing butterflies. "Good morning, Amanda," he spoke softly.

The sound of another human voice unnerved her; she was not expecting anyone to be outside this early in the morning. The sun was just beginning its slow ascent to the east of the café. She jumped and turned around. "Geeeezzz, Doug! You scared the holy crap out of me!"

Doug titled his head before shaking it in denial. "There's no such thing…"

"What?" Amanda puzzled while placing a hand over her heart and catching her breath.

"There's no such thing as *holy* crap…it's all just…*regular*…crap…" his fist covered his mouth to suppress a fake cough and to hide the grin that threatened to spread across his face.

Amanda wrinkled her brows together and shook a finger at him. "If Bertie was here, she'd punch you for that one! What are you doing out here so early? You don't usually check in until later in the day."

Doug could not keep the grin suppressed. "I know, but, there was a crowd waiting in the parking lot this morning, so Bertie opened up a little early. I decided to help out for a while…at least until she ordered me to take a break. I just stepped outside for a quick confabulation," he said, looking upward toward Heaven.

"Confabulation, huh?" Amanda teased as she took his hand and led him back to the steps. She sat down and patted the spot beside her. "That's an interesting word…"

"It means…" Doug began.

"I know what it means, Doug, but most folks today would just refer to it as a *chat*," her voice held a tease-like quality to it.

"Well, young lady…you have to remember that I died in 1953, and in 1953…it was a common word in my family's household. My Dad, especially, loved to say it. He said he liked the way it rolled off his tongue."

"You know," Amanda smiled. "I know a little about Bertie's background, but, you've never talked much about your own. Neither has Max for that matter, but Bertie filled me in on his Gladiator status."

Doug smiled and shrugged. "I'm an open book, Amanda. What would you like to know?"

"Well..." Amanda began slowly. "One thing has always intrigued me. So...it's like...Max has been dead a gazillion years and even Bertie died over a hundred years ago. You say you died in 1953, and that was like..." she wrinkled her nose as she did the math in her head, "only sixty years ago..."

"And you figured that out without a calculator...I am impressed, young lady!" Doug laughed.

"Don't make fun of me...what I'm getting at is...if you've only been dead for sixty years, don't you ever worry that you might run into someone who...you know...might recognize you?"

"That was a concern for Martin, yes..."

"Martin is the mentor guy...in Heaven, right?" Amanda's curiosity was heightened.

"You could call him that, yes..." Doug smiled down at her. "You have to remember...I was only twenty when I died. This body that I was given in Heaven," he placed his hands on his chest, "Well, it's not the same body I had when I was twenty...and, it's true...there could be an eighty-year old classmate or comrade out there somewhere who might still remember what I looked like in 1953, but the chances of that happening are pretty slim; slim enough that Martin decided to take a chance on me for the assignment to the Heavenly Grille."

"What about your parents? Did you have any brothers or sisters?" Amanda was eager to learn more about Doug's past.

"Yes, as a matter of fact, I did have parents!" Doug grinned.

Amanda took a page from Bertie's book and punched him hard against his shoulder. "Dang it! Bertie was right...that's like hitting a concrete wall!"

"Sorry," Doug said as he took her wounded hand and kissed the top of it. "I was born on January 1, 1933...my parents were Joseph and Camille..."

"Last name?" Amanda queried.

Doug shook his head firmly. "No...angels do their best to never use last names...they no longer really matter to us, and it's probably best if you mere mortals were not privy to that information. Anyway, let's see…I was the youngest of three children…I have two older sisters, Emily and Rachel."

"Were y'all close?" Amanda asked. "That's one thing I always wished for…a brother or sister; I think it would have made losing my parents so much easier if I had not been an only child."

Doug nodded. "I know what you mean…yes, the three of us were very close. Our entire family was close; there were no rebellious teenagers in our family. The Korean War was going on when I finished high school, so I walked downtown one Saturday afternoon and enlisted in the Army. I saw two years of heavy action, and was scheduled to return home at the end of July 1953."

"What happened...or is it too painful to talk about?" Amanda touched Doug's shoulder.

He placed his hand on top of hers and shook his head. "No, those memories are not painful for me at all. It was…July 16, 1953…and it was the last day of battle for what history has written about as the Battle of Pork Chop Hill…the enemy did not kill me…friendly fire did…"

"Oh, no…" Amanda slapped her hand against her mouth.

Doug bowed his head and closed his eyes. "It was a young soldier by the name of Charlie; he had only been on the ground for four months and had not seen any real action. My platoon got caught in the cross-fire between the enemy and another American platoon. Charlie panicked when I stood up to run after another comrade who had been shot. He tried to run after me, but he slipped and fell. When he fell, his finger pulled reflexively against the gun's trigger, and…I was shot in the back…the bullet pierced my lungs."

Tears were streaming down Amanda's cheeks. "I'm sorry I asked, Doug...it must be hard for you to have to relive that..."

"No, not at all, Amanda…not at all, because, you see…my life did not really begin until the day I died. Heaven…it's…"

Max cracked open the back door and smiled at the duo

leaning against each other. "Why don't you save that story for another time, Doug? Good morning, Princess. If you don't mind, I need the two of you to come inside and help Bertie out…I've never seen so many people here so early in the morning…lots of strange faces, too…"

Amanda wiped away a tear and allowed Doug to help her up. She smiled at Max and said, "Good morning, Max…sure thing, I'll be glad to help out."

"Strange faces?" Doug pondered. "I wonder if some of them are here for the fights tonight?"

The crew at the Abbott ranch had all been assigned their specific duties to ready the ranch for the upcoming fight; so, by noon, Tyler found himself all alone in the training area with the dogs. He suspected that Little John might be at the cabin, and, he knew that Clint was overseeing the set-up for the arena. He had overheard Clint instructing some of the crew on how to set animal traps in the woods that surrounded the fight area. Yellow taping would be put up and spectators would be told to stay within the confines of the marked areas. Bubba and the rest of the crew were all busy doing the manual labor needed for the night's fight, which also included the unpleasant duty of disposing of the bait animals.

Tyler looked around to make sure he was alone with the dogs. He looked at their empty water bowls and quickly grabbed a hose and began to fill all their bowls with cool water. It was one thing not to feed them for two days leading up to a fight, but Tyler knew that the dogs needed water. He watched as every bowl was quickly drained, erasing evidence that Tyler had broken any rules…all bowls, except for one.

Tyler walked over to Sam's cage and bent down until he was looking the large black pit squarely in the eye. "You need to drink the water, fella…please…"

The dog appeared to be smiling at him again and Tyler fell on his butt when Sam's eyes glowed a brilliant gold.

"My, God…it's true, isn't it? What Amanda told me about you…you're not a real dog, are you? That's why you don't need food or…water." He watched as Sam's eyes returned to their normal color. "Man, I'd give anything if you could talk to me…tell me that everything is going to go according to plan tonight…that Spartacus will be okay…"

Spartacus was in the cage next to Sam and barked excitedly when he heard his name.

Tyler reached inside the cage and rubbed the back of Spartacus' neck. "I'd give anything if you didn't have to fight again, Spartacus. I can't believe that God saved you once only to send you back here to die tonight…"

Tyler never heard Sam's cage door open, but he immediately sensed the presence of something behind him. He spun around sharply, still on his knees, and fell backwards on his butt again when Sam moved slowly toward him. "How the hell are you doing that!" Tyler practically shrieked.

Sam stopped and lay down at Tyler's waist. He lifted his head and saw the perplexed look on the young man's face and grinned again, showing all his teeth this time. He stared intensely at Tyler and decided to transport his thoughts to the man who might one day marry Amanda. *"We are all creatures of God, Tyler Foster…and He will be here beside each and every one of us tonight…you have to know that Amanda will not listen to what she was told…she will do everything in her power to be here tonight, and…you must protect her…will you do that, Tyler Foster…for me?"*

Tyler could not swallow the lump that had formed in his parched throat, so he just nodded in dumfounded agreement.

Sam stood up and stretched each of his hind legs in turn. *"That's good…I knew I could count on you…now, why don't you fill up all these bowls one more time…"*

CHAPTER 35

Friday Night Fight Begins

The rest of the day went way too quickly for Tyler's liking. He had managed to get away for a couple of hours and went to the café to check on Amanda; he needed to know that she would do as she was told, and stay away from the fight that night. He knew that he would have his hands full with what he needed to do; Amanda would be a distraction that he simply did not need tonight. After sharing a late lunch with her and discussing his father's plan in more detail, he felt relatively reassured that she would remain at the café until the fight was over and Tyler returned to her.

Amanda, on the other hand, spent the remainder of the day helping the angels around the café, and doing her best to block out her thoughts and plans so that Max could not read her mind. It was best if the angels did not suspect her of any intentions to get involved. She felt like she had pulled it off when she untied her apron at six o'clock and told the angels she was going to take Buster for a long walk, shower, and get some rest before Tyler returned to them. She told them to let her know, immediately, if they heard from Tyler before she did. She knew they would be busy with the dinner crowd by the time she was able to slip away without them seeing her.

Little John made his final inspection of the fighting arena and surrounding areas at five-thirty, and called his main contact to notify all fighters and spectators of the exact location and time for the fight. He drove to the training area and walked among his prized champions, dragging his truck keys against their cages as he strolled past each one. Teeth bared and the dogs lunged at the intrusion; Little John smiled in satisfaction…until he came to the cages that held Spartacus and the newest addition. Spartacus did not snarl and bare teeth as the other fighter dogs had done; instead, he inched as far backward in his cage as he could get, tucked his tail between his legs and cowered in fear. Little John shook his head and said, "Tonight will be your last fight, and I pity the fools who place their bets on you…"

Sam, in direct contrast to Spartacus, stood erect and moved as close to the front of his cage as he could get. *"You're right about one thing…it will be his last fight…it will be all of their last fights…"*

Little John stared down at the large, black dog that seemed to be staring back at him with…what…defiance? He squatted down and returned the dog's glare. "We still need a name for you, don't we? Well, let's see…Michael Vick had a champion fighter named Lucas, but…no, that doesn't suit you. How about…Duke or, Zebo, Zeus, Frisco, Matrix…?" Little John suddenly slammed the front of Sam's cage with his bare fist, but the dog never flinched; it just continued to look at him with disdain and defiance. "Well…" Little John spoke softly. "That's it…we'll call you Defiance…and, since I'm still not sure how you're going to perform out there tonight against the champion from North Carolina, I probably shouldn't put you as the last, star performer, but…you will be, and, if you know what's good for you, you will win your fight…" He kicked the cage with his boot as he stood to leave. He walked past the cage that held Czar, the champion he had recently purchased, and the one that Spartacus had lost his last fight against. The dog growled at him when he knelt down, and Little John smiled proudly. "I have no doubt you will win your match, Czar…it will be a long time before you meet the burning pit…"

As Little John's truck pulled away from the training area, Spartacus looked over at Sam and said, *"I don't think he likes you very much…"*

Sam offered his best look of defiance and grinned back at his cell mate. *"I didn't come here to make friends…"*

Tim Breydan and Ross Taylor limped nervously around the small, dark cabin. Ross was still in severe pain from his bruised and broken ribs, but he was standing more erect than he had been since his initial beating. "It's a good thing I'm not claustrophobic…" he mumbled. "You'd think they would have put at least one window in this damn cabin." He glanced at the small space between the floor and the bottom of the door. "Sun's going down…"

Tim had been walking the floor and praying. He kept rehashing the phone call that Little John had forced him to make the night before, while a knife had been held against Ross' neck. His supervisor had answered on the third ring and had been concerned that he had not heard from the two men since their regular check-in on Tuesday night. The call lasted less than three minutes, but Tim felt confident that he had convinced his boss that the dog-fighting ring in Thomasville was not on a large enough scale to be included in the scheduled bust for the following Friday. He told him that they had discovered a larger operation, located closer to Albany, Georgia, that they might have time to include in the sting. He ended the conversation with assurance that he would check in again before the weekend was over.

Ross stopped walking and nudged Tim lightly against the shoulder. "Why do I have the feeling you haven't heard a word I've said?"

Tim opened his eyes and looked over at the younger man who had become a good friend to him. "Sorry…I was…"

"Praying?" Ross grinned. "How's that working out for you, buddy?"

Tim smiled back. "We're still alive, aren't we?"

Ross nodded and said, "Yeah…that was some pretty good acting on your part last night when you called McRoberts and convinced him that the Abbott operation was too small-time to waste our time on. Are you sure he believed you?"

"Pretty sure, yes…" Tim answered back. "There was something strange about his voice, though."

"What do you mean? You didn't say anything about that after Abbott left last night."

Tim shook his head. "I don't know, really…it may be nothing…I mean, it was a little hard to concentrate on the conversation while seeing that blade press into your neck…but, I keep re-hashing the call, and there was something just a little *off* in the way Mr. McRoberts sounded…I don't know…something in the *tone* of his voice. It was almost like he was trying to tell me something without actually telling me something…"

"Well, that makes perfect sense!" Ross tried to laugh but the sharp pain stopped him short. "Hey…have you noticed that nobody has been here today? I mean, it's almost dark, and no one has brought us any food or water."

Tim nodded. "I know…and the dogs have been howling and barking more than usual, it seems. Would be nice to have some water, though…"

"Well, look on the bright side," Ross quipped. "No water means we won't have to piss in that nasty hole for a while. Man, that thing is just gross…the smell around it is strong enough to make you pass out."

Tim held up a finger to his lips and motioned for Ross to look toward the front door.

A shadow walked in front of the door, disappeared for a moment, and then returned…a shadow with four legs.

□ □ □

The crowd had settled into a dull roar by seven-thirty, the referee was announced, and twenty-four dogs had been paired off by size and weight. Only one owner had to forfeit his $1,000 down payment because his dog was overweight; a replacement dog had been quickly added to the fighting list. Bets for the first fight were being placed and monies collected. The spectators were in their folding chairs or on the bleachers provided; some preferred to remain standing as close to the ring as they were allowed to be. The handlers for the two dogs matched for the first fight flipped a coin to see who would wash their opponent's dog first. The winner of the flip was provided two towels, baking soda, milk, and soap to wash their opponent's dog; this was done to make sure the animals' coats were not covered with any slick substance or poison. Each handler was required to bare their arms to the elbow and use the same warm water to wash and rinse the opponent dog.

After the dogs were cleaned, a timekeeper was chosen, and, the two dogs were placed in their respective corners behind the scratch lines. Their faces were turned away from each other. The spectators grew quiet and waited for the referee to shout, "FACE YOUR DOGS!" The handlers then turned their dogs and positioned them to stand full head and shoulders between their legs. The two dogs growled and pulled, but their handlers held them firmly until the referee shouted, "LET'S GO!"

The handlers released their dogs and the first fight between two new fighters began. Both dogs were young, less than two years old, and this was the first fight for both of them. The crowd cheered when the white boxer immediately jumped on the brown cur-mix and went for the throat. He missed but still managed to rip away one side of the cur's cheek. The cur-mix jumped up and turned his head and shoulders away. Its handler claimed the "turn" and the referee made the call. Each handler returned their dog to their assigned corner and turned their faces away so that they, once again, faced the corner. Twenty-five seconds passed and the referee called out again, "FACE YOUR DOGS!" The handlers turned to show their dogs. Five more seconds passed until the referee shouted, "LET'S GO!" Since the cur-mix was the first fighter to "turn", he would be required to cross the scratch line first. He did, and for the next 20 minutes, the two dogs took turns trying to destroy each other. By the time the first match ended, the white boxer had been declared the winner, and the brown cur-mix was shot in the head by its owner and dumped in the disposal pile.

Tyler couldn't watch the match, especially the end, when he knew that the losing dog would most likely be beaten or destroyed by its owner, so he walked among the spectators. He glanced at the crowd, nonchalantly, and tried to determine which of them, if any, might be law enforcement or animal control investigators. If they were in attendance, they managed to blend perfectly into the crowd. He glanced into the wood line and tried to distinguish any unusual sounds or movements. There weren't any. He turned his Atlanta Braves cap so that it was facing backward on his head and exhaled softly. He continued walking through the crowds until the fifth fight ended; it was then that he saw Little John and Clint Meacham watching him. It only took one look into the cold, steely eyes of John Abbott for Tyler to realize something. He didn't know how or when it had happened, but he suddenly knew that his short acting career was over. *"Holy crap..."* he panicked. *"They know..."*

Amanda's plan had gone more smoothly than she had hoped, and she had sat snugly, through the first five fights, wedged between two, burly rednecks from Alabama. She had been watching Tyler intensely and saw the exact moment that panic crossed his handsome face. She turned to see what had caused his panicked expression, and recognized the man that Tyler had described to her…Little John Abbott. It had to be him. She watched as Tyler backed slowly away and disappeared into the dark wood line. She turned back in time to see Little John say something to the wiry, older man who stood beside him. The man spit on the ground, grinned widely, and nodded before moving off in the same direction as Tyler.

"Not, no…but Hell, no!" Amanda thought as she pushed and squirmed away from her two bookends, jumped off the short bleachers, and dashed into the same wood line into which Tyler had just vanished.

CHAPTER 36

Change of Plans

Tyler pulled a small flashlight from his back pocket and made his way quickly through the woods toward the cabin. It was only nine o'clock, and the plan had been for him to wait until the eleventh fight between Spartacus and the champion fighter from South Carolina; however, Tyler was certain that Little John was suspicious of him now, and he did not want to take the chance that Clint Meacham would get to the two investigators before he did.

He moved slowly through the woods and kept his flashlight toward the ground in order to avoid stepping on the any of the traps the crew had set throughout the woods. He knew what to look for…three medium sized stones to the side of the trap which would be covered with leaves and pine straw. He had just passed a sixth trap when he heard a slight rustling of leaves about a hundred feet behind him. He turned around quickly and did not see anyone, but the sound of rustling leaves was getting closer. He moved to hide behind a large oak tree and squatted down in attack mode. The rustling grew louder; whoever was following him was almost upon him.

Tyler assumed that it must be Clint Meacham and he knew that he would have to stop him. He waited until the rustling of the leaves was less than five feet from him. He raised himself up to a half-standing position, and head-butted Clint in the stomach, knocking him to the ground. He quickly pressed his left hand against Clint's throat and raised his right fist to pummel the older man's face.

"Tyler Foster! Don't you dare hit me or I will kick your butt all the way back to Brooksville!"

Amanda gasped for air but still managed to shove her right knee deep into Tyler's groin. "Now, get off me, you big oaf!"

Tyler groaned and grabbed his manly jewels as he began to roll off her. "Damn you, Amanda…" he croaked. "What the hell are you doing here…I told you to stay away tonight…"

Amanda completed the push off, stood up, and began brushing the leaves off her clothes. She held her stomach; it hurt, but wasn't anything she couldn't endure. "I don't take kindly to being told what to do, Mr. Foster…that's something you had best learn about me. Besides…I thought I might be able to help."

"There are plenty of law enforcement and animal control reps to help with this, Amanda." Tyler had rolled onto his back, but was now attempting to sit up. He saw her holding her stomach. "I'm really sorry…are you okay?" He shook his head. "Never mind…you've got to get out of here…*now*. I can't be sure how any of this is going to go down tonight…it could go either way. Please…go back to the café. These woods aren't safe…they're full of animal traps…I can't believe you didn't step into one of them already…"

Amanda released her stomach and held out a hand to help him up. "I'm fine…a little head-butt isn't going to stop me, and…why does everyone forget that I *am* a cop! Do you honestly think that I can't find my way through a bunch of dark woods? These idiot rednecks and their ridiculous animal traps are so conspicuous and predictable. I'm assuming you're talking about the pile of leaves with the rocks beside them, right?"

Tyler took her offered hand and managed a semi-erect position. He exhaled and shook his head. "I don't even want to know how you knew that..." He stopped mid-sentence when he heard more rustling of the leaves, coming from the direction of the fighting arena. "Come on...we've got to get to the cabin...I only hope it's not too late..."

The cabin was located about two miles from the fighting arena. Tyler and Amanda continued to tread their way carefully through the dense woods. They never looked back; if they had, they would have seen that it was not a two-legged creature that followed closely behind them.

The lantern inside the cabin offered a dull glow for the two men who had been trapped inside it for three long days.

Ross shook the lantern. "Guess we should have been more conservative in our use of this thing, huh?"

Tim moved closer to the door. "I don't think we're going to need it much longer anyway..."

"What do you mean?" Ross asked as he moved slowly toward the door.

"Listen..." Tim spoke softly. "Can you hear it?"

Ross put his ear to the door and shook his head.

"Listen again," Tim said. "It sounds a long way off, but..."

Ross nodded. "Sounds like a cheering crowd...yeah...I hear it now, but...what do you think is going on? The fight is scheduled for next Friday..."

Tim looked at his friend and co-worker. He smiled sadly. "My guess is...fights are subject to change...I would be willing to bet that Abbott moved the fight up a week, maybe...to throw the agency off...to give himself plenty of time to get rid of all the evidence before next Friday..."

"Son-of-a-bitch..." Ross growled. "That means..."

Tim started to place a hand on his friend's shoulder, but stopped when he heard the sound of a loud engine pull up outside the cabin. He waited until the engine shut off, and one door creaked open and quickly slammed shut again. "That means our time may be up..."

"Not if I can help it..." Ross gritted his teeth and quickly shut off the lantern. "They may not have considered it when they left us this lantern, but, they also provided us a weapon. Quick, Tim...go stand in the corner...I'll hide behind the door..."

"You're too weak, Ross...let me do it..."

"No!" Ross whispered loudly. "Your conscience may not allow you to do what has to be done. If you think my ribs have taken a beating, buddy, you have no idea what all this has done to my conscience. Now, go! Get in the corner!"

The key turned in the padlock and Clint Meacham kicked open the door with his boot. He was surprised to see the room in complete darkness, especially since he knew they had provided the men with a lantern. "Damn, fellas...don't tell me the battery has run down already..."

Ross moved silently from behind the door and swung wildly into the darkness. He could make out Clint's silhouette but could not judge how far away he was. He missed Clint's head by a few millimeters and was more than a little shocked at the older man's reflexive response.

Clint felt something heavy whiz past his head and heard it crash into the door behind him. He sensed, rather than saw, a movement to his left. He turned and threw a hard punch directly into the stomach of his attacker. He heard more movement off to his right, turned, and fired his gun into the darkness.

The firing of the gun was sloppy, but the bullet somehow managed to hit its target. Both men fell heavily to the floor and groaned. Clint pulled out a flashlight and moved it around the room. "Stupid sons-of-bitches..." he muttered as he backed out of the door and moved toward his truck where he still had the old, kerosene lantern. He brought it back inside the cabin and lit it.

Ross Taylor lay in a crumpled pile gasping for air. Tim

Breydan lay in another crumpled pile, pressing both hands against his stomach. Blood seeped quickly between his fingers as he stared back at Clint for a moment…before closing his eyes and passing out.

Tyler and Amanda were still a mile away from the cabin when Tyler stopped abruptly, causing Amanda to bump into his backside.

"What are you stopping for?" Amanda asked hurriedly. "Come on, we've got to get to that cabin."

"You didn't hear that?" Tyler asked.

"Hear what?" Amanda moved in front of him. "Come on, let's go!"

Tyler grabbed her arm and pulled her back toward him. "I could have sworn I heard a gunshot," Tyler steered her behind him. "Sounded like it came from the direction of the cabin…"

"But, who…" Amanda began, but stopped.

Tyler shook his head. "I don't know…but come on…stay behind me…we've got to get to that cabin."

They were running so fast that neither of them was aware that they were being followed.

CHAPTER 37

Clint Takes Matters In His Own Hands

Clint's hands shook slightly. He knew, without a doubt, that Little John would not be happy about what had just happened; but, he had done what he had to do. His breathing was heavy and labored as he paced nervously around the room. Neither of the downed men had made a move to stand, and Clint was pretty sure that the one he shot was either dying or already dead.

He had dropped the key to the padlock during his scuffle with the man at the door, and he knew that he couldn't leave the men unattended in an unlocked cabin. He continued his nervous pacing and finally made a decision. He holstered his gun and moved to the man closest to him...the one crumpled on the floor behind the door. He grabbed the man's arm and heard a low moan coming from him. "Well, good, you ain't dead yet..." He turned the man over on his back and pulled him into the door way. There were plenty of stars in the sky, but no visible moon, so the night was much darker than usual. Clint left Ross lying in the doorway and rushed to his truck. He started it up and positioned it so that it was facing the cabin. He turned on the truck lights so that he would be able to see what had to be done next.

"Tim…" Ross turned his head in the last direction he saw his friend. There was no sound coming from the right corner of the cabin.

Clint ran back inside the cabin and grabbed Ross underneath both arms. He began dragging him toward the burning pit. He was not as young as he once was, and Ross Taylor was a heavy man, so it took him almost ten minutes to drag him to the edge of the pit. He left him there and ran back inside for the other investigator.

Ross turned his head slightly toward the pit and wished he hadn't. The smell of rotting animal corpses quickly overwhelmed him. His brain, along with training he had received, automatically registered the smell as a combination of sulfur dioxide, methane, benzene derivatives, and long chain hydrocarbons that were produced when body parts were in their decomposing phase. The smell was so utterly disgusting and sickening, that he quickly associated the stench with the smell of death. Ross Taylor was grateful that he had not had anything to eat in the past twenty-four hours.

Ross tried to turn on his side to see what was causing the stomach-wrenching stench, even though he was fairly certain of what it might be. He and Tim had recently attended a class on the various stages of animal decomposition. The first phase began approximately four minutes after death and lasted for about 3 days. Putrefaction was the second stage of decomposition, and occurred 4 to 10 days after death. Black putrefaction, also known as active decay, usually began between 10 to 25 days after death. The fourth stage was called butyric fermentation, and began 20 to 25 days after death. The final stage in animal decomposition - dry decay – began between 25 to 50 days after death and could take as long as one year. The only remnants of the animal, during this final and last phase of decomposition, would be dried skin, hair, and bones.

Ross could barely make out a powdery substance that covered the top layer of corpses; he guessed that it was, most likely, quick lime. He fell back and looked up into a sky full of stars but no moon. "Stupid sons-of-bitches..." he gasped and closed his eyes. *"These Georgia rednecks probably think that applying quick lime will speed up the decomposition...idiots...if they only knew that it helps in controlling some of the odor but does nothing to speed up decomposition..."* he thought. *"What these fools don't realize is that, by using quick lime, they have actually helped to preserve these bodies...and, this evidence. The more lime used, the better the preservation...resulting in more physical evidence to be used against them when they get caught...and...they WILL be caught..."*

The night air actually felt good against Ross' battered body. It was the first time he had been outside since their capture on Wednesday, and, as bad as the pit stench was, he welcomed the opportunity to be lying outside instead of being cooped up in that dark cabin. He didn't know how long it had been since Clint Meacham had dragged him outside. He had hit his head on the floor when he fell inside, and his eyes still burned with pain. He heard movement and the sound of something being dragged toward him. He turned his head to the right and saw Clint's backside inching toward him. He winced when Tim's body was rolled roughly up against his own. He saw the pool of blood on Tim's shirt and the paleness of his face. He felt a second of relief when Tim's eyes opened slightly. His friend was still alive!

That sense of relief did not last long, because in the next instant, Ross felt his feet and legs being lifted. His hands grasped at the earth beneath him, but he could not stop Clint from pushing him backwards...backwards into the stench-filled pit that was filled with the rotting corpses of deceased animals. He screamed in agony when his bruised ribs made contact with the soft, squishy bodies of recently killed bait dogs.

Tyler heard the scream and took off at a faster sprint. He was within fifty feet of the pit when he saw Clint Meacham push a body into the burning pit. "NOOOOOO!" he screamed. He knew that Amanda was right behind him, but still hidden in the darkness of the woods. He turned around quickly and whispered, "Stay back, Amanda...*please*!" He continued running toward the pit but stopped abruptly when he saw the gun in Meacham's hands.

"Well, well..." Clint grinned. "Look at who's come to the rescue. Well, you're too late pretty boy...move over by the truck...nice and slow...I would hate to have to waste another bullet. Come on...MOVE!"

Tyler did not dare to look back to see if Amanda had listened to him; he did not want to give away her presence. There was still a chance she could make it out of here alive, and he would do everything in his power to see that she did. He held his hands up in the air. "Take it easy, Clint. Why don't you put that gun down? Nobody has to get hurt..." He walked slowly toward the truck and prayed that Clint's full attention would be on him...and him alone.

"Too late for that, pretty boy...okay, stop," he ordered when Tyler reached the truck. "Take off your jacket and boots, and empty your pockets."

"I don't have any weapons on me, Clint..." Tyler began.

"Shut up!" Clint ordered. He was enjoying this much more than he had imagined he would. He had never killed anyone before, but the power he felt when he pulled the trigger on the investigator was unlike any he had ever felt before.

Tyler removed his jacket and shoes, and turned his pockets inside out to show Clint that he had been telling the truth about not having any weapons. "See...no weapons...come on, Clint...let's talk about this."

"The time for talking ended the minute you showed up here tonight, kid. Now, move over there...that's right...toward the pit..." He waited for Tyler to comply with his order. "Now, it's up to you...you can do this the easy way, or...I can just shoot you, and push you in along with your two accomplices..."

"I don't know what you're talking about..." Tyler fought for a way to delay the inevitable. He glanced quickly into the pit and saw the outline of two bodies.

"Don't even try to talk your way out of this, Jones. Oh, wait...no...Jones isn't even your real name, is it? You see...Little John had his own investigator working on you all this time...and, he finally found out about an hour ago who you really are. It didn't take him long to put all the pieces together...to know that you were working as the inside man, with those two, to bust up his dog-fighting business. You gotta know that he's not happy about that."

"What are you going to do with me?" Tyler was doing his best to stall for time, but knew that it could still be an hour or more before anyone noticed his absence at the fights. The authorities would allow the fights to play out in their entirety before making the bust, so it would probably be closer toward midnight before the fights ended and the bust began.

"That's for Little John to decide. I know what I would like to do to you, but he gave me specific instructions to save you for himself...you can bet it won't be pretty, though. So...until then, I need you to jump down into that pit. Go ahead now...either jump or I'll shoot your legs out from under you and push you in myself...your choice..."

Amanda had listened to Tyler's plea and remained hidden in the woods, but she was close enough to hear the conversation taking place between her future husband and Abbott's skinny side-kick. She was about to stand up and announce her presence when she suddenly felt something cold and wet against her neck. She turned around sharply and stared into the soulful eyes of her long-lost pet. She sighed and closed her eyes when Sam's eyes turned a brilliant gold and he moved stealthily around her.

Tyler had moved to the edge of the pit, as Clint had instructed him to. He breathed heavily as Clint advanced toward him, and waved the gun carelessly at Tyler's head. His foot was already at the edge of pit and he felt some of the dirt giving way beneath it. He was ready to follow Clint's orders and jump into the pit when he saw a flash of gold creeping slowly toward Clint. He didn't know how he knew what was about to happen, but he did.

"Well, it looks like I'm going to have to waste another bullet after all..." Clint gleamed. He lowered the gun toward Tyler's kneecap and fired his gun. The brunt force of an 70-pound angel dog, barreled hard into his spine, and forced the intended bullet into the ground beside Tyler's foot.

Tyler jumped out of the way just in time. Clint dropped his gun and fell forward, but managed to stand up again; however, before he could turn around to see who or what had hit him, he took another hard pounding in his spine. This last pounding sent him over the edge into the burning pit. He landed squarely on his stomach beside a large German Shepherd that had been tossed there a few hours before.

Clint Meacham soiled his pants when the Shepherd emitted a weak, but definite growl.

Amanda came running from the woods and wrapped her arms around Tyler. She rubbed her hands up and down his sides and cried out, "Oh, God...are you okay...did he shoot you...tell me you're okay!"

Tyler took her in his arms and held her until her breathing, as well as his own, began to steady. "I'm okay...I'm okay...really...you can let go now, Amanda..."

Amanda released her hold on him and stood back to inspect him, to reassure herself that he was really okay. She looked around for Sam and saw him standing on the other side of the pit, looking down into it. She thought that he looked especially sad when he looked up at her and began backing away into the wood line. "Sam! Come back here! Where are you going?"

Tyler held her arm tightly when she tried to turn and follow Sam. "Let him go, Amanda. His job isn't finished yet." He looked down into the pit and shook his head. "I don't think this was on Sam's To-Do list for tonight, but he did what he had to do to save us. I think he's probably headed back to the fight...to be there when it all comes crashing down around Little John Abbott...to be there for Spartacus and the other dogs..."

Amanda nodded her head. "Okay...okay...I get that..." She turned to look down into the pit and gasped. "Oh, my, God! Tyler... we've got to get them out of there."

"The pit's too deep, Amanda. I don't have anything to get them out, but, I need you to listen to me. I need you to stay here with them until I get back. There's nothing you can do to help get them out of there, but if they regain consciousness, it might help them to know that someone is coming to help them. Whatever you do, *do not* try to get them out by yourself; trust me, you'll just end up in there with them, and you *do not* want to be inside that pit. I will be back as quick as I can. Don't go into the cabin, either. If you hear anyone coming, head back into that wood line and hide. There's plenty of rope back at the bunk house. I can take Clint's truck and be back in less than thirty minutes. Promise me you can stay out of trouble for thirty minutes?"

"Okay, okay...go!" Amanda shouted. "But hurry! I don't care whether that scumbag gets out or not, but those other two don't look so good. I'll be fine...don't worry about me."

Tyler pulled on his shoes and rushed toward Clint's truck. He was thankful that Clint had left the keys in the ignition. "Thirty minutes!" he shouted out the driver's window as he backed the truck up and sped away. He was so intent on reaching his destination that he never saw Little John's truck pulled off on a side road, with its headlights off.

Clint Meacham was cursing and shouting at Amanda. He was causing so much ruckus that she never heard Little John Abbott's silent approach behind her. She began kicking her legs wildly when she was swept up in an incredibly tight hold, and tried in vain to connect to her attacker's family jewels.

Little John held her securely in his left arm while he reached in his pocket for the handkerchief that he had soaked in chloroform before he left the truck. He had left the fight about thirty minutes after Clint, and followed him to the cabin. He had, instinctively, parked on the side road and soaked the handkerchief with the chloroform; he thought it might be useful if they needed to forcibly subdue the investigators. He was about to emerge from the thicket when he witnessed the dog he named Defiance knock Clint Meacham into the pit. He waited until Tyler drove off in Clint's truck before making his move on the young woman who had embraced Tyler so fervently just minutes ago.

Little John had been uneasy for several days about tonight's fight. He had no real proof, but he had his own suspicions about what was about to happen on his ranch. He suspected that Tyler was in the middle of the whole bust and that the bust was going to happen tonight instead of a week from now. He was a realist, so he also knew that it was too late for him to stop the bust from happening, but once he saw the obvious connection between Tyler and the woman he had called "Amanda", he decided he might be able to use her as a bartering tool, if need be. She might, also, prove to be a valuable avenue for his spiraling need for vengeance.

Little John Abbott took a moment to look around at the darkness that surrounded him…at the land that had been in his family for four generations. Yes, the need for vengeance was growing rapidly, and he was determined that it would be his before the night was over. He threw Amanda's limp body over his broad shoulders and carried her back to his truck. He would be well on his way out of Thomasville before Tyler Jones-Foster made it back to the burning pit.

CHAPTER 38

Tyler and Sam's Tough Decision

By ten o'clock the fights were progressing faster than usual; the longest fight had lasted thirty-seven minutes, while the shortest one had been over in less than three minutes. There were only three more fights to go before the grand finale between the dogs known as Defiance and Kong. Czar had initially been scheduled to fight against Kong, but Little John had decided to take his chances on the unknown fighting abilities of Defiance. He had created a false-win document outlining the recent wins of Defiance, stating that no opponent dog had lasted more than seven minutes in the ring with him. He knew the odds would be in favor of Defiance; however, he had no intentions of betting on his own dog. He had invested twenty-five thousand on Kong to win.

Spartacus' and Sam's cages were sitting on the ground next to each other; dark covers had been placed over the cages to keep distraction to a minimum. Spartacus paced nervously inside his own cramped cage and cringed whenever the crowd roared with approval at the defeat of another doomed fighting dog.

"Sam? I hate to admit it, but I'm scared to death of getting in

that ring again. I can smell Czar's aggression, and all I can say is that...I'm glad I don't have to fight him again, but that dog from South Carolina may be just as bad...I heard that he's a Corso, and they're even meaner than pit bulls or mastiffs...Sam?"

Spartacus could not see inside Sam's cage, so he had no idea that Sam was not even inside it. He had no clue that Sam was currently dealing with the toughest decision of his mortal and eternal lives.

After Sam had pushed Clint Meacham into the deep burning pit, he had looked longingly at his former mistress. He wanted to run to her...to protect her...but he knew that he had to honor his assignment to protect the animals fighting that night. It was vital that he be there when each animal took its last breath; if he wasn't there with them, then he would not be able to bring them back to life later. Eight had already been killed for losing their fights, so he did not have the luxury of being held in Amanda's warm embrace.

Sam felt the moment of alarm within seconds of transporting himself back to the fighting arena. He knew, immediately, that Amanda was in trouble...that she needed his help. He sensed that Little John Abbott had his sweet Amanda and that he intended to hurt her badly. His body remained in limbo for several moments while he deliberated his options. He could save Amanda, or he could save the lives of eleven of his comrades. He dropped his head and sighed before he transported himself back inside his cage. *"I'm here, Spartacus...do not worry, my friend...everything will turn out the way God intends it to."*

"But look at all of them, Sam...shot or beat to death with ball bats...dumped in a pile so they can be burned later...they didn't deserve to die like that, Sam...no animal deserves to die that way..."

The ninth fight was beginning; the odds were that it would not last any longer than the ones before it. Spartacus would be next to face his opponent, followed by Czar, and finally, the grand finale fight between Defiance and Kong.

□ □ □

Tyler had spent precious minutes searching for any rope or cable he could use to haul Tim Breydan and Ross Taylor from the burning pit. Most of the rope had been taken to the fighting arena, but Tyler found enough of it, along with an old, rusted extended ladder and two large boards of heavy wood behind the Abbott's horse barn. He hastily threw the rope, wood, and ladder into the bed of the truck. He looked at his watch and realized he had already been gone for almost thirty minutes. A shiver suddenly coursed through his body and he knew that he had to get back to the pit and make sure Amanda was alright. He sped down the long driveway and noticed a vehicle, in the distance, speeding south toward the main highway. His first thought was that it looked like Little John's truck, but he couldn't be sure…it was too far away, and…he felt certain that Little John was still at the arena, overseeing the fights.

It took Tyler less than ten minutes to make the normal, 15-minute trip to the burning pit. He left the headlights facing the pit and jumped out of the truck. He looked in every direction for Amanda, but did not see her anywhere. He raced to the edge of the pit and looked down. The investigators had not moved; their bodies were in the same position they had been in earlier, and that worried Tyler to no end. Clint Meacham, on the other hand, had turned over on his back and grinned up at Tyler in wicked silence.

Tyler spun around and stared into the darkness that surrounded him. The cabin door was still open and he rushed toward it. "AMANDA!" he yelled. She was not inside the cabin. He ran around to the back of the cabin and yelled into the woods. "AMANDA! WHERE ARE YOU!" He listened to the black calm that surrounded the cabin. No sounds came from the woods…no rustling leaves…no scurrying animals…nothing. He ran back to the front of the cabin and looked in every direction. The only sound he heard was the distant cheering coming from the fighting arena.

Panic flooded his handsome face. He rushed back to the burning pit.

The pain in his back was searing and he couldn't feel his legs, but Clint managed to push himself up to a sitting position, and spat a wad of tobacco into the moistened lime. "She ain't here, asshole," he laughed bitterly and spat again. "Boss man done took her away…pretty little thing, but you can bet she won't be that way after he gets through with her."

"Damn it!" Tyler hissed. "Damn it…" Tyler, like Sam had experienced earlier, now faced a tormented dilemma. He could jump in the truck and head south, hoping he could catch up with Abbott; or, he could climb into the pit and rescue the two investigators, who could already be dead for all he knew. "Where did he take her…did you kill them?" Tyler demanded, pointing to Tim and Ross.

Clint's tobacco-stained grin smiled up at Tyler through the darkness. He spat another wad of juice and said. "Ain't got no idea where he took that pretty little thing…wouldn't tell you if I did know…as for them…why don't you come on down and see for yourself, pretty boy? You don't have to worry about me none…I can't hurt you right now…can't seem to move my damn legs…" The smell from the decomposing animals was so overpowering that Clint couldn't finish his challenge to Tyler. He began coughing and gagging. "You gotta get me outta here, too…you can't leave me here…"

Tyler threw his cap on the ground and ran both hands over and around his head. He was so torn on what to do, on who to help first. He closed his eyes and offered a quick prayer to the God that had saved him so many times in the past. "Please let me make the right decision, Lord…"

In less than a minute, Tyler's decision was made. He tried to call 911 to tell them about Amanda and the two investigators but his cell phone's reception was out of range. He couldn't risk jeopardizing the sting by reaching out to the detectives and investigators at the fight, and the local police were in Abbott's back pocket, so they would be of no help to him now. He rushed back to Clint's truck and grabbed the ladder, ropes, board, and the gun that Meacham had dropped earlier when Sam pushed him into the pit. He ran around to the opposite side of the pit, as far away from Clint Meacham as he could get, and lowered the twenty-foot ladder into the pit; the men were fifteen feet deep inside the pit. He tucked the gun inside the back of his jeans and began his descent. The smell of rot and decay made his eyes and sinuses burn, so he pulled a bandana from his back pocket and wrapped it around his head, covering his nose as much as possible. It wasn't much, but it helped some.

Tyler jumped off the ladder when he was within two feet of where the investigators lay. His feet sunk into mushy skin and fur; he felt bones breaking beneath his weight. He felt his stomach lurch and thought he was going to lose it, but somehow managed to squelch the vomiting reflex.

He looked quickly in the direction where Clint Meacham still sat upright, about fifteen feet away from Tim and Ross. "Too bad that dog didn't kill you..." he said.

Clint tried to move but the pain in his back was too severe. He wasn't going anywhere without Tyler's help, and, he was suddenly concerned that he might not receive that help. "You can't leave me here, you know...you gotta help get me out, too. They're probably dead by now, anyway, so don't waste your time with them...I know where Little John keeps his stash...there's enough money in his safe for the two of us...get me out of here and I'll disappear and you can..."

Tyler glared at the man he had been forced to take orders from for months now. "SHUT UP! Trust me, Meacham...*you* are the least of my concerns right now. A low mumble beside him drew him back to the task at hand. Tyler jumped when a hand reached out and grabbed his ankle. The hand belonged to the younger of the two investigators, Ross Taylor.

Ross had landed on his stomach when he had been pushed into the pit. He squeezed Tyler's ankle and wheezed, "Get Tim...he's been shot...gotta get him help...quick..."

Tyler bent lower and squeezed Ross' hand. "I tried calling 911, buddy, but I'm not getting any reception in these woods. I'm getting you both out of here and taking you to the ER myself. Just hang on, okay? You're going to make it..."

"Get...Tim...first..." Ross mumbled before his head fell forward and he lost consciousness once again.

Tyler searched for a pulse on the older man and exhaled gratefully when he found one; it was extremely slow and weak, but it was there. He rolled Tim Breydan onto one of the narrow boards and secured him to it with the ropes. He exhaled deeply again and looked upward into the star-lit sky. "Okay, Lord...you provided the means...now, please...give me the physical strength to get these men out of here..." He took a deep breath and began a slow, backward ascent up the ladder, dragging the man secured to the board behind him. It didn't take as long as he thought it would, but by the time Tyler had placed both investigators in the truck bed, twenty-five, precious minutes had already sped by.

The last thing he heard as he sped away was the frantic screams from Clint Meacham. Tyler was at the ER thirty minutes later before he realized he had left the ladder inside the pit.

CHAPTER 39

Spartacus Fights Again

"What do you want me to do with him, Boss?" the handler of the losing dog from the ninth fight asked the owner.

The owner's bloodshot eyes glared at the white pit bull's mangled face and legs. "He's worthless now. Chain him to the back of the truck. If he survives the ride home, use him as bait tomorrow for his replacement. If he doesn't...dump him in the woods and let the buzzards eat him. Damn loser just cost me fifteen grand."

The dog used his one remaining eye to look pleadingly at his owner. He whimpered and tried to move toward him, but the owner's swift kick to his back side sent his legs collapsing beneath him. He whimpered again when the handler dragged him by a chain toward the area where the owners had parked their vehicles.

Sam growled when the handler tugged hard at the dog's chain, and didn't back away when the man kicked at his cage.

The handler spit on the ground at Sam's cage and hissed. "You had better win your fight...I've got a month's salary bet on you…" He continued to drag the whimpering dog to a dusty, old F-150 and secured him to the trailer hitch.

Sam closed his eyes when the white pit whimpered its last breath.

Spartacus had watched quietly while the dog had been dragged away. *"He's dead, isn't he?"*

Sam paced inside his cage. His nostrils flared widely and his eyes glowed their brilliant gold. *"Yes…for now…"*

"I'm going to die, too, aren't I, Sam…that's okay…you don't have to answer. I know that's why I had to come back. I have to die so that others might live…so that others won't have to live their lives in fear, day after day…will it hurt, Sam?"

Sam stopped his pacing and moved to the side of his cage, to be as close to Spartacus as he could get. *"I told you, Spartacus…you are not going to die…none of them are…not tonight…"*

"Well, in case you haven't been paying attention, good buddy…" Spartacus tried to sound flippant, but his fear was more than evident. *"Nine of our partners in crime have already died. Don't you angels have something like the five-second rule? Like…don't you have to save them within seconds of their dying in order to bring them back?"*

Sam was only half-listening to Spartacus and his concerns. He was still torn on helping his sweet Amanda and doing what he had been assigned to do. He had sensed Amanda's initial fear, but for the last half hour or so, he had not been able to sense her presence at all, and that worried him more than he cared to admit.

"Hey, Sam…you listening to me?" Spartacus whispered. *"Oh, no…they're announcing the next fight…that's me, Sam…Sam? Please tell me you're still there…"*

Sam listened to the announcements to place bets on fight number ten between Little John Abbott's former champion fighter, Spartacus, and the three-time winner, Lucifer, a liver-brown Corso from Greenville, South Carolina.

"Oh, that's just great…" Spartacus sighed. *"His name would have to be Lucifer…"*

"Whatever happens, Spartacus…just go with it and know that I am close by…I will not let anything happen to you…or to the others…they will not die tonight…"

"Okay, then…" Spartacus conceded. *"That's all I needed to know…well…here goes nothing…"*

Spartacus jumped back when his cage door opened, and, in spite of his newfound confidence, his bladder failed him.

"They're not expecting you to win, Spartacus," Sam whispered as Spartacus was literally dragged from his cage by his handler. *"The odds are against you…trust me, my friend…a lot of people are going to lose a lot of money on your fight…"*

Spartacus' fight was over before it ever really began. For some strange reason, the former fearless Corso known as Lucifer, turned away from Spartacus, time and time again. The dogs were returned to their scratch positions three times; each time, Lucifer turned away and would not engage in fight. His owner was speechless, and could not explain why his formidable champion fighter seemed to cower in fear. The referee called the fight after Lucifer's third turn, and Spartacus was declared the winner.

Spartacus held his head up high as he was led back to his cage. The booing jeers from the unhappy crowd did nothing to dampen his renewed spirit. He winked at Sam before he entered his cage. *"Well…that was easy enough!"*

Sam grinned at his new friend. Spartacus' win, by default, was not the way that fight was supposed to go down. There might be consequences to pay for Sam's part in changing the outcome of that fight; but, it was imperative that the fights be speeded up so that he could get to Amanda. He could feel the distance growing between them with each passing moment. He could no longer sense her essence and that worried him. He continued pacing his cage throughout the next fight between Czar and his worthy opponent. The two dogs were evenly matched and, for some unexplainable reason, Sam was not able to speed up that fight. It lasted for thirty-three minutes, with Czar finally being declared the winner.

Spartacus heard the approaching footsteps. *"They're coming for you, Sam..."*

"I wish they would get a move on it..." Sam growled. *"I need to help the dogs that lost their fights...there is a six-hour time limit on their resurrection...that first one died almost five hours ago."*

"What do you mean...there's a time limit on how long a dog can be dead before you can bring it back to life?" Spartacus squealed. *"You didn't tell me there was a time limit! I was just kidding about that five-second rule! I mean...you're an angel dog...I thought you could do anything!"*

"We do have our limitations, Spartacus. The angels at the café cannot interfere with a mortal's destiny...at all...and they are not allowed to resurrect any human life. I, on the other hand, and only by the authority of God Himself, have the limited ability to resurrect the dogs involved with this assignment...but, yes, a time limit has been established...no more than six hours can lapse from the time of death to the time of resurrection. I would have done it already, but there are far too many people here..."

"You mean...too many non-believers, don't you?" Spartacus asked. *"Wouldn't God see the resurrection of those animals as a way to turn them all into believers?"*

"I suppose that is possible, Spartacus...but...it is not my place to question His intentions. He gave me my instructions before I came down...as well as my limitations. I've already interfered with destiny when I pushed Clint Meacham into the burning pit..."

"Well, hot damn!" Spartacus cheered. *"You didn't tell me you did that!"*

"You don't understand, my friend...it was not my place to interfere with that encounter. When I interfered, it may have changed destiny's intended course for all those involved...I'm not sure how things will turn out now because of my actions. Amanda may not have been kidnapped had I not interfered..."

"What! Amanda's been taken? Who took her? Where did they go? I'll help you get her back!"

"Be ready to move quickly, Spartacus...we won't have much time..."

The door to Sam's cage was jerked open and a wire loop

hooked around his neck. He was growling and snarling when he was pulled out into the open. The crowd went wild with enthusiasm when Sam showed his long fangs to their best advantage. The betting began as Sam and Kong were weighed and received their mandatory baths from the opposing handler.

Sam's black fur glistened under the bright lights. His dark eyes were alert as he bared his teeth to the crowd when he was led to his corner. He saw the many streaks of blood that soaked the canvas flooring and his body grew stiff and rigid with anger. His handler turned him away to face the corner of the ring.

Cheering rang out again when the handler of the red pit-bull from North Carolina was practically dragged into the ring by his dog. He turned Kong to face the opposing corner. The crowd quieted and the announcer proclaimed the history of each fighting dog. He paused for a moment before finally yelling out, "FACE YOUR DOGS!"

Kong immediately lunged forward, snarling and eager for the fight to begin, and had to be dragged behind the scratch line.

Sam stood stoically between his handler's legs. His eyes never left those of the red pit-bull. *"Forgive me for what I must do..."*

Kong paused and blinked. He stared at his opponent and saw Sam's eyes change from brown-black to a soft golden hue. He didn't have time to ponder what that might mean before the referee yelled, "LET'S GO!" He lunged at Sam quickly the moment his handler released him. His mouth opened wide and he aimed for the throat. He never saw it coming, but the next thing he felt was an immense pressure to his head when Sam head-butted him, and he was thrown half-way across the ring.

The crowd cheered when Kong quickly regained his balance and lunged at his opponent once again. He made contact with Sam's throat this time and the crowd went crazy when Sam yelped and went down. The crowd expected to see a lot of blood as Kong stood over Sam and shook him from side to side, tearing at his throat. They began to boo when no blood ever appeared.

The crowd's booing ceased abruptly when Sam suddenly stood up with Kong's massive jaws still attached to his throat. They watched in awe as the huge, black pit-mix walked slowly in a circle, dragging the red pit bull along with him. They began to cheer again when Sam swiftly swung his head in a downward motion, causing Kong to release his hold on Sam's throat; two of Kong's teeth flew out of his mouth when he was slammed hard against the canvass-covered ground.

Sam knew that time was of the essence. He had to resurrect the animals that had lost their fights before he could begin his search for Amanda. He stood over Kong and uttered a low growl. The crowd could not see the changing color of his eyes, but he knew that Kong saw it and finally recognized Sam for what he truly was. *"I promise…this will not hurt…"* Sam assured his opponent just before he grabbed Kong's throat between his own sharp teeth. It only took one quick shake for Sam to break the champion fighter's neck.

The formerly cheering crowd was stunned into silence. There was no more cheering because they were all in shock at what had just happened during the final fight of the night. The referee was speechless, too; he had never seen the neck of a dog Kong's size snapped like it was a twig. The handlers of both dogs were dumbfounded, and neither made a move toward their respective dogs.

Sam backed away slowly from Kong's body and looked around slowly at everyone in attendance. His eyes still glowed golden, and a similar hue now engulfed his entire body as he moved slowly around the ring. He was mesmerizing the crowd into a semi-conscious state that was similar to hypnotism. The crowd could still see but they could not move, and only those who were true Christians would ever remember what they had just witnessed…and what they were about to witness. Sam suspected there might be a handful of people in attendance who fell into that category; most of the believers were part of the law enforcement and animal protection group who had immersed themselves into the crowd of spectators.

"Whoa..." Spartacus mumbled as he watched the clip from his cage door slide sideways. He pushed against it and moved slowly among the dazed crowd. He made his way toward the ring where Sam was still walking around it in a slow circle. *"Whoa...what have you done to them, Sam? Did you hypnotize them or something?"*

"Something like that, my friend..." Sam sighed. *"We have to move quickly. I need your help. I need you to push the pile of dogs off one another...I need them lying side-by-side...quickly, Spartacus!"* Sam moved first to Kong and lay down beside the massive red pit bull until their heads, shoulders, and hips lined up together. Sam closed his eyes and the golden hue from his body began to spread outward until it covered Kong's body. In a matter of seconds, Kong gasped and tried to stand. *"Easy..."* Sam instructed him. *"Easy, now...okay...once you feel strong enough, I need you to stand and move into the wood line...over there...there will be some nice officers coming to get all of you and take you to safety. You will instruct the others of this and wait for the officers to find you...do you understand?"*

Sam stood up when Kong's eyes began to clear and he regained the strength to stand. Kong's legs still felt a bit wobbly, but he looked into Sam's golden eyes and said, *"Yes...yes, I understand. Don't worry...I will lead them all to safety until the officers find us. I...I don't know what just happened, but...thank you..."*

"You are very welcome, my friend. You and the others will have a very different life from here on out...you will have a second chance...make it count..."

Sam left the ring and found the F-150 where the mangled white, pit lay dead behind it; it was still chained to the trailer hitch. He repeated his healing ritual and waited until the dog's mangled face transformed to its former clarity, and its legs grew strong with renewed life and strength. The chain simply fell away from the dog's neck and he slowly made his way toward the wood line where Kong waited patiently. He looked back as Sam once and barked his gratitude.

It was eleven-thirty by the time Sam had completed the resurrection process on the seven other dogs. He opened the cages of the winning dogs and instructed them to follow the others into the wood line. Czar had waited patiently in his cage and watched in amazement at each resurrection Sam had performed. He hung his head in shame when Sam approached his cage. He had known nothing but fighting all his life, and had grown to love it. It had never bothered him one bit when he carelessly took the lives of the smaller bait dogs, or the stronger fighter dogs he had defeated over the past couple of years. He felt that he did not deserve to be saved now.

"Look at me, Czar..." Sam spoke softly.

Czar shook his head and lowered it even farther toward the bottom of his cage. *"I...can't..."*

"Look at me, Czar!" Sam spoke more sharply. He waited until Czar had lifted his head and met his gaze. *"None of this is your fault, Czar...none of it. This life is all you have ever known, but...if you want...you can have a very different life. You can have a real home...with a family who loves and cherishes you...a family you can honor and protect...a place to feel safe and...loved..."*

Czar sighed and lifted his head. He returned Sam's stare and said, *"I don't deserve all that...I don't deserve to be...loved..."*

Sam motioned for Czar to step outside his cage, and when he did, he moved to stand beside him. Sam was slightly taller, so he quietly laid his head upon Czar's. *"Everyone deserves to be loved, my friend, and...you...are no exception. Now...I need you to follow the others into the woods and wait for the officers to find you. I'm trusting in you and Kong to keep the others quiet and safe until you are all found."*

A tear escaped Czar's eye and flowed down the side of his face. He watched as the other dogs, winners and losers, moved into the wood line to wait with Kong. He nodded and looked back at Sam and Spartacus. *"I can do that...thank you,*

Sam." He smiled sheepishly at Spartacus. *"I'm sorry I ever hurt you...please forgive me..."*

Spartacus simply nodded and watched while the group of dogs moved silently into the woods. His glance skewed over the people in the crowd and the groups clustered around the ring. *"What about all of them? Are you just going to leave them like that?"*

Sam watched the group of dogs until they had all disappeared safely into the wood line. *"They will remain like this for a few more minutes...long enough for us to be far away from here. Well...correction...long enough for ME to be far away from here. You my friend, unfortunately, will have to make the trip on your own."*

Spartacus pouted. *"Why can't you just wiggle your nose or something and take me with you?"*

"It doesn't work that way, Spartacus. I need you to make your way back to the café. Stay on the road...someone will stop along the way and pick you up..."

"Who? Who's going to pick me up? I want to go with you, Sam. You might need my help..."

Sam looked back at Spartacus for just an instant before he transported himself away. His eyes glowed golden and he winked at his new friend.

Spartacus stood beside Czar's empty cage and looked around. *"Yeah, right...sure...like YOU need MY help...I..."*

"SPARTACUS! GO! QUICKLY!" The voice boomed from the heavens above.

Spartacus yelped, lost control of his bladder once again, and took off running. *"Jesus, Christ...you scared me to death!"* That voice had not belonged to Sam!

CHAPTER 40

Rescue or Recovery

It was almost eleven forty-five. A lot would happen before the dawn of a new day.

The Emergency Room doctors at Archbold Memorial Hospital worked quickly and fervently on the two men that had been brought in fifteen minutes ago by a young man who had given his name as Tyler Foster. Tim Breydan had been rushed immediately into surgery; his wound was life-threatening and the doctors did not hold out much hope for him making it through the surgery. Ross Taylor remained unconscious while x-rays were taken and his wounds were being thoroughly examined. The young man expressed regret at not being able to wait, but had given the nurse on duty a quick report of who the men were and what had transpired. He had asked her to contact the authorities and provided his contact number before rushing out into the night.

Little John Abbott was never one to panic in any given

situation, and he did not panic when he drugged Amanda Turner and tossed her into the back seat of his truck. He had looked into the burning pit before he drove off and assured his foreman that he would be back to help him out. He recognized the look of doubt that had crossed Clint Meacham's face; maybe the man knew him better than he thought and realized how dire his own situation really was. Little John had no intention of returning to help Clint out of the pit. If he had more time, he would have set fire to the pit to eliminate the bodies of the two investigators from being identified; however, time was not on his side this night, and he did not want to draw any attention to the pit area until he was well out of range.

He had listened briefly to the distant cheering of the crowd from the fighting arena before he reluctantly turned his truck toward the main house. He had more than two hundred thousand dollars in cold, hard cash in his safe. He was a realist...he knew that life as he knew it was probably over, but he did not intend to spend what was left of it locked behind bars with his own father. He had felt his blood pressure rise and his anger intensify as he thought about who was to blame for all this. He intended to get that money, and then he would find a way to get even with Tyler Foster. He had thrown a few clothes into a suitcase, gathered the money and his passport, looked around the home that he was sure he would never return to, and began driving south on Highway 19. He had connections in Tampa that, for enough money, could get him on a cargo ship leaving the United States. He had glanced at the pretty blonde sprawled upon his back seat. She was indeed very pretty, and he briefly contemplated the idea of taking her aboard the ship with him, but that would have cut into his cash. He shook his head and decided she wasn't that pretty after all; that meant he would have to...dispose of her.

Twenty-two dogs had gathered together in the wood line.

Kong stood in front of them all, determined to honor his promise to Sam that he would see that they remain together until help arrived. Sam and Spartacus were long gone by the time the crowd of spectators, owners, handlers, law enforcement, and animal control investigators immersed from their ten-minute catatonic state. Sam had immediately transported himself to the Heavenly Grille Café, and Spartacus had begun a fast, physical sprint in the same direction.

"Hey…where are the damn dogs?" one fat-bellied, bearded man yelled from the sidelines of the fighting ring. "I want my damn money back! What the hell is going on here?"

The murmuring from the crowd began as a soft whisper, but it didn't take long for others to begin feeling the same ire as the fat-bellied, bearded man. Five investigators displaced themselves from the crowd and came together in a small circle. One of them looked around and shook his head. "I'm with him," he said, nodding toward the fat-bellied, bearded man. "What *is* going on? Did we miss something? Where *are* the dogs…"

Fifteen men in dark uniforms suddenly rushed from the wood line and circled the fighting arena. Their guns were drawn and the leader of group issued a quick order to everyone there. "NOBODY MOVES!" This is a bust for illegal dog-fighting and everyone here…EVERYONE…is under arrest!"

Several burly men on the bleachers jumped down with intentions to run; however, another twenty law enforcement personnel emerged from the opposite wood line and halted their escape. The spectators heard the sound of blaring sirens, and their breathing became more labored as the sounds got closer. The five investigators spread out and began a search for the animals. It only took a couple of minutes until one of them shouted out, "Hey! Over here! They're all over here…they look like they're…waiting for us…"

Kong and twenty-one other dogs sat quietly just inside the

wood line. Once Kong was sure that the authorities had control of the situation, he stood up and motioned for the other dogs to follow him. He wagged his tail when he saw an investigator move cautiously toward him.

"Well, I'll be damned..." the investigator spoke under his breath. "You'd never know that these were fighter dogs. Just look at them," he told the other four investigators when they arrived by his side. "Every single one them...wagging their tails." He pulled a leader leash from a clip on his belt and moved cautiously toward Kong. "Easy fella...we're not here to hurt you guys...come on, now..."

Kong moved toward the investigator. It was imperative that he prove to the investigators that he and the other dogs were not a threat to them. He lowered his head when he was within two feet of the investigator and allowed the leader leash to be placed over his massive neck. He took four more steps toward the investigator and licked the man's hand.

"Jesus!" the man almost shrieked. "Is this the same dog that had the one called Defiance by the throat just a little while ago?" He held out a tentative, shaking hand and allowed Kong to sniff his scent. When the dog didn't growl or attempt to bite him, the man kneeled and slowly placed his hand on Kong's head. He used his thumb to rub the dog's forehead between its brows.

It was the first kind touch that Kong had ever experienced. He whimpered and lay down at the man's feet.

The other dogs moved forward while the other four investigators looped leashes around their necks. Five law enforcement officers appeared and took more leashes from the investigators. Each man looped two dogs and began leading them away. The last two dogs didn't even wait for leashes; they simply followed the pack of dogs and officers back to their crates.

Enrique Ramos was the investigator holding the leashes of Kong and the white pit bull whose face and legs had been badly mangled in the ninth fight. He was one of only four Christians at the fights to witness the resurrection of the dogs that had lost their individual fights. They had witnessed their mangled bodies being returned to healthy flesh and bone. They had watched the transformation of the dog named Defiance, seen the heavenly glow that had enveloped him as he lay beside the deceased dogs, and watched as those same dogs were restored to a glorious health they had never before experienced. The truth and reality of what they had witnessed took some time to sink in, but when it did, each and every one of them turned their eyes toward the night sky and gave silent thanks to their God above. They had witnessed a miracle at an illegal dog fight tonight, and they would share their stories with anyone who wanted to listen.

Enrique led Kong to his crate and slid the lock closed on it. He leaned down and whispered, "It won't be long, fella. You'll have to stay locked up until everything gets processed, reports are submitted, you get checked out by a vet…all that stuff…but, then…I want you to know that you will have a home with me and my family for the rest of your days."

Kong whimpered and licked at the man's fingers. He looked over at the cage that held the white pit bull from the ninth fight. He looked back at the man.

Enrique laughed softly. "Don't worry…we always have room for one more…"

"Ramos!" the voice came from Enrique's supervisor, who was handling the transportation of the dogs to the agency's vet. He held a sheet of paper in his hands. "Looks like two are unaccounted for…best we can tell…they are both Abbott's dogs…the one called Defiance and the smaller, black pit…Spartacus. I have someone searching the woods for them."

Ramos looked back at Kong. If he didn't know better he would have sworn the dog had raised his brows in mockery. He shook his head and smiled. "Something tells me those two are long gone, Boss…probably miles away from here by now."

"Well, let's get the word out for everyone to be on the lookout for them, just in case…wouldn't want them attacking anyone before we can catch them."

Enrique felt another lick against the top of his hand. He grinned and winked at Kong. "Somehow, I don't think we have to worry about that happening..." he spoke softly.

Clint Meacham had cursed Little John Abbott when he left him in the pit; he knew that Little John never had any intentions of returning to help get him out. He cursed again when Tyler had sped away, rushing to get the two investigators to the hospital. He lay in that gut-stenching pit until he thought he would gag on his own breath. He listened to the cheering of the crowds and knew that the fights would probably be over in less than two hours, and he knew that help was not coming for him; he had to help himself. He grinned when he realized that Tyler had forgotten to pull up the ladder from the pit, but that grin had faded when he contemplated how difficult it would be to pull himself up twenty feet to the ground above, even with the help of the five-foot cushion of dead and decomposing animals.

Clint rolled over and belly-crawled his way to the foot of the ladder. His hands dug into soft, decomposing flesh and fur as he rallied to get a grip on the top layer of animals. He gagged each time his fingers became lodged in rotted heads and bellies, but he finally managed to reach the ladder. He was stronger than most men gave him credit for, and he had actually pulled himself up to the sixth rung of the ladder before the gooey gore on his hands caused him to slip backward. He screamed out in pain when he landed on his back; the pain started in his back and spiraled downward into each leg and foot. His bottom extremities felt on fire with the pain. He took four, deep labored breaths and began pulling himself up again. He continued to do this time and time again until it suddenly dawned on him that he no longer heard any cheering from the crowd. When had it stopped? Why had it stopped? "To hell with this!" he grunted as he began a final attempt to pull himself up. His arms and chest were burning with having to bear all his weight, but Clint bit his bottom lip in relief when his fingers finally dug into the earth at the top of the pit. "Only a little bit more...come on...you can do this..." he encouraged himself. He had no earthly idea what he would do when he reached the top, or where he could go; all he knew was that he had to get out of that pit.

The ladder moved slightly to the left when he placed both hands on the ground and began his final separation from it. He kept pulling at the earth and moving forward until he knew his feet had cleared the top of the pit. His head fell forward and he began to laugh hysterically. "Oh...thank, God...so glad I'm outta there..." he moaned as he eagerly inhaled the fresh air.

Two uniformed officers stood motionless on the other side of the pit and waited until Clint had pulled himself out. "Yep," one of them nodded. "So are we...cause we were getting ready to flip a coin to see which of us was going to have to go in to haul you out."

"Imagine our surprise," the other officer grinned in acknowledgement, "When we searched and searched, but neither of us could come up with a coin!"

Little John had decided to stay on the local back roads, travelling south on Highway 19, instead of getting on the interstate. The interstate would have been much quicker in getting him to Tampa, but he figured he would be more visible to law enforcement on the main roads. He could get to Tampa in about four hours, get on the cargo ship, and be on open water before the sun came up.

He was still pondering what to do with Amanda, and was regretting the decision to bring her along. His first instinct had been to have his way with her, strangle her, and dump her body in some swampy wooded area. There were plenty of those type areas between here and Tampa, and it would take weeks, maybe even months, before her body was found...if it was ever found. There were plenty of wild coyotes, bears, gators, and other land critters out there who would love to sample this tasty little appetizer, especially along a 30-mile stretch of dark nothingness just south of Perry, Florida. He would probably save a small piece of her as a souvenir to send Tyler; it was important to him that Tyler know that his little girlfriend had suffered a horrible death.

His rambling thoughts and plans were thwarted by a bright glow that suddenly appeared from above the trees, just around the bend in the road ahead. He saw the huge halo that seemed to float above what might be a restaurant, to the right, just past the curve. He saw the flashing marque in the empty parking lot that read- HEAVENLY GRILLE CAFÉ - open 7 - 11. He glanced at the clock on his dash...it was eleven-thirty...the place was probably closed, but all the lights were still on. He glanced back at Amanda to make sure she was still knocked out. He had bound her hands and feet with duct tape, every redneck's surefire remedy for anything that needed to be fixed. "I've got a long ride ahead of me...maybe I can get some coffee if they're still open..."

He should have kept going and stopped at a gas station for coffee, but something compelled Little John to pull into the café parking lot at the same time that Sam transported himself to the back porch.

Little John's fate and destiny had arrived right on time.

If the police had been hiding with their radar on, they could have made quite a chunk of money on Tyler Foster. By eleven forty-five, he was more than half-way to the Heavenly Grille Café. He couldn't explain *why* he was headed to the café; it would be closed by now, but he felt obligated to let the people closest to Amanda Turner know what was going on...he dreaded telling them, especially Bertie, that Amanda had been taken by Little John Abbott and could be anywhere by now. He had called the local police from the Emergency Room and told them about his suspicions, but they were reluctant to take him seriously over the phone. They had suggested that he wait twenty-four hours and then come in to make an official missing persons report. He had hung up on them and knew that saving Amanda was up to him, but he felt helpless not even knowing if he was driving in the right direction. Little John could have gotten on the interstate by now and headed God knows where.

Tyler was about ten minutes away from the café when he took a curve in the road too fast and almost lost control of his truck; he had swerved to avoid hitting a dog that was running fast on the side of the road. Tyler barely missed hitting the dog and somehow managed to keep his four wheels firmly on the road. "Jeez!" he growled and looked in his rearview mirror. The dog was black and it was hard to make it out in the dark and against the pavement, but something about the way it moved seemed so familiar to Tyler. He slowed the truck and looked in the rear-view mirror again; the dog was lagging a good hundred feet behind the truck now, but… "Oh, my God!" Tyler yelled when it suddenly dawned on him that the dog was Spartacus. "What the hell…" He slammed on his brakes and threw open his door.

"Oh, boy…oh, boy!" Spartacus gasped. *"Whew! I sure am glad it's a friendly face!"*

"Spartacus!" Tyler yelled into the total blackness that surrounded them. "It is you! Come here, boy!" He grunted and fell backward as the mass of solidness that was Spartacus barreled into his chest. He held the dog firmly against him and picked him up quickly. He placed him on the passenger seat and pulled a half-bottle of water and a small, plastic bowl from underneath. "Here you go, fella…slow now…drink it slow…" He patted the dog's head and wondered how in the world the dog had escaped from his cage at the fighting ring. He would love to know what was happening there at this very moment, what had happened to all the dogs, who had been arrested, if the bust had been successful, but he didn't have the luxury of finding out the answers to all those things.

Tyler waited a precious two minutes, allowing the dog to

cool down and waiting for him to get his heavy breathing under control. He kissed the top of the dog's head and said, "I guess you're coming with me, fella. I can't leave you out here in the middle of nowhere, now can I?"

"Nope...nope, you sure can't do that, Tyler! Come on, we've got to get going! I sure hope you're headed where I need you to be headed!"

Tyler started the truck and glanced sharply at the dog who was now riding shotgun. His brows drew together and he shook his head. "Damn...I could have sworn you said something..."

Max was wiping down his stove and counters when he sensed a presence at the back door. Bertie and Doug were locking things up out front, so he knew it wasn't either of them. He sensed who it was before he opened the screen door that lead to the back porch.

Sam grinned up at him. *"It's all coming to an end, Max."*

"So..." Max answered back. "I take it you accomplished your assignment? Everything went according to plan at the fights? Is Spartacus with you? Where are all the other dogs?" He looked into the empty back yard and listened. He heard the barking of one dog, and one dog only. He stepped out onto the porch and looked upward. There was a light on in Amanda's room and Buster was barking up a storm. "Hmmm...I wonder why Amanda isn't taking him out? She doesn't normally allow him to bark like that."

"Yeah...about that, Max. I hate to tell you, but Amanda isn't in her room..."

"Of course she is," Max laughed. She told us she was turning in early tonight, but for us to let her know if we heard anything from Tyler before she did. She's been in her room for most of the night..."

"Max...think about who you're talking about...Amanda...our sweet, NOSY, Amanda," Sam closed his eyes. He tensed for a moment when he sensed another presence close by. He

looked across the back yard but did not see anything that looked out of place.

"She's really not in her room, is she?" Max pursed his lips together. "Bertie is not going to be happy about this. She warned that girl not to get involved with the dog-fighting bust. She went, didn't she? Is she still there? Why isn't she with you? Where's Tyler?"

"You're an angel, Max! I thought you would already know the answers to all these questions..." Sam tensed again when that same, uneasy feeling crept over him again. *"I'm worried about her, Max. I saw her earlier tonight...with Tyler, but...I couldn't stay with her...I had to return to the fights. I don't know where she is right now, but I got an uneasy feeling about things while I was finishing up my assignment...I hope and pray she's with Tyler, but I don't think she is..."*

"Just because we're angels doesn't mean we're privy to what's going on in everyone's life at any given time, Sam." Max opened the door wide. "Come on inside..."

Sam stepped inside the kitchen and lifted his nose at the leftover aromas of the night's meal...spare ribs with sauerkraut, sweet potato casserole with marshmallows, and grilled corn on the cob. Sam loved marshmallows, but he re-routed his senses when he heard voices coming from the front of the café. His spine stiffened, his ears flattened against his head, and his tail became erect. *"Wait, Max! I know that voice...it's Little John Abbot! What's he doing here..."*

Max tensed and inhaled sharply. "I don't know, but... I intend to find out. Stay here, Sam. I don't want him to see you...STAY!"

"I'm staying! I'm staying..." Sam muttered beneath his breath. He lay down and belly-crawled behind Max so that he could hear what was going on.

Max pushed open the swinging half-door and stopped in his tracks. The man that he supposed was Little John Abbott was holding a gun to Bertie's head.

□ □ □

Tyler made it to the café in record time and immediately cut his lights when he recognized Abbott's truck in the parking lot. It was the only vehicle there, other than the café's van. The lights inside the café, as well as the floating halo, provided sufficient lighting to make it hard to sneak up on Abbott's vehicle. "Sweet, Jesus..." he whispered. "I don't believe it...I found him. Please don't let me be too late...please, God...let Amanda be with him..." Tyler opened his door as quietly as he could and crept alongside the passenger side of Abbott's truck. He almost tripped over Spartacus when he lifted his head to look inside. "Spartacus! No, boy...go back!" he whispered as loudly as he dared.

Spartacus shook his head and slobber splashed against Tyler's jeans. *"No way, Jose...nope, nope, nope...I'm not staying on the sidelines for this!"*

Tyler flicked some slobber off his jeans and looked disgusted. "Really? You're picking now to be obstinate? Fine, okay, but try to stay out of the way..." He stretched up and looked inside the truck. He wasn't sure what he expected to see, but it wasn't Amanda stretched out on the back seat, with her eyes closed, and her hands and feet tied together with tape. "Son of a bitch..." he hissed.

He didn't expect that Abbott would have left the door unlocked, so he was startled when he squeezed the door handle and the door opened with a slight squeak. Spartacus pushed between his legs and dashed into the front seat before Tyler could stop him. He watched in awe as the dog quickly bounded into the back seat and began licking Amanda's face. She didn't wake up, but Tyler heaved a giant sigh of relief when he saw her head move and her eyelids flutter. "Okay, okay..." he exhaled and looked upward. "Thank you, God...she's okay." He looked at Spartacus and began talking to him like he knew the dog would understand everything he said. "I have to find Abbott, so it's important that you stay with Amanda, okay? Do you understand what I'm saying, Spartacus? You have to stay with her and make sure nothing happens to her until I get back."

Spartacus appeared to shrug his shoulders. He returned Tyler's intent stare and growled softly. *"Do you really think I would be anywhere else? Really?"*

Tyler watched the dog's expression and closed the door softly. "If I didn't know better, I would swear that dog understood every word I said…"

He stayed as low to the ground as possible as he moved quickly and closer to the café. He stood among the bushes that lined the front of the café, and rose as high as he dared to get a look inside. His gaze riveted to the front door where he saw Abbott holding a gun to Bertie's head. He exhaled and quickly made his way around to the back of the cafe. "He obviously does not know who he's dealing with…I *almost* feel sorry for him," he smirked. "Bertie is not going to be happy with him…"

Max pushed open the swinging kitchen door and moved slowly toward the front counter where Doug stood with his hands in the air. Max looked at Little John and said, "There's no need for the gun, Mr. Abbott."

Little John pulled his arm tighter against Bertie's neck and pressed the gun closer against her temple. "How the hell do you know who I am?" he spoke loudly. "Damn! All I wanted was some coffee to go…until this bitch got too damn nosy for her own good."

"I wasn't being nosy!" Bertie choked out. "Let go of me, you big oaf!" She stomped on his foot which only served to make him choke her tighter.

"Shut up, bitch!" Abbott bellowed. "Asking all those questions about whether I had attended the dog fight…looking at my truck and wanting to know if anyone was out there waiting for me…" He pointed the gun at Max. "You didn't answer my question…how do you know me?" He saw Doug's slight movement to the left of Max and did not hesitate. He moved the gun quickly from Bertie's temple, aimed it at Doug, and…fired twice in rapid secession.

Tyler had entered the café through the back door and moved silently into the kitchen. He pushed through the swinging door just as the second bullet passed through Doug's shoulder. "Nooooo!" he screamed as he ran recklessly toward Little John.

Abbott saw Tyler running toward him and a sickening grin crossed his face. Fate was with him; he would have his revenge against Tyler Jones-Foster after all, and face-to-face revenge at that. He pushed Bertie roughly to the floor and turned the gun toward Tyler. Tyler was about thirty feet from him when Little John raised his gun and fired again. Everything seemed to move in slow motion as the bullet raced toward Tyler's head.

The bullet was within ten feet of hitting Tyler squarely in the center of his forehead; everything truly was moving in slow motion. Tyler watched helplessly as Bertie and Doug fell to the floor simultaneously. He was now within five feet of the slow-moving bullet when, out of nowhere, Sam flew through the air, soared in front of Tyler, and took the bullet that was intended to kill Tyler Foster. Everyone in the room saw the bullet hit the right side of Sam's head, between his ear and eye. The slow motion effect of what was happening even allowed Tyler to see the bullet exit on the left side on Sam's head.

Sam landed with a hard thud at the feet of Little John Abbott. Tyler had never stopped his running approach; the slow motion effect suddenly ceased and everything returned to rapid movement. Tyler dove his entire body into the solid concrete wall that was Little John Abbott's massive chest.

The big man went down and the next thing Tyler and Little John saw was Sam's huge mouth clamping down on Abbott's neck.

"What the hell!" Little John screamed.

It would have been comical to Tyler to hear a tough guy like Little John Abbott screaming like a scared little girl, except for the fact that a dead dog had been the one to cause his hysterics. All he could do was repeat Little John's expletive. "What the hell?"

Max had helped Doug and Bertie to their feet and hugged each of them to him. He smiled down at Sam and said, "Easy, Sam…don't hurt him…just hold him there until the authorities arrive, which should be any minute now…I called them from the kitchen when I saw what was going on out here," he attempted an explanation that Tyler might believe.

Tyler looked at Sam closely while Little John struggled in vain to escape the dog's jaws. "He was shot…I saw him…I saw the bullet go straight through his head…" He looked back at Max and at Doug who was standing next to him. "And, you…" he pointed at Doug. "He shot you, too, TWICE!" He plopped down heavily on the floor next to Sam and grabbed Little John's gun. He looked over at Bertie and exhaled. "Who the hell are you people…"

Bertie pulled away from Max and straightened her uniform and adjusted her halo headband. She walked slowly over to Tyler and squatted down next to him. She looked him directly in the eye and winked as a golden hue surrounded her entire body. She punched him hard against his arm and laughed out loud. "I'm guessing you might already know the answer to that question, handsome!"

Everyone was so engrossed in subduing Little John that they never noticed when Sam walked slowly behind them, through the kitchen, out the back door, and to Little John's pick-up truck. The back door opened on its own, and he jumped inside where Amanda was still sleeping on the back seat, with Spartacus guarding her. Spartacus looked up and said, *"I heard shots inside...is everyone okay?"*

Sam moved closer to Amanda and licked her forehead. *"Everyone is just fine, my friend. Everything will be fine from here on out."* A golden glow filled the inside of the truck's cab.

Amanda stirred and blinked her eyes open. She smiled at Sam and reached out to wrap a limp arm around his neck. "Hey there, you..." she said sleepily. "So glad you're okay..."

Sam put his head against hers and whined softly. He raised a paw and draped it across her shoulder.

Amanda opened her eyes again, and a single tear slid down her cheek. "You've got to go now, don't you, Sam? Oh, how I wish you could stay...even if for just a little while..."

The golden glow brightened and Sam whined again. He licked her cheek and looked toward Spartacus. *"I'm depending on you to look after her for me..."*

"I won't let you down, Sam...I promise..." Spartacus choked back his own tears. *"Thank you for everything...thank you for saving us all..."*

"You are very welcome, my friend...I have to go now...until we meet again, Spartacus..."

Amanda reached out to Sam just as the golden glow shimmered and he began to vanish. "I love you, Sam...I always will..."

EPILOGUE

Six Months Later

The last two months of 2013 were happy and hectic ones for the angels of the Heavenly Grille Café. Thanksgiving had always been Max's favorite holiday because it gave him an official reason to produce his mouth-watering meals and desserts. The holiday also held a very special, though not totally unexpected, announcement from Amos Brown and Isabelle Ghent. The happy couple knew that whatever time they had left on earth may be limited, so they mutually decided on a quick wedding after their announcement on Thanksgiving. Izzy presented Amos with an early Christmas present so that he was able to proudly show off his new set of dentures in their wedding pictures on Christmas Day. The couple moved into Izzy's home and quickly settled into a comfortable routine – one of which included at least one daily meal at the Heavenly Grille Café.

The twenty-three dogs that had been rescued from the final illegal dog fight on the Abbott ranch had all been placed in loving foster, rescue, or fur-ever homes. Engrique Ramos quickly adopted Kong and the white pit bull that had died and been chained to the back of the F-150; he renamed them Hank and Willie after two of his favorite country singers. The two dogs bonded immediately with Enrique's twelve grandchildren and spent their weekends romping and playing on the Ramos' small farm. Ten of the remaining twenty-one dogs, to include Spartacus, went to live on the Foster Farm; two of those ten had been so traumatized that B.B. and Jean decided it would be in the dogs' best interest to remain with them permanently. The remaining eleven dogs all found their fur-ever families...some locally, while others were transported as far north as Michigan. They would be well cared for and loved for the remainder of their earthly lives. Only one dog had been unaccounted for, and that was the huge black pittie-mix that had fought the final fight of the night. A thorough search of the woods and surrounding area had been done, but the dog had never been found. Of course, the handful of Christians that had been in attendance during the fight, had their own suspicions about what had happened to Sam.

Tim Breydan had miraculously survived his gunshot wound, and spent several months resting and recuperating before returning to his job as an animal control investigator. Ross Taylor spent a lot of time by Tim's bedside after his friend's surgery. Tim awoke during one of those visits to find Ross with his head bent and hands pressed together in prayer. Tim spoke with Ross constantly and answered all of his questions about God, the Bible, and organized religion. It was a slow, gradual process, but Ross Taylor accepted Jesus Christ as his Lord and Savior on Christmas Day. He left the agency after the first of the year and accepted a job heading a larger, independent group of people responsible for the rescue of abandoned and neglected animals.

Little John Abbott, along with several of his ranch hands, had been captured and incarcerated while awaiting their upcoming trial, which was scheduled to begin in May 2014. Some of those ranch hands had been fined and placed on probation, and prohibited from ever owning a domestic pet of any kind. Bail had been denied for Little John and Clint Meacham; Clint could not afford bail, and Little John was deemed to pose a threat for fleeing the country, so he was denied bond. Once a jury was formed, the prosecutors felt sure that justice would be served. Violation of Georgia's dogfighting statutes was a felony, with a mandatory fine of $5,000 and/or imprisonment of one to five years. Any subsequent convictions brought fines of not less than $15,000 and imprisonment of one to ten years. The prosecution had done their job well and would provide documentation of the total number of illegal fights over the past ten years at the Abbott ranch. They would also provide an estimation of the number of dogs that were stolen, abused, neglected, and killed in support of Abbott's illegal operation. The Abbott ranch was currently in foreclosure status. Everything on it would be auctioned off, and all proceeds would be contributed to local rescue organizations, specifically to those credited for caring for rescued bait and fighter dogs.

Amanda had returned to her job on the Tampa police force, but her heart wasn't really in it. She made sure to visit her angels at least one weekend every month and discussed her thoughts about quitting the force and going back to school to become a veterinarian. The angels listened to her, but were careful to keep their opinions to themselves. They knew better than to interfere with whatever God's plan had in store for their sweet Amanda. Amanda had spent Thanksgiving with the angels, and celebrated with Amos and Izzie when they announced their plan to marry. She was so happy for them, but in the back of her mind, she wondered when it would be her turn to find that special someone. She thought she had found that person when she met Tyler Foster, but she had only heard from him about once a month since he and Sam had rescued her from Little John in late October.

Amanda returned to Monticello for the Christmas holidays and wept with joy during the small wedding ceremony for Amos and Izzie. Max, Bertie, and Doug had showered her with attention and gifts; they even had gifts for Buster, who had gained another ten pounds over the past couple of months. Max had suggested that Amanda stop by the Foster Farm on her way home to say hello to the family, and Amanda had reluctantly agreed to do just that. She had been received warmly by the entire family, even by Tyler, and loved spending time with all the rescued animals. They had convinced her to spend New Year's Eve with them and she agreed. When the ball dropped in New York City, celebratory kisses and hugs went around the entire room. Amanda quickly found herself locked in Tyler's embrace and had closed her eyes in anticipation of the kiss. She had felt the hesitation in Tyler's body and tried not to cry when he pulled her toward him and kissed the top of her forehead.

Tyler called her twice in January and again in February, to say hello and to see how she was doing. Their conversations were always long and filled with easy, non-committal subjects. It took everything Amanda had not to just come out and ask him what the hell was going on, but she managed to bite her tongue and continued to go with the flow. If all he wanted was friendship from her, then she would have to be satisfied with that kind of relationship.

March brought a new man into Amanda's life. He was ten years older than Amanda; his name was Jason, and he was an undercover detective that had transferred to Tampa from Atlanta. They began dating on a fairly regular basis, and Amanda even took him to meet her angels when spring arrived in March 2014. Once again, the angels had to keep their opinions to themselves and not interfere with the decisions Amanda made for her life.

The Heavenly Grille had another visitor the weekend after Amanda and Jason visited…Tyler Foster. Tyler had traveled to Thomasville to go over his testimony again with the prosecutors, specifically about his role in the illegal dog fighting, the subsequent sting operation, and the rescue of Amanda from her kidnapper. He decided to stop and enjoy some of Max's cooking on the way back home. Bertie had been quick to feel him out, get all of the latest gossip on his love life, and, to let him know that Amanda was dating Jason. She had punched him hard on the arm when he left and suggested that he do a better job of keeping in touch…with *everyone*!

Tyler had been fighting his own demons regarding Amanda. Part of him was being stubborn because everyone in his family was constantly telling him that he had better not let that one get away…that there was something special about her. Tyler had spent the past four months trying to get Amanda out of his head, and…yes, out of his heart, too. He didn't know when she had managed to wedge herself into his heart, but she had, and he had continually fought against the desire to keep her there. He had dated several different women since he returned home, some of whom, he had slept with on occasion…none of whom, had he felt any real connection. On those rare occasions when he dreamed, the dreams were always about Amanda Turner. Those were the times when he would break down and call her, to say hello, and to see how she was doing…to hear her voice…to remember her kisses. Something finally began to break in him when he stopped by the Heavenly Grille in March for a meal, and to talk with Max, Bertie, and Doug. That was when Bertie made it a point to let him know that Amanda was seeing another man; that was, also, when Tyler's phone calls to Amanda began to increase. Instead of once or twice a month, his calls gradually increased to once a week; by the end of April, he was calling her on a daily basis.

Amanda was volunteering at Pet Haven Rescue in Tampa on Saturday, April 26. Earl Stocker had passed away in his sleep two months earlier, and Amanda spent more time than usual helping out his wife, Sharon. Pet Haven was in the process of closing down and Sharon Stocker was determined to find good homes for the last few dogs she had. Amanda had volunteered to drive six of the remaining twelve dogs to the Foster Farm, in Brooksville. B.B. Foster had offered to take all twelve dogs, but Sharon Stocker felt confident that she would be able to find local families for six of them before she had to shut down her rescue organization.

Amanda had recently called things off with Jason, after an episode when she saw him shoving Buster. She had walked in to her bedroom for a sweater, and had left Buster sleeping on the couch beside Jason. The bedroom door was left ajar, and she heard a soft thump coming from the living room. She started to shout out and ask what was going on, but instead, she moved to the bedroom door and glanced out in time to see Buster sprawled on the living room floor. He attempted to jump back up to his comfortable spot and blanket on the couch, when Jason shoved him away again. Amanda had stormed out of her room and told Jason to leave. He had made some comment about it being "just a dog", and it took all of her self-control not to hurl the television at him. Needless to say, things had been a little uncomfortable between them at work since the incident happened.

Buster had grown considerably over the past six months and still enjoyed riding shotgun beside his sweet Amanda. His ears and jowls flapped happily as he extended his head out the window to enjoy the warm, spring air rush against his face. Amanda enjoyed the hour-long ride to Brooksville even more by listening to her father's collection of Patsy Cline CDs. She was still singing along with Patsy when she pulled the van into the long drive way that led to the Foster's log home.

She honked her horn when she saw the entire clan gathered on the large front porch. Everyone had gathered for a family cookout. All the Foster sons…Scott, Rick, Matthew…and their wives and children were playing games on the porch and in the front yard. Jean was sitting in B.B.'s lap, and Spartacus was lying beside the huge rocking chair they sat in. Amanda performed a rapid scan of the entire area until she spotted the person for whom she was really searching.

Tyler straddled one of the wide railings on the porch and had his Atlanta Braves baseball cap pulled low over his eyes.

She watched carefully for his reaction when she and Buster exited the van. She had specifically told the Fosters not to tell Tyler she was coming today; she wanted to surprise him. Her palms felt clammy, and she felt like a school girl experiencing her very first crush; and, she thought she might be physically sick from the queasiness that settled in the pit of her stomach.

Tyler jumped off the railing and adjusted his cap. A wide grin spread across his face when he saw Amanda. He laughed when Buster began barking and running around in circles. Spartacus looked over at him and Tyler nodded, "Go get him, fella!"

"I've missed that little fella!" Spartacus barked and ran to meet up with Buster. He stopped long enough to accept hugs and kisses from the pretty blond woman who owned the boisterous pup.

Jean got up off her husband's lap and smiled over at Tyler. "Well, would you look who's here!"

B.B. shook his head and feigned surprise at Amanda's arrival. "Yep…it's Amanda Turner alright. It's good to see you, young lady. Come on over here and give me a hug. We've missed you…and Buster!"

Amanda exchanged hugs with all of them, saving Tyler for last. "It's really good to see all of you again…it's been a long time."

"Too long…" Tyler mumbled too softly for anyone to hear. He moved between his mother and father and walked down the steps to meet Amanda at the bottom. "Hey there, you," he smiled at her and relaxed when she eagerly accepted his hug.

Amanda squinted up at him and smiled back. "It's one thing to hear your voice every day, but it's even better to finally see you in person again…"

It was another couple of hours before everyone had eaten and split up into various groups…some resumed game playing while others relaxed in comfortable chairs on the porch. Amanda and Tyler took the opportunity to slip away and go for a walk along the lake behind the main house. Tyler pointed to an old canoe on the bank. "Want to take it out?"

"You bet I do!" Amanda laughed. "I can't remember the last time I was in one of these. My Dad use to take me fishing in an old one he had."

"I didn't know you knew how to fish," Tyler grinned.

"Well, I don't, really," Amanda shrugged. "My Dad would always bait my lines for me, and I always felt so sorry for the poor fish when he hauled them in...I couldn't stand to see that hook in their mouths, and the look on their scared faces...so, I would cry until he took the hook out and threw the fish back into the water. It was really more about spending time with my Dad than it was about fishing, I guess."

"Hmmm..." Tyler mocked. "Does that mean you want to spend time with me, too?"

Amanda put her hands on her slim hips and stared up at him. "I think we've pussy-footed long enough, don't you, Tyler Foster?"

Tyler pushed the canoe half-way into the water and took her hand in his. "Care to elaborate, Amanda Turner?"

Amanda stepped into the canoe, sat down, and waited for Tyler to push off and hop in. She watched the muscles flex in his arms while he rowed them to the middle of the lake. "Sure, I'll elaborate...be happy to. I don't know why you distanced yourself from me after the dog-fighting sting last October, but you did. At first, I decided to give you the space you needed, and some time to adjust being back home. I didn't understand why you didn't want to see me..."

Tyler locked the oars in place and stretched his shoulders. "It's hard to explain, Amanda. I felt like everyone expected us to be together...like I didn't have any say in the matter...I was confused about how or what I felt about you. I dated other women, but found myself comparing them to you...none of them ever measured up. None of them made me...*laugh*. My family was pushing me to see you, and the more they pushed, the more I was determined that I wasn't going to allow them to make that decision for me."

"Hmmm..." Amanda nodded. "So, I guess you didn't believe what I said when we first met...when I told you that you and I were going to be married one day?"

Tyler shook his head. "No...I never really believed that...well...maybe, I did, for a brief moment when we rescued you from Abbott. I have to tell you...that whole episode had me scared to death...thinking about what he might have done to you..."

"So...you saved my life and then ran like hell from me, huh?"

Tyler exhaled. "I guess I did, but...something changed when I stopped in to see Max, Bertie, and Doug last month."

"I didn't know you had seen them," Amanda began. "I see them at least once a month...they never mentioned seeing you.

"They told me that you were seeing someone special...and, something clicked inside this empty head of mine when Bertie told me that...something unpleasant...I didn't know why I was feeling the way I was...angry, hurt, disappointed. It took me a few days to realize that I didn't have anyone but myself to blame for those feelings. I had pushed you away enough times, until you found someone else to fill my spot."

Amanda shrugged. "Yeah...well...that man is definitely not in the picture any more..."

Tyler perked up and grinned a victor's grin. "He's not? What happened? I mean...it's none of my business really, but..."

Amanda waved him off. "The man doesn't like animals, specifically, my Buster. He's lucky I didn't give him a concussion when I saw him shove my sweet boy!"

Tyler looked out at the golden red sky. He would always remember this day...April 26...as the day he finally acknowledged to himself that he loved the dizzy blond sitting across from him. He didn't know what the future held for them, but he knew beyond all doubt that they could face anything...as long as they were together.

"Amanda..." he cleared his throat. "Your Dad isn't here for me to do the honorable thing, so if you would like, I could row us back to shore and get Buster."

"What *are* you talking about, Tyler Foster?" Amanda laughed.

"Well, he's the main man in your life, so I think it only right that he be the one that I should ask for your hand in marriage..."

Amanda jumped up and dragged Tyler along with her. The old canoe rocked dangerously from side to side, and within mere seconds, they both fell sideways into the lake. Tyler surfaced first and looked around for Amanda. She bounced to the surface seconds later, spitting water from her nose and mouth. She looked down and was shocked to find herself holding a small fish in her hands. She looked back and forth from Tyler and the flopping fish before bursting out in laughter. She threw the fish back into the lake and looked toward Heaven, before locking her arms around Tyler's neck. "I think that was my Dad's sick sense of humor...giving his own approval!"

Tyler held her around her waist as they treaded water, and slowly lowered his mouth to hers. It was a kiss worth waiting for...when their lips finally parted and they had caught their breaths, he smiled down at her and asked, "Then...does that mean...?"

Amanda laughed out loud again before dunking his head beneath the water. She was still laughing when he bobbed up again and shook the water off. "YESSSSS! Yes, Tyler Foster...I will most definitely marry you!"

At that precise moment, the dinner crowd was pushing through the front door of the Heavenly Grille Café. Bertie tensed, grinned broadly, and winked at Max who was watching her from the kitchen. "Well, I'll be damned!" she beamed as she punched one of the truckers hard against his massive forearm.

"**B-E-R-T-I-E**!!!"
"Oops…" Bertie whispered. "My bad…"

The End…Until the Next Angelic Encounter!

Author's Request:

Our four-legged friends depend on us to be their voice. Please don't be afraid to step forward and get involved if you see one of them being neglected, abused, or abandoned. Contact your local shelter and/or law enforcement and report your findings. If you suspect any animal is being used for illegal dogfighting, pick up your phone and call the national Dog Fighting Hotline, sponsored by the Humane Society of the United States: 1-877-847-4787.

READERS: If you enjoyed this book, please take time to leave a review of it on Amazon.com or BarnesandNoble.com